THE REALITIES OF LOVE, PASSION AND LIFE!

Emile Zola was the world's first great naturalistic writer. The truth was his God—the exact, uncompromising truth about the way people lived. Willing to risk jail or ostracism, he was determined to describe the world as he knew it to be and not as censors and moralists told him it ought to be. He dared to record the authentic language of the people. Alone among his contemporaries, he dared to describe the realities of love between man and woman. With ruthless honesty, he chronicled the fantastic corruption and decay which marked the reign of Napoleon III.

NANA

is one of Zola's greatest masterpieces—a brilliant portrait of the underground world of Paris where writers and whores, aristocrats and workers met as equals in their frantic pursuit of vice; and of the woman they acknowledged as their Queen, the incomparable NANA.

NANA

BY EMILE ZOLA

A new, brilliant, complete translation by
LOWELL BAIR

NANA

A Bantam Book / published August 1964

Library of Congress Catalog Card Number: 64-20905

NANA

1

At nine o'clock the Variety Theater was still almost empty. A few people were waiting in the balcony and the orchestra, lost among the garnet-colored velvet seats, in the dim light of the half-extinguished gas chandelier. The vast red curtain was drowned in shadow, no sound came from the stage, the footlights were unlit, and the music stands were scattered in disorder. Up in the third gallery, however, around the domed ceiling on which naked women and children were soaring across a sky that had been turned green by gas, shouts and laughter rose above a continuous hum of voices, and there were rows of heads wearing bonnets and caps beneath the broad round windows with their gilded frames. Occasionally an attendant holding tickets in her hand could be seen busily conducting a couple who walked in front of her and finally sat down, the man in evening clothes, the woman thin and arched, slowly looking over the theater.

Two young men appeared in the orchestra. They stood looking around them.

"What did I tell you, Hector?" exclaimed the older of the two, a tall man with a small black mustache. "We've come too early. You could have let me finish my cigar."

An attendant was passing by. "Oh, Monsieur Fauchery," she said familiarly, "it won't start for another half-hour!"

"Then why do they say nine o'clock on the posters?" complained Hector, his long, thin face taking on a look of annoyance. "Only this morning Clarisse, who's in the cast, swore to me that they were going to begin at nine o'clock sharp."

They fell silent for a moment and stared at the shadowy boxes, whose green wallpaper made them darker still. The ground-floor boxes under the balcony were hidden in total darkness. In the balcony boxes there was no one except a fat lady leaning on the velvet-covered railing. To the left and right, between tall pillars, the stage boxes with their long-fringed drapery remained empty. The entire inside of the theater, decorated in white and gold set off by pale green, was blurred as though it were filled with a kind of fine dust by the short flames of the great crystal chandelier.

"Did you get your stage box for Lucy?" asked Hector.

"Yes," replied the young man, "but not without a lot of trouble. . . . Oh, there's no danger that Lucy will come too early!" He stifled a slight yawn, then went on after a silence: "You're lucky, since you've never been to a first night before. *The Blond Venus* will be the sensation of the year. People have been talking about it for six months. Ah, what music! And such vivacity! Bordenave knows what he's doing: he saved it for the Exposition."

Hector had been listening religiously. He asked a question: "And do you know Nana, the new star who's going to play Venus?"

"Oh! So you're going to start that too!" cried Fauchery, throwing up his arms. "Everyone has been harassing me with Nana ever since this morning. I've met over twenty people, and it's been nothing but Nana this and Nana that! How should I know anything about her? Do you think I know every girl in Paris? Nana is one of Bordenave's discoveries. She must be something magnificent!"

He became calmer. But he was irritated by the emptiness of the theater, by that church-like tranquillity filled with the sound of whispering voices and closing doors.

"No!" he said suddenly. "It's too boring in here. I'm going out. . . . Maybe we'll find Bordenave downstairs. He'll give us some details."

Downstairs in the large marble-floored lobby where the box office was located, the public was beginning to arrive. Through the three open grilles, the ardent life of the boulevards could be seen passing by, swarming and blazing in the beautiful April night. Rumbling carriages stopped abruptly, their doors were slammed noisily, and people entered in little groups, standing in front of the box office or climbing the double staircase at the rear, where women lingered with swaying hips. In the harsh glare of the gaslights, on the pale, bare walls of that room whose meager Empire decorations gave it the appearance of the peristyle of a cardboard temple, there were high, garish posters bearing Nana's name in big black letters. Men were reading them as though they had been caught and held as they were walking past; others were blocking the doorways as they stood talking to one another, while near the box office a thickset man with a broad, clean-shaven face was giving blunt answers to some people who insisted on having seats.

"There's Bordenave," said Fauchery as he came down the stairs.

But the producer had already seen him. "You're a nice one!" he called out to him from a distance. "So that's how you write a notice for me! I opened the *Figaro* this morning —nothing!"

"Wait!" replied Fauchery. "I have to see your Nana before I can talk about her! Besides, I didn't promise you anything."

Then, to change the subject, he introduced his cousin, Monsieur Hector de la Faloise, a young man who had come to complete his education in Paris. The producer sized up the young man with a glance. But Hector examined him with emotion. So this was Bordenave, that exhibitor of women who treated them like slaves, whose brain was always turning out some new publicity scheme, a cynic who shouted, spat, slapped his thighs, and had the coarse mind of a trooper! Hector felt that he ought to make some pleasant remark.

"Your theater—" he began in a piping voice.

Bordenave calmly interrupted him in the tone of a man who likes unequivocal situations: "Call it my whorehouse."

Fauchery laughed approvingly, while La Faloise stood with his compliment stuck in his throat, deeply shocked yet trying to look as though he appreciated the joke. The producer had hurried over to shake hands with a drama critic whose writings had great influence. When he returned, La Faloise was recovering his composure. He was afraid of being regarded as a provincial if he appeared to be too disconcerted.

"I've been told," he began again, determined to find something to say, "that Nana has a delightful voice."

3

"Nana?" exclaimed the producer, shrugging his shoulders. "She sings like a crow!"

"And I hear she's an excellent actress," the young man hastened to say.

"She's an awkward clod! She doesn't know what to do with her hands and feet!"

La Faloise blushed slightly. He was bewildered. "I wouldn't have missed this first night for anything in the world," he stammered. "I knew that your theater—"

"Call it my whorehouse," Bordenave interrupted again, with the cool obstinacy of a convinced man.

Fauchery had been calmly watching the women as they entered. He came to his cousin's aid when he saw him gaping, not knowing whether to laugh or be angry.

"Make Bordenave happy: call his theater what he wants you to, since it amuses him. . . . And you, my dear friend, don't try to fool us. If your Nana can neither sing nor act, you'll have a fiasco, that's all. And that's just what I'm afraid you *will* have."

"A fiasco!" cried the producer, his face turning purple. "Does a woman need to know how to act and sing? Ah, my boy, you're too stupid! . . . Nana has something else, something that replaces everything! I smelled it, and she has a strong dose of it, or else I have the nose of a fool. . . . You'll see, you'll see: all she has to do is walk onto the stage and she'll have the whole audience with their tongues hanging out." He had raised his big hands, quivering with enthusiasm; now, feeling relieved, he lowered his voice and muttered to himself, "She'll go far. Yes, by God, she'll go far! Her skin. . . Oh, what skin she has!"

Then, when Fauchery questioned him, he consented to give details, using crude expressions that embarrassed Hector de la Faloise. He had come to know Nana and decided to give her a start in the theater. It so happened that he was looking for a Venus at the time. He never bothered with a woman for long; he preferred to let the public enjoy her immediately. But Nana's arrival in his theater had turned everything upside down, and she was still causing all kinds of trouble. Rose Mignon, his star, a clever actress and an adorable singer, was furious because she felt that she now had a rival. Every day she threatened to leave him in the lurch. And the playbills—good God,

4

what an uproar there had been about that! He had finally decided to print the names of the two actresses in letters of equal size. He wouldn't stand for being annoyed. Whenever one of his little women, as he called them—Simonne or Clarisse, for example—stepped out of line, he gave her a kick in the behind. Otherwise he would never have had any peace. He bought and sold them, so he knew what they were worth, the bitches!

"Look, there's Mignon and Steiner," he said, interrupting himself. "They're always together. Steiner is beginning to get sick of Rose, you know, so her husband stays with him all the time, for fear he'll slip away."

The row of gas jets flaming along the cornice of the theater cast a patch of bright light on the sidewalk outside. Two green little trees stood out sharply, a white pillar was so brightly illuminated that the posters on it could be read from a distance as easily as in broad daylight, and the dense darkness of the boulevard beyond was broken only by pinpoints of light and the vague outlines of a moving crowd. Many of the men did not come directly into the theater, but stayed outside to talk and finish a cigar beneath the gaslights, which made their faces look pale and silhouetted them in short black shadows on the asphalt. Mignon, tall and broad, with the square head of a circus strong man, was making his way through the groups, pulling the banker Steiner by the arm. The latter was a short man with a bulging paunch and a round face framed by graying whiskers.

"Well, you saw her yesterday in my office," Bordenave said to the banker.

"Ah, so that was her!" said Steiner. "I thought it might have been. But I hardly got a glimpse of her, because I was going out as she was coming in."

Mignon listened with his eyes lowered, nervously turning a big diamond ring around his finger. He had understood that they were talking about Nana. Then, when Bordenave began giving a description of his new star that made the banker's eyes sparkle, he decided to intervene:

"Never mind, she's nothing but a cheap whore! The public will soon send her back where she came from. . . . Steiner, my boy, you know my wife is waiting for you in her dressing room."

5

He tried to lead him away, but Steiner refused to leave Bordenave. In front of them, a line of people was pressing against the box office and there was a rising hubbub of voices in which Nana's name was constantly repeated with the melodious vivacity of its two syllables. The men standing in front of the posters read it aloud; others uttered it in a questioning tone as they passed, while women, uneasy and smiling, repeated it softly with an air of surprise. No one knew Nana. Where had this Nana come from? Stories and jokes were whispered from ear to ear. Her name was like a caress. It was a little name whose familiarity suited everyone's lips. Merely pronouncing it made the crowd feel cheerful and good-humored. They were all driven by a fever of curiosity, that Parisian curiosity that has the violence of a fit of madness. They wanted to see Nana. A lady had the flounce of her dress torn off; a gentleman lost his hat.

"Ah, you're asking too much!" cried Bordenave, besieged with questions from a score of men. "You'll see her. . . . I have to go, I'm needed backstage."

He disappeared, delighted at having stirred up his public. Mignon shrugged his shoulders and reminded Steiner that Rose was waiting to show him the costume she would wear in the first act.

"Look, there's Lucy getting out of her carriage," La Faloise said to Fauchery.

It was Lucy Stewart, an ugly little woman in her forties; her neck was too long, her face was thin and drawn, and she had thick lips, but she was so lively and gracious that she had great charm. She was with Caroline Héquet and her mother. Caroline was coldly beautiful; her mother looked dignified and strait-laced.

"Come with us, I've reserved a seat for you," she said to Fauchery.

"So I can't see anything?" he answered. "No, thanks! I have a seat in the orchestra; I like it better there."

Lucy became angry. Was he afraid to be seen with her? Then she abruptly calmed down and skipped to another subject:

"Why didn't you tell me you knew Nana?"

"Nana? I've never seen her!"

"Really? I was told you'd gone to bed with her."

6

But just then Mignon motioned them to be silent. When Lucy questioned him he pointed to a young man who was passing by and murmured, "That's Nana's gigolo."

They all looked at him. He had an attractive appearance. Fauchery recognized him: his name was Daguenet; he had squandered three hundred thousand francs on women, and he now dabbled in stocks so that he could afford to buy them flowers and take them out to dinner now and then. Lucy thought he had handsome eyes.

"Ah, there's Blanche!" she cried. "She's the one who told me you'd gone to bed with Nana."

Blanche de Sivry, a big blond girl whose pretty face was growing too fat, was coming toward them with a slender, well-groomed, distinguished-looking man.

"That's Count Xavier de Vandeuvres," Fauchery whispered to La Faloise.

The Count shook hands with the journalist while a lively argument took place between Blanche and Lucy. They blocked the passage with their flounce-laden skirts, one blue, the other pink, and they repeated Nana's name so shrilly that the crowd began listening to them. The Count led Blanche away. By this time Nana's name was being echoed all over the lobby, with an eagerness heightened by waiting. Would the performance never begin? Men were looking at their watches, latecomers were leaping from their carriages before they had stopped, groups were leaving the sidewalk, where passers-by were slowly crossing the empty lighted space, craning their necks to look into the theater. A street urchin stood whistling in front of one of the posters at the door, then cried out "Oh, Nana!" in a husky voice and went on his way, swaying his hips and dragging his feet. There was a wave of laughter. Several well-dressed gentlemen repeated "Nana, oh, Nana!" The crush grew tighter, a quarrel broke out at the box office, and there was a swelling clamor composed of voices calling for Nana, demanding Nana, in one of those surges of stupidity which sometimes pass through crowds.

Then the sound of a bell rose above the uproar. Word was passed along all the way to the boulevard: "The bell has rung." There was a wild rush for the door, with everyone trying to get through at once while theater attendants made frantic efforts to maintain order. Mignon, looking worried, again took hold of Steiner, who had not gone to see Rose's costume. As soon as the bell had rung, La Faloise had forced his way through the crowd, dragging Fauchery with him, in order not to miss the overture. Lucy Stewart was irritated by this eagerness on the part of the public. What a rude mob, shoving women around like that! She stayed behind with Caroline Héquet and her mother. The lobby was empty; the endless rumble of the boulevard could be heard outside.

"As though their shows were always funny!" Lucy said as she climbed the stairs.

Fauchery and La Faloise stood in front of their seats and looked around again. The theater was now resplendent. The great crystal chandelier was ablaze with pink and yellow reflections from the high gas flames that sent down a rain of light from the ceiling to the floor. The garnet-colored velvet of the seats was mottled with patches of deeper red, while the glitter of the gilding was softened by the pale green decorations beneath the garish paintings on the ceiling. The footlights vividly illuminated the curtain whose heavy crimson cloth suggested the richness of a fairy palace and contrasted with the shabbiness of the frame around it, in which there were cracks showing the plaster under the gilding. It was already very warm. The musicians were in their places, tuning their instruments. Amid the growing uproar of voices rose the delicate trills of the flutes, the muffled sighs of the horns, and the singing tones of the violins. All the spectators were talking, jostling one another and finding room for themselves in the general rush for seats; and the crush in the corridors was so violent that the seemingly inexhaustible flow of people had difficulty in passing through the doors. There were waving hands, rustling cloth, and a procession of women's skirts and hats, occasionally broken by the black of a frock coat. Meanwhile the seats were gradually filling; here and there a light-colored dress stood out, and a head with a delicate profile lowered a chignon adorned by a flashing gem. In one of the boxes a bare shoulder shone like white silk. Other women were calmly and languidly fanning themselves as they watched the surging crowd, while young gentlemen stood in the orchestra with their vests open and

8

gardenias in their buttonholes, looking through opera glasses held with the tips of their gloved fingers.

The two cousins began searching for familiar faces. Mignon and Steiner were sitting side by side in a ground-floor box, with their wrists resting on the velvet-covered railing. Blanche de Sivry seemed to be alone in one of the stage boxes. But La Faloise particularly scrutinized Daguenet, who had an orchestra seat two rows in front of his. Near him a very young man, fresh out of school and no more than seventeen years old, was staring at everything with his angelic eyes opened wide. Fauchery smiled when he saw him.

"Who's that lady in the balcony?" La Faloise suddenly asked. "The one sitting beside a girl in a blue dress."

He pointed to a fat woman tightly laced into her corset, a former blond whose hair had turned white and was now dyed yellow. Her round face, reddened by make-up, was bloated beneath a cascade of childish curls.

"That's Gaga," Fauchery answered simply. Then, since this name apparently meant nothing to his cousin, he added, "Haven't you ever heard of Gaga? She was the delight of the early years of Louis-Philippe's reign. Now she takes her daughter with her everywhere she goes."

La Faloise scarcely glanced at the young girl. The sight of Gaga affected him deeply and he kept his eyes on her. He thought she was still quite attractive, but he did not dare to say so.

Meanwhile the conductor raised his violin bow and the orchestra struck up the overture. People were still coming in. The noise and bustle increased. In that special first-night audience, which did not change, there were intimate little corners where friends smiled as they met each other again. Veteran theatergoers casually exchanged familiar greetings without taking off their hats. Paris was there: the Paris of letters, of finance and pleasure; there were many journalists, a few writers, several financiers, and more prostitutes than respectable women. It was a singularly mixed society, composed of all talents and tainted with all vices, in which the same weariness and the same fever appeared on every face. Fauchery, questioned by his cousin, pointed out the boxes of the various newspapers and clubs, then began naming the drama critics: a lean, dried-out man with thin, malicious lips, and particularly a fat man with a good-natured face who was leaning on the shoulder of his companion, an artless young girl whom he gazed at with a fond, paternal expression.

But Fauchery stopped short when he saw La Faloise greet some people in one of the center boxes. He looked surprised.

"What!" he exclaimed. "Do you know Count Muffat de Beuville?"

"Yes, I've known him for a long time," replied Hector. "The Muffats used to have an estate near ours. I often go to see them. . . . The Count is with his wife and her father, the Marquis de Chouard."

And out of vanity, for he was delighted by his cousin's astonishment, he went into details: the Marquis was a state councillor, the Count had just been appointed chamberlain to the Empress. Fauchery raised his opera glasses and looked at the Countess, a plump brunette with white skin and beautiful black eyes.

"You must introduce me during the intermission," he said at last. "I've already met the Count, but I'd like to go to their Tuesday receptions."

Energetic shouts of "Quiet!" came from the upper galleries. The overture had begun, and people were still coming in. Latecomers forced entire rows of spectators to stand up, the doors of boxes were banging, loud voices were quarreling in the corridors. And the sound of conversations did not cease; it was like the chattering of a flock of talkative sparrows at sundown. Everything was in confusion; there was a jumble of moving arms and heads as some people sat down and tried to make themselves comfortable, while others persisted in remaining on their feet to take one last look around. An outcry arose violently from the rear of the orchestra: "Sit down! Sit down!" A thrill of excitement had run through the audience: at last they were going to see that famous Nana, whom everyone in Paris had been talking about for a week.

The hum of voices gradually died down, with an occasional resurgence. And in the midst of those fading murmurs and sighs, the orchestra burst into the lively little notes of a waltz whose raffish rhythm was like ribald laughter. The audience, titillated, was already smiling. The claque in the first rows of the orchestra seats applauded wildly. The curtain was going up.

"Look," said La Faloise, who was still talking, "there's a man with Lucy."

He pointed to one of the stage boxes on the right. Caroline and Lucy were sitting in the front of it. Behind them could be seen the dignified face of Caroline's mother and the profile of a tall, impeccably dressed young man with handsome blond hair.

"Look," La Faloise repeated insistently, "there's a man with her."

Fauchery consented to turn his opera glasses toward the stage box. But he immediately turned them away.

"Oh, that's Labordette," he murmured casually, as though that gentleman's presence ought to seem natural and inconsequential to anyone.

Someone behind them shouted, "Quiet!" They fell silent. The audience now became motionless. A sea of heads, upright and attentive, rose from the orchestra to the upper galleries.

The first act of *The Blond Venus* took place on Olympus, a cardboard Olympus with painted clouds and Jupiter's throne on the right. Iris and Ganymede first appeared, aided by a group of celestial attendants who sang a chorus as they arranged the seats of the gods for the council. The paid claque again applauded all alone; the rest of the audience waited in mild bewilderment. La Faloise, however, had applauded Clarisse Besnus, one of Bordenave's "little women," who was playing the part of Iris, dressed in light blue with a large scarf of seven colors wrapped around her waist.

"She takes off her chemise to put that on," he said to Fauchery, loudly enough to be heard by those around him. "We tried it this morning. . . . Her chemise showed under her arms and on her back."

But just then there was a slight tremor in the audience. Rose Mignon had come onto the stage, as Diana. Although she had neither the face nor the figure for the part, being thin and dark, with the adorable ugliness of a Paris street urchin, she was charming, for she was like a mockery of the character she represented. Her entrance song had appallingly stupid words. In it she complained

of Mars, who was neglecting her in favor of Venus. She
sang it with a modest reserve so full of licentious sugges-
tiveness that the audience began to warm up. Steiner and
Rose's husband, sitting side by side, laughed with satisfaction. And everyone burst out laughing when Prullière, the
beloved actor, appeared in the uniform of a general, a
masquerade Mars, wearing a gigantic plume and dragging
a sword that came up to his shoulder. He said he had had
enough of Diana: she was always putting on airs. Diana
swore to keep an eye on him, and to take vengeance. The
duet ended with some farcical yodeling, which Prullière
performed very amusingly in the voice of an angry tomcat.
He had the ludicrous conceit of a young actor who has just
made an amorous conquest, and he rolled his eyes in a
dashing way that brought shrill feminine laughter from
the boxes.

Then the audience became cold again: the scenes that
followed were boring. There were a few smiles, though
only for a moment, when old Bosc, as an imbecile Jupiter
staggering beneath an enormous crown, had a conjugal
quarrel with Juno over the cook's accounts. The procession
of gods—Neptune, Pluto, and the others—almost spoiled
everything. An ominous murmur slowly arose; the spectators became impatient, lost interest, and began looking
around the house. Lucy was laughing with Labordette; the
Count de Vandeuvres was craning his neck behind
Blanche's broad shoulders; Fauchery was examining the
Muffats out of the corner of his eye: the Count was very
solemn, as though he had understood nothing, while the
Countess smiled vaguely, her eyes lost in revery. But suddenly the applause of the claque burst forth with the regularity of volley firing. All eyes turned to the stage. Was
Nana coming at last? She had kept everyone waiting long
enough!

It was a delegation of mortals who had been brought to
Olympus by Ganymede and Iris. They were all respectable
middle-class citizens, and all deceived husbands. They had
come to the ruler of the gods to lodge a complaint against
Venus, who was inflaming their wives with too much ardor.
The chorus, sung in a simple, plaintive tone and filled with
significant silences, caused great amusement. A phrase was
whispered all over the house: "The cuckolds' chorus, the

cuckolds' chorus." The name caught on and there were shouts of "Encore!" The singers' faces were funny. The audience found that they really looked like cuckolds, especially one fat man with a face as round as the moon. Vulcan appeared on the scene, furiously seeking his wife, who had been gone for three days. The chorus began singing again, appealing to Vulcan, the god of cuckolds. Vulcan was played by Fontan, a comedian of roguish and original talent who walked with a whimsical swaying gait. He was dressed as a village blacksmith, with a flaming red wig, and his bare arms were tattooed with hearts pierced by arrows. A woman's voice exclaimed loudly, "How ugly he is!" and all the other women laughed and applauded.

The next scene seemed endless. Jupiter took an inordinate amount of time to assemble the council of the gods in order to present the deceived husbands' request. And still no Nana! Was she being kept for the last scene? The long wait had finally irritated the audience. The murmurs began again.

Mignon was radiant. "It's going badly," he said to Steiner. "There's going to be an uproar, you'll see!"

Just then the clouds at the back of the stage parted and Venus appeared. Nana, very tall and well-developed for her eighteen years, in the white tunic of a goddess, with her long blond hair hanging loosely over her shoulders, walked toward the footlights with calm self-assurance, smiling at the audience. She began her main song:

"When Venus roams at night . . ."

By the time she had come to the second line, the spectators were looking at one another. Was this some sort of joke on Bordenave's part? Was he doing it on a bet? Never had such a tuneless voice been heard before, or one used with less art. The producer had judged her correctly when he had said that she sang like a crow. And she did not even know how to conduct herself on the stage: she thrust her hands forward and swayed her whole body in an indecent and ungraceful manner. People were already beginning to hiss and shout "Oh! Oh!" when from one of the orchestra seats a voice like that of a molting young rooster cried out with conviction, "She's wonderful!"

Everyone looked. It was the cherub, the schoolboy. His

attractive eyes were open wide and his fair-skinned face was inflamed by the sight of Nana. When he saw everyone turn toward him he blushed deeply at having unintentionally spoken aloud. Daguenet, who was sitting next to him, looked at him with a smile. The audience laughed, as though disarmed, and thought no more of hissing. The young gentlemen in white gloves, also captivated by Nana's curves, applauded ecstatically.

"Yes, that's right! Bravo!"

Seeing the audience laughing, Nana laughed also. The gaiety redoubled. This girl was funny as well as beautiful! She had an adorable little dimple in her chin when she laughed. She waited, not in the least embarrassed. She had immediately placed herself on a familiar footing with the audience, and she seemed to be saying with a wink of her eye that she had no talent at all, but that it didn't matter, because she had something else. Then, after making a gesture to the conductor which signified, "All right, let's go on," she began the second verse:

"At midnight, Venus passes by . . ."

It was still the same rough voice, but it now scratched the audience in the right place and occasionally gave them a little shiver of pleasure. Nana kept her smile, which lit up her small red mouth and glowed in her big, light blue eyes. When she sang certain suggestive lines, her pink nostrils quivered with delight and a flame passed over her cheeks. She continued to sway her body, not knowing what else to do. And it was no longer considered ungraceful, far from it: the men stared at her through their opera glasses. As she was finishing the second verse, her voice failed her completely and she realized that she could not go through to the end. Without being at all disturbed, she moved her hip in a way that revealed its curves beneath her thin tunic, then arched her back, making her breasts stand out, and stretched forth her arms. There was a burst of applause. She immediately turned around and walked away from the footlights, showing the red hair that covered the back of her neck like the fur of an animal. The applause became deafening.

The end of the act aroused less enthusiasm. Vulcan tried to slap Venus. The gods held council and decided to make

14

an inquiry on earth before giving satisfaction to the deceived husbands. It was then that Diana, overhearing some tender words between Venus and Mars, swore not to take her eyes off them during the journey. There was also a scene in which Cupid, played by a twelve-year-old girl, replied to every question: "Yes, mama . . . No, mama . . ." in a whining tone, with her finger in her nose. Then Jupiter, with the sternness of an angry schoolmaster, shut Cupid up in a dark closet and ordered her to conjugate the verb "to love" twenty times. A better reception was given to the finale, a chorus that was brilliantly performed by the orchestra and the entire troupe. But when the curtain had fallen the claque vainly tried to obtain an encore: everyone stood up and began moving toward the doors.

The crowd exchanged impressions as they trampled and jostled their way between the rows of seats. One remark was repeated everywhere: "It's idiotic." A critic said that the whole thing needed a great deal of cutting. But the play itself was unimportant: the talk was chiefly about Nana. Fauchery and La Faloise, who had been among the first to leave, met Steiner and Mignon in the corridor leading to the orchestra seats. The air was stifling in that gas-lit passage, as narrow as a mine shaft. They stopped for a moment at the foot of the staircase on the right, protected by the curve of the railing. The spectators from above were coming down with a constant clumping of heavy shoes, there was a steady stream of black frock coats, and an attendant was making frantic efforts to divert the shoving crowd from a chair on which she had piled up clothes.

"But I know her!" cried Steiner as soon as he saw Fauchery. "I'm sure I've seen her somewhere. . . . At the Casino, I think, and she was so drunk she was picked up by the police."

"I don't know exactly," said the journalist, "but I'm like you: I'm sure I've met her . . ." He lowered his voice and added, laughing, "Maybe it was at Tricon's."

"Or in some other foul place!" exclaimed Mignon, who seemed exasperated. "It's disgusting the way the public accepts any slut who comes along. Soon there won't be any decent women left in the theater. . . . Yes, some day I may have to make Rose leave the stage."

Fauchery could not help smiling. Meanwhile the clatter of heavy shoes on the stairs continued, and a short man wearing a cap said in a drawling voice, "She's got curves in all the right places! She looks good enough to eat."

In the corridor, two young men with carefully curled hair, looking very correct in their wing collars, were quarreling. One of them kept repeating "Wretched!" without giving any reason, while the other replied with "Magnificent!" and also disdained any argument.

La Faloise was deeply impressed by Nana; he did, however, venture to remark that she would be better if she cultivated her voice. At this point Steiner, who had stopped listening, seemed to awake with a start. They would have to wait. Perhaps everything would be spoiled in the following acts. The audience had shown good will, but it was certainly not yet captivated. Mignon swore that the whole audience would walk out before the last act. When Fauchery and La Faloise left them to go up to the lounge, he took Steiner's arm, pressed against his shoulder and whispered in his ear, "Just wait till you see my wife's costume in the second act! It's positively indecent!"

Upstairs in the lounge, three crystal chandeliers were burning brightly. The two cousins hesitated for a moment; through the open glazed door they could see waves of heads being moved by two different currents from one end of the room to the other. They went in. Five or six groups of men, talking loudly and gesticulating, were stubbornly holding their ground in the middle of the crush; the others were walking in rows, occasionally turning on their heels, which resounded on the waxed floor. To the left and right, between mottled marble pillars, women were sitting on red velvet seats, watching the passing crowd with an air of weariness, as though they were exhausted by the heat; and their chignons could be seen in the tall mirrors behind them. At the far end of the room, in front of the buffet, a man with a fat stomach was drinking a glass of fruit syrup.

Fauchery had gone to the balcony for a breath of fresh air. La Faloise, who had been studying the framed photographs of actresses that alternated with mirrors between the pillars, finally followed him. The row of gaslights in front of the theater had just been extinguished. It was dark and cool on the balcony, which seemed empty to them.

They saw only one young man, wrapped in shadow, leaning on the stone balustrade of the recess to the right, smoking a glowing cigarette. Fauchery recognized Daguenet. They shook hands.

"What are you doing here?" asked the journalist. "Why are you hiding in a corner, when you usually never leave the orchestra during a first night?"

"I'm smoking, as you can see," replied Daguenet.

Then, to embarrass him, Fauchery asked, "And what do you think of the new star? The comments I've heard about her haven't been very good."

"They must have been made by men she refused to have anything to do with," murmured Daguenet.

That was his entire judgment of Nana's talent. La Faloise leaned forward and looked down at the boulevard. Across the street, the windows of a hotel and a club were brightly illuminated, and a dark mass of customers occupied the sidewalk tables of the Café de Madrid. Despite the lateness of the hour, there was a dense crowd moving slowly along the sidewalks and continuously emerging from the Passage Jouffroy. Carriages followed one another so steadily that people had to wait five minutes before being able to cross the street.

"What noise and movement!" exclaimed La Faloise, who was still astonished by Paris.

A bell rang for a long time and the lounge became empty. People hurried through the corridors. Even after the curtain had risen they were still entering in groups, to the annoyance of those who were already seated. Everyone returned to his seat with an expression of animation and renewed attention. La Faloise immediately looked at Gaga; he was amazed to see her with the tall, blond young man who had been in Lucy's stage box during the first act.

"What did you say that man's name is?" he asked.

Fauchery did not see him at first. "Oh, yes, Labordette," he finally said, with the same casual gesture.

The scenery of the second act was a surprise. It represented a low dance hall named the Boule-Noire, on the outskirts of Paris, during Mardi Gras. A group of masqueraders were singing a rondelet, accompanying the refrain by tapping their heels. This down-to-earth scene, which no one had expected, aroused such amusement that the rondelet was given an encore. And it was to this place that the gods, led astray by Iris, who had falsely boasted that she knew the earth well, came to pursue their inquiry. They had disguised themselves in order to preserve their incognito. Jupiter was dressed as King Dagobert, with his breeches inside out and a huge tin crown on his head, Phoebus appeared as the Postillion of Lonjumeau, and Minerva as a Norman wet nurse. Shouts of mirth greeted Mars, who was fantastically dressed as a Swiss admiral. But the laughter became uproarious when Neptune, wearing overalls and a high, bulging cap, with little curls stuck to his temples, shuffled onto the stage and said, "When a man's as handsome as I am, he can't stop women from loving him!" There were a few exclamations of "Oh! Oh!" while the ladies raised their fans a little. Lucy, in her stage box, laughed so loudly that Caroline Héquet silenced her with a tap of her fan.

From then on, the play was saved, and even promised to be a great success. The audience was delighted by this carnival of the gods, by the sight of Olympus being dragged in the mud and of a whole religion and poetry being scoffed at. The fever of irreverence took possession of even the most literate first-night spectators: legends were trampled underfoot, ancient images were shattered. Jupiter had a likable face, Mars was a little crazy. Royalty became a farce, the army a joke. When Jupiter, having suddenly fallen in love with a little laundress, began dancing a wild cancan, Simonne, who was playing the part of the laundress, kicked up her foot to the nose of the ruler of the gods and called him her "big daddy" in such a funny way that the whole house was shaken by a fit of laughter. While the others danced, Phoebus treated Minerva to mulled wine, and Neptune was surrounded by seven or eight women who regaled him with pastry. Every allusion was eagerly seized upon, obscenities were added, inoffensive words were given different meanings by the exclamations of the audience. It had been a long time since the theatergoing public had wallowed in such disrespectful stupidity. It rested them.

Meanwhile the plot was developing in the midst of all this foolishness. Vulcan, as an elegant young man wearing a monocle, dressed entirely in yellow, even to his gloves, was still running after Venus, who had finally appeared dressed as a fishwife, with a kerchief on her head and big gold ornaments on her protruding breasts. Nana was so white and plump, so natural in the role of a broad-hipped, loud-mouthed fishwife, that she instantly won over the whole audience. Rose Mignon, appealingly dressed as a child, with a little hat and a short muslin skirt, was entirely forgotten, even though she had just sung Diana's complaints in a charming voice. Nana, that buxom girl who slapped her thighs and clucked like a hen, was so full of life and female vigor that the audience was carried away by her. From the second act onward, she could do no wrong: she moved awkwardly, sang off key, and forgot her lines, yet she had only to turn to the audience and smile in order to bring forth enthusiastic cheers. Whenever she moved her hips in her own special way, a wave of warmth rose from the orchestra seats to the topmost gallery. And so it was a complete triumph when she led the dance. She was in her element; hands on hips, dropping Venus into the gutter. And the music seemed made for her earthy voice: it was vulgar music, reminiscent of the Saint-Cloud Fair, with sneezing clarinets and capering flutes.

Two more numbers were encored. The waltz of the overture, with its roguish rhythm, came back and carried the gods away. Juno, dressed as a peasant woman, caught Jupiter with his laundress and boxed his ears. Diana overheard Venus arranging a rendezvous with Mars and hurried to reveal the time and place to Vulcan, who cried, "I have my plan!" The rest did not seem very clear. The inquiry ended with a final galop, after which Jupiter, now without his crown, out of breath and bathed in perspiration, declared that the women of earth were delightful and that the men were entirely in the wrong.

As the curtain was falling, a number of voices rose above the general cheering: "Everyone! Everyone!"

The curtain rose again and the whole cast reappeared, holding one another by the hand. Nana and Rose Mignon were in the middle, bowing side by side. There was great applause, the claque shouted acclamations, and then the house slowly became half empty.

"I must go and pay my respects to Countess Muffat," said La Faloise.

"Good! You can introduce me," replied Fauchery. "We'll go downstairs afterward."

It was not easy to reach the balcony boxes. The corridor at the top of the stairs was packed with people. They had to elbow their way through the groups. Leaning against the wall beneath a copper gas lamp, the fat critic was giving his opinion of the play in front of an attentive circle. People murmured his name to one another as they passed. It was rumored that he had laughed during the whole act; he now showed great severity, however, and spoke of good taste and morality. Further on, the thin-lipped critic was full of benevolence that had an unpleasant aftertaste, like sour milk.

Fauchery was moving along, glancing into each box through the round opening in the door, when the Count de Vandeuvres stopped him and questioned him. When he learned that the two cousins were on their way to greet the Muffats, he directed them to box number seven, which he had just left. He then leaned close to the journalist's ear and said, "Listen, I'm sure this Nana is the girl we saw one night on the corner of the Rue de Provence. . . ."

"Yes, you're right!" exclaimed Fauchery. "I knew I'd seen her before!"

La Faloise introduced his cousin to Count Muffat de Beuville, who received him very coldly. But when the Countess heard Fauchery's name, she looked up and discreetly complimented him on his articles in the *Figaro*. Leaning on the velvet-covered railing, she turned halfway around, with a graceful movement of her shoulders. They talked for a few moments and the conversation turned to the Exposition.

"It will be admirable," said the Count, whose square, regular face maintained an official gravity. "I visited the Champ-de-Mars today. I came back amazed."

"I hear it won't be ready on time," La Faloise ventured to remark. "Things are in confusion—"

But the Count interrupted in his stern voice: "It will be ready on time. The Emperor desires it."

Fauchery told gaily how he had nearly become lost in the aquarium, which was then under construction, one day when he had gone there in search of material for an article. The Countess smiled. She occasionally looked around the theater, raising an arm with its white glove reaching to the elbow, and slowly fanning herself. The seats were nearly all empty; a few gentlemen in the orchestra had unfolded newspapers; women were receiving friends, perfectly at ease, as though they were at home. There were now only well-bred whispers beneath the chandelier, whose light was softened as it passed through the fine dust raised by the stir that had followed the end of the act. Men were crowding around the doorways to see the women who had remained seated; they stood there motionless for a minute or so, craning their necks, their shirt fronts looking like great white hearts.

"We'll expect to see you next Tuesday," the Countess said to La Faloise.

She also invited Fauchery, who responded with a bow. They did not speak of the play; Nana's name was not mentioned. The Count maintained such icy dignity that one might have thought him to be at a meeting of the legislature. He said simply, to explain their presence, that his father-in-law liked the theater. The door of the box had remained open. The Marquis de Chouard, who had gone out to make room for the visitors, now returned. He was a tall old man with a pale, flabby face, wearing a broadbrimmed hat. His dim eyes followed all the women as they passed.

As soon as the Countess had given her invitation, Fauchery withdrew, feeling that it would not be proper to discuss the play. La Faloise was the last to leave the box. He had just seen the fair-haired Labordette comfortably installed in the Count de Vandeuvres' stage box, talking at very close range with Blanche de Sivry.

"Tell me, does this Labordette know all women?" he said as soon as he had rejoined his cousin. "Now he's with Blanche."

"Of course he knows them all," Fauchery replied calmly. "Where have you been keeping yourself, my friend?"

The corridor was a little less crowded. Fauchery was about to go downstairs when Lucy Stewart called him. She was at the end of the corridor, in front of the door of her stage box. The heat was terrible in there, she said. She, Caroline Héquet, and her mother occupied the entire width of the passage, nibbling pralines. An attendant was talking maternally with them. Lucy reprimanded the journalist; he wasn't at all nice: he went up to see other women, but he didn't even come to ask them if they were thirsty! Then, dropping this subject: "You know, I think Nana is very good."

She wanted him to stay in her stage box for the last act, but he escaped, promising to come for them at the end of the performance. Outside, in front of the theater, Fauchery and La Faloise lit cigarettes. A small crowd blocked the sidewalk, a line of men who had come down the steps and were breathing in the cool night a' amid the diminished rumble of the boulevard.

Meanwhile Mignon had just led Steiner into the Café des Variétés. Seeing Nana's success, he had begun talking about her with enthusiasm, watching the banker out of the corner of his eye. He knew him well; he had twice helped him to deceive Rose, and each time, when the caprice was over, he had brought him back repentant and faithful. In the café, the too numerous customers were squeezed around marble tables. A few men were standing up, drinking hurriedly. Broad mirrors reflected this jumble of heads to infinity, inordinately enlarging the narrow room with its three chandeliers, its artificial leather seats, and its spiral staircase draped in red. Steiner sat down at a table in the first room, which opened onto the boulevard; its doors had been removed a little too early in the season. As Fauchery and La Faloise were passing by, the banker stopped them.

"Come and have a glass of beer with us."

But he was preoccupied by one idea: he wanted to have a bouquet thrown to Nana. Finally he summoned one of the waiters, whom he familiarly called Auguste. Mignon, who was listening to him, looked at him so pointedly that he became disconcerted and stammered, "Two bouquets, Auguste, and give them to the attendant. One for each of the ladies, at the right moment, eh?"

At the other end of the room, with her head leaning against the frame of a mirror, a girl who could not have been more than eighteen was sitting motionless in front of an empty glass, as though numbed by a long and futile wait. Beneath the natural curls of her beautiful ash-blond hair, she had a virginal face with soft, velvety, candid eyes. She was wearing a faded green silk dress and a round hat that had been knocked out of shape. The chilly evening air had made her very pale.

"Look, there's Satin," Fauchery murmured when he saw her.

La Faloise asked about her. She was nothing but a streetwalker, but she was so vulgar that it was amusing to make her talk. The journalist called out to her, "What are you doing here, Satin?"

"Just sitting here bored as hell," she replied calmly, without moving.

The four men, delighted, burst out laughing.

Mignon assured the others that there was no need to hurry: it would take at least twenty minutes to set up the scenery for the third act. But the two cousins had finished their beer and decided to go back to the theater; they felt cold. When Mignon was left alone with Steiner, he put his elbows on the table and spoke to him from close up: "We'll go to see her, right? I'll introduce you. . . . But this is just between you and me—my wife doesn't need to know about it."

As soon as they returned to their seats, Fauchery and La Faloise noticed a pretty, modestly dressed woman sitting in one of the boxes of the second tier. She was with a serious-looking gentleman, a department head in the Ministry of the Interior, whom La Faloise knew from having met him at the Muffats'. As for Fauchery, he thought he recognized her as Madame Robert, an honorable woman who never had more than one lover at a time, and always chose a respectable man.

But they had to look away. Daguenet was smiling at them. Now that Nana had succeeded, he no longer concealed his status: he had just triumphed in the corridors. Beside him, the young man fresh from school had not left his seat, for Nana had plunged him into a stupor of admiration from which he had not yet emerged. To him, she was Woman. He blushed, absent-mindedly putting on and taking off his gloves. Then, since the man sitting next to him had talked about Nana, he ventured to question him:

"Excuse me, sir, but do you know the lady who's playing the part of Venus?"

"Yes, a little," replied Daguenet, surprised and hesitant.

"And do you know her address?"

Asked of him, the question seemed so crude that Daguenet felt like answering it with a slap.

"No," he said curtly, turning away.

The young man realized that he had just done something improper; he blushed still more deeply and was overcome with bewilderment and dismay.

The three knocks announcing the raising of the curtain resounded through the theater. In the midst of the entering crowd, the attendants, laden with cloaks and coats, were stubbornly trying to put away the garments. The claque applauded the scenery, which represented a grotto on Mount Etna, hollowed out of a silver mine whose sides glittered with the brilliance of newly minted coins. At the back, Vulcan's forge glowed like the setting sun. In the second scene Diana worked out a plan with Vulcan: he was to pretend to go off on a journey in order to leave the way clear for Venus and Mars. Scarcely had Diana been left alone when Venus arrived. A quiver ran through the audience. Venus was naked. She was naked with calm audacity, certain of the omnipotence of her flesh. A piece of gauze was draped over her, but her round shoulders, her Amazonian breasts whose pink tips were firmly tilted upward like two lances, her broad, voluptuously swaying hips, her plump, fair-skinned thighs, her whole body, in short, could be seen, white as foam, through the transparent cloth. She was Venus rising from the waves, with no other veil than her hair. And when she raised her arms the footlights revealed the golden hair of her armpits. There was no applause. No one laughed now. The men strained forward with serious faces, their nostrils contracted, their mouths irritated and dry. A soft wind seemed to have passed, laden with secret menace. The good-natured girl had suddenly been transformed into a disquieting woman who brought with her all the madness of her sex and opened the unknown depths of desire. Nana was still smiling, but it was the sharp smile of a destroyer of men.

"My God!" Fauchery said to La Faloise.

Meanwhile Mars, in his plumed helmet, hurried to his rendezvous and found himself between the two goddesses. There followed a scene which Prullière performed very skillfully: caressed by Diana, who wanted to make one last effort to win him back before delivering him into Vulcan's hands, and cajoled by Venus, who was stimulated by the presence of her rival, he abandoned himself to these blandishments with a blissful look on his face. The scene ended with a trio, and it was then that an attendant appeared in Lucy Stewart's box and threw two enormous bouquets of white lilacs onto the stage. There was a burst of applause; Nana and Rose Mignon bowed while Prullière picked up the bouquets. Some of the spectators in the orchestra seats turned around and smiled at the box occupied by Steiner and Mignon. The banker's face was aflame and his chin was moving convulsively, as though something were stuck in his throat.

The audience was overwhelmed by what took place next. Diana had left in a fury. Venus, seated on a bed of roses, immediately called Mars to her side. Never before had anyone dared to present such a passionate seduction scene on the stage. Nana had her arm around Prullière's neck and was drawing him toward her when Fontan, comically enraged, exaggerating the expression of an outraged husband who has caught his wife in the act, appeared at the far end of the grotto. He was holding the famous iron net. He swung it for a moment like a fisherman about to cast, then Venus and Mars were skillfully ensnared: the net enveloped them and held them fast in their posture as happy lovers.

A murmur arose like a single swelling sigh. A few people applauded, and all the opera glasses in the house were fixed on Venus. Little by little, Nana had taken possession of the audience, and every man was now in her power. The lust that emanated from her, as from an animal in heat, had spread until it filled the house. Her slightest movement now breathed desire. She could stir the flesh with a gesture of her little finger. Men's backs were arched, vibrating as though invisible bows had been drawn across their muscles; wisps of hair rose on their necks as though blown by a woman's warm breath. In front of him, Fauchery saw the young schoolboy lifted from his seat by passion. His curiosity led him to look at other men: the Count de Vandeuvres was very pale and his lips were pinched; fat Steiner's apopletic face seemed to be on the point of bursting; Labordette was staring with the astonished expression of a horse trader admiring a perfect mare;

Daguenet's ears were blood-red and trembling with enjoyment. Then he turned around for a moment and was amazed by what he saw in the Muffats' box: the Countess was pale and serious; behind her, the Count had half risen to his feet, with his mouth open and his face covered with red blotches; beside him in the shadows, the Marquis de Chouard's dim eyes had become like those of a cat, phosphorescent and flecked with gold.

The heat was suffocating; hair weighed heavily on perspiring heads. For the past three hours the breathing of the audience had warmed the air with a human odor. The dust suspended in the air was growing thicker beneath the blazing chandelier. The whole audience was unsteady, on the verge of dizziness, weary and excited, in the grip of those drowsy midnight desires that are haltingly expressed in the depths of alcoves. And Nana, facing that ecstatic audience, that dense mass of fifteen hundred people engulfed in the weakness and nervous exhaustion that come with the end of a performance, was still victorious with her marble flesh, her sex strong enough to destroy them all and remain unscathed.

The play was ending. In response to Vulcan's triumphant calls, all Olympus paraded past the two lovers with exclamations of amazement and lascivious delight. Jupiter said, "My son, I think you acted lightly in calling us here to see this." Then there was a shift of feeling in favor of Venus. The chorus of cuckolds, brought in again by Iris, begged the ruler of the gods to cease complying with their request: since wives had begun staying home, life had become unbearable for men; they preferred to be deceived and satisfied, which was the moral of the play. Venus was then released. Vulcan was given a legal separation from her. Mars and Diana were reconciled. Cupid was finally taken from his prison, where he had been making paper birds instead of conjugating the verb "to love." The curtain fell on the grand finale, with the chorus of cuckolds kneeling and singing a hymn of gratitude to Venus, who was smiling and exalted in her sovereign nudity.

The spectators were already on their feet and moving toward the doors. The authors were named and there were two curtain calls amid a thunder of bravos. The cry, "Nana! Nana!" had been repeated wildly. Then, before the house was completely empty, it became dark. The footlights went out, the chandelier was dimmed, and the long gray coverings slipped from the stage boxes and enveloped the gildings of the galleries. The theater, so agitated and noisy only a short time before, suddenly fell into a deep sleep and became filled with a musty, dusty odor. Countess Muffat, wrapped in her furs, was standing erect in front of her box, staring into the shadows as she waited for the crowd to leave.

In the corridors the attendants were becoming frantic among jumbled heaps of garments. Fauchery and La Faloise had hurried to watch the people coming out. In the lobby, men were standing in rows while two endless, regular, compact lines came down the double staircase. Steiner, led by Mignon, had been among the first to leave. The Count de Vandeuvres went out with Blanche de Sivry on his arm. For a moment, Gaga and her daughter seemed to be in difficulty, but Labordette quickly found them a cab and gallantly held the door for them. No one saw Daguenet leave. The schoolboy, his cheeks aglow, was determined to wait at the stage door. Satin was standing on the sidewalk as he ran toward the Passage des Panoramas, whose gate he found locked. She went over to him and brushed her skirt against him. But he was in such despair that he violently rejected her advances and disappeared into the crowd with tears of desire and helplessness in his eyes. Men were lighting cigars, and walking away from the theater humming "When Venus roams at night. . . ." Satin went back to the Café des Variétés, where Auguste let her eat the lumps of sugar left by the customers. A fat man who had just left the theater in a state of excitement finally took her away into the shadows of the slowly quieting boulevard.

People were still coming downstairs. La Faloise was waiting for Clarisse. Fauchery had promised to escort Lucy Stewart, with Caroline Héquet and her mother. They arrived in the lobby, occupying a whole corner and laughing very loudly, when the Muffats passed by with an icy expression. Bordenave had just opened a little door and was making Fauchery promise to write an article. He was sweating, his face was flushed, and he seemed to be intoxicated by success.

"You're good for two hundred performances," La Faloise said to him obligingly. "Everyone in Paris will come to your theater."

But Bordenave angrily made a quick movement of his chin toward the crowd that filled the lobby, toward that mob of men with dry lips and ardent eyes, still burning to possess Nana, and cried out violently, "Call it my whorehouse, you stubborn fool!"

Paris used, for two months performances. La
she said offhandedly, "Everyone in Paris will dine at
your theater.

2

*A*t ten o'clock the next morning, Nana was still asleep. She occupied the third floor of a big new house on the Boulevard Haussmann whose owner had decided to rent to single ladies until the plaster was dry. A rich merchant from Moscow, who had come to spend a winter in Paris, had installed her there, paying the rent for six months in advance. The apartment was too big for her and had never been furnished completely. Gaudy luxury—gilded chairs and console tables—contrasted with second-rate odds and ends such as mahogany pedestal tables and zinc candelabra that tried to imitate Florentine bronze. It all told the story of a girl who had been abandoned too soon by her first serious gentleman and had then fallen back on shabby lovers, of a difficult beginning and early efforts hampered by refusals of credit and threats of eviction.

Nana was sleeping on her stomach with her bare arms around the pillow in which her face, pale with fatigue, was buried. The bedroom and the dressing room were the only rooms to which the neighborhood upholsterer had given careful attention. A streak of light beneath a curtain revealed rosewood furniture and the brocaded damask of the hangings and chairs, with big blue flowers against a gray background. But in the damp, drowsy air of that bedroom, Nana awoke with a start, as though surprised to feel an empty place next to her. She looked at the pillow beside her own. In the midst of its lace was a hollow made by a head; it was still warm. With her groping hand she pressed the button of an electric bell at the head of her bed.

"Is he gone?" she asked the maid who appeared.

"Yes, Madame, Monsieur Paul left less than ten minutes ago. Since you were tired he didn't want to wake you up. But he asked me to tell you he'll come tomorrow."

Zoé, the maid, had opened the blinds as she spoke. Bright daylight streamed into the room. Zoé's dark hair was held in place by little headbands. Her pale, scarred face was long and pointed, like a dog's; she had a snub nose, thick lips and black eyes that were constantly in motion.

"Tomorrow . . . tomorrow . . ." repeated Nana, still only half awake. "Is tomorrow his day?"

"Yes, Madame, Monsieur Paul has always come on Wednesday."

"No, I remember now!" cried Nana, sitting up. "Everything's changed. I wanted to tell him this morning. . . . He'd run into the blackhead and we'd have trouble on our hands."

"You didn't tell me, Madame, so I couldn't know," murmured Zoé. "It would be a good idea to let me know when you change your days. . . . So the old miser won't come on Tuesday any more?"

Between themselves they unsmilingly gave the names of "the old miser" and "the blackhead" to Nana's two paying visitors. One was a parsimonious businessman from the Faubourg Saint-Denis; the other was a Walachian who claimed to be a count and whose money, always very irregular, had a suspicious odor. Daguenet had reserved for himself the mornings after the old miser's departure. Since the businessman had to be at his establishment by eight o'clock, Daguenet waited in Zoé's kitchen until he had gone, then took his place, which was still warm, until ten o'clock. He and Nana considered it a pleasant arrangement.

"It doesn't matter," she said, "I'll write to him this afternoon. . . . And if he doesn't get my letter, don't let him in tomorrow."

Zoé walked softly around the room. She spoke of the great success of the previous evening. Madame had shown such talent! She had sung so well! Ah, Madame had no need to worry now!

With her elbow sunk into the pillow, Nana answered only with a nod. Her nightgown had slipped down and her loose, tangled hair hung over her shoulders.

"Yes," she said thoughtfully, "but how can we manage to wait? I'm going to have all kinds of annoyances today. . . . Has the concierge come up yet this morning?"

They both began talking seriously. Nana was nine months behind in her rent and the landlord was speaking of seizing her belongings. And there was a throng of creditors: a livery-stableman, a linen-draper, a dressmaker, a coal merchant, and others. They came every day and sat on a bench in the anteroom. The coal merchant was particularly violent: he shouted on the stairs. But Nana's greatest worry was her little Louis, a child she had had when she was sixteen. She had left him with a wet nurse in a village near Rambouillet. The nurse was demanding three hundred francs and refused to give Louiset back before she had been paid. Ever since her last visit to her child, Nana had been seized with a fit of maternal love, and she was in despair at not being able to carry out a plan that had become an obsession with her: to pay the nurse and place the child with her aunt, Madame Lerat, in Les Batignolles, where she would go to see him whenever she wished.

Her maid hinted that she should have told the old miser about her needs.

"Oh, I've told him everything!" said Nana. "He told me he had too many bills to pay. He never goes beyond his thousand francs a month . . . The blackhead has no money at all right now; I think he's been losing at cards. . . . As for poor Mimi, he needs a loan himself. He was wiped out by a drop in the stock market and he can't even bring me flowers any more."

She was speaking of Daguenet. In her moments of abandon just after awakening, she kept no secrets from Zoé, who, accustomed to such confidences, received them with respectful sympathy. Since Madame deigned to talk to her about her affairs, she would take the liberty of saying what she thought. First of all, she was very fond of Madame. That was why she had left Madame Blanche, and God knew that Madame Blanche was doing everything she could to get her back! She could always get a job; she was known by enough people to be sure of that, but she would have stayed with Madame even in poverty, because she believed in Madame's future. And she finally gave her advice. When one was young, one did foolish things. It was now time to be careful, because men thought only of amusing themselves. Oh, there would be plenty of them!

31

Madame would have only to say a word to quiet her creditors and get the money she needed.

"All that doesn't give me three hundred francs," said Nana, plunging her fingers into her tousled hair. "I need three hundred francs today, right away. . . . It's stupid not to know anyone who'll give you three hundred francs."

She racked her brain. She was expecting Madame Lerat that morning, and she would have sent her to Rambouillet. Her triumph of the night before was spoiled by her inability to carry out her whim. To think that among all those men who had acclaimed her, there was not one who would bring her three hundred francs! Anyway, she couldn't accept money like that. Oh, how unlucky she was! And her thoughts always returned to her baby: he had angelic blue eyes, he said "Mama" in such a funny way that it almost made her die laughing.

Then the electric doorbell rang with its rapid, tremulous vibration. When Zoé returned she said confidentially, "It's a woman." She had seen that woman at least twenty times before, but she always pretended not to recognize her or to know anything about her dealings with ladies in distress. "She told me her name," she added: "Madame Tricon."

"Tricon!" exclaimed Nana. "Yes, of course, I'd forgotten about her. . . . Show her in."

Zoé brought in a tall old woman with her hair in ringlets; she looked like a countess who haunted lawyers' offices. Zoé then slipped away and disappeared without a word, with the lithe, snakelike movement with which she left a room when a gentleman arrived. She might just as well have stayed, however. Tricon did not even sit down. There was only a brief exchange of words.

"I have someone for you today. Are you interested?"

"Yes. How much?"

"Four hundred francs."

"At what time?"

"Three o'clock. . . . Then it's settled?"

"Yes."

Tricon immediately began talking about the weather; it was dry and good for walking. She still had four or five people to see. She left after looking at a little notebook. As soon as she had been left alone, Nana seemed to feel relieved. A slight shiver passed over her shoulders and she got back into her warm bed, indolently, with the languor of a cat. Her eyes gradually closed as she smiled at the idea of dressing Louiset in pretty clothes the next day. Then, in the sleep which finally overtook her, the feverish dream that had stayed with her all night—a dream of endless cheers and applause—returned like a figured bass and lulled her lassitude.

At eleven o'clock, when Zoé showed Madame Lerat into the bedroom, Nana was still asleep. But she awoke at the sound and said immediately, "Ah, it's you . . . I want you to go to Rambouillet today."

"That's why I came," replied her aunt. "There's a train at twenty past twelve. I have time to take it."

"No, I won't have the money till this afternoon," said Nana, stretching her arms with her back arched. "You'll have some lunch, then we'll see."

Zoé brought her a negligee and said, "Madame, the hairdresser is here."

But Nana did not want to go into the dressing room. She called out, "Come in, Francis."

A very correctly dressed gentleman opened the door. He bowed just as Nana was getting out of bed, her legs bare. She unhurriedly held out her hands so that Zoé could pull on the sleeves of her negligee. Francis, looking dignified and perfectly at ease, waited without averting his eyes. Then, when she was sitting down and he had passed the comb through her hair, he spoke: "Perhaps you haven't seen the newspapers, Madame. . . . There's a very good article in the *Figaro*."

He had brought the newspaper. Madame Lerat put on her glasses and read the article aloud, standing in front of the window. She drew her military figure erect and contracted her nostrils each time she read a racy adjective. It was an article by Fauchery, written immediately after leaving the theater: two very warm columns filled with witty sarcasm about the performer and forthright admiration of the woman.

"Excellent!" Francis kept repeating.

What did Nana care whether anyone made fun of her voice? He was nice, that Fauchery; she would repay him for his pleasant manner. After rereading the article, Madame Lerat declared abruptly that all men had the devil in the calves of their legs; and she refused to explain any further, satisfied with this ribald allusion that she alone understood. Francis had finished combing up and tying Nana's hair. He bowed and said, "I'll keep my eye on the evening papers. . . . At half-past five, as usual?"

"Bring me a jar of pomade and a pound of pralines from Boissier's!" Nana called out to him through the drawing room as he was closing the door.

Then the two women, left alone together, remembered that they had not embraced; they warmly kissed each other on the cheek. The article had roused them. Nana, who had not been fully awake, again felt all the fever of her triumph. Ah, Rose Mignon must have been spending a lovely morning! Madame Lerat had not gone to the theater because, she said, all the excitement upset her stomach, so Nana began telling her about the evening, becoming intoxicated by her own story, as though all Paris had wildly applauded her. Then she stopped short and asked, laughing, if anyone would ever have believed it when she was a little girl on the Rue de la Goutte-d'Or. Her aunt shook her head. No, nobody could ever have predicted it. She now began to talk, taking on a serious expression and calling Nana her daughter. Wasn't she her second mother, since her real mother had gone to join her father and her grandmother? Nana, deeply moved, was on the verge of tears. But Madame Lerat said that the past was the past—and it was a dirty past, too, with things in it that shouldn't be stirred up every day. For a long time she had stopped seeing her niece, because the family had accused her of ruining herself with the girl. As though that were possible! She didn't ask Nana to confide in her, she believed she had always lived decently. And now it was enough for her to find her in a good position, and to see that she had motherly feelings for her son. Nothing mattered in this world except honesty and hard work.

"Who's the father of your baby?" she asked abruptly, her eyes glowing with keen curiosity.

Nana, surprised, hesitated for a second, then replied, "A gentleman."

"Oh?" said her aunt. "I was told he was a bricklayer who used to beat you. . . . Well, you can tell me about it some day. You know how discreet I am! . . . Anyway, I'll

34

take care of him as though he were the son of a prince."

She had given up her trade as a maker of artificial
flowers and was now living on an income of six hundred
francs a year derived from the savings she had hoarded up
sou by sou. Nana promised to rent a nice apartment for
her; in addition to that, she would give her a hundred
francs a month. When she heard this figure, Madame Lerat
was so carried away that she cried out to her niece that
she ought to squeeze them for all they were worth, since
she now had them in her power; she was speaking of men.
They kissed each other again. But in the midst of her
joy, when the conversation turned back to Louiset, Nana
seemed to be saddened by a sudden recollection.

"How annoying!" she said. "I have to go out at three
o'clock! What a bore!"

Zoé had just come in to say that lunch was ready. They
went into the dining room, where an old lady was already
sitting in front of the table. She had not taken off her hat,
and she was wearing a dark dress of an indecisive color,
somewhere between puce and gosling green. Nana did not
seem surprised to see her there. She merely asked her why
she had not come into her bedroom.

"I heard voices," replied the old lady. "I thought you
had company."

Madame Maloir, who had a respectable appearance and
good manners, served as Nana's elderly friend; she gave
her companionship and accompanied her when she went
out. At first, Madame Lerat's presence seemed to make
her uneasy. When she learned, however, that she was
Nana's aunt, she gave her a friendly look and a faint smile.
Nana, who had said she was starving, began devouring
some radishes without bread. Madame Lerat ceremoniously
refused the radishes; she said they caused heartburn. Then,
when Zoé brought in the cutlets, Nana merely toyed with
her meat and contented herself with sucking the bone.
Now and then she examined her friend's hat out of the
corner of her eye.

"Is that the new hat I gave you?" she finally asked.

"Yes, I altered it," Madame Maloir answered with her
mouth full.

It was an ostentatious hat, flared widely in front and
adorned with a big feather. Madame Maloir had a mania

for remaking all her hats; she knew what suited her, and she could quickly turn the most elegant hat into a vulgar bonnet. Nana nearly lost her temper, for she had bought her that hat precisely because she did not want to feel embarrassed by her when she went out with her.

"You could at least take it off!" she cried.

"No, thank you," the old lady replied with dignity. "It doesn't bother me. I can eat very well with it on."

After the cutlets came some cauliflower and the remains of a cold chicken. But Nana turned up her nose at each dish, hesitated, sniffed, and finally left everything on her plate. She finished her lunch with some jam.

Dessert took a long time. Zoé did not clear the table before serving coffee. The ladies had simply pushed back their plates. They again talked about Nana's triumph. Nana rolled cigarettes and smoked them, tilting back her chair. And since Zoé had remained in the room, leaning against the sideboard with her arms dangling, they finally began listening to the story of her life. She said she was the daughter of a Bercy midwife who had gotten into trouble. First she had worked for a dentist, then for an insurance broker; but that hadn't suited her. Next she mentioned, with a touch of pride, the ladies for whom she had worked as a maid. She spoke of them as though she had held their fortunes in her hands. If it hadn't been for her, more than one of them would have been in a fine mess. One day when Madame Blanche was with Monsieur Octave, for example, the old man had suddenly come in. What did Zoé do? She deliberately fell as she was walking through the drawing room, the old man rushed up to her, then went into the kitchen to get her a glass of water, and Monsieur Octave escaped.

"Ah, that's a good one!" said Nana, who had been listening with affectionate interest and a kind of docile admiration.

"As for me, I've had my share of trouble," said Madame Lerat. She drew closer to Madame Maloir and began confiding in her. They were both eating lumps of sugar dipped in brandy. But Madame Maloir listened to the secrets of others without ever revealing anything about herself. She was said to be living on a mysterious pension in a room which no one else ever entered.

· Suddenly Nana burst out angrily: "Don't play with knives, aunt! You know it upsets me!"

Without thinking of what she was doing, Madame Lerat had just crossed two knives on the table. Nana claimed not to be superstitious: spilled salt meant nothing to her, and neither did Fridays; but she couldn't help believing in the significance of crossed knives. It had never failed. Something unpleasant was surely going to happen to her. She yawned and said with profound annoyance, "It's already two o'clock. I'll have to leave soon. What a nuisance!"

The two old women looked at each other. All three of them nodded without speaking. No, life wasn't always amusing. Nana leaned back in her chair again and lit another cigarette while the others discreetly and philosophically pursed their lips.

"We'll play bezique while you're gone," Madame Maloir said after a silence. "Do you know the game, Madame?"

Of course Madame Lerat played bezique; she played it perfectly, in fact. There was no need to trouble Zoé, who had disappeared; one corner of the table would be enough. They folded back the tablecloth over the dirty dishes. But just as Madame Maloir was about to take the cards from a drawer of the sideboard, Nana said she would appreciate it if she would write a letter for her before beginning the game. She didn't like to write, and besides, she wasn't sure of her spelling, whereas her old friend could write beautiful letters full of feeling. She went off to her bedroom to get some fancy stationery. A cheap bottle of ink and a rusty pen were already in the dining room. The letter was for Daguenet. Madame Maloir began in her graceful handwriting: "My dearest darling." She told Daguenet not to come the next day because it was "impossible," but that "near or far, at every moment," she was "with him in thought."

"And I'll end with 'a thousand kisses,'" she said.

Madame Lerat had approved each phrase with a nod. Her eyes were aglow; she loved being involved in affairs of the heart. She was inspired to make a suggestion of her own: "How about 'a thousand kisses on your beautiful eyes'?" she cooed tenderly.

"That's it, 'a thousand kisses on your beautiful eyes'!"

said Nana, while a blissful expression came over the faces of the two old women.

Nana rang for Zoé, gave her the letter, and told her to take it to a messenger. Zoé said she had just been talking with a messenger from the theater who had brought Madame a schedule that had been forgotten that morning. Nana had the man brought in and asked him to deliver the letter to Daguenet on his way back. Then she began to question him. Oh, Monsieur Bordenave was very pleased! The house was already sold out for a week. Madame couldn't imagine how many people had been asking for her address all day. When he had left, Nana said she would be gone no more than half an hour. If any visitors came, Zoé was to ask them to wait. As she spoke, the doorbell rang. It was a creditor, the livery-stableman. He had sat down on the bench in the anteroom; he could sit there and twiddle his thumbs for the rest of the day, there was no hurry!

"I must pull myself together," Nana said lazily, yawning and stretching again. "I ought to be there now."

Yet she did not move. She was following the game, in which her aunt had just announced a hundred in aces. She watched attentively, with her chin in her hand. But she started suddenly when she heard the clock strike three.

"Good God!" she exclaimed loudly.

Madame Maloir, who was counting the aces, encouraged her in her languid voice: "You'd do better to get your business over with as soon as possible."

"Yes, hurry," said Madame Lerat, shuffling the cards. "I'll take the four-thirty train if you come back with the money by four o'clock."

"Oh, it won't take that long," said Nana.

Ten minutes later, with Zoé's help, she had put on a dress and a hat. She didn't care how she looked. As she was about to leave, the doorbell rang again. This time it was the coal merchant. Well, he could keep the livery-stableman company! They could entertain each other! Fearing a scene, however, she went through the kitchen and left by the back stairs. She often went down them, holding up her skirts.

"If a woman is a good mother, she can be forgiven for anything," Madame Maloir said sententiously when she had been left alone with Madame Lerat.

"I have eighty in kings," replied Madame Lerat, who loved to play cards. And they both plunged into an endless game.

The table had not been cleared. The room was filled with cigarette smoke and the smell of lunch. The two ladies had begun eating brandy-soaked lumps of sugar again. They had been playing cards and sipping brandy for twenty minutes when the doorbell rang a third time. Zoé burst into the room and spoke to them brusquely, as though they were friends of hers: "There's the doorbell again! You can't stay here. If a lot of people come, I'll need the whole apartment. Come on, out you go!"

Madame Maloir wanted to finish the game, but when Zoé threatened to grab the cards she decided to move them without disarranging them while Madame Lerat took the bottle of brandy, the glasses, and the sugar. They hurried into the kitchen and sat down at one end of the table, between some towels that had been hung up to dry and a pan still full of dirty dishwater.

"Let's see now: three hundred and forty . . . It's your turn."

"Hearts."

When Zoé came back she found them absorbed in their game again. After a silence, while Madame Lerat was shuffling the cards, Madame Maloir asked, "Who was it?"

"Oh, no one," the maid answered casually. "Just a boy. . . . I was going to send him away, but he's so good-looking, with his blue eyes and his girlish face without a single whisker, that I finally told him to wait. He's holding a big bouquet and won't let go of it. He deserves a spanking—a youngster like that who should still be in school!"

Madame Lerat went to get some water with which to make a hot toddy; the sugar had made her thirsty. Zoé murmured that she wouldn't mind having a hot toddy herself. She had a taste in her mouth as bitter as gall, she said.

"And where did you put him?" asked Madame Maloir.

"In the little unfurnished room at the back. There's nothing in it except one of Madame's trunks and a table. That's where I usually put stingy visitors."

She was lavishly putting sugar into her hot toddy when she was startled by the doorbell. Damn it! Couldn't she even have a drink in peace? With so many visitors already, what was it going to be like later? She hurried to the door nevertheless. When she returned, she said in answer to Madame Maloir's questioning look, "Nothing, only a bouquet."

The three women nodded to one another and drank. While Zoé was finally clearing the table and bringing the dirty dishes to the sink one by one, the doorbell again rang twice in rapid succession. But it was nothing serious. She kept her friends in the kitchen informed, and twice repeated her disdainful phrase, "Nothing, only a bouquet."

However, the two ladies had a good laugh in the middle of their card game when Zoé told them how the creditors in the anteroom had looked when the flowers arrived. Madame would find the bouquets on her dressing table. It was a shame they cost so much, yet couldn't be sold for more than ten sous! Well, there was a lot of money wasted in the world.

"I'd be happy if I had only the amount of money that men spend on flowers for women in Paris every day," said Madame Maloir.

"I should think you would be!" said Madame Lerat. "You don't ask much! Why, if I had only the money that's spent on wire to hold the bouquets together . . . Sixty in queens, my dear."

It was ten minutes to four. Zoé expressed surprise that Madame should have been gone so long. Usually when she had to go out in the afternoon she got it over with in no time. But Madame Maloir pointed out that one did not always do things as one wished. Life was full of snags, declared Madame Lerat. The best thing to do was to wait; if her niece was late, it was surely because her business had detained her. Anyway, they had no reason to complain. They were quite comfortable in the kitchen. And since she had no more hearts, Madame Lerat played a diamond.

The doorbell began again. When Zoé reappeared she was all excited.

"It's fat Steiner, girls!" she said softly as soon as she came in. "I put him in the little drawing room."

Madame Maloir said a few words about the banker to Madame Lerat, who knew nothing about such gentlemen. Was he going to drop Rose Mignon? Zoé made a gesture with her head; she knew a thing or two. But then she had to go to the door again.

"What a mess!" she said when she came back. "It's the blackhead! I kept telling him Madame was out, but he went into the bedroom anyway. . . . We weren't expecting him till tonight."

At a quarter past four Nana had still not returned. What could she be doing? It didn't make sense. Two more bouquets were delivered. Zoé, bored, looked to see if there was any coffee left. Yes, the ladies would be glad to finish the coffee, it would wake them up. They were getting drowsy, slumped in their chairs, constantly drawing cards with the same movement. The clock struck half-past. Something must have happened to Nana. They began whispering to one another.

Suddenly forgetting everything else, Madame Maloir cried out triumphantly, "Five hundred! Quint major in trumps!"

"Quiet!" Zoé said angrily. "What will all those gentlemen think?"

In the silence that followed, broken only by a muffled argument between the two old women, they heard footsteps swiftly coming up the back staircase. It was Nana at last. They could hear her heavy breathing even before she opened the door. Her face was red when she came in, and her movements were abrupt. The laces of her skirt had apparently broken; it was dragging on the floor and it had just been soaked in a puddle of something dirty that had flowed down from the second floor, where the maid was a slovenly wench.

"It's about time!" said Madame Lerat, still annoyed by Madame Maloir's five hundred points. "You really know how to keep people waiting!"

"You're not reasonable, Madame!" said Zoé.

Nana, already in a bad mood, was exasperated by these reproaches. So this was how they welcomed her, after the unpleasantness she had just been through!

"Leave me alone!" she cried.

"Sh, Madame, there are people waiting," said Zoé.

Nana lowered her voice and said haltingly, still out of breath, "Do you think I've been enjoying myself? I thought it was never going to end. I wish I could have seen you in

41

my place. . . . I was boiling, I felt like slapping him. . . . And then I couldn't find a cab to come back. Fortunately it's not far. Just the same, I did a lot of running."

"Do you have the money?" asked her aunt.

"I've been waiting for that question!"

Nana sat down on a chair near the stove. Her legs were still weak from having run so far. Without catching her breath, she reached into the front of her dress and took out an envelope containing four one-hundred-franc notes. She had previously ripped it open to make sure the money was there. The three women around her stared at the dirty, rumpled envelope in her little gloved hand. It was too late; Madame Lerat would not be able to go to Rambouillet until the following day. Nana began to give long explanations.

"Madame, there are people waiting," Zoé repeated.

Nana became angry again. They could go right on waiting! She would deal with them later, after she had finished what she was doing.

When her aunt reached out her hand toward the money she said, "No, not all of it! Three hundred francs for the nurse and fifty for your traveling expenses, that makes three hundred and fifty. I'm keeping fifty francs."

The great difficulty was to get change. There was less than ten francs in the apartment. No one even bothered to ask Madame Maloir, who listened with an uninterested look, because she never carried more than the six sous she needed for the omnibus. Finally Zoé left the room, saying that she was going to look in her trunk. She came back with a hundred francs in five-franc coins. They were counted on one end of the table. Madame Lerat left immediately, after promising to bring Louiset back the next day.

"You say there are people waiting?" asked Nana, still sitting down and resting.

"Yes, Madame, three people."

She gave the banker's name first. Nana made a face. Did that Steiner think she was going to let him bore her just because he had thrown her a bouquet the night before?

"Anyway," she said, "I've had enough. I won't see any of them. Go tell them you no longer expect me to come home."

"Think it over, Madame, and I'm sure you'll decide to see Monsieur Steiner," Zoé said gravely without moving, annoyed to see her mistress about to behave foolishly again. She then spoke of the Walachian: time must be hanging heavy on his hands in the bedroom. Nana flew into a rage and became still more stubborn. No! She wouldn't see anyone! How had she ever gotten herself involved with such a clinging leech of a man?

"Throw them all out! I'm going to play bezique with Madame Maloir. I like that much better."

She was interrupted by the doorbell. This was the last straw! Another pest! She forbade Zoé to go to the door. The maid left the kitchen without listening to her. When she returned, she handed Nana two cards and said firmly, "I told these gentlemen you were at home, Madame. They're in the drawing room."

Nana furiously leapt to her feet. But she became calmer when she looked at the cards and saw the names of the Marquis de Chouard and Count Muffat de Beuville.

"Who are they?" she asked at length. "Do you know them?"

"I know the old one," replied Zoé, discreetly pursing her lips. And when her mistress continued to question her with her eyes, she added simply, "I've seen him somewhere."

These words seemed to decide Nana. She regretfully left the kitchen, that warm refuge where she could talk and be at ease in the odor of the coffee heating over the embers. Behind her she left Madame Maloir, who was now playing solitaire; she still had not taken off her hat, although she had just made herself comfortable by untying its strings and throwing them over her shoulders.

In the dressing room, where Zoé quickly helped her to put on a negligee, Nana avenged herself for the annoyances that were being inflicted on her by mumbling curses against all men. These crude words upset her maid, for she was pained to see that Madame was slow in throwing off the vulgarity of her origins. She even dared to beg Madame to calm down.

"Oh, don't worry," Nana replied bluntly, "they're all pigs: they like it."

However, she took on what she called her princess look.

Zoé had held her back as she was about to go into the drawing room; she now showed the Marquis de Chouard and Count Muffat into the dressing room. It would be much better that way.

"Gentlemen," said Nana with studied politeness, "I'm sorry I kept you waiting."

The two men bowed and sat down. The light in the room was softened by an embroidered tulle blind. It was the most elegant room in the apartment, with light drapery, a big marble dressing table, a mirror with an inlaid frame, a chaise longue and armchairs covered with blue satin. On the dressing table, the bouquets of roses, lilacs, and hyacinths were like a cascade of flowers, and their scent was strong and penetrating, while in the damp air, in the stale exhalations from the basins, a sharper smell could occasionally be detected, coming from a few springs of dried patchouli broken into small pieces at the bottom of a cup. And as she huddled in her chair, drawing her loosely fastened negligee around her, Nana seemed to have been surprised during her toilet. Her skin was still moist, she was smiling, and she looked almost startled in the midst of her laces.

"Madame," Count Muffat said gravely, "please excuse us for having insisted. . . . We've come to ask for a donation. . . . The Marquis and I are members of the charity committee for this district."

The Marquis de Chouard hastened to add gallantly, "When we learned that a great artist was living in this house, we decided to come and plead the cause of our poor people to her in person. Talent is never without a heart."

Nana made a show of modesty. She replied with little movements of her head, making rapid reflections at the same time. It must have been the old man who had brought the other one; he had lecherous eyes. Yet she must also be careful of the other one, whose temples were bulging quite noticeably; he might have come all by himself. Probably the concierge had given them her name and they had egged each other on, each with his own ends in view.

"You were quite right to come, gentlemen," she said graciously. Just then the sound of the doorbell made her start. Another visitor, and Zoé kept letting them in! She went on: "I'm always happy when I can give."

At the bottom of her heart, she was flattered.

"Ah, Madame," said the Marquis, "if you only knew! Such poverty! There are over three thousand poor people in our district, and it's one of the richest. You can't imagine such distress: children without food, sick women without any assistance whatever, dying of cold . . ."

"Oh, the poor people!" cried Nana, deeply moved.

Her pity was so great that tears blurred her beautiful eyes. She leaned forward, forgetting to study her movements. Her open negligee revealed her neck, and her knees stretched the thin cloth, outlining the roundness of her thighs. A slight flush appeared on the Marquis' ashen cheeks. Count Muffat, who had been about to speak, lowered his eyes. The air was too warm in that room; it had the heavy, sultry warmth of a greenhouse. The roses were wilting and an intoxicating smell was rising from the patchouli in the cup.

"I'm sure everyone would like to be very rich on such occasions," said Nana. "But each person does what he can. Believe me, gentlemen, if I'd known. . ."

She realized that her emotion was about to make her say something foolish, so she did not finish her sentence. She was perplexed for a moment, trying to remember where she had put her fifty francs when she took off her dress. Then it came back to her: the money was on one corner of her dressing table, under a pomade jar that had been turned upside down. As she was standing up, the doorbell rang for a long time. Another one! Wasn't it ever going to stop? The Count and the Marquis had also stood up, and the latter's ears seemed to be straining toward the door; he had no doubt recognized the manner in which the bell had been rung. Muffat looked at him, then they both turned their eyes away, each embarrassed by the other. They became cold again, the one stocky and solid, with his thick head of hair, the other drawing back his narrow shoulders over which fell his crown of thin white hair.

"I'm afraid I'm going to give you a heavy burden, gentlemen," said Nana, laughing, as she brought the ten big silver coins. "This is for the poor. . ." And the adorable little dimple appeared in her chin. Her face had a relaxed, good-natured expression and she held the pile of coins in her open hand, offering it to the two men as though saying to them, "Well, who wants it?" The Count was the quicker of the two: he took the fifty francs. But one coin remained in her hand, and as he picked it up he touched her skin, a skin so warm and smooth that it sent a little tremor through his body. Nana, amused, was still laughing.

"There you are, gentlemen," she said. "Next time I hope to give more."

No longer having any pretext for staying, they bowed and walked toward the door. Just as they were about to leave, the doorbell rang again. The Marquis could not hide a faint smile, while a shadow passed over the Count's face and made it still more solemn. Nana retained them for a few seconds to give Zoé time to find a place for the new-comer. She did not like men to meet one another in her apartment. By now, though, it was probably full to over-flowing. She was relieved when she saw that the drawing room was empty. Had Zoé been stuffing them into the closets?

"Good-by, gentlemen," she said, stopping on the thresh-old of the drawing room.

She enveloped them in her smile and her clear gaze. Count Muffat bowed, troubled despite his great social experience. He needed air: he felt dizzy from having been in that small dressing room with its overpowering odor of woman and flowers. And behind him the Marquis de Chouard, sure of not being seen, dared to wink at Nana. His features had suddenly become contorted, and he had his tongue between his lips.

When Nana returned to her dressing room, where Zoé was waiting for her with letters and calling cards, she laughed still more loudly and exclaimed, "Those two beggars walked off with my fifty francs!"

She was not angry: it seemed amusing to her that men had taken her money. Just the same, they were a couple of pigs; now she didn't have a single sou. The sight of the letters and calling cards brought back all her ill-humor. She did not mind the letters so much: they came from men who, after having applauded her the night before, were now making passionate declarations to her. As for the visitors, they could go to hell!

Zoé had placed them everywhere; and she pointed out that the apartment was conveniently arranged, since each room opened onto the hall. It was not like Madame Blanche's apartment, where everyone had to go through the drawing room. Madame Blanche had had a lot of trouble because of that.

"Send them all away," said Nana, pursuing her thought. "Begin with the blackhead."

"Oh, I sent him away a long time ago, Madame," Zoé answered with a smile. "He only wanted to tell you he couldn't come tonight."

Nana clapped her hands with joy. He wasn't coming! What good luck! She was going to be free! She heaved a sigh of relief, as though she had been spared a harrowing ordeal. She immediately thought of Daguenet. Poor boy, she'd just written him to wait till Thursday! Quick, Madame Maloir would have to write another letter! But Zoé said that Madame Maloir had slipped away unnoticed, as usual. Nana spoke of sending a messenger, but then she became hesitant. She was very tired. It would be so good to be able to sleep for a whole night! The idea of this treat finally prevailed. For once she could allow herself that pleasure.

"I'll go to bed as soon as I come back from the theater," she said with a greedy expression, "and don't wake me up before noon." She raised her voice: "And now, throw them all out!"

Zoé did not move. She would never have taken the liberty of openly advising Madame, but she managed to give her the benefit of her experience whenever she seemed to be carried away by her headstrong character.

"Including Monsieur Steiner?" she asked curtly.

"Of course!" replied Nana. "Throw him out before any of the others!"

Zoé went on waiting, to give Madame time to reflect. Monsieur Steiner was a very rich man, known in all the theaters—wouldn't Madame be proud to take him away from her rival, Rose Mignon?

"Hurry," said Nana, who understood perfectly, "and tell him he's a nuisance." But she abruptly reconsidered: she

47

might want him the next day. She cried out with a childish gesture, laughing and winking her eyes, "After all, if I want to have him, throwing him out will be the quickest way to get him!"

Zoé was struck by these words. She gave Nana a look of sudden admiration, then went off to send Steiner away without hesitation.

Nana waited patiently for a few minutes to give her time to sweep the place out, as she put it. Her apartment had been invaded by a whole army! She looked into the drawing room; it was empty. So was the dining room. But as she was continuing her inspection, reassured, certain now that there was no one left, she opened the door of a small unfurnished room and found herself face to face with an adolescent boy. He was calmly sitting on a trunk with an enormous bouquet on his lap.

"Good God!" she cried. "There's still one in here!"

The boy had jumped to the floor as soon as he saw her. His face was as red as a poppy, and he did not know what to do with his bouquet; he passed it back and forth from one hand to the other, choking with emotion. Nana was touched by his youth, his embarrassment and the comical appearance he presented with his flowers. She burst into melodious laughter. What! Children too? Were men coming to her now as soon as they were out of the cradle? She slapped her thighs and said to him in a familiar, maternal tone, "Do you want me to wipe your nose for you, little boy?"

"Yes," he answered softly and pleadingly.

This reply amused her all the more. He was seventeen and his name was Georges Hugon. He had been at the Variety Theater the night before. He had now come to see her.

"Are those flowers for me?"

"Yes."

"Then give them to me, you silly fool!"

But as she took the bouquet he seized her hands with all the impetuous gluttony of his age. She had to strike him to make him let go. The little brat had his nerve! She scolded him, but her face had turned pink and she was smiling. She sent him away, after giving him permission to come back. He was unsteady on his feet and had difficulty in finding the doors.

She went back to the dressing room. Francis came in almost immediately to give her hair its final arrangement. She never got dressed before evening. She sat down in front of the mirror and bowed her head beneath the hairdresser's nimble hands. She was silent and thoughtful when Zoé came in and said, "Madame, there's one who refuses to leave."

"Then you'll have to let him stay," Nana replied calmly.

"And others are still coming."

"Well, tell them to wait. When they get too hungry they'll go away."

Her mood had changed. She was delighted to keep all those men waiting. She had a thought that brought her amusement to its peak. She slipped out from under Francis' hands and bolted the door. Now they could pile up in the other rooms. They surely wouldn't break through the walls! Zoé could come in through the little door that led to the kitchen. Meanwhile the doorbell was still going. It rang loud and clear every five minutes, with the regularity of a smoothly functioning machine. Nana diverted herself by counting the rings.

She had a sudden recollection: "What about my pralines?"

Francis had also forgotten about them. He took a bag from his coat pocket with the discreet gesture of a man offering a gift to his mistress; he never failed to put the pralines on his bill, however. Nana put the bag between her knees and began to eat, moving her head beneath the hairdresser's gentle pushes.

"My God, what a crowd!" she exclaimed after a silence.

The doorbell had just rung three times in quick succession. Its calls were becoming more and more frequent. There were modest rings that stammered with the trembling of a first avowal; bold ones that vibrated beneath some brutal finger; hurried ones that pierced the air with a rapid quiver. There was almost a continuous peal, enough to alert the whole neighborhood, as Zoé said, a steady stream of men pushing the ivory button one after another. Bordenave had carried the joke too far; he must have given her address to everyone in the audience.

"By the way, Francis," she said, "do you have a hundred francs?"

He stepped back, examined her hair, then said calmly, "A hundred francs? That depends."

"Look, if you want a guarantee. . ." Without finishing her sentence, she made a broad gesture in the direction of the adjoining rooms. Francis lent her a hundred francs. Zoé, during her moments of respite, came in and made preparations for Madame's toilet. Soon she began helping her to dress while Francis waited to give the finishing touches to her hair. But Zoé was constantly being called away by the doorbell, so that she had to leave Madame only half laced up, or with only one shoe on. She almost lost her head, despite her experience. After having put men all over the apartment, making use of the smallest nooks and crannies, she was finally forced to put them together in groups of three or four, which was contrary to all her principles. If they ate each other up, so much the better—it would make more room! And Nana, sheltered behind her bolted door, made fun of them, saying she could hear them panting. She could imagine what a fine sight they must be, with their tongues hanging out, like dogs sitting around on their haunches! Her success of the night before was still going on: this pack of men had followed her trail.

"I hope they don't break anything," she murmured. She was beginning to feel uneasy; it seemed to her that she could feel all those hot breaths passing through the crack under the door. She uttered an exclamation of relief when Zoé brought in Labordette. He wanted to talk to her about an account he had settled for her at the office of the justice of the peace. She did not listen to him. "I'll take you with me," she said. "We'll have dinner together, then you'll go to the theater with me. I don't go on till nine-thirty."

Good old Labordette! He had come at just the right time! *He* never asked for anything. He was only a friend of women, and took care of their little affairs for them. He had just sent the creditors away, for example, as he was coming through the anteroom. Anyway, those worthy people did not want to be paid; on the contrary, they had insisted on waiting only so that they could compliment

Madame and personally offer her their services after her great success.

"Let's go, let's go," said Nana, who was now dressed.

Just then Zoé came in and said, "I'm not even going to the door any more, Madame! They're lined up on the stairs."

Lined up on the stairs! Even Francis laughed, despite the English impassivity he affected, as he put away his combs. Nana took Labordette's arm and pushed him toward the kitchen. She hurried away, free from men at last, happy, knowing she could be alone with Labordette anywhere without having to fear any unwanted advances on his part.

"I want you to take me home from the theater," she said as they were going down the back stairs. "That way I'll be sure. . . Just think: I'm going to sleep all night, a whole night to myself! It's a whim of mine."

3

Countess Sabine, as Madame Muffat de Beuville had come to be called in order to distinguish her from the count's mother, who had died the year before, received every Tuesday in her house on the Rue Miromesnil, at the corner of the Rue de Penthièvre. It was a large square building that had been occupied by the Muffats for more than a hundred years. Its tall, dark façade had the sleepy, melancholy look of a convent, with enormous blinds that were nearly always closed. At the rear, in a damp little garden, a few trees rose up in search of sunlight, so thin and tall that their branches could be seen above the roof.

On this particular Tuesday, toward ten o'clock in the evening, there were no more than a dozen people in the drawing room. When she was expecting only her close friends, the Countess did not open either the little drawing room or the dining room. The atmosphere was more intimate, and they could chat beside the fire. The drawing room was high and spacious; four windows overlooked the garden, whose dampness could be felt on that rainy late-April evening despite the big logs that were blazing in the fireplace. The sun never shone into that room. During the day a greenish light did little to relieve its gloom, but at night, when the lamps and the chandelier had been lit, it merely looked solemn, with its solid mahogany Empire furniture and its hangings and chair coverings of yellow velvet with gold embroidered designs. On entering it, one stepped into cold dignity and ancient customs, into a vanished age that exhaled an odor of piety.

On one side of the fireplace, however, opposite the armchair in which the Count's mother had died, a square armchair with stiff woodwork and hard upholstery, Countess Sabine sat in a deep chair whose padded red silk was as soft as eiderdown. It was the only modern piece of furniture in the room, a bit of whimsey that clashed with all the surrounding austerity.

"And so," said the Countess, "we'll have the Shah of Persia. . . ."

They were talking about all the royalty that would come to Paris for the Exposition. Several ladies were seated in a semicircle in front of the fire. Madame Du Joncquoy, whose brother, a diplomat, had fulfilled a mission in the East, gave a few details about the court of Nasr-ed-Din.

"Are you feeling unwell, my dear?" asked Madame Chantereau, wife of an iron manufacturer, seeing the Countess shiver slightly and turn pale.

"No, not at all," replied the Countess, smiling. "I'm a little chilly. . . . This room takes so long to get warm!"

She raised her dark eyes, scanning the walls from floor to ceiling. Estelle, her thin, insignificant daughter, still in the awkward age at eighteen, stood up from the stool on which she had been sitting and silently went over to push back one of the logs that had rolled off the fire. Madame de Chezelles, a convent-school friend of Sabine's, five years younger than she, exclaimed, "Oh, how I wish I had a drawing room like yours! You, at least, can receive guests. . . . They only make little boxes nowadays. If only I were in your place!"

She talked giddily, with animated gestures, explaining how she would change the hangings, the chairs, and everything else; then she would give balls that everyone in Paris would be eager to attend. Her husband, a magistrate, was seated behind her, listening with a solemn expression. It was rumored that she deceived him without even bothering to hide it; but everyone forgave her and continued to receive her because, it was said, she was mad.

Countess Sabine contented herself with smiling faintly and murmuring, "Oh, Léonide!" And she completed her thought with an indolent gesture. She certainly had no intention of changing her drawing room after having lived in it for seventeen years. It would stay as her mother-in-law had wished to preserve it during her lifetime.

"I've been told that we'll also have the King of Prussia and the Emperor of Russia," she said, returning to the conversation.

"Yes, some magnificent festivities have been announced," said Madame Du Joncquoy.

The banker Steiner, recently introduced into the house by Léonide de Chezelles, who knew everyone in Paris, was talking on a sofa between two windows. He was questioning a deputy from whom he was adroitly trying to extract some news about a development in the stock market of which he had certain suspicions. Count Muffat, standing in front of them, listened to them in silence, his face even gloomier than usual. Four or five young men formed another group near the door, surrounding Count Xavier de Vendeuvres, who was talking to them in a hushed voice. He was no doubt telling them some racy story, for they were choking with laughter. All alone in the middle of the room, a fat man, head of a department in the Ministry of the Interior, was seated heavily in an armchair, sleeping with his eyes open.

"You're too skeptical, Foucarmont," Vandeuvres said, raising his voice, when one of the young men seemed to doubt his story. "You'll spoil your own pleasures."

He laughed and returned to the ladies. The last of a great family, effeminate and witty, he was engaged in squandering a fortune with a frenzy of appetites that nothing could allay. His racing stable, one of the most famous in Paris, cost him an enormous amount of money; his losses at the Cercle Impérial reached alarming figures each month; every year his mistresses carved off another slice from his vast domains in Picardy by forcing him to sell a farm and several acres of meadow or forest.

"You don't believe in anything, so what right do you have to call anyone else a skeptic?" said Léonide, making room for him beside her. "It's you who spoil your own pleasures."

"Precisely," he replied. "I want to give others the benefit of my experience."

But silence was imposed on him: he was shocking Monsieur Venot. Some of the ladies moved aside and Vandeuvres saw a little man in his sixties with bad teeth and a shrewd smile; he had been sitting on a chaise longue, perfectly at ease, listening to everyone without saying a word. He made a gesture indicating that he was not shocked. Vandeuvres resumed his lordly manner and said gravely, "Monsieur Venot knows very well that I believe what I ought to believe."

It was an act of religious faith. Even Léonide appeared to be satisfied. At the far end of the room, the young men had ceased laughing. It was a prim drawing room and they found little amusement in it. A coldness seemed to have settled over everything. In the midst of the silence, Steiner's nasal voice could be heard; the deputy's discretion was beginning to exasperate him. Countess Sabine looked at the fire for a few moments, then resumed the conversation.

"I saw the King of Prussia last year at Baden. He's still quite vigorous for his age."

"Count Bismarck will accompany him," said Madame Du Joncquoy. "Do you know the Count? I had lunch with him at my brother's house a long time ago, when he was representing Prussia in Paris. . . . I can't understand that man's recent successes."

"Why not?" asked Madame Chantereau.

"How can I explain it? . . . I don't like him. He seems brutal and ill-bred. And I find him stupid."

Everyone began talking about Count Bismarck. Opinions were divided. Vandeuvres was acquainted with him and said that he was a great drinker and gambler. But in the thick of the discussion the door opened and Hector de la Faloise appeared. Fauchery, who had come with him, went up to the Countess, bowed, and said, "Madame, I did not forget your gracious invitation."

She smiled and gave him a friendly greeting. After bowing to the Count, the journalist felt out of place for a few moments, for he recognized no one else in the drawing room except Steiner. Then Vandeuvres turned around and came over to shake hands with him. Glad to see him and feeling a need to communicate, Fauchery drew him aside and said to him softly, "It's going to be tomorrow. Are you coming?"

"Of course!"

"Midnight, in her apartment."

"I know, I know. . . I'm going with Blanche."

He wanted to return to the ladies and give another argument in Count Bismarck's favor, but Fauchery held him back.

"She asked me to invite someone. You'll never guess who it is." And he nodded discreetly toward Count Muffat, who was discussing the budget with the deputy and Steiner.

"Impossible!" Vandeuvres exclaimed with mingled stupefaction and amusement.

"I give you my word! She made me promise to bring him. That's one reason why I'm here."

They both laughed silently. Vandeuvres hurried back to the circle of ladies.

"I assure you that, on the contrary, Count Bismarck is quite witty," he said. "One night, for example, he made a delightful remark in my presence. . ."

Meanwhile La Faloise, having heard the few words that had been quickly exchanged in an undertone, looked at Fauchery, expecting an explanation which did not come. To whom had they been referring? What were they going to do at midnight tomorrow? He stayed with his cousin, who had gone over to a chair and sat down. He was especially interested in Countess Sabine. Her name had often been mentioned in front of him. He knew that she had been married at seventeen, that she must now be thirty-four, and that ever since her marriage she had led a cloistered life between her husband and her mother-in-law. In society, some said she had the coldness of pious virtue, others pitied her, recalling her charming laughter and her big, fiery eyes in the days before she was shut up in that old house. Fauchery examined her and hesitated. One night after dinner a friend of his, a captain who had left for Mexico the following day and had recently died there, had bluntly told him one of those personal secrets that even the most discreet men sometimes reveal. But this memory was vague; they had dined well that evening, and he now had doubts as he saw the Countess dressed in black, with her peaceful smile, in that old-fashioned drawing room. Her dark hair and the profile of her plump face were outlined in the light of a lamp behind her. Only rather thick lips gave evidence of a kind of imperious sensuality.

"Can't they talk about anything else except their Bismarck?" said La Faloise, who always tried to give the impression that he was bored in society. "It's unbearably dull here. It was an odd idea of yours to come."

Fauchery questioned him abruptly: "Tell me, does the Countess go to bed with anyone?"

"No, no, of course not!" he stammered, obviously disconcerted, forgetting his pose. "Where do you think you are?" Then he realized that his indignation showed a lack of sophistication. He leaned back on the sofa and said, "I say she doesn't, but actually I don't know anything about it. There's a man by the name of Foucarmont—the one sitting over there—who's always somewhere around her. Stranger things have happened. Anyway, I don't care. . . . One thing is certain, though: if she does have her little fling now and then, she's very clever about it, because it's never become known. There's never been any gossip about her."

Then, without Fauchery's having to take the trouble to question him, he told him what he knew about the Muffats. While the ladies continued their conversation in front of the fire, the two men lowered their voices; seeing them with their white gloves and ties, one would have thought they were carefully discussing some serious subject. Muffat's mother, whom La Faloise had known well, was an insufferable old woman, always involved with priests; she was very self-important and had an authoritative manner that bent everyone to her will. As for Muffat, the belated son of a general who had been given the title of count by Napoleon I, he had naturally found himself in favor after the Second of December. He also had a dismal personality, but he was known as a very honest, forthright man. Along with his other-worldly opinions, he had such a lofty idea of his post at court, his dignities, and his virtues, that he carried his head as though it were the Blessed Sacrament. His mother had given him a fine upbringing: confession every day, no escapades, no youth of any kind. He was a practicing Catholic; he had fits of faith so violent that they were like attacks of fever. Finally, to finish his description with a last detail, La Faloise whispered something in his cousin's ear.

"Impossible!" said Fauchery.

"I was assured of it, I give you my word! . . . He still had it when he got married."

Fauchery laughed and looked at the Count, whose face, framed by side whiskers and without a mustache, looked squarer and harder as he quoted figures to Steiner, who was now arguing with him.

"Yes, he looks like that kind of man," said Fauchery. "What a nice present he gave his wife! . . . Poor woman, how he must have bored her! I'm willing to bet she doesn't know anything at all!"

Just then Countess Sabine spoke to him. He was so surprised and amused by what he had just learned about the Muffats that he did not hear her. She repeated her question:

"Monsieur Fauchery, didn't you once publish an article on Count Bismarck? You've spoken to him, haven't you?"

He quickly stood up and went over to the ladies, trying to recover his composure. He managed to reply with casual ease.

"Madame, I must admit that I wrote that article on the basis of biographies published in Germany. I've never seen Count Bismarck."

He remained next to the Countess. He continued his reflections while he talked with her. She did not look her age; he would have said she was twenty-eight at the most. Beneath the blue shadows of her eyelids, her eyes had kept the flame of youth. After growing up in a divided family, spending one month with the Marquis de Chouard and the next with the Marquise, she had married at an early age, shortly after her mother's death. Her father had no doubt pushed her into the marriage, for she had become a burden to him. The Marquis was a terrible man; strange stories were beginning to be told about him, despite his lofty piety. Fauchery asked the Countess if he would have the honor of seeing him. Yes, of course her father would come, but very late—he had so much work! The journalist, who felt sure he knew where the old man spent his evenings, kept his serious expression. But he was surprised by a birthmark he noticed on the Countess's left cheek, near her mouth. Nana had exactly the same kind of birthmark. It was odd. There were little curly hairs on it, only Nana's were blond while the Countess's were jet black. In any case, the Countess didn't go to bed with anyone.

"I've always wanted to know Queen Augusta," she said. "They say she's so good, so pious. . . . Do you think she'll accompany the King?"

"It's said that she won't, Madame."

She didn't go to bed with anyone, that was obvious. It was enough to see her there next to her daughter, so insipid and prim on her stool. That sepulchral drawing room, with its church-like odor, clearly spoke of the iron hand and the rigid existence that held her fast. She had put nothing of herself into that ancient house, darkened by dampness. It was Muffat who imposed himself on it, who dominated everything with his devout upbringing, his penances, his fasts. But the sight of the little old man with bad teeth and a shrewd smile, whom he suddenly discovered in his armchair behind the ladies, seemed to him a still more decisive argument. He knew the man, Théophile Venot, a former lawyer who had specialized in ecclesiastical cases. He had retired with a large fortune and now led a rather mysterious life. He was received everywhere, treated with deep respect, and even feared a little, as though he represented some great, occult power that could be felt behind him. Yet he behaved with great humility. He was a churchwarden at the Madeleine church, and he had merely accepted a position as deputy mayor of the Ninth Arrondissement to occupy his leisure, he said. Yes, the Countess was well protected! There was no use trying anything with her.

"You're right, it's unbearably dull here," Fauchery said to his cousin when he had escaped from the circle of ladies. "Let's go."

But Steiner, whom Count Muffat and the deputy had just left, was coming toward Fauchery, furious and sweating. "Why can't they just keep quiet if they don't want to tell me anything?" he grumbled. "I'll find people who will talk!" Then, pushing the journalist into a corner and changing his tone of voice, he said triumphantly, "It's going to be tomorrow. I'll be there, my friend!"

"Ah!" murmured Fauchery, surprised.

"You didn't know . . . Oh, I had a lot of trouble finding her at home! And Mignon kept sticking to me like a leech."

"But the Mignons are coming too."

"Yes, she told me. . . . Anyway, she received me, and she invited me. Twelve o'clock sharp, after the theater."

The banker was radiant. He blinked his eyes and added,

giving the words special significance, "And have you made out all right?"

"What do you mean?" said Fauchery, pretending not to understand. "She wanted to thank me for my article, so she came to see me."

"Yes, yes. . . . You journalists are lucky, you get rewarded. . . . By the way, who's going to pay tomorrow?"

Fauchery spread his arms, as though to declare that he had never been able to find out. But Vandeuvres was calling Steiner, who knew Count Bismarck. Madame Du Joncquoy was almost convinced. She concluded with these words: "He made a bad impression on me. His face struck me as malicious. . . . But I'm willing to believe he's intelligent. That explains his success."

"No doubt," said the banker, a Jew from Frankfort, with a faint smile.

Meanwhile La Faloise finally dared to question his cousin. He pursued him and whispered in his ear, "You're having supper at a woman's house tomorrow night, aren't you? Who is it? Who?"

Fauchery signaled that people were listening; they had to behave properly. The door had just opened again and an old lady was entering, followed by a young man. The journalist recognized him as the same young man who, during the opening performance of *The Blond Venus,* had called out the famous "She's wonderful!" that was still being talked about. The lady's arrival caused a stir in the drawing room. Countess Sabine quickly stood up, walked forward to meet her, took both her hands, and called her "my dear Madame Hugon." Seeing that his cousin was watching this scene with curiosity, La Faloise gave him a brief explanation: Madame Hugon, widow of a notary, was living in retirement at Les Fondettes, an old family estate near Orléans. She kept a small apartment in Paris, in a house she owned on the Rue de Richelieu. She was now spending a few weeks there in order to help her younger son settle himself in the city, where he was in his first year of law school. She had been a close friend of the Marquise de Chouard and had known the Countess since she was a baby. Sabine had lived with her for several months before her marriage, and they were still on intimate terms with each other.

60

"I've brought Georges," Madame Hugon said to Sabine. "He's grown a little since the last time you saw him!"

The young man, with his bright eyes and blond, girlish curls, greeted the Countess without shyness and reminded her of a game of battledore they had played two years earlier at Les Fondettes.

"Philippe isn't in Paris?" asked Count Muffat.

"Oh, no," replied the old lady. "He's still in garrison at Bourges."

She sat down and talked proudly about her elder son, a tall, husky young man who, after enlisting on the spur of the moment, had quickly reached the rank of lieutenant. The ladies all surrounded her with respectful affection. The conversation began again, more gracious and delicate. And when Fauchery saw the respectable Madame Hugon, with her motherly face brightened by a kindly smile beneath its broad sweep of white hair, he felt ridiculous at having suspected Countess Sabine for a moment.

His attention was drawn to the big chair covered with padded red silk on which the Countess was sitting. He found it disturbingly garish and whimsical in that smoky drawing room. That voluptuously indolent chair had surely not been placed there by the Count. It was like an attempt, the beginning of a desire and an enjoyment. Fauchery's mind began to wander and, in spite of himself, he again thought of that vague story which had been confided to him one night in a private room at a restaurant. Driven by a sensual curiosity, he had sought to become acquainted with the Muffats. Since his friend had died in Mexico, who could tell? He would have to wait and see. The whole thing was probably foolish, but the idea tormented him; he felt attracted, and all his depravity had been awakened. He was now amused by the rumpled look and slanted back of the big chair.

"Well, shall we go?" asked La Faloise, expecting to learn the name of the woman at whose house the supper party was being given as soon as they were outside.

"In a little while," replied Fauchery.

He was no longer in a hurry; he gave as an excuse the invitation he had been asked to make, for which it was not easy to find an opportunity. The ladies were talking about a girl who had become a nun. The ceremony had been very touching, and all of Parisian society had been deeply moved by it for the past three days. The girl was the eldest daughter of the Baroness de Fougeray. She had joined the Carmelites in response to an irresistible calling. Madame Chantereau, who was distantly related to the Fougerays, said that the Baroness had been so choked by tears that she had had to stay in bed the next day.

"I had a very good seat during the ceremony," said Léonide. "I found it quite interesting."

Madame Hugon pitied the poor mother. How painful it must be to lose a daughter that way! "I'm accused of being pious," she said with her calm frankness, "but just the same I think children who insist on committing that kind of suicide are very cruel."

"Yes, it's a terrible thing," murmured the Countess with a chilly little shiver, huddling deeper into her big chair in front of the fire.

The ladies launched into a discussion, but their voices remained discreet, and the gravity of the conversation was occasionally relieved by gentle laughter. The two lamps on the mantelpiece, covered with pink lace, cast only a dim light on them. There were only three other lamps, placed far apart on various pieces of furniture, so that the vast drawing room was left in soft shadow.

Steiner was bored. He was telling Fauchery about an adventure of that little Madame de Chezelles, whom he familiarly called Léonide. She was a real terror, he said, lowering his voice behind the ladies' chairs. Fauchery looked at her in her pale blue satin dress, perched on one corner of her chair, as slender and bold as a boy. He was finally surprised to see her there; more decorum was observed in Caroline Héquet's house, which had been seriously regulated by her mother. He could write an article on the subject. What a strange world Paris society was! The most rigid drawing rooms were being invaded. Of course, that silent Théophile Venot, who contented himself with smiling and showing his bad teeth, was no doubt a legacy from the late Countess, along with the elderly ladies, Madame Chantereau, Madame Du Joncquoy, and four or five old men who sat motionless in their corners. Count Muffat had brought some government officials who maintained the correctness of dress and bearing that was expected of men in the Tuileries; among others, there was the department head, still alone in the middle of the room, with his clean-shaven face and lackluster eyes, so tightly buttoned up in his coat that he could hardly risk making a gesture. Nearly all the young men, and some of the individuals with aristocratic manners, had been introduced by the Marquis de Chouard, who had kept in close touch with the legitimist party after accepting the current régime to the point of becoming a member of the Council of State. There remained Léonide de Chezelles, Steiner, and a whole group of other ambiguous people who formed a strange contrast with Madame Hugon's charming serenity. And Fauchery, who was still thinking about his article, called them "Countess Sabine's clique."

"On another occasion," Steiner continued softly, "Léonide had her tenor come down to Montauban. She was living in the Château de Beaurecueil, five miles away, and every day she came in a two-horse carriage to see him at the Lion-d'Or, where he was staying. The carriage would wait at the door of the hotel while Léonide stayed inside for hours, and a crowd would gather to look at the horses."

There was a silence; a few solemn seconds went by beneath the high ceiling. Two young men were whispering, but they soon ceased, and then nothing could be heard except Count Muffat's soft footsteps as he walked across the room. The lamps seemed to have dimmed, the fire was dying down, a stern shadow fell over the old friends of the family sitting in the chairs they had occupied there for the past forty years. It was as if, between two sentences, the guests had suddenly felt the Count's mother coming with her grave, icy manner.

Then Countess Sabine went on: "At any rate, there was a rumor to that effect. . . . The young man died, it was said, and that explained the poor girl's decision to become a nun. It was also said that Monsieur de Fougeray would never have given his consent to the marriage."

"A lot of other things are said, too!" Léonide exclaimed thoughtlessly.

She laughed and refused to explain what she meant. Her gaiety spread to Sabine, who put her handkerchief to her lips. Fauchery was struck by the sound of their laughter in the solemnity of that vast room; it was like the sound of breaking glass. And it actually did indicate the beginning of a kind of break. Then everyone began talking again; Madame Du Joncquoy protested, Madame Chantereau knew that a marriage had been planned, but that nothing further had been done; even the men ventured to state their views. For several minutes there was a confusion of opinions in which the various elements in the drawing room—the Bonapartists and the legitimists, mingled with the worldly skeptics—rubbed shoulders with one another and all spoke at the same time. Estelle rang for a servant to put more wood on the fire, the lamps were turned up, and it was as if everyone had suddenly begun to awaken. Fauchery was smiling, apparently at ease again.

Vandeuvres had gone over to join Fauchery. "Yes, they marry God when they can't marry their cousins," he said between his teeth, thoroughly bored with the subject. "Have you ever seen a woman become a nun when there was a man in love with her?" He did not wait for an answer; he had had enough. "Tell me," he said in an undertone, "how many will there be tomorrow? There will be the Mignons, Steiner, you, Blanche and I . . . Who else?"

"Caroline, I think . . . Simonne . . . probably Gaga. . . . You never know exactly. If you're expecting twenty people on these occasions, you end up with thirty."

Vandeuvres was looking at the ladies. He abruptly changed the subject: "Madame Du Joncquoy must have been quite a woman fifteen years ago. . . . That poor Estelle has grown still taller. What a nice plank to put in a bed!" He stopped short, and came back to the supper: "The trouble with these affairs is that the same women always turn up at them. . . . We need some new ones. Try to find one . . . Ah! I've got an idea. I'm going to ask that fat man to bring the woman he was with the other night at the Variety."

He was referring to the department head who was dozing in the middle of the room. Fauchery amused himself by watching this delicate negotiation from a distance. Vandeuvres had sat down next to the fat man, who continued to look very dignified. For a few moments they both seemed to be sedately discussing the question of the moment, namely, what had been the true feelings which had led the young girl to become a nun. Then Vandeuvres came back and said, "He won't bring her. He says she's virtuous and would refuse. . . . But I could have sworn I'd seen her at Laure's."

"What! You go to Laure's?" said Fauchery, laughing. "You venture into such places? I thought it was only poor devils like myself who—"

"A man ought to experience everything, my friend."

They both laughed, and their eyes glowed as they talked about the place on the Rue des Martyrs where fat Laure Piédefer served three-franc meals to women who were down on their luck. A fine place! All the women kissed Laure on the mouth. When Countess Sabine turned her head, having overheard a few words, they stepped back, rubbing against each other, gay and excited. They had not noticed that Georges Hugon was standing near them, listening. He was blushing so deeply that he had turned pink from his ears to his girlish neck. He was filled with shame and delight. Ever since his mother had turned him loose in the drawing room, he had been hovering behind Madame de Chezelles, the only woman who seemed attractive to him. But even so, she couldn't compare to Nana!

"Georges took me to the theater last night," Madame Hugon said. "Yes, to the Variety. I hadn't set foot in it for ten years. He loves music. I didn't enjoy it very much, but he was so happy! . . . Some very strange plays are being presented nowadays. . . . But I admit I'm not fascinated by music."

"What, Madame, you don't like music!" cried Madame Du Joncquoy, raising her eyes to the ceiling. "How can anyone not like music?"

There was a general exclamation. No one said anything about the play at the Variety Theater, which the good Madame Hugon had not understood at all. The other ladies knew about it, but they did not even mention it. They immediately gave the conversation an aura of sentiment and began expressing refined, ecstatic admiration of the great masters. Madame Du Joncquoy liked only Weber; Madame Chantereau preferred the Italians. The ladies' voices became soft and languid. The group in front of the fireplace had the contemplative look of a church congregation, and their talk had the hushed, discreet sound of chanting in a little chapel.

"Look," said Vandeuvres, leading Fauchery to the middle of the room, "we must find a new woman for tomorrow. Why don't we ask Steiner?"

"Oh, Steiner!" said the journalist. "He never gets a woman until no one else in Paris wants her!"

Vandeuvres began looking around. "Wait," he said; "the other day I met Foucarmont with a charming blond. I'll tell him to bring her."

And he called Foucarmont. They quickly exchanged a few words. A complication apparently arose, for, carefully stepping over the ladies' skirts, they went to join another young man with whom they continued the conversation in a window recess. Fauchery, left alone, decided to go over to the fireplace just as Madame Du Joncquoy was saying that she could never hear Weber's music without immediately seeing lakes, forests, and the sun rising over a dewy landscape; but a hand touched him on the shoulder while a voice said behind him, "It's not nice of you."

"What?" he asked, turning around and recognizing La Faloise.

"That supper tomorrow . . . You could have had me invited."

Fauchery was about to reply when Vandeuvres came back and said to him, "It seems she's not one of Foucarmont's women. She belongs to that gentleman over there. She won't be able to come. What bad luck! . . . But I've recruited Foucarmont anyway. He'll try to bring Louise, from the Palais-Royal."

"Monsieur de Vandeuvres," said Madame Chantereau, raising her voice, "wasn't Wagner's music hissed last Sunday?"

"Yes, horribly, Madame," he replied, stepping toward her with his exquisite politeness. Then, since no one detained him, he moved away and whispered to the journalist, "I'm going to recruit some more. . . . Those young men must know some girls."

Smiling and affable, he went up to various men and talked to them in all four corners of the drawing room. He mingled with the groups, murmured a few words over someone's shoulder here and there, turned around with a wink or some other sign of complicity. It was as though he were giving out a watchword, in his easy manner. The word spread, appointments were made, and the feverish sound of this recruiting was covered by the ladies' sentimental dissertations on music.

"No, don't talk to me about your Germans," said Madame Chantereau. "Song and gaiety are like sunlight. . . . Have you heard Patti in the *Barber?*"

"Delightful!" exclaimed Léonide, who played only musical comedy numbers on her piano.

Meanwhile Countess Sabine had rung for tea, which was served in the drawing room on Tuesdays when the visitors were not numerous. As she was instructing a servant to clear the table, she watched Vandeuvres. She kept that vague smile which showed a little of the whiteness of her teeth. And when he came near her she questioned him: "What are you plotting, Monsieur de Vandeuvres?"

"I, Madame?" he replied calmly. "I'm not plotting anything."

"Oh? I saw you so busy. . . . Here, you can make yourself useful."

She handed him an album and asked him to put it on the piano. But he still managed to whisper to Fauchery that they would have Tatan Néné, who had the finest breasts that had been seen all winter, and Maria Blond, who had just made her début at the Folies-Dramatiques. La Faloise kept stopping him at every step, expecting an invitation. He finally said outright that he wanted to come. Vandeuvres accepted him at once, but made him promise to bring Clarisse. When La Faloise pretended to have misgivings, he quieted him by saying, "I've invited you, haven't I? That's enough."

La Faloise still wanted to know the name of the hostess, but the Countess had summoned Vandeuvres to ask him how the English made tea. He often went to England to enter his horses in races there. According to him, only the Russians knew how to make tea, and he told how they did it. Then, as though he had been pursuing another train of thought while he spoke, he interrupted himself to ask, "By the way, aren't we going to see the marquis tonight?"

"Yes, of course, my father promised to come," replied the

Countess. "I'm beginning to worry, though. . . . His work must have detained him."

Vandeuvres smiled discreetly. He, too, seemed to have some suspicion of the nature of the Marquis de Chouard's work. He had thought of a pretty woman whom the marquis sometimes took to the country with him. Perhaps they could get her to come.

Fauchery finally decided that the time had come to hazard his invitation to Count Muffat. It was getting late.

"Seriously?" asked Vandeuvres, who thought he was joking.

"Very seriously. . . . If I don't invite him she'll scratch my eyes out. She's taken it into her head that he must be there."

"Then I'll help you."

The clock struck eleven. The Countess, aided by her daughter, was serving tea. Since the company was composed almost entirely of close friends, the cups and the plates of little cakes were casually handed around. Even the ladies remained in their chairs in front of the fire, sipping their tea and holding their cakes between their fingertips. From music, the conversation had turned to tradesmen. There was no one like Boissier for bonbons, or Catherine for ices; Madame Chantereau, however, was a partisan of Latinville. The talk was becoming slower; a drowsy lassitude was settling over the drawing room. Steiner had quietly resumed his attack on the deputy, whom he had blocked in one corner of a sofa. Monsieur Venot, whose teeth had probably been ruined by sweets, was eating hard cookies one after another, making a noise like a gnawing mouse, while the department head, with his nose in his cup, seemed to be drinking endlessly. And the Countess went from one person to another, never insisting, staying a few seconds to look at the men with an air of silent interrogation, then smiling and passing on. The blazing fire had made her face pink; she seemed to be the sister of her daughter, who looked so skinny and awkward beside her. As she was about to offer a cup of tea to Fauchery, who was talking with her husband and Vandeuvres, she noticed that they fell silent at her approach; she did not stop, but continued on her way and gave the cup to Georges Hugon.

68

"It's a lady who wants you to come for supper," the journalist said gaily to Count Muffat.

The Count, whose face had remained somber all evening, seemed greatly surprised.

"Who is this lady?"

"It's Nana!" said Vandeuvres, to get the invitation over with.

The Count became still more solemn. His eyelids fluttered slightly, while a little wave of uneasiness passed over his forehead like the shadow of a headache.

"But I don't know her," he murmured.

"Come, come, you've already paid her a visit," Vandeuvres pointed out.

"What! I've paid her a visit? Oh, yes, the other day, for the charity committee. I'd forgotten about it. . . . Even so, I don't know her, so I can't accept the invitation."

He had taken on his icy expression to make them understand that he considered their joke to be in bad taste. A man of his rank could not sit at the table of such a woman. Vandeuvres protested: it was going to be a supper party of artists, and talent excused everything. But without listening to Fauchery, who began telling him about a dinner at which a Scottish prince, the son of a queen, had sat beside a former music-hall singer, the count emphatically repeated his refusal. He even made a gesture of annoyance, despite his great politeness.

Georges and La Faloise, drinking their tea standing up in front of each other, had overheard the words that had been exchanged near them.

"Ah, so it's going to be at Nana's!" said La Faloise. "I should have known!"

Georges said nothing, but he was aflame; he was so excited by the sensuality that had been in possession of him for the past few days that his blue eyes shone like candles and his blond hair was in disorder. At last he was going to plunge into everything he had been dreaming of!

"But I don't know the address," said La Faloise.

"Boulevard Haussmann, between the Rue de l'Arcade and the Rue Pasquier, fourth floor," said Georges, all in one breath. And when La Faloise looked at him in surprise, he added, blushing still more deeply, bursting with conceit and embarrassment, "I'm going too. She invited me this morning."

Just then there was a great commotion in the drawing room. Vandeuvres and Fauchery were forced to stop pressing Count Muffat. The Marquis de Chouard had just arrived, and everyone was hastening to greet him. He walked in slowly and unsteadily and stood in the middle of the room, pale, blinking his eyes as though he had just left some dark alley and was blinded by the light of the lamps.

"I'd given up hope of seeing you, father," said the Countess. "I'd have been worried till tomorrow."

He looked at her without answering, apparently not understanding what she had said. His lower lip was drooping and his nose looked like an enormously swollen pimple on his clean-shaven face. Full of kindliness, Madame Hugon felt sorry for him when she saw how exhausted he was.

"You work too hard," she said. "You ought to rest. . . . At our age, we must leave work to young people."

"Work . . . Ah, yes, work," he stammered at length. "I always have a great deal of work. . . ."

He began to pull himself together. He straightened his back and, with a gesture that was habitual to him, passed his hand through the thin, curly white hair behind his ears.

"What kind of work were you doing so late?" asked Madame Du Joncquoy. "I thought you were at the reception given by the Minister of Finance."

The Countess intervened: "My father had to study the draft of a proposed law."

"Yes, precisely, a proposed law," he said. "I was in my study. . . . It concerns factories: I'd like them to be closed on Sundays. It's truly shameful that the government has been unwilling to take vigorous action. The churches are becoming empty. We're headed for a catastrophe."

Vandeuvres glanced at Fauchery. They were both standing behind the Marquis, listening to him with suspicion. When Vandeuvres was able to take him aside to talk to him about the pretty woman he occasionally took to the country, the old man made a great show of surprise. Perhaps he had been seen with Baroness Decker, at whose house in Viroflay he sometimes spent a few days. Solely for revenge, Vandeuvres suddenly asked him, "Tell me, where have you been? Your elbow is covered with cobwebs and plaster."

"My elbow?" he murmured, somewhat perturbed. "Why, yes, so it is. . . . A little dirt . . . I must have picked it up on my way downstairs from my study."

Several people were leaving. It was nearly midnight. Two servants were quietly taking away the cake plates and the empty cups. In front of the fireplace, the ladies had narrowed their circle and were talking more freely in the languor that had descended over them as the end of the evening approached. The room itself seemed to be sleepy; shadows dropped heavily from its walls. Fauchery spoke of leaving, but then he again became engrossed in looking at Countess Sabine. She was sitting in her usual place, resting from her duties as a hostess. As she silently watched a log that was burning to embers, her face was so pale and impenetrable that his doubts returned. In the glow of the fire, the black hairs on the birthmark at the corner of her mouth seemed lighter. It was exactly the same as Nana's birthmark, even to the color. He could not resist whispering a few words about it to Vandeuvres. Yes, it was true; Vandeuvres had never noticed it before. And they continued to draw parallels between Nana and the Countess. They found a vague resemblance in the chin and mouth; but the eyes were not at all similar. And Nana had an open, good-natured expression, while there was something mysterious about the Countess: she was like a sleeping cat with its claws drawn in and its paws almost imperceptibly agitated by a nervous tremor.

"Even so, I wouldn't mind going to bed with her," declared Fauchery.

Vandeuvres undressed her with his eyes. "No, neither would I," he said. "But you know, I'm suspicious of her thighs. Would you like to bet she doesn't have any worth talking about?"

He stopped: Fauchery had quickly touched his elbow and motioned toward Estelle, who was sitting on her stool in front of them. They had raised their voices without realizing it, and she must have heard them. But she remained stiff and motionless; not one hair had moved on her neck, whose thinness showed that she had grown too fast.

They walked three or four steps away from her. Vandeuvres swore that the Countess was a virtuous woman.

Just then voices were raised in front of the fireplace. Madame Du Joncquoy was saying, "I've granted you that Count Bismarck may be an intelligent man, but if you go so far as to call him a genius . . ."

The ladies had returned to their first topic of conversation.

"What! Bismarck again?" said Fauchery. "This time I'm really going to leave."

"Wait," said Vandeuvres, "we must get a final word from the Count."

Count Muffat was talking with his father-in-law and a group of solemn men. Vandeuvres took him aside and insistently repeated the invitation, adding that he himself was going to be present. A man could go anywhere he chose; no one would ever dream of seeing evil where there was nothing more than curiosity. The Count listened to these arguments with his eyes lowered and his face impassive. Vandeuvres was beginning to sense a certain hesitation in him when the Marquis de Chouard came up to them with a questioning look. When the Marquis had been informed of the subject under discussion, and when Fauchery had invited him also, he cast a furtive glance at his son-in-law. There was an embarrassed silence; but they encouraged each other, and they would no doubt have ended by accepting if Count Muffat had not noticed that Monsieur Venot was staring at him. The little old man was no longer smiling; his face was ashen, his eyes were as bright and sharp as steel.

"No," the Count said immediately in such a curt tone that it was clearly useless to insist.

The Marquis then refused with still more severity. He spoke of morality. The upper classes ought to set a good example. Fauchery smiled and shook hands with Vandeuvres. He would not wait for him: he was leaving at once, because he had to stop by the office of his newspaper.

"Midnight at Nana's, right?"

La Faloise also withdrew. Steiner had just taken leave of the Countess. Other men were following them. They all repeated the same words: "Midnight at Nana's," as they went to get their overcoats in the anteroom. Georges, who was waiting to leave with his mother, stood in the doorway and gave them the exact address: fourth floor, the door on the left. Before leaving, Fauchery took one last look around the drawing room. Vandeuvres had gone back to his place among the ladies and was jesting with Léonide de Chezelles. Count Muffat and the Marquis de Chouard were taking part in the conversation. The good Madame Hugon was sleeping with her eyes open. Half concealed behind the skirts, Monsieur Venot now looked small again and had resumed his smile. The clock slowly struck midnight in the vast solemn room.

"What!" exclaimed Madame Du Joncquoy. "You think Count Bismarck will make war on us and beat us? How fantastic!"

They were laughing around Madame Chantereau, who had just repeated this remark, which she had heard in Alsace, where her husband owned a factory.

"We still have the Emperor, fortunately," Count Muffat said with his official gravity.

These were the last words Fauchery heard. He closed the door after looking once again at Countess Sabine. She was talking calmly with the department head and seemed to be interested in what that fat man was saying. He must have been mistaken: there was no break. It was a pity.

"Well, aren't you coming?" La Faloise called out to him from the vestibule.

And outside, as they parted, the men repeated once more, "Tomorrow night, at Nana's."

4

Since morning Zoé had given over the apartment to a
steward who had come from Brébant's with a staff of as-
sistants and waiters. Brébant was to furnish everything: the
supper, the dishes, the crystal, the linen, the flowers, even
the chairs and stools. Nana could not have found a dozen
napkins in all her closets. Since she had not yet had time to
establish herself in keeping with her new success, and since
she disdained to go to a restaurant, she had preferred to
make the restaurant come to her. That seemed more elegant
to her. She wanted to celebrate her great success as an actress with a supper that everyone would talk about. Since
the dining room was too small, the steward had had a table
put in the drawing room, a table set for twenty-five people
placed rather close together.

"Is everything ready?" Nana asked when she returned
at midnight.

"Oh, I don't know!" Zoé replied gruffly. She appeared to
be beside herself with irritation. "I have nothing to do with
it, thank God! They're making a terrible mess in the
kitchen and all over the apartment! And then I had to have
an argument! The two others came again. I threw them
out."

She was referring to the two gentlemen, the businessman
and the Walachian, whom Nana had decided to get rid of,
now that she was sure of her future and wanted to start
over again from scratch, as she put it.

"What leeches!" she said. "If they come back, threaten to
go to the police."

She called Daguenet and Georges, who had remained
behind in the anteroom, where they were hanging up their
coats. They had met at the stage door in the Passage des
Panoramas and she had brought them home with her in a

74

cab. Since no one else had arrived yet, she told them to come into the dressing room while Zoé got her ready. Hurriedly, without changing her clothes, she had her hair done up and put white roses in her chignon and on her dress. The room was cluttered with furniture that it had been necessary to remove from the drawing room: a pile of tables, sofas and chairs with their legs in the air. She was all ready when her skirt caught on a caster and tore. She swore furiously; such things happened only to her. She pulled off her dress in a rage. It was a simple white silk dress, so thin and supple that it clung to her like a long chemise. But, not finding another one to her taste, she put it on again, almost weeping, saying that she looked like a ragpicker. Daguenet and Georges had to patch up the tear with pins while Zoé arranged her hair again. All three of them busied themselves around her, particularly Georges, who was kneeling on the floor with his hands buried in her skirt. She finally calmed down when Daguenet assured her it must be no later than a quarter past twelve; she had drastically shortened the third act of *The Blond Venus* by hurrying through her lines and skipping whole verses.

"It was still too good for those idiots," she said. "Did you see? What faces there were tonight! . . . Zoé, I want you to wait here. Don't go to bed, I may need you. . . . Ah, there's somebody at the door. It's about time!"

She left the room. Georges remained kneeling, his coattails resting on the floor. He blushed when he saw Daguenet looking at him. However, they had begun to feel affection for each other. They rearranged their ties in front of the big mirror and brushed each other off, for they were covered with white powder from having rubbed against Nana.

"It's like sugar," said Georges, laughing like a greedy baby.

A footman, hired for the night, showed the guests into the little drawing room, where only four chairs had been left, in order to make more room for the people. From the adjoining main drawing room came a clatter of dishes and silverware, while a streak of bright light shone from under the door. When Nana entered, she found Clarisse

75

Besnus, whom La Faloise had brought, already seated on one of the chairs.

"What! You're the first!" said Nana, who now treated her familiarly, since her success.

"It's because of him," replied Clarisse. "He's always afraid of being late. . . . If I'd listened to him, I wouldn't even have taken time to take off my make-up and my wig."

The young man, meeting Nana for the first time, bowed, complimented her, and began talking about his cousin, hiding his agitation beneath an exaggerated politeness. But Nana, without listening to him, without even knowing who he was, shook his hand and quickly stepped forward to meet Rose Mignon. She immediately assumed an extremely genteel manner.

"Ah, dear Madame, how kind of you! I was so hoping you'd be able to come!"

"I'm delighted to be here, I assure you," said Rose, with equal gentility.

"Do sit down. Is there anything you'd like?"

"No, thank you. . . . Ah, I've left my fan in my coat. Steiner, look in the right-hand pocket."

Steiner and Mignon had come in behind Rose. The banker went out and returned with the fan, while Mignon gave Nana a brotherly kiss and forced Rose to kiss her also. Did they not all belong to the same family in the world of the theater? Then he winked as though to encourage Steiner, but the latter, disconcerted by Rose's clear gaze, contented himself with kissing Nana's hand.

At that moment the Count de Vandeuvres appeared with Blanche de Sivry. There were deep bows. Nana ceremoniously led Blanche to a chair. Vandeuvres laughingly said that Fauchery was having an argument downstairs because the concierge had refused to let Lucy Stewart's carriage enter the courtyard. In the anteroom, Lucy was heard calling the concierge a dirty skunk. But when the footman opened the door she walked in with a gracious smile, announced her name, and took both of Nana's hands, saying that she had liked her as soon as she had seen her and that she thought she had great talent. Nana thanked her, truly embarrassed despite the pride she took in her role as hostess. However, she had seemed preoccupied ever since Fauchery's arrival. As soon as she was able to get near him she asked softly, "Is he coming?"

"No, he refused," the journalist replied bluntly; he had been taken off guard, even though he had prepared a story to explain Count Muffat's refusal. He became aware of his mistake when he saw Nana turn pale. He tried to make up for it: "He couldn't come. He's taking the Countess to a ball at the Ministry of the Interior tonight."

"All right," murmured Nana, who suspected him of not having tried; "you'll regret it, my friend."

"Listen," he said, offended by this threat, "I don't like that kind of errand. Next time, ask Labordette."

They angrily turned their backs on each other. Just then Mignon pushed Steiner over to Nana. When she was alone for a moment he said to her in a low voice, with the good-natured cynicism of a man who wants to assure a friend's pleasure, "You know he's dying to have you, but he's afraid of my wife. You'll protect him, won't you?"

Nana seemed not to have understood. She smiled, looked at Rose, her husband, and Steiner, then said to the banker, "Monsieur Steiner, you'll sit next to me."

From the anteroom came the sound of laughter, whispering, and an outburst of gay, chattering voices, as though a whole convent had been emptied there. Labordette appeared with five women behind him, his boarding school, as Lucy maliciously termed them. There was Gaga, majestic in her tight blue velvet dress, Caroline Héquet, always in black ribbed silk trimmed with Chantilly lace, Léa de Horn, outrageously dressed as usual, Tatan Néné, a big, good-humored blond with the bosom of a wet nurse, which often gave rise to jokes, and finally little Maria Blond, a girl of fifteen, as thin and depraved as a street urchin, who was on her way up in the world after her début at the Folies-Dramatiques. Labordette had brought them all in a single carriage; they were still laughing at the way they had been squeezed together, with Maria Blond sitting on the others' knees. But then they pinched their lips and quite properly exchanged handshakes and greetings. Gaga behaved like a child, and even lisped in her strained attempt at decorum. Tatan Néné, however, who had been told on the way that the supper was going to be served by six completely naked Negroes, grew uneasy and asked to see them. Labordette called her a fool and told her to keep quiet.

"Where's Bordenave?" asked Fauchery.

"Oh, I'm terribly sorry about him," said Nana; "he won't be able to come."

"Yes," said Rose Mignon, "he caught his foot in a trap door and gave himself a bad sprain. You should have heard him cursing, with his leg all bandaged up and stretched out on a chair!"

Everyone expressed regret. No supper party was complete without Bordenave. Well, they would try to get along without him. They were already talking about other things when they heard a loud voice:

"Well? What kind of a welcome is this? Did you think I was dead and buried?"

There were exclamations and everyone looked around. It was Bordenave, red-faced and enormous, standing in the doorway with his leg stiff, leaning on Simonne Cabiroche's shoulder. For the moment, he was going to bed with her. She was a pretty little blond who had received a certain amount of education and could play the piano and speak English. Although she was so delicate that she bent beneath Bordenave's weight, she continued to smile submissively. He stood still for a few seconds, feeling that they presented an attractive picture.

"This shows how much I like you," he went on. "I was afraid I'd be bored, so I said to myself, 'I'll go—'" He stopped short to utter an oath: "God damn!"

Simonne had stepped forward too quickly and he had put his weight on his lame leg. He jostled her roughly. Without ceasing to smile, she lowered her pretty face like an animal afraid of being beaten, and supported him with all the strength of her plump little body. The others cried out and hurried to assist him. Nana and Rose Mignon brought out an armchair into which Bordenave let himself fall, while the other women slipped a second chair under his leg. And all the actresses who were there kissed him, of course. He grunted and sighed.

"God damn it! . . . Anyway, there's nothing wrong with my stomach, as you'll soon see."

Other guests had arrived. The room was so tightly packed that no one could move. The clatter of dishes and silverware had ceased, but the sound of a quarrel could be heard from the drawing room, where the steward was shouting furiously. Nana was becoming impatient; since she was not expecting any more guests, she was surprised that supper had not yet been served. She had just sent Georges to find out what was wrong when she was astonished to see still more men and women come in. She did not know them all. Somewhat embarrassed, she questioned Bordenave, Mignon, and Labordette. They did not know them either. When she spoke to the Count de Vandeuvres he suddenly recalled that they were the young people he had recruited at Count Muffat's house. Nana thanked him. Good, good. Only they were going to be crowded. She asked Labordette to go and have seven more places laid at the table. Scarcely had he left the room when the footman ushered in three more people. Now it was becoming ridiculous! There wasn't going to be room for everyone, she was sure of it. She began to lose her temper and said in her loftiest manner that it was hardly proper. But when she saw two more arrive she burst out laughing: it was too funny. They would just have to find room for themselves as best they could! Everyone was standing except Gaga, Rose Mignon, and Bordenave, who had two chairs all to himself. There was a steady hum of voices; everyone was speaking softly, occasionally stifling a little yawn.

"Look, why don't we sit down at the table?" asked Bordenave. "Isn't everyone here now?"

"Oh, yes, everyone's here, all right," replied Nana, laughing.

She looked around the room. Then she became serious, as though surprised not to have seen someone. There was apparently a guest missing about whom she had not spoken. The others would have to wait. A few minutes later, they saw a tall gentleman with a noble face and a handsome white beard. And the odd part of it was that no one had seen him come in; he must have slipped into the little drawing room through a bedroom door that had been left ajar. There was a silence broken only by rapid whispers. The Count de Vandeuvres clearly knew who the gentleman was, for they had discreetly shaken hands with each other, but he replied to the women's questions only with a smile. Then Caroline Héquet softly stated her conviction that he was an English lord who was going back to London the next day to get married; she knew him well, because she had once had him. This story circulated among the ladies. Maria Blond, however, maintained that she recognized him as a German ambassador. She was sure of it because he often went to bed with one of her friends. The men quickly passed judgment on him. He seemed to be a respectable man. Maybe he was paying for the supper. Probably. It looked that way. Well, as long as it was a good supper! . . . The question was left in doubt. The old man with the white beard was already being forgotten when the steward opened the door of the main drawing room.

"Supper is served, Madame."

Steiner offered Nana his arm. She took it without seeming to notice a movement on the part of the old man, who began walking behind her, alone. Anyway, it was impossible to organize a ceremonial entry. The men and women entered in disorder, joking with homely good humor about this lack of formality. The vast drawing room was bare except for a long table that extended from one end of it to the other; and this table had proved to be too small, for the plates were touching one another. It was lighted by four candelabra with ten candles each. One of them was silverplated and had clusters of flowers on either side. The table was laid with the luxury of a restaurant: china without monograms, but decorated with gold lines; silverware that had been worn and dulled by constant washing; glasses that could be matched in any cheap store. It gave the impression of a house bought with a suddenly acquired fortune and thrown open to guests too soon, before anything was yet in place. There was no chandelier, and the candelabra, whose tall candles had just been lighted, cast a pale yellow glow over the dishes and bowls, in which fruit, pastry, and preserves alternated symmetrically.

"You can all sit wherever you like," said Nana. "It's more amusing that way."

She was standing at the middle of the table. The old gentleman whom no one knew had placed himself on her right and she kept Steiner on her left. Some of the guests were already sitting down when loud cursing was heard from the little drawing room. It was Bordenave: he had been forgotten. He was having terrible difficulty in getting up from his two armchairs, and as he did so he shouted for that little bitch Simonne, who had gone off with the others. The women hurried in to him, full of pity. Bordenave appeared, supported and almost carried by Caroline, Clarisse, Tatan Néné, and Maria Blond. Getting him seated was a complicated affair.

"In the middle, facing Nana!" cried someone. "Bordenave in the middle! He'll preside over us!"

The ladies seated him at the middle of the table. Two women lifted his leg and gently placed it on a second chair. It would be all right: he could eat sideways.

"Damn it," he grumbled, "it's a tight fit! . . . Well, girls, you'll have to take care of papa."

He had Rose Mignon on his right and Lucy Stewart on his left. They promised to take good care of him. Everyone was now getting settled. Vandeuvres sat down between Lucy and Clarisse, Fauchery between Rose Mignon and Caroline Héquet. On the other side, Hector de la Faloise had hurried to sit down next to Gaga, despite Clarisse's calls from across the table, and Mignon, still staying close to Steiner, was separated from him by Blanche, while Tatan Néné sat on his left. Then came Labordette. Finally, at both ends of the table there were several young men and some women, Simonne, Léa de Horn, Maria Blond, all jumbled up together, without any order. It was there that Daguenet and Georges Hugon were becoming more and more friendly as they looked at Nana and smiled.

Two people remained standing and there was some joking about it. The men offered their knees. Clarisse, who could not move her elbows, told Vandeuvres that she was counting on him to feed her. And Bordenave took up so much room with his two chairs! There was a final effort and everyone was able to sit down; but, as Mignon exclaimed, they were packed like herrings in a barrel.

"Asparagus purée à la comtesse, consommé à la Deslignac," said the waiters as they carried full plates behind the guests.

Bordenave was loudly recommending the consommé when shouts of protest and anger arose. The door had opened and three latecomers, a man and two women, had just entered. Oh, no, this was too much! Without leaving her chair, however, Nana squinted her eyes and tried to see if she knew them. The woman was Louise Violaine. But she had never seen the men before.

"My dear," said Vandeuvres, "this gentleman is Monsieur de Foucarmont, a naval officer and a friend of mine, whom I invited."

Foucarmont bowed, perfectly at ease. "And I took the liberty of bringing one of my friends," he said.

"Ah, good, very good," said Nana. "Please sit down. . . . Come, Clarisse, move down a little. You've got lots of room there. It won't be hard. . . ."

They squeezed together still more tightly. Foucarmont and Louise got a little segment of the table for themselves, but Foucarmont's friend had to sit at some distance from his plate and eat by reaching out his arms between his neighbors' shoulders. The waiters took away the soup plates and brought rabbit sausages with truffles and dumplings with parmesan cheese. Bordenave caused a general commotion by saying that for a moment he had considered bringing Prullière, Fontan, and old Bosc. Nana resumed her dignity and said curtly that she would have given them a reception they would not have forgotten. If she had wanted all her theatrical colleagues to come, she would have invited them herself. No, she didn't want any ham actors. Old Bosc was always drunk; Prullière was too conceited; as for Fontan, he was unbearable in society, with his loud voice and stupid remarks. And after all, third-rate actors were always out of place among gentlemen.

"Yes, it's true," declared Mignon.

All around the table, the men looked very correct in their evening coats and white ties. Their pale faces had a distinguished air that was refined still more by fatigue. The old gentleman moved deliberately and had a subtle smile, as though he were presiding over a diplomatic conference. Vandeuvres was so exquisitely polite to the women on either side of him that it seemed as though he were still in Countess Muffat's drawing room. Only that morning Nana had said to her aunt that it would have been impossible to find a better collection of men: they were either noblemen or rich, and were all quite fashionable. As for the ladies, they behaved very well. A few—Blanche, Léa,

Louise—had come in low-cut dresses; only Gaga, however, showed a little too much, especially since at her age she would have done better to show nothing at all. Now that everyone had managed to find a seat, the laughter and joking began to die down. Georges reflected that he had attended gayer dinner parties in the homes of middle-class citizens in Orléans. There was scarcely any conversation; the men who did not know each other exchanged stares; the women sat quietly. This was what most astonished Georges. He found them prosaic and sedate; he had expected them to begin kissing one another immediately.

The next course, consisting of a Rhine carp à la Chambord and an English-style saddle of venison, was being served when Blanche said loudly, "Lucy, my dear, I saw your Ollivier last Sunday. . . . How he's grown!"

"Yes, he's eighteen now," replied Lucy. "It doesn't make me any younger. . . . He went back to his school yesterday."

Her son Ollivier, of whom she spoke with pride, was a student in the naval school. The talk turned to children. The ladies became sentimental. Nana told them of her own happiness: her baby, little Louis, was now living with her aunt, who brought him to her every morning at about eleven o'clock; and she took him into her bed, where he played with Lulu, her terrier. She almost died laughing every time she saw the two of them crawling under the covers all the way to the foot of the bed. It was amazing how smart Louiset was already.

"What a day I had yesterday!" said Rose Mignon. "I went to get Charles and Henri at their boarding school, and they absolutely insisted on going to the theater in the evening. They jumped up and down and clapped their little hands and said, 'We'll see mama on the stage! We'll see mama on the stage!' Oh, they were so excited!"

Mignon smiled complacently, his eyes moist with paternal tenderness.

"And they were so funny during the performance!" he said. "They sat there looking as serious as men. They kept staring at Rose and asking me why mama's legs were naked like that."

Everyone laughed. Mignon was radiant, flattered in his pride as a father. He adored the children; he had only one preoccupation: to increase their fortune by managing, with the strictness of a faithful steward, the money Rose earned in the theater and elsewhere. When he had married her, he had been the orchestra leader in the music hall where she was singing. They had been passionately in love with each other at the time. Now they were good friends. It was all arranged between them: she worked as hard as she could, with all her talent and all her beauty, and he had given up the violin in order to devote his full attention to her success as an actress and as a woman. One could not have found a more bourgeois or closely united couple.

"How old is the eldest?" asked Vandeuvres.

"Henri is nine," replied Mignon. "But he's a big boy for his age!"

Then, with tranquil audacity, he mockingly told Steiner, who did not like children, that if he were a father he would not squander his fortune so stupidly. As he spoke, he watched the banker over Blanche's shoulder, to see how things were working out between him and Nana. But for the past few minutes he had been irritated by Rose and Fauchery, who were talking very close to each other. Surely Rose wasn't going to try to waste her time on anything so foolish as that! In such cases he always put his foot down. Wearing a diamond ring on the little finger of one of his shapely hands, he finished his venison steak.

The conversation about children continued. La Faloise, disquieted by Gaga's presence, asked her about her daughter, whom he had had the pleasure of seeing with her in the Variety. Lili was in good health, but she was still so childish! He was surprised to learn that Lili was nearly nineteen. It made Gaga seem more imposing to him. When he tried to find out why she had not brought Lili with her, she said stiffly, "Oh, no, never! Less than three months ago she insisted on leaving boarding school. I'd been dreaming of finding a husband for her right away. . . . But she loves me so much that I had to take her back with me, although it was very much against my will."

Her blue eyelids, with their singed lashes, blinked as she spoke of getting her daughter settled in life. If, at her age, she hadn't saved a single sou and was still working, still having men, especially young ones who could have

84

been her grandsons, it showed that a good marriage was worth much more. She leaned toward La Faloise, who blushed beneath the enormous, bare, plastered shoulder with which she crushed him.

"You know," she murmured, "if she weakens it won't be my fault. . . . But girls are so odd when they're young!"

There was a great deal of movement around the table. The waiters were bustling back and forth. The entrées were brought in: chicken à la maréchale, filets of sole with ravigote sauce, and slices of goose liver. The steward, who until then had had the waiters serve only Meursault wine, now offered Chambertin and Léoville. During the slight hubbub between courses, Georges, more and more surprised, asked Daguenet if all those ladies had children. Amused by this question, Daguenet gave him some details about them. Lucy Stewart was the daughter of a railroad greaser of English origin who worked in the Gare du Nord. She was thirty-nine, had a long, horselike face, but was adorable nevertheless. Although she was consumptive, she was still very much alive. She was the most successful of all the ladies there: she had had three princes and a duke. Caroline Héquet, born in Bordeaux, was the daughter of a little clerk who had died of shame. She was lucky enough to have as her mother a capable woman who cursed her at first, but finally made up with her after a year's reflection, wishing at least to save a fortune for her. Caroline, aged twenty-five and cold by nature, was known as one of the most beautiful women who could be had for a fixed price. Her mother was of a very orderly turn of mind; she kept strict account of all income and expenditures and managed the entire establishment from her small apartment two flights up, where she had set up a sewing shop for making dresses and linen. As for Blanche de Sivry, whose real name was Jacqueline Baudu, she came from a village near Amiens. Although magnificent physically, she was stupid and untruthful: she claimed to be the granddaughter of a general and would not admit that her age was thirty-two; she was highly appreciated by Russians because of her plumpness. Daguenet then added a few words about the others: Clarisse Besnus had been brought from Saint-Aubin-sur-Mer to work as a maid for a lady whose husband had launched her on her present career; Simonne Cabiroche, daughter of a furniture dealer in the Faubourg Saint-Antoine, had been educated in a large boarding school to prepare her to become a governess; and Maria Blond, Louise Violaine, and Léa de Horn, who had all grown up on the sidewalks of Paris, and Tatan Néné, who had tended cattle in the barren regions of Campagne until she was twenty. Georges listened, looking at the women, bewildered and excited by this blunt recital of facts being whispered in his ear, while behind him the waiters were saying respectfully, "Chicken à la maréchale . . . Filets of sole with ravigote sauce . . ."

"My friend," said Daguenet, imposing his experience on him, "don't take any of that fish: it shouldn't be eaten this late at night. And stick to the Léoville wine, it's less treacherous."

Heat was rising from the candelabra, the dishes that were being passed around, and the whole table at which thirty-eight people were almost suffocating. The waiters had become careless and now hurried across the rug, which already had several grease spots on it. Yet the company had not become any livelier. The ladies toyed with their food, leaving half their meat on their plates. Only Tatan Néné ate everything, gluttonously. At that late hour of the night there were only nervous appetites, the caprices of disordered stomachs. Sitting beside Nana, the old gentleman refused all the dishes that were offered to him. He had taken only a spoonful of soup. He was now staring in silence, in front of his empty plate. There were discreet yawns. Now and then eyelids would close, and faces would go blank. Vandeuvres remarked that the evening was a deadly bore, as usual. To be amusing, such supper parties should not be so proper. If they took place in an atmosphere of virtue and respectability, one might as well eat in good society, where the boredom was no greater. If it had not been for Bordenave's constant shouting, everyone would have fallen asleep by now. The rascal was acting like a sultan as he sat there with his leg propped up, letting himself be waited on by Lucy and Rose. They were completely occupied with him, taking care of him, pampering him, making sure his glass and plate were always full. All this did not prevent him from complaining.

"Who's going to cut my meat for me? I can't do it myself, the table is a mile away."

Simonne kept standing up and stepping behind him to cut his meat and bread. All the women were interested in what he ate. The waiters were called back, and he was stuffed to the bursting point. Simonne wiped his mouth, while Rose and Lucy changed his plate and silverware. This struck him as being nice, and he finally deigned to express satisfaction: "There, you're right, my girl! That's what a woman is made for."

The others woke up a little and the conversation became general. They had just finished some tangerine sherbet. The hot roast was a fillet with truffles, the cold roast a gelatine of guinea fowl. Nana, annoyed by her guests' lack of animation, began talking loudly:

"Did you know that the Prince of Scotland has already had a stage box reserved for him so that he can see *The Blond Venus* when he comes to Paris for the Exposition?"

"I hope all the princes will see it," Bordenave said with his mouth full.

"The Shah of Persia is expected to arrive on Sunday," said Lucy Stewart.

Rose Mignon began talking about the Shah's diamonds. He wore a tunic completely covered with precious stones; it was a marvel, a blazing star, worth millions of francs. And the ladies, with pale faces and eyes glowing with covetousness, leaned forward and named the other kings and emperors who were expected. They were all dreaming of a royal caprice, of a night that would be paid for with a fortune.

Caroline Héquet moved closer to Vandeuvres and said, "Tell me, my dear, how old is the Emperor of Russia?"

"Oh, he's ageless!" replied the Count, laughing. "You won't get anywhere with him, I warn you."

Nana made a pretense of being offended. The remark seemed too crude; there were murmurs of protest. But then Blanche began talking about the King of Italy, whom she had seen once in Milan; he wasn't handsome, but that didn't stop him from being very successful with women. She was disappointed when Fauchery told her that Victor Emmanuel would not be able to come. Louise Violaine and Léa stated their preference for the Emperor of Austria.

Suddenly little Maria Blond was heard saying, "What an old bag of bones the King of Prussia is! I was at Baden last year. He was always with Count Bismarck."

"Ah, Bismarck!" interrupted Simonne. "I knew him once. . . . He's a charming man."

"That's what I was saying yesterday," cried Vandeuvres, "and no one would believe me."

There was a long discussion of Count Bismarck, just as there had been at Countess Sabine's. Vandeuvres repeated the same remarks. For a time he felt that he was back in the Muffats' drawing room, except that the ladies had changed. And, just as before, the conversation turned to music. Then, when Foucarmont mentioned Mademoiselle de Fougeray, whose decision to become a nun was the talk of Paris, Nana became interested and insisted on knowing more about her. Poor girl, burying herself alive like that! But then, maybe she had a real calling. . . . All around the table, the women were deeply touched. Georges, bored at hearing these things a second time, was questioning Daguenet about Nana's intimate habits when the conversation inevitably came back to Count Bismarck. Tatan Néné leaned close to Labordette's ear and asked him who this Bismarck was; she knew nothing about him. Labordette coolly began telling her outrageous stories: Bismarck ate raw meat; whenever he met a woman near his lair he carried her off on his back; in this way, he had already had thirty-two children at the age of forty.

"Thirty-two children at forty!" cried Tatan Néné, astounded and convinced. "He must be terribly worn out for his age."

There was a burst of laughter and she realized that he had been making fun of her. "You're so stupid!" she said. "How am I supposed to know if you're joking?"

Meanwhile, Gaga was still talking about the Exposition. Like all the other ladies, she was delighted by it and was already preparing for it. It was going to be a good season, with all the provincials and foreigners rushing to Paris. And after the Exposition, if business had been good, maybe she could retire to Juvisy, in a little house she had had her eye on for a long time.

"What else can I do?" she said to La Faloise. "I never get what I want. . . . If only I were still loved!"

She was behaving tenderly because she had felt the young man's knee touch her own. His face was very red. As she continued to lisp, she sized him up with a glance. He didn't amount to much, but she was no longer hard to please. He obtained her address.

"Look," Vandeuvres said to Clarisse, "I think Gaga is taking your Hector away from you."

"She can have him!" replied the actress. "I've already thrown him out of my place three times. . . . It disgusts me to see a young man running after old women." She paused, then discreetly called his attention to Blanche, who, since the beginning of the meal, had been affectedly holding herself in an uncomfortable position for the purpose of displaying her shoulders to the distinguished old gentleman seated three places away from her. "You're being abandoned too, my friend," she said.

Vandeuvres smiled subtly, with a gesture of indifference. He certainly had no desire to prevent poor Blanche from making a conquest. He was more interested in the spectacle Steiner was presenting to everyone at the table. The banker was noted for his sudden infatuations; that terrible German Jew, that great financier who had made and spent millions, became a fool as soon as he began to desire a woman—and he wanted them all! He could not see one on the stage without buying her, no matter what the price. Great sums were quoted. His insatiable appetite for women had already ruined him twice. As Vandeuvres said, women avenged morality by emptying his coffers. A big transaction involving the Landes salt works had restored his power in the stock market, so for the past six weeks the Mignons had been taking great bites out of the salt works. But offers were being made to bet that the Mignons would not finish them off, because Nana was now showing her white teeth. Steiner had been caught again, and this time so violently that he seemed to be dazed as he sat beside Nana; he ate without appetite, his lower lip hung down and his face was mottled. She had only to name her price. She was in no hurry, however; she played with him, breathing laughter into his hairy ear, amusing herself by watching the tremors that occasionally passed over his fat face. There would always be time to deal with him if that miserable Count

Muffat should turn out to be really determined to preserve his virtue.

"Léoville or Chambertin?" asked a waiter, putting his head between Nana and Steiner just as the latter was beginning to say something to her in a low voice.

"Eh? What?" he stammered in bewilderment. "Whatever you like, I don't care."

Vandeuvres gently nudged Lucy Stewart, who had an evil tongue and a ferocious temperament when she was aroused. Mignon had been exasperating her all evening.

"He'd be glad to lead Steiner into bed with Nana," she said to the Count. "He hopes to do the same as he did with Jonquier. You remember: Jonquier was Rose's lover when he fell for Laure. Mignon arranged for him to have Laure, then brought him back to Rose like a husband who's been allowed to go off on a little spree. . . . But this time it's not going to work. I don't think Nana gives back the men who are lent to her."

"What's the matter with Mignon?" asked Vandeuvres. "Why is he looking at his wife so sternly?" He leaned forward and saw that Rose was showing great tenderness for Fauchery. That explained to him why Lucy was being so spiteful. "My God!" he exclaimed, laughing. "Are you jealous?"

"Jealous!" Lucy said furiously. "Look, if Rose wants Léon, I'll be glad to give him to her. He's not worth much! A bouquet once a week, and not always even that! . . . Those actresses are all the same. Rose wept with rage when she read Léon's article on Nana, I know that for a fact. So she has to have an article too, you see, and she's earning it. . . . As for me, I'm going to tell Léon to go away and never come back, you'll see!"

She stopped to specify "Léoville" to a waiter standing behind her with two bottles. Then she went on, lowering her voice, "I don't want to shout, that's not my style. But just the same, she's a dirty slut. If I were her husband, I'd give her a beating she'd never forget. . . . If she thinks Fauchery is going to do her any good, she'd better think again! She doesn't know him. He's as slimy as they come. He's always using women to improve his position in the world. . . . Oh, they're a fine bunch of people!"

Vandeuvres tried to calm her. Bordenave, neglected by

Rose and Lucy, angrily cried out that they were letting papa die of hunger and thirst. This provided a welcome diversion. The supper was dragging. Almost everyone had stopped eating; platefuls of Italian mushrooms and pineapple tarts à la Pompadour were going to waste. But the champagne that all the guests had been drinking ever since the soup was gradually animating them with a kind of nervous intoxication. They were beginning to behave a little less properly. The women leaned their elbows on the disorderly table, the men pushed back their chairs so that they could breathe more freely. Black coats moved closer to light-colored dresses, half-turned shoulders gleamed like silk. The room was too warm. Above the table, the light of the candles was becoming thick and still more yellow. Now and then, when a woman tilted her head, the back of her neck gave off a golden glow beneath a rain of curls and the glitter of a diamond clip illuminated a high chignon. There were broad jokes which set off sparks of gaiety, laughing eyes, glimpses of white teeth, reflections of the candelabra burning in glasses of champagne. The guests gesticulated, indulged in loud banter, asked questions that received no answer, and called out to one another across the room. But it was the waiters who made the most noise, thinking they were still in the corridors of their restaurant, jostling each other, serving the ices and the dessert with guttural exclamations.

"Listen, girls," shouted Bordenave, "don't forget that we have a performance tomorrow. Be careful! Don't drink too much champagne."

"I've drunk every kind of wine you can think of, in every part of the world," said Foucarmont. "And I've had some extraordinary liquids, liquors capable of killing a man. But nothing has ever had any effect on me. I can't get drunk. I've tried, but I can't."

He was very pale, very calm, leaning back in his chair and continuing to drink.

"Even so, you'd better stop," said Louise Violaine. "You've had enough. I wouldn't enjoy taking care of you the rest of the night."

Intoxication had brought a bright consumptive flush to Lucy Stewart's cheeks. Rose Mignon's eyes were moist, and she was becoming more and more amorous. Tatan Néné, sluggish from having eaten too much, was smiling vaguely at her own stupidity. The others—Blanche, Caroline, Simonne, Maria—were all talking together, telling each other about their affairs: a quarrel with a coachman, a planned trip to the country, complicated stories about lovers stolen and returned. A young man sitting near Georges tried to kiss Léa de Horn. She slapped him, and said with noble indignation, "What do you think you're doing? Let go of me!" Georges, very drunk by now, and more excited than ever by the sight of Nana, hesitated over an idea he had been seriously considering, namely, to crawl under the table and lie down at her feet like a little dog. No one would have seen him and he would have stayed there quietly. When, at Léa's request, Daguenet told the young man to behave himself, Georges suddenly felt grieved, as though he himself had just been reprimanded; everything was stupid, sad and worthless. Daguenet jokingly forced him to drink a big glass of water, asking him what he would do if he were alone with a woman, since three glasses of champagne were enough to knock him flat.

"In Havana," Foucarmont went on, "they make a brandy out of some kind of wild berry. It's like swallowing fire. Well, I drank over a quart of it one night and it didn't do anything to me. Or better still, one day on the Coromandel Coast the natives gave us something that tasted like a mixture of pepper and vitriol. That had no effect on me either. I can't get drunk."

For some time now he had been developing an aversion to La Faloise, who was sitting across the table from him. He began sneering at him and making unpleasant remarks. La Faloise, whose head was spinning, moved around a great deal and kept pressing up against Gaga. Then a great anxiety increased his agitation: someone had just taken his handkerchief. He began asking for it with drunken persistence, questioning those around him, leaning down to look under their chairs and between their feet. When Gaga tried to calm him he said, "This is absurd. It has my initials and my crest on one corner. . . . It may compromise me."

"Look here, Monsieur Falamoise, Lamafoise, Malafoise!" cried Foucarmont, who felt that it was extremely witty to garble the young man's name in this manner.

La Faloise became angry. He stammered a few remarks about his ancestors and threatened to throw a pitcher at Foucarmont. Vandeuvres had to intervene: he assured La Faloise that Foucarmont was very funny. And everyone was indeed laughing. The bewildered young man was shaken by this; he consented to sit down, and he obediently began eating when his cousin loudly ordered him to do so. Gaga drew him close to her again. From time to time, however, he cast a sullen, anxious glance at the other guests, still looking for his handkerchief.

Then Foucarmont, in a witty mood, attacked Labordette across the whole table. Louise Violaine tried to silence him, because, she said, whenever he started teasing someone like that it always ended badly for her. He had found a joke which consisted in calling Labordette "Madame." It seemed to amuse him greatly, for he repeated it again and again. Labordette calmly shrugged his shoulders each time and said, "Be quiet, my friend, it's stupid."

But when Foucarmont continued, and even became insulting for some reason that no one understood, he stopped answering him and addressed Vandeuvres instead: "Make your friend be quiet, Monsieur. I don't want to lose my temper."

He had fought two duels. He was bowed to and received everywhere. There was a general surge of feeling against Foucarmont. Everyone had become gayer, and he was considered to be very witty, but that was no reason for him to spoil the night. Vandeuvres, whose delicate face had darkened, demanded that he give Labordette back his true sex. The other men—Mignon, Steiner, Bordenave—excitedly intervened also, drowning out his voice with their shouts. Only the old gentleman, who had been forgotten in his seat beside Nana, kept his distinguished air and his silent, weary smile as his pale eyes watched this tumultuous ending of the meal.

"Why don't we have our coffee in here?" said Bordenave. "We're all quite comfortable."

Nana did not answer immediately. Since the beginning of the meal she had felt that she was no longer in her own home. She was dazed and overwhelmed by all those people who kept calling the waiters, talking and putting themselves at ease as though they were in a restaurant.

She had forgotten her role as the hostess, and had begun to devote all her attention to fat Steiner, who was almost bursting with apoplexy beside her. She listened to him, still shaking her head in refusal, with the provocative laugh of a buxom blond. The champagne she had drunk had turned her face pink, moistened her lips, and made her eyes glow; and each time she made a winsome movement of her shoulders, each time her neck swelled voluptuously when she turned her head, the banker offered her a greater sum. Near her ear he saw a delicate little corner, a patch of velvety skin that drove him mad. Occasionally, when something disturbed her, she would remember her guests and try to be gracious in order to show that she knew how to entertain.

By the end of the meal she was very drunk. It was so annoying: champagne always made her drunk right away. Then she had an idea which exasperated her: those women were deliberately playing a dirty trick on her by behaving so badly in her apartment. Oh, she had seen what was going on! Lucy had winked at Foucarmont to incite him against Labordette, and Rose, Caroline, and the others had stirred up the men. The noise was now so great that you couldn't hear yourself think, and they were doing it just so they could say it didn't matter what you did when you had supper at Nana's! Well, she would show them! She might be drunk, but she was still the most elegant and proper woman there.

"Tell them to serve the coffee in here," said Bordenave. "It'll be better for me, because of my leg."

But Nana had leapt to her feet, muttering under her breath to Steiner and the old gentleman, who were both taken aback, "It serves me right; this will teach me to invite such vulgar people!" Then she pointed to the door of the dining room and said loudly, "If you want coffee, there's some in there."

Her guests left the table and crowded toward the dining room without noticing her anger. Soon there was no one left in the drawing room except Bordenave, steadying himself on the walls as he cautiously moved along, cursing those damned women who didn't care about papa now that they were drunk. Behind him, the steward was giving loud orders to the waiters, who were already clearing the table. They bustled back and forth, jostling one another, and finally made the table disappear, like stagehands removing scenery at a signal from the stage manager. The ladies and gentlemen were going to return to the drawing room when they had finished their coffee.

"Oh! It's not so warm in here!" said Gaga, shivering slightly as she entered the dining room.

The window had been left open. Two lamps illuminated the table on which coffee and liqueurs had been set out. There were no chairs. Everyone drank his coffee standing up, while the noise made by the waiters in the next room became still louder. Nana had vanished, but no one was concerned about her absence. Her guests got along quite well without her: they served themselves and reached into the drawers of the sideboard for spoons, which were lacking on the table. Several groups had formed. People who had been separated during supper now rejoined one another to exchange glances, significant smiles, or brief remarks that summed up various situations.

"Monsieur Fauchery should come and have lunch with us one of these days, shouldn't he, Auguste?" said Rose Mignon.

Mignon, who was toying with his watch chain, looked at the journalist sternly for a second. As a good manager, he would put a stop to such waste. For an article, yes; but after that, the door would be closed. However, since he knew how headstrong his wife could be, and since he made it a rule to give his paternal consent to her foolish whims whenever he could not prevent her from indulging them, he answered amiably, "Yes, of course, I'll be delighted. . . . Why don't you come tomorrow, Monsieur Fauchery?"

Lucy Stewart, talking with Steiner and Blanche, overheard this invitation. She said to the banker, raising her voice, "It's a mania all those women have. One of them even went so far as to steal my dog. . . . After all, my friend, is it my fault if you abandon her?"

Rose turned her head. She stared at Steiner, very pale, slowly sipping her coffee, and all the repressed anger she felt over her abandonment flashed in her eyes like a flame. She saw things more clearly than Mignon. It was stupid of him to try that Jonquier maneuver again; those things never worked twice. Well, at least she would have Fauchery. She had been wanting him ever since the beginning of supper. If Mignon didn't like it, it would teach him a lesson.

Vandeuvres went over to Lucy Stewart and said, "You're not going to fight, are you?"

"No, don't worry. But she'd better watch her step or I'll really give her a piece of my mind."

She summoned Fauchery with an imperious gesture.

"I have your slippers at home," she said to him. "I'll have them delivered to your concierge tomorrow."

He tried to joke about it. She walked away with a queenly air. Clarisse, who had leaned against a wall to drink a glass of kirsch in peace, shrugged her shoulders. What a fuss to make over a man! As soon as two women were together with their lovers, didn't each always begin trying to take the other's lover away from her? It never failed. If she, for example, had wanted to take offense, she would have scratched Gaga's eyes out because of Hector. But what did she care? When La Faloise passed by, she contented herself with saying to him, "You like them well aged, don't you? You don't want them ripe, you want them rotten!"

La Faloise showed irritation, then anxiety. Since Clarisse was making fun of him, he suspected her.

"The joke's gone far enough," he said. "You took my handkerchief. Give it back."

"You're getting on my nerves with that handkerchief of yours!" she cried. "Why should I have taken it, you idiot?"

"I'll tell you why," he said mistrustfully. "You took it so you could send it to my family, to compromise me."

Meanwhile Foucarmont was attacking the liqueurs. He continued to sneer whenever he looked at Labordette, who was drinking his coffee in the midst of the ladies. And he muttered disconnected phrases: son of a horse dealer, others said the bastard son of a countess; no income, and always with five hundred francs in his pocket; all women's servant, and never went to bed with any of them.

"Never, never!" he cried, becoming angry. "Yes, I'll have to slap him."

He emptied a little glass of chartreuse. Chartreuse didn't bother him at all, not that much, he said, and he clicked his thumbnail against the edge of his teeth. But suddenly, just as he began to walk toward Labordette, he turned pale and fell in a heap in front of the sideboard. He was dead drunk. Louise Violaine was in despair. She had known very well it was going to end badly for her; now she would have to spend the rest of the night taking care of him. Gaga reassured her; after examining the officer with the eye of an experienced woman, she declared that it was nothing, that he was going to sleep for twelve or fifteen hours without any trouble. He was taken away.

"What's happened to Nana?" asked Vandeuvres.

Yes, as a matter of fact, she had slipped away as soon as she left the table. Everyone now recalled her and began asking about her. Steiner became worried; he questioned Vandeuvres about the old gentleman, who had also vanished. But the Count reassured him: he had just shown the old gentleman to the door. He was a foreigner whose name it was not necessary to mention, a very rich man who contented himself with paying for supper parties. Then, when everyone was beginning to forget Nana again, Vandeuvres saw Daguenet motioning him through a doorway. He found the hostess sitting stiff and white-lipped in the bedroom while Daguenet and Georges stood looking at her in consternation.

"What's wrong?" he asked, surprised.

She did not answer; she did not even look at him. He repeated his question.

"I don't like people trying to make a fool of me, that's what's wrong!" she cried out at length.

She poured out everything that came into her mind. No, she wasn't stupid, she could see what was going on. They'd made fun of her during supper, they'd said all kinds of horrible things to show they despised her. A bunch of filthy sluts who weren't fit to lick her boots! It would be a long time before she'd go to all that trouble again, just so they could stab her in the back! She didn't know what kept her from throwing them all out. Her rage choked her; her voice faltered and she burst into sobs.

"Come, come, my dear, you're drunk," Vandeuvres said affectionately. "You must be reasonable."

No, she refused in advance. She was going to stay where she was.

"I may be drunk, but I want to be respected."

For the past quarter of an hour, Daguenet and Georges had been vainly begging her to return to the dining room. She had stubbornly repeated that her guests could do whatever they liked; she despised them too much to go back to them. Never, never! Nothing in the world could make her leave her bedroom.

"I should have known better," she said. "That bitch Rose is the one who's behind the plot. I was expecting a respectable woman tonight, and I'm sure Rose stopped her from coming."

She was referring to Madame Robert. Vandeuvres gave her his word of honor that Madame Robert had declined the invitation of her own accord. He listened and talked, without laughing. He was used to such scenes, and he knew how to deal with women when they were in that state. But as soon as he tried to take Nana's hands to pull her up from her chair and lead her out of the room, she struggled with increased fury. No one would ever make her believe, for example, that Fauchery hadn't made Count Muffat decide not to come. He was a snake in the grass, that Fauchery, an envious man who would keep after a woman until he had destroyed her happiness. She knew very well that the Count had fallen in love with her. She could have had him.

"Muffat? Never!" cried Vandeuvres, forgetting himself and laughing.

"Why not?" she asked seriously, sobering up a little.

"Because the priests have too strong a hold on him. If he so much as touched you with the tip of his finger, he'd go and confess it the next day. . . . Let me give you some advice: don't let the other one get away."

She reflected in silence for a moment. Then she stood up and bathed her eyes. When Vandeuvres tried to lead her into the dining room, however, she again refused furiously. He left the bedroom with a smile, without insisting any further. As soon as he was gone she had a fit of tenderness: she threw herself in Daguenet's arms and said, "Oh, my Mimi, there's no one but you! You know I love you, I really love you. . . . It would be so good if we could live together forever! Ah, women are so unlucky!"

Then, noticing that Georges was turning very red from

seeing them kiss each other, she kissed him also. Mimi couldn't be jealous of a baby. She wanted Paul and Georges always to get along well, because it would be nice for the three of them to stay like that, knowing they all liked each other. But they were disturbed by a strange noise: someone was snoring in the bedroom. After looking around for a few moments they discovered Bordenave, who had apparently installed himself comfortably there after drinking his coffee. He was sleeping on two chairs, with his leg stretched out and his head resting on the edge of the bed. Nana thought he looked so funny, with his mouth open and his nose moving each time he snored, that she was shaken by wild laughter. She left the bedroom, followed by Daguenet and Georges, walked through the dining room, and entered the drawing room, laughing more and more.

"Oh, my dear," she said, almost throwing herself in Rose's arms, "you have no idea . . . Come and see for yourself!"

All the women had to go with her. She caressingly took hold of their hands and dragged them away with such forthright gaiety that they all began laughing without yet knowing why. The group disappeared, then returned after having stayed for a minute with bated breath, looking at Bordenave majestically stretched out on his chairs. They all burst into laughter again. When one of them called for silence, they heard Bordenave snoring in the distance.

It was nearly four o'clock in the morning. A card table had just been placed in the dining room. Vandeuvres, Steiner, Mignon, and Labordette were sitting around it, while Lucy and Caroline stood behind them, making bets. Blanche, sleepy and dissatisfied with her night, kept asking Vandeuvres every five minutes if they would soon be leaving. In the drawing room, others were trying to dance. Daguenet was at the piano, "at the commode," as Nana said. She did not want any "banging"; Mimi would play as many waltzes and polkas as anyone wished. But the dancing languished. The ladies talked among themselves, sitting drowsily on sofas. Suddenly there was an uproar. Eleven young men had arrived in a group. They were laughing loudly in the anteroom and pushing their way toward the door of the drawing room. They had just left the ball at the Ministry of the Interior, wearing evening coats, white ties, and the decorations of several unknown orders. Nana, annoyed by this rowdy arrival, called the waiters, who were still in the kitchen, and ordered them to throw those gentlemen out. She swore she had never seen them before. Fauchery, Labordette, Daguenet, and all the other men had stepped forward to force them to respect their hostess. There were angry words and threatening gestures. For a moment it looked as though there might be a general exchange of blows. But then a blond, sickly-looking little man said insistently, "Come now, Nana, the other night at Peters', in the big red room . . . Don't you remember? You invited us."

The other night at Peters'? She did not remember it at all, which night? And when the blond little man had told her it was Wednesday, she remembered having had supper at Peters' then, but she hadn't invited anyone, she was almost sure of it.

"And yet if you did invite them," said Labordette, who was beginning to have doubts, "you may have been a little tipsy at the time."

Nana laughed. It was possible, she couldn't say for sure. Anyway, since those gentlemen were there, they could come in. The tension subsided; several of the newcomers found friends in the drawing room, and the scene ended with handshakes. The sickly-looking little man bore one of the greatest names in France. Furthermore, they announced that others were to follow them; and, true enough, the door opened every few moments to admit men wearing white gloves and ceremonial evening clothes. They had all come from the ball at the ministry. Fauchery jokingly asked if the minister himself was going to come. Nana irritably replied that the minister visited people who were certainly worth less than she was. What she did not say was that she had conceived the hope of seeing Count Muffat arrive in that stream of people. He might have changed his mind. She kept her eye on the door as she talked with Rose.

The clock struck five. The dancing had ceased, but the gamblers were still at their game. Labordette had yielded his place and the women had gone back to the drawing room. The air there was heavy with the somnolence of a long sleepless night. The lamps glowed dully, their charred wicks giving a reddish tinge to their gloves. The ladies had reached that state of vague melancholy in which each felt a need to relate the story of her life. Blanche de Sivry spoke of her grandfather, the general, while Clarisse invented a tale about a duke who had seduced her at her uncle's house, where he came to hunt wild boars; and, with their backs turned to each other, they both shrugged their shoulders and asked how anyone could tell such lies. As for Lucy Stewart, she calmly admitted her humble origins and freely talked about her childhood, when her father, the greaser in the Gare du Nord, used to treat her to an apple tart on Sundays.

"Oh, I must tell you!" little Maria Blond suddenly exclaimed. "There's a gentleman who lives across the street from me, a Russian. He's terribly rich. Well, yesterday I received a basket of fruit. I never saw anything like it! Huge peaches, grapes this big . . . It was fantastic for this time of year. And in the middle of it I found six thousand-franc notes. It came from the Russian. Naturally I sent it all back to him, but it made me a little sad, because of the fruit."

The other women looked at each other, trying not to smile. That Maria Blond had plenty of nerve for her age! As though such things ever happened to little whores like her! They felt profound contempt for her. They were all jealous of Lucy, infuriated by the thought of her three princes. Ever since she had begun riding in the Bois de Boulogne every day, which was what had started her on the road to success, they had all been seized with a mania for horseback riding.

It was nearly dawn. Nana lost hope and stopped watching the door. Everyone was thoroughly bored. Rose Mignon had refused to sing "The Slipper." She was curled up on a sofa, talking softly with Fauchery while she waited for Mignon, who had already won a thousand francs or so from Vandeuvres. A fat gentleman, wearing decorations and a serious expression, had just recited "Abraham's Sacrifice" in Alsatian dialect. In it, when God swore He said, "By Myself!" and Isaac always replied, "Yes, papa." However, since no one understood it, it had fallen flat. No one knew what to do in order to be gay, to finish the night on a note of wild abandon. For a moment Labordette considered denouncing the women to La Faloise so that he would prowl around each one of them to see if she had his handkerchief tucked into the top of her dress. Then, since there were still some bottles of champagne in the sideboard, the young men began drinking again. They shouted and tried to stir each other up, but a dreary, abysmally stupid drunkenness was inexorably invading the drawing room. Finally the little blond man, the one who bore one of the greatest names in France, at his wits' end and desperate at not having been able to think of anything amusing, had an idea: he picked up a bottle of champagne and emptied it into the piano. The others were convulsed with laughter.

"Why is he putting champagne in the piano?" asked Tatan Néné, watching him with astonishment.

"What! Don't you know?" Labordette replied gravely. "There's nothing as good for pianos as champagne. It improves the tone."

"Oh," murmured Tatan Néné, convinced.

And when everyone laughed at her she became angry. How was she supposed to know? They were always trying to confuse her!

Things were rapidly going from bad to worse. The night threatened to end unpleasantly. In one corner of the room, Maria Blond was quarreling with Léa de Horn, whom she accused of going to bed with men who were not rich enough. They began using coarse language and making derogatory remarks about each other's faces. Lucy, who was ugly, silenced them. A woman's face meant nothing, she said; a good figure was all that mattered. Some distance away, on a sofa, a diplomatic attaché had put his arm around Simonne's waist and was trying to kiss her neck; but Simonne, tired and irritable, pushed him away each time, struck him across the face with her fan, and said, "Stop bothering me!" The other women refused to let anyone touch them. After all, they weren't streetwalkers! Gaga, however, had caught La Faloise and was almost holding him on her lap. Clarisse was hidden between two gentlemen, laughing nervously like a woman who is being tickled. Around the piano, the little game continued in a fit of stupid folly; the men jostled one another, each trying to pour out the remaining contents of his bottle. It was all quite simple and good-natured.

"Here, old boy, have a drink. . . . What a thirsty piano! . . . Careful, here's another bottle. We mustn't waste a drop."

Nana had her back to them and did not see them. She had definitely decided to concentrate her efforts on Steiner, who was sitting beside her. What else could she do? It was Muffat's fault for refusing to come. In her white silk dress, light and rumpled like a chemise, with dark circles under her eyes and a touch of intoxication which had turned her face pale, she offered herself to Steiner with her usual good-humored expression. The roses in her hair and on her dress had shed their petals; only the stems remained. Steiner suddenly withdrew his hand from her skirt, where he had just encountered the pins placed there by Georges. A few drops of blood appeared. One of them fell on her dress and stained it.

"Now it's sealed," Nana said seriously.

Dawn was growing brighter. An uncertain, hideously sad light was creeping in through the windows. The guests began to leave. It was a disorderly departure, filled with uneasiness and rancor. Caroline Héquet, annoyed at having wasted her night, said she was going to leave before some really disgusting things began to happen. Rose was pouting as though her honor had been compromised. It was always the same with those women: they didn't know how to behave, they were obnoxious from the start. When Mignon had cleaned out Vandeuvres, the couple left without showing any concern for Steiner, after having again invited Fauchery to lunch the next day. Lucy then refused to let the journalist take her home, and loudly told him to go back to his ham actress. Rose turned around and retorted sharply, "You filthy pig!" But Mignon, always paternal in quarrels between women, with a superiority born of long experience, pushed his wife outside and told her to keep quiet. Behind them, Lucy regally descended the stairs, all alone. Then Gaga led La Faloise away. He felt sick and he was sobbing like a baby, calling for Clarisse, who had long since gone off with her two gentlemen. Simonne had also disappeared. Only Tatan, Léa, and Maria

were left. Labordette obligingly offered to take charge of
them.

"I'm not at all sleepy," said Nana. "We ought to do
something."

She looked at the sky through the window. It was a livid
sky, with sooty clouds drifting across it. It was six o'clock
in the morning. On the other side of the Boulevard Haussmann, the damp roofs of sleeping houses stood out in the
dim light. A group of street sweepers were clattering
along the deserted pavement in their wooden shoes. As she
watched this dismal awakening of the city, she felt a surge
of girlish tenderness, a longing for the country, for idyllic
scenes, for something soft and white.

"Oh! I'll tell you what," she said, going back to Steiner.
"I want you to take me to the Bois de Boulogne. We'll
drink milk there!"

She clapped her hands with childish joy. Without waiting for a reply from the banker, who consented, of course,
although he was inwardly annoyed and had other things
in mind, she hurried off to get her coat. There was no one
left in the drawing room with Steiner except the group of
young men. Having emptied even their glasses into the
piano, they were speaking of leaving when one of them
triumphantly appeared with a last bottle, which he had
brought in from the pantry.

"Wait, wait!" he cried. "Here's a bottle of chartreuse!
. . . There, the poor piano needed some chartreuse; it'll
make him feel better. . . . And now, my friends, let's go.
We've been acting like fools."

Nana had to awaken Zoé, who had dozed off on a chair
in the dressing room. The gas was still burning. Zoé shiv-
ered as she helped Madame to put on her hat and coat.

"Well, I've done what you wanted me to," Nana said
with expansive familiarity, relieved at having come to a
decision. "You were right: it may as well be the banker
as anyone else."

The maid was sullen and still drowsy. She grumbled that
Madame should have made up her mind the first night.
Then, as she followed her around the bedroom, she asked
her what she was to do with those two: Bordenave was still
snoring, and Georges, who had slipped in to bury his
head in a pillow, had finally gone to sleep, breathing as

lightly as an angel. Nana told her to let them sleep. Then her tenderness returned when she saw Daguenet come in. He had been waiting for her in the kitchen. He looked very sad.

"Come, Mimi, be reasonable," she said, taking him in her arms and kissing him with all sorts of caresses. "Nothing has changed, you know my Mimi is still the one I love. . . . I had to do it. You understand, don't you? We'll be even happier than before, I promise you. Come tomorrow and we'll decide on the hours. . . . Hurry, kiss me to show me how much you love me. . . . Oh, more, more than that!"

She slipped away from him and went back to Steiner, happy and once again possessed with her idea of drinking milk. In the empty apartment, Vandeuvres remained alone with the decorated man who had recited "Abraham's Sacrifice." They were both glued to the card table, not knowing where they were, not seeing the daylight. Blanche had decided to lie down on a sofa and try to sleep.

"Ah, Blanche will come too!" cried Nana. "We're going to drink milk, my dear. . . . Come with us; Vandeuvres will still be here when we get back."

Blanche got up lazily. The banker's flushed face lost some of its color: he was irritated by the thought of taking that big girl who was going to get in his way. But the two women already had hold of him and were saying, "We want them to milk the cow in front of us."

a word, he crossed his left leg over the right, and began
slowly to stretch his limbs. . . . Then, with the air of the
veteran of gloomina, and a long beard, began gravely to
mumble incoherence to his kingly deportment. . . . Old

5

𝒯he thirty-fourth performance of *The Blond Venus* was
being given at the Variety Theater. The first act had just
ended. In the greenroom, Simonne, dressed for her part as
the little laundress, was standing in front of a console
table surmounted by a mirror, between the two corner
doors opening obliquely onto the corridor leading to the
dressing rooms. She was alone. She examined herself and
passed her finger under her eyes to correct her make-up
while the two gaslights on either side of the mirror warmed
her with their glare.

"Has he come yet?" asked Prullière, entering the room
in his Swiss admiral's costume, with his big saber, his
enormous boots, and his gigantic plume.

"Who?" said Simonne without turning around, smiling
at the mirror to see her lips.

"The Prince."

"I don't know, I'm about to go down. . . . Oh, he'll come.
He comes every day!"

Prullière walked over to the fireplace opposite the console table. A coke fire was burning in it, and two other
gaslights were blazing above it. He raised his eyes and
looked at the clock and the barometer, accompanied by
gilded Empire-style sphinxes, to his left and right. Then
he stretched out in a big armchair whose green velvet,
worn down by four generations of actors, had taken on a
yellowish hue in spots. He sat still, staring into space, in
the weary, resigned attitude of an actor accustomed to
the waits between his appearances on the stage.

Old Bosc also came in, shuffling and coughing, wearing
an ancient yellow box coat which had slipped down off
one shoulder, revealing King Dagobert's gold-spangled
cloak. After putting his crown on the piano without saying

a word, he stamped his feet for a few moments, looking gloomy yet affable. His hands trembled with the first beginnings of alcoholism, and a long white beard gave a venerable appearance to his red drunkard's face. Then, when the silence was broken by the sound of a sudden downpour striking against the panes of the big square window that overlooked the courtyard, he made a gesture of disgust and grunted, "What miserable weather!"

Simonne and Prullière did not move. Four or five paintings—landscapes, a portrait of the actor Vernet—were slowly turning yellow in the heat of the gaslights. On the shaft of a column, a bust of Potier, one of the bygone glories of the Variety Theater, looked on with its empty eyes. Suddenly a loud voice rang out. It was Fontan, in his second-act costume, that of a stylish young man dressed in yellow, even to his gloves. "Don't you know?" he cried, gesticulating. "Today is my name day!"

"Oh?" said Simonne, approaching him with a smile, as though attracted by his big nose and broad, comical mouth. "Is your first name Achille?"

"That's right! And I'm going to tell Madame Bron to bring up some champagne after the second act."

For the past few moments a bell had been ringing in the distance. The prolonged sound died away, then returned; and when it had stopped, a cry went up and down the stairs and became lost in the corridors: "On stage for the second act! . . . On stage for the second act! . . ." This cry drew nearer until a pallid little man passed by the door of the greenroom, where he shouted at the top of his high-pitched voice, "On stage for the second act!"

"My God, champagne!" said Prullière, seeming not to have heard this noise. "You must be in good shape!"

"If I were you, I'd have it sent from the café," old Bosc declared slowly, sitting on a green velvet bench with his head resting against the wall.

But Simonne said they ought to let Madame Bron have her little profit. She excitedly clapped her hands, devouring Fontan with her gaze, while his goatlike face was animated by a constant movement of his eyes, nose, and mouth. "Oh, that Fontan!" she said. "There's nobody like him!"

The two doors of the greenroom were open wide onto

the corridor leading to the wings. Along the yellow wall, brightly illuminated by an unseen gas lantern, figures were swiftly passing: costumed men, half-naked women wrapped in shawls, the whole chorus of the second act, the masqueraders of the Boule-Noire dance hall; and at the end of the corridor their feet could be heard thumping on the five wooden steps that led down to the stage. As Clarisse was running past, Simonne called out to her; but she said she would come back right away. And she reappeared almost immediately, shivering beneath the thin tunic and scarf of Iris.

"Damn it!" she said. "It's cold in here, and I left my fur coat in my dressing room!" Then, standing in front of the fire to warm her legs, whose tights were mottled with bright pink, she added, "The Prince is here."

"Ah!" the others exclaimed with interest.

"Yes, that's why I was running: I wanted to see. . . He's in the first stage box on the right, the same as Thursday. This is the third time in a week, isn't it? That Nana is so lucky! . . . I was willing to bet he wouldn't come again."

Simonne opened her mouth, but her words were drowned out by a new cry that burst forth near the greenroom. In the corridor the callboy's shrill voice was shouting, "Curtain going up!"

"Three times: that's starting to get impressive!" said Simonne when she was able to speak again. "He won't go to her place, you know; he takes her to his. And they say it costs him a lot of money."

"Of course—it always costs money to go out on the town," Prullière said maliciously, standing up and glancing at himself in the mirror. It was obvious that he considered himself a handsome man who was adored by the ladies in the boxes.

"Curtain going up! Curtain going up!" repeated the callboy's voice, gradually dying away as he hurried along the corridors and staircases.

Fontan, who knew what had happened the first time between Nana and the Prince, told the story to the two women. They pressed up against him, laughing loudly when he leaned down to give certain details. Old Bosc, filled with indifference, did not move. Such things no longer interested him. He was stroking a big reddish cat that was blissfully curled up on the bench. He finally picked it up in his arms with the tender benevolence of a senile king. The cat arched its back and sniffed his big white beard for a long time; then, apparently repelled by the smell of glue, it curled up on the bench again and went to sleep. Bosc remained solemn and thoughtful.

"Even so, if I were you I'd get the champagne from the café; it's better," he suddenly said to Fontan as the latter was finishing his story.

"The curtain's up!" cried the callboy's quavering voice. "The curtain's up! The curtain's up!"

The cry echoed for an instant. There was a sound of rapid footsteps. The corridor door opened abruptly, admitting a burst of music and a distant clamor; then the padded door closed with a thud.

Once more a heavy quiet reigned in the greenroom, as though it were a hundred miles away from the stage and the applauding audience. Simonne and Clarisse were still talking about Nana. There was one girl who never hurried herself! Only the night before she had missed her entrance cue. But they stopped speaking when a tall girl put her head in through the door, then, seeing that she was mistaken, hurried off to the end of the corridor. It was Satin, wearing a hat and veil, acting like a lady paying a social call. "A pretty whore!" murmured Prullière, who had been seeing her for the past year in the Café des Variétés. And Simonne told how Nana, having recognized Satin, a former schoolmate of hers, had taken a great fancy to her and had begun plaguing Bordenave to give her a chance on the stage.

"Hello, good evening," said Fontan, shaking hands with Mignon and Fauchery, who had just come in. Even old Bosc held out his fingers while the two women kissed Mignon.

"Is there a good house tonight?" asked Fauchery.

"Oh, magnificent!" replied Prullière. "You should see how they're taking it all in!"

"Tell me," Mignon said to them, "isn't it almost time for you to go on?"

Yes, almost. They did not go on until the fourth scene. Only Bosc stood up, with the instinct of an old theatrical veteran who feels his cue approaching. And just then the callboy appeared in the doorway. "Monsieur Bosc! Mademoiselle Simonne!" he cried.

Simonne quickly threw a fur-lined cloak over her shoulders and walked out. Bosc unhurriedly went over to get his crown, put it on his head, and gave it a pat; then, dragging his coat, unsteady on his feet, he went off grumbling with the angry look of a man who has been disturbed.

"You were very nice in your last article," Fontan said to Fauchery. "But why did you say that actors are vain?"

"Yes, my boy, why did you say that?" cried Mignon, bringing his enormous hands down on the slender shoulders of the journalist, who bent beneath the force of the blow.

Prullière and Clarisse repressed a burst of laughter. For some time now everyone in the theater had been amused by a comedy that was being performed backstage. Mignon, furious over his wife's caprice, and annoyed at seeing Fauchery contribute nothing to their household except some questionable publicity, had conceived the idea of taking vengeance by overwhelming him with demonstrations of friendship. Every evening, when he met him backstage, he pounded him vigorously, as though carried away by great affection; and Fauchery, puny beside that colossus, had to accept the blows with a constrained smile, in order not to quarrel with Rose's husband.

"Aha, my lad, you've insulted Fontan!" said Mignon, continuing the farce. "On guard! One, two, and right in the chest!" He lunged and gave Fauchery such a violent thrust that for a few moments he was pale and unable to speak. But, with a wink, Clarisse drew the others' attention to Rose Mignon, who was standing on the threshold of the greenroom. Rose had witnessed the scene. She walked straight up to Fauchery, as though she had not noticed her husband. In her baby costume, with her arms bare, she stood on tiptoe and presented her forehead to him with childish tenderness.

"Good evening, Baby," said Fauchery, familiarly kissing her.

This was his compensation. Mignon did not even seem to have noticed the kiss; everybody kissed his wife in the theater. But he laughed and cast a quick glance at the journalist. Fauchery was no doubt going to pay dearly for Rose's defiance.

In the corridor, the padded door opened and closed, admitting the sound of a storm of applause to the green-room. Simonne came back after her scene.

"Oh, old Bosc made a hit!" she cried. "The Prince nearly laughed himself to death, and he was clapping along with the others, as if he'd been paid. . . . Listen, do you know the tall man sitting beside the Prince in his stage box? He's handsome and looks very dignified, and he has magnificent side whiskers."

"That's Count Muffat," replied Fauchery. "I know that day before yesterday, at the Empress's, the Prince invited him to dinner this evening. He must have corrupted him afterward."

"Count Muffat! We know his father-in-law, don't we, Auguste?" Rose said to Mignon. "You know: the Marquis de Chouard. I once went to his house to sing. . . . He's in the audience too. I saw him at the back of a box. Now there's an old man . . ."

Prullière, who had just put on his enormous plumed hat, turned around to call her: "Rose! Let's go!"

She ran after him without finishing her sentence. Just then the concierge of the theater, Madame Bron, passed by the door with a huge bouquet in her arms. Simonne jokingly asked if it was for her. Without answering, the concierge pointed her chin toward Nana's dressing room at the end of the corridor. That Nana! They were always covering her with flowers! Then, when Madame Bron returned, she handed a letter to Clarisse, who swore under her breath. That pest La Faloise again! There was a man who wouldn't let go! And when she learned that he was waiting for her in the concierge's room she cried out, "Tell him I'll come down when the act is over. I'll give him a good slap in the face!"

Fontan rushed forward, saying, "Madame Bron, listen . . . Listen, Madame Bron. . . . Bring up six bottles of champagne during the intermission."

But the callboy had reappeared, out of breath, repeating in a singsong tone, "Everyone on stage! Everyone on stage! . . . Come on, Monsieur Fontan! Hurry! Hurry!"

"Yes, yes, we're coming, Barillot," replied Fontan, taken

aback. He ran after Madame Bron and said, "Have you got it straight? Six bottles of champagne in the greenroom during the intermission. I'll pay for it; today is my name day."

Simonne and Clarisse had gone off with a great rustling of skirts. They all rushed away. When the padded door had closed, another shower could be heard striking against the window. Barillot, a pale little old man who had been a callboy for thirty years, familiarly went over to Mignon and held out his open snuffbox. This pinch of snuff offered and accepted gave him a minute's rest in his constant running up and down the backstage staircases and corridors. There was still Madame Nana, as he called her, but she did only as she pleased and cared nothing about fines; when she wanted to miss her entrance cue, she missed it. He stopped in astonishment and said, "Look, she's ready! Here she comes . . . she must know the Prince is in the audience."

Nana had appeared in the corridor, dressed as a fishwife, her arms and face white, with two pink spots under her eyes. She nodded to Mignon and Fauchery without coming into the greenroom.

"Hello, how are you?"

Only Mignon shook the hand she held out. And she went on her way, regally, followed by her dresser, who was bending down to arrange the folds of her skirt as she walked along at her heels. Behind the dresser, bringing up the rear of the procession, came Satin, trying to look very sedate but already bored to tears.

"What about Steiner?" Mignon asked abruptly.

"Monsieur Steiner left for Loiret yesterday," said Barillot, who was going back toward the stage. "I think he's going to buy an estate there."

"Ah, yes, I know: Nana's estate."

Mignon's face became serious. That Steiner had once promised Rose a house in the city! Well, there was no use quarreling with anyone; the important thing was to find the opportunity again. Thoughtful, but still retaining his sense of superiority, Mignon walked back and forth between the fireplace and the console table. Only he and Fauchery were left in the greenroom. The journalist, tired, had just stretched out in a big armchair. He sat there quietly with his eyes half closed while Mignon glanced at him occasionally as he passed. When they were alone together, Mignon disdained to pummel him. What would have been the point of it if there was no one there to enjoy the scene? He had too little interest in the matter to continue performing his farce as a mocking husband when no one else was present.

Fauchery, glad of this brief respite, languidly rested his feet in front of the fire while his eyes wandered from the barometer to the clock. Mignon stopped walking, stood in front of the bust of Potier, looked at it without seeing it, then went over to the window and stared out at the dark pit of the courtyard. The rain had stopped. The silence of the room was made still heavier by the heat of the coke fire and the flaming of the gaslights. Not a sound could be heard from the wings. The staircase and the corridors seemed dead. It was the hushed peace that comes with the end of an act, when the whole company is on stage, joining in the deafening uproar of some finale, while the empty greenroom drowses in humming asphyxia.

"Oh, the bitches!" Bordenave's husky voice suddenly cried out.

He was still in the corridor, but he was already bellowing out his rage against two chorus girls who had almost fallen down on the stage because they had been playing foolish pranks. When he saw Mignon and Fauchery he called them to show them something: the Prince had just asked permission to come and pay his respects to Nana in her dressing room during the intermission. But as he was leading them toward the stage, the callboy passed by.

"Slap a fine on those two bitches Fernande and Maria!" Bordenave said furiously.

Then he calmed down and tried to recover the dignity of a noble father. After passing his handkerchief over his face, he said, "I'm going to receive His Highness."

The curtain fell amid a prolonged salvo of applause. There was a stampede in the semidarkness of the stage, which was no longer illuminated by the footlights; the actors and members of the chorus hurried back to their dressing rooms while the stagehands began rapidly changing the scenery. Simonne and Clarisse, however, remained in one corner, talking in low voices. On stage, during the intervals between their lines, they had made an arrangement. After thinking it over, Clarisse had decided that she would rather not see La Faloise, who could not make up his mind to abandon her in favor of Gaga. Simonne would go to him and simply explain to him that he would have to stop hanging onto Clarisse that way. In short, she would get rid of him.

Simonne, dressed as a comic-opera laundress, put her fur-lined cloak over her shoulders and walked down the narrow, winding staircase, with its slippery steps and damp walls, which led to the concierge's room. This room, placed between the actors' staircase and the manager's staircase, closed on either side by broad glazed partitions, was like a big transparent lantern in which two gas flames were burning violently. Letters and newspapers were piled up in a set of pigeonholes. On the table there were bouquets of flowers waiting beside forgotten dirty dishes and an old blouse whose buttonholes the concierge was mending. The whole room was like a neglected closet. In the midst of this disorder, four fashionably dressed gentlemen sat on straw-bottomed chairs, looking patient and docile, quickly turning their heads whenever Madame Bron came downstairs with answers. She had just given a letter to a young man who had hastened to open it in the vestibule, beneath the gaslight. He had turned slightly pale when he saw this classic sentence, which had been read so many times in that place: "Not tonight, darling, I'm busy." La Faloise was sitting on one of the chairs at the back of the room, between the table and the stove. He seemed determined to spend the evening there, although he also showed considerable anxiety. He kept his feet under his chair because a whole litter of black kittens were engaged in lively play around him while their mother, sitting on her haunches, stared at him with her yellow eyes.

"Ah, so it's you, Mademoiselle Simonne," said the concierge. "What do you want?"

Simonne asked her to send La Faloise out. But Madame Bron was not able to grant her request immediately. In a kind of deep cupboard under the stairs, she kept a little bar where the members of the chorus came down to drink during the intermissions. Since there were five or six husky men there, still wearing their masquerade costumes from the Boule-Noire scene, dying of thirst and in a hurry, she had begun to lose her head a little. A gaslight was burning in the cupboard, revealing a table covered with a sheet of tin and shelves on which there were partly emptied bottles. Each time she opened the door of this little hole in the wall, a violent smell of alcohol burst from it and mingled with the odor of burnt fat in her room and the penetrating scent of the bouquets lying on the table.

"Now, then," said the concierge when she had finished serving her customers, "that dark little man over there is the one you want, isn't he?"

"No, no, don't be silly!" said Simonne. "He's the skinny one beside the stove, the one your cat is sniffing."

Madame Bron led La Faloise into the vestibule while the other gentlemen sat in silent resignation, half suffocated by the smells in the room, and the masqueraders stood drinking on the stairs, slapping each other on the back and jesting in hoarse, drunken voices.

Upstairs, on the stage, Bordenave was angrily shouting at the stagehands because they were taking too long to change the scenery. They were doing it on purpose! A piece of scenery was sure to fall on the Prince's head!

"Come on, pull!" cried the foreman.

At last the backdrop was raised and the stage was clear. Mignon, who had been watching for Fauchery, took the opportunity to begin pummeling him again. He grabbed him in his big arms and shouted, "Look out! That pole almost fell on you." Then he carried him away and gave him a good shaking before putting him down again. Hearing the stagehands' exaggerated laughter, Fauchery turned pale; his lips quivered and he was on the verge of rebelling. Mignon again assumed his good-natured manner. He gave Fauchery an affectionate pat that nearly broke his shoulder, and said, "I have to take good care of you! My God, what would become of me if anything happened to you?"

Just then a murmur arose: "The Prince! The Prince!" All eyes turned toward the little door leading to the auditorium. Nothing could yet be seen except Bordenave's thick neck and round back, bobbing up and down in a series of obsequious bows. Then the Prince appeared. He was tall and broad, with a blond beard, pink skin, and the distinguished air of a confirmed pleasure-seeker. His solid build was clearly discernible beneath his impeccably cut frock coat. He was followed by Count Muffat and the Marquis de Chouard. They entered a dark corner of the theater and became almost invisible among the moving shadows. To speak to the son of a queen, to the future inheritor of a throne, Bordenave had adopted a showman's voice, quavering with false emotion: "If Your Highness will be so kind as to follow me . . . Will Your Highness deign to come this way? . . . I beg Your Highness to be careful. . . ."

The Prince was not hurrying in the least; on the contrary, he lingered to watch the stagehands with great interest. They had just lowered a beam supporting a row of gas jets that cast a broad streak of light across the stage. Muffat, who had never been behind the scenes in a theater before, was particularly lost in astonishment; he also felt a kind of uneasiness and vague repugnance mingled with fear. He looked up and saw other rows of gas jets whose flames were burning low, making constellations of little bluish stars in the chaos of the upper flies, where there were ropes of all sizes, flying bridges, and backdrops spread out in the air like enormous sheets hung up to dry.

"Lower away!" suddenly shouted the foreman of the stagehands.

The Prince himself had to warn the Count. A backdrop was being lowered. The scenery for the third act—the grotto on Mount Etna—was being set up. Men were fixing poles in holes cut into the floor, others went to get the flats that were leaning against the walls and fastened them to the poles with strong ropes. At the back of the stage, a lampman had placed a row of gas jets covered by red glass globes to produce the glare of Vulcan's fiery forge, and was now lighting them. Everything seemed to be in bustling confusion, yet each movement was carefully regulated. Amid all this haste, the prompter was slowly walking back and forth to take the stiffness out of his legs.

"Your Highness is too kind," said Bordenave, still bowing. "The theater isn't large, but we do the best we can. . . . And now, if Your Highness will deign to follow me . . ."

Count Muffat was already walking toward the corridor leading to the dressing rooms. The rather sharp slope of the stage had surprised him, and a large part of his uneasiness came from that floor, which seemed to be mobile beneath his feet. Through the open holes in it he could see gaslights burning underneath. There was a whole underground world down there, with dark depths, men's voices, and the musty odor of a cellar. Then, as he was about to leave the stage, an incident detained him. Two chorus girls, in their third-act costumes, were talking in front of the peephole in the curtain. One of them, leaning forward and widening the hole with her fingers so that she could see better, was looking around the house.

"I see him!" she exclaimed. "Oh, what a face!"

Bordenave, horrified, had to restrain himself from giving her a kick in the behind. But the Prince smiled, happy and excited at having heard the remark, looking affectionately at the girl who had made fun of His Highness. She laughed brazenly. Bordenave persuaded the Prince to follow him. Count Muffat had just taken off his hat, for he was beginning to sweat. What bothered him most was the suffocating heat of the air, laden with a strong smell, that backstage smell composed of the stench of gas, the glue of the scenery, the dirt in dark corners, and the dubious underwear of the chorus girls. In the corridor, his suffocation was increased still more by the acrid scent of toilet water and perfumed soap, and a thick accumulation of foul-smelling breath. He looked up the staircase as he was passing by, startled by the sudden flood of light that had fallen upon him. From above him came the sounds of water splashing in basins, laughter, shouts, and a constant slamming of doors that, each time they opened, allowed a puff of female odor to escape, a mixture of musk, grease paint, and the animal reek of hair. He did not stop; he quickened his pace, almost fleeing, carrying with him the shudder aroused in him by that glimpse into a feverish world that was unknown to him.

"A theater is a fascinating place," said the Marquis de Chouard, with the delighted expression of a man who has found himself at home again.

But Bordenave had finally reached Nana's dressing room at the end of the corridor. He calmly turned the doorknob, then stood aside and said, "If Your Higness will be so good as to enter . . . "

They heard the cry of a startled woman, and saw Nana, naked to the waist, run behind a curtain. Her dresser, who had been drying her, stood with her towel in her hand.

"What's the matter with you, coming in like that?" cried Nana, hiding behind the curtain. "Go out and close the door; you can see you can't come in!"

Bordenave seemed annoyed by her flight.

"Come back, my dear, it doesn't matter," he said. "It's His Highness. Come, don't be childish." She refused to show herself, for she was still startled, although she had already begun to smile. "My God, these gentlemen know how a woman is made!" he added. "They won't eat you."

"That's not certain," the Prince said slyly.

Everyone laughed exaggeratedly, to curry favor with him. It was an exquisite, thoroughly Parisian remark, said Bordenave. Nana made no reply. The curtain was moving; she was no doubt making up her mind to come out. Count Muffat, whose cheeks were flushed, looked around the dressing room. It was a square room with a very low ceiling, hung entirely with light brown cloth. The curtain of the same material, supported by a brass rod, cut off one end of the room. Two broad windows opened onto the courtyard of the theater, no more than ten feet away from a leprous-looking wall on which the panes cast bright yellow squares in the darkness of the night. A big mirror faced a white marble dressing table on which there was a disorderly array of bottles and glass boxes for oils, scents, and powders. The Count walked up to the mirror. When he saw that his face was red and that there were little drops of sweat on his forehead, he lowered his eyes and stood in front of the dressing table for a few moments, apparently absorbed in examining the basin full of soapy water, the scattered ivory implements, and the damp sponges. He was again seized with the feeling of dizziness that he had experienced during his visit to Nana in her apartment on the Boulevard Haussmann. He felt the thick carpet growing softer beneath his feet; the gaslights burning beside the mirror and the dressing table seemed to project hissing flames around his temples. Fearing that he might faint in that feminine odor, which was heated and intensified by the low ceiling, he sat down on the edge of a soft sofa between the two windows. But he stood up again almost immediately and went back to the dressing table, although this time he did not look at anything. His eyes were vague; he was thinking about a bouquet of tuberoses that once withered in his bedroom and nearly killed him. When tuberoses decay, they have a human smell.

"Hurry up!" Bordenave whispered, putting his head behind the curtain.

The Prince was listening politely to the Marquis de Chouard, who had picked up a hare's foot from the dressing table and was explaining how make-up was applied. In one corner, Satin, with her pure, virginal face, was staring at the gentlemen, while Madame Jules, the dresser, was preparing Venus's tights and tunic. Madame Jules was ageless; she had the shriveled skin and motionless features of an old maid whom no one knew when she was young. She had been dried out in the heated air of dressing rooms, amid the most celebrated thighs and breasts in Paris. She always wore a faded black dress, with a forest of pins on her flat, sexless chest, over her heart.

"Please excuse me, gentlemen," said Nana, pushing back the curtain, "but you took me by surprise. . . ."

They all looked at her. She had not covered herself at all; she had merely buttoned a little percale blouse that only half hid her breasts. When the gentlemen put her to flight, she had only begun to undress, having quickly taken off her fishwife costume. Her chemise was still pulled out of her drawers in back. She stood there with her arms and shoulders bare, the tips of her breasts pointing outward, in all the adorable freshness of her plump blond beauty, still holding the curtain with one hand, as though to draw it shut again at the slightest cause for alarm.

"Yes, you took me by surprise . . . I'll never dare to . . ." she stammered with feigned modesty and an embarrassed smile, blushing down to her neck.

"Come, come," said Bordenave, "you look good to us just the way you are!"

She ventured another of her hesitant, guileless expressions, writhed as though she were being tickled, and said, "You honor me too much, Your Highness. Please excuse me for receiving you like this."

"It's I who must apologize for this intrusion, Madame,"

said the Prince, "but I couldn't resist the desire to pay my compliments to you."

Then, to go to her dressing table, she calmly walked through the midst of the gentlemen in her drawers. They all stepped aside for her. Her drawers tightened over her broad hips, and her breasts protruded as she bowed to them with a subtle smile. Suddenly she seemed to recognize Count Muffat for the first time. She held out her hand to him in a friendly manner and scolded him for not having come to her supper party. His Highness deigned to make a few jesting remarks to Muffat, who stuttered an incoherent reply, still shivering from having held that little hand, as cool as toilet water, in his own burning hand. The Count had dined well with the Prince, a great eater and drinker. They were both a little tipsy, in fact, although they behaved quite correctly. To hide his agitation, Muffat could think of nothing except a comment on the heat.

"It's so hot in here!" he said. "How can you live in such heat, Madame?"

The conversation was about to continue on this topic when loud voices were heard outside the door. Bordenave drew back the covering of a grated peephole of the kind to be found in convents. It was Fontan, followed by Prullière and Bosc, all three carrying bottles under their arms, with their hands full of glasses. Fontan knocked, shouting that it was his name day and that he was treating everyone to champagne. Nana gave the Prince a questioning look. Of course! He would be only too delighted! He didn't want to be in anyone's way. But Fontan came in without waiting for permission.

"Me not stingy," he said childishly, "me pay for champagne!"

He had not known the Prince was there. When he noticed him, he stopped short, took on an expression of farcical solemnity, and said, "King Dagobert is outside and would like to have a drink with Your Royal Highness."

The Prince smiled, whereupon the others found Fontan's little performance charming. But the dressing room was too small for all those people. They had to pack themselves in tightly, Satin and Madame Jules standing against the curtain, the men crowding around Nana, who was still half naked. The three actors were still wearing their second-act costumes. Prullière took off his Swiss admiral's hat, whose enormous plume was too high for the ceiling. Bosc, in his crimson cloak and tin crown, steadied himself on his drunken legs and bowed to the Prince like a monarch receiving the son of a powerful neighbor. The glasses were filled and everyone clinked them together.

"I drink to Your Highness!" old Bosc said regally.

"To the army!" added Prullière.

"To Venus!" cried Fontan.

The Prince courteously swung his glass. He waited, then bowed three times and murmured, "Madame . . . Admiral . . . Sire . . ."

He emptied his glass. Count Muffat and the Marquis de Chouard followed suit. There was no more jesting now: they were all at court. The real world was being extended into this world of the theater, in a solemn farce enacted beneath the glowing haze of the gaslights. Nana, forgetting that she was in her drawers with her chemise hanging out, acted the part of a great lady, Queen Venus, opening her private apartment to the dignitaries of the State. She used the words "Royal Highness" in every sentence, she bowed with conviction, she treated the two masqueraders, Bosc and Prullière, as though the first were a sovereign and the second his minister. And no one smiled at the strange sight of a genuine prince, heir to a throne, drinking a common actor's champagne, perfectly at ease in that carnival of gods, in that masquerade of royalty, amid a crowd of dressers, chorus girls, third-rate actors, and exhibitors of women. Bordenave, carried away by the scene, was thinking of the money he would make if His Highness would consent to appear like that in the second act of *The Blond Venus*.

"I know what!" he said expansively. "I'll have my little women come down here!"

Nana opposed the idea. She herself was becoming more relaxed, however. She was attracted to Fontan, with his grotesque face. She rubbed up against him with the look of a pregnant woman who has a desire to eat something unsavory.

"Don't just stand there: fill up the glasses!" she said to him with sudden familiarity.

Fontan poured the champagne again. They drank, repeating the same toasts:

"To Your Highness!"

"To the army!"

"To Venus!"

Nana motioned for silence. She raised her glass very high and said, "No, no, to Fontan. Today is his name day. To Fontan, to Fontan!"

They clinked their glasses together a third time and acclaimed Fontan. The Prince had seen Nana gaze longingly at the comedian. "Monsieur Fontan," he said to him with great politeness, bowing to him, "I drink to your success."

Meanwhile the tail of His Highness's frock coat swept the marble top of the dressing table. The room was like an alcove or a narrow bathroom, with the vapor from the wash basin and the sponges, the strong perfume of the scents, mingled with the tart, slightly intoxicating smell of the champagne. Nana was wedged in between the Prince and Count Muffat. They had to raise their hands to avoid brushing against her hips or her breasts each time they made a gesture. Madame Jules was standing stiffly, waiting, without a single drop of perspiration. Satin, with all her vice, was surprised to see a prince and gentlemen in frock coats pursuing a naked woman in the company of a group of costumed actors. She reflected that fashionable people were not so respectable after all.

But the tinkling of Barillot's bell was approaching in the corridor. When he reached the door of the dressing room he was horrified to see the three actors still wearing their second-act costumes.

"Oh, gentlemen, gentlemen," he said, "hurry! The bell has just rung in the lounge!"

"Well, the audience can wait," Bordenave said calmly.

However, since the bottles were empty, the actors bowed once again and went upstairs to change their costumes. Bosc, having soaked his beard in champagne, had just taken it off, and beneath that venerable beard the drunkard had suddenly reappeared, with the ravaged, empurpled face of an old actor who has taken to drink. At the foot of the stairs he was heard saying to Fontan in his husky voice, referring to the Prince, "I really impressed him, didn't I?"

No one was left in Nana's dressing room except His Highness, the Count, and the Marquis. Bordenave had gone off with Barillot, after telling him not to give the signal for the raising of the curtain without first notifying Madame.

"Please excuse me, gentlemen," said Nana. She began making up her arms and face with particular care because of the nude scene in the third act.

The Prince sat down on the sofa with the Marquis de Chouard. Count Muffat remained standing. Their intoxication had been increased by the two glasses of champagne they had drunk in that suffocating heat. On seeing the gentlemen shut themselves in with her friend, Satin had discreetly disappeared behind the curtain. She was now waiting there, sitting on a trunk, annoyed at having nothing to do while Madame Jules calmly came and went without saying a word to her, or even looking at her.

"You sang your rondelet wonderfully," said the Prince.

A conversation followed, but it was composed only of short phrases interrupted by silences. Nana could not always reply. After spreading cold cream over her face and arms with her hand, she applied grease paint with the corner of a towel. For a moment she stopped looking at herself in the mirror, smiled, and glanced at the Prince, without letting go of the grease paint.

"Your Highness is too kind," she murmured.

Her preparations were complicated. The Marquis de Chouard watched her for a time with an expression of blissful enjoyment, then said, "Couldn't the orchestra play more softly when it accompanies you? It covers your voice, and that's an unforgivable crime."

This time Nana did not turn around. She had picked up the hare's foot and was attentively passing it over her face, bending above the dressing table in such a way that the white roundness of her drawers, with her chemise hanging out, was very much in evidence. She swayed her hips to show her appreciation of the old man's compliment.

There was silence. Madame Jules had noticed a tear in the right leg of Nana's drawers. She took a pin from over her heart and knelt for a few moments on the floor, busying herself around Nana's thigh, while Nana, without seeming to know she was there, covered herself with powder, being careful not to put any over her cheekbones. Finally the Prince said that if she came to sing in London all England would want to applaud her. She laughed graciously and turned around for a second, her left cheek very white, in a cloud of powder. Then she suddenly became serious: it was time to put on her rouge. Putting her face near the mirror again, she dipped her fingers into a jar, applied the rouge under her eyes and gently spread it to her temples. The gentlemen maintained a respectful silence.

Count Muffat had not yet said anything. He was thinking of his youth. The bedroom he had had when he was a child had been very cold. Later, at sixteen, when he kissed his mother every evening he could still feel the icy touch of that kiss even in his sleep. One day as he was passing a half-open door he had caught a glimpse of a maid washing herself. This was the only memory that had troubled him from the time he reached puberty to the day of his marriage. Then he had found in his wife a strict obedience to conjugal duty, while he himself felt a kind of devout repugnance. He had grown up and matured in ignorance of the flesh, submitting to rigid religious practices, having regulated his life in accordance with precepts and laws. And now he had suddenly found himself in an actress's dressing room, in front of a half-naked girl. He, who had never seen Countess Muffat put on her garters, was now watching the intimate details of a woman's toilet, surrounded by jars and basins, in the midst of that strong, sweet odor. His whole being rebelled. The slow possession that Nana had been taking of him for some time frightened him by reminding him of the pious stories he had read in his childhood about people who were possessed by the devil. He believed in the devil. He had a confused feeling that Nana was the devil, with her laughter, with her breasts and buttocks swollen with vices. But he promised himself he would be strong. He would be able to defend himself.

"Then it's agreed," said the Prince, quite at ease on the sofa; "you'll come to London next year and we'll give you such a good reception that you'll never return to France.

. . . Ah, my dear count, you don't value your pretty women highly enough. We'll take them all away from you."

"That won't bother him," the Marquis de Chouard said maliciously, venturing to reveal himself in private. "The count is virtue personified."

When she heard this remark about Muffat's virtue, Nana gave him such a strange look that he felt greatly annoyed. Then this feeling surprised him and made him angry with himself. Why did the idea of being virtuous bother him in front of that girl? He felt like beating her. But she had just dropped a brush, and as she bent down for it he hurried to pick it up for her. They felt each other's breath and Venus's hair fell loosely over his hands. He experienced keen pleasure mingled with remorse, the kind of pleasure known only to Catholics who, in the midst of sin, are goaded by the fear of hell.

Just then Barillot's voice was heard outside the door: "May I give the signal to raise the curtain, Madame? The audience is getting impatient."

"In a little while," Nana replied calmly.

She had dipped the brush into a jar of black paint. Pressing her nose against the mirror and closing her left eye, she passed it delicately between her eyelashes. Muffat watched her from behind. He saw her in the mirror, with her round shoulders and her breasts covered by a pink shadow. Despite all his efforts, he could not look away from that face made so provocative by its closed eye, full of dimples, and seemingly transported by desires. When she closed her right eye and began painting its lashes, he realized that he belonged to her.

"Madame," cried the callboy's breathless voice, "they're stamping their feet! They'll start breaking the seats before long! May I give the signal?"

"Go ahead!" Nana said impatiently. "I don't care! If I'm not ready, they'll just have to wait for me." She calmed down, turned to the gentlemen, and added with a smile, "It's a pity we can't even talk for a few minutes."

She had finished making up her face and arms. With her finger she added two broad streaks of carmine on her lips. Count Muffat felt more agitated than ever, seduced by the perversion of powders and paints, seized with an inordinate desire for that painted young woman, with her mouth too red and her face too white, her eyes enlarged, burning, and ringed with black, as though after a night of love. Nana stepped behind the curtain for a moment to take off her drawers and put on Venus's tights. Then, with tranquil immodesty, she came out, unbuttoned her little percale blouse and held out her arms to Madame Jules, who slipped on the short sleeves of the tunic.

"Hurry, since they're getting angry," she said.

The Prince contemplated the swelling outlines of her breasts with the eye of a connoisseur. The Marquis de Chouard involuntarily nodded his head. Muffat looked down at the floor to avoid seeing her. Venus was now ready, for she wore only that gauze over her shoulders. Madame Jules hovered around her, looking like a little old woman carved out of wood, with her clear, empty eyes. She quickly took some pins from the inexhaustible cushion over her heart and pinned Venus's tunic, passing her bony hand over all that plump nudity without a single memory, as though she had no interest in her sex.

"There!" said Nana, taking one last look at herself in the mirror.

Bordenave came in and said anxiously that the third act had begun.

"Well, I'm going," she said. "Why make such a fuss? I always have to wait for the others."

The gentlemen left the drawing room, but they did not say good-by, for the Prince had expressed a desire to watch the third act from the wings. When she had been left alone, Nana looked around in surprise.

"Where is she?" she asked.

She was looking for Satin. When she found her behind the curtain, waiting on the trunk, Satin said to her calmly, "I didn't want to get in your way, with all those men." And she added that she was now going to leave. But Nana held her back. How could she even think of leaving? Bordenave had promised to hire her! It would all be settled after the performance. Satin hesitated. She felt out of place there; everything was so complicated. . . . However, she remained.

As the Prince was going down the little wooden staircase, he heard strange sounds from the other side of the theater: there were muffled curses and the scuffling of feet, as though someone were fighting. An occurrence was taking place that alarmed the actors waiting for their cues. Mignon had begun his joke again, pummeling Fauchery with affectionate blows. He had also invented a little game which consisted in flicking Fauchery's nose, to protect him from flies, he said. This game naturally amused the actors greatly. But then, carried away by success and giving free rein to his whimsey, Mignon had suddenly given the journalist a slap, a real and vigorous slap. This time he had gone too far. In the presence of others, Fauchery could not accept such a slap with a smile. Putting an end to the farce, the two men had leapt at each other's throats, their faces livid and filled with hatred. They were now rolling over and over on the floor behind a scenery frame, each calling the other a pimp.

"Monsieur Bordenave! Monsieur Bordenave!" cried the stage manager, running up to the producer in alarm.

Bordenave followed him, after asking the Prince to excuse him. When he recognized Fauchery and Mignon on the floor, he made an angry gesture. They had really chosen the right time, with His Highness on the other side of the scenery, and a whole audience who could hear them! To make things complete, Rose Mignon arrived, out of breath, just as it was time for her to go on stage. Vulcan gave her her cue, but she stood petrified when she saw her husband and her lover at her feet, wallowing on the floor, kicking and choking each other, with their hair in disorder and their coats white with dust. They were blocking her way. A stagehand had caught Fauchery's hat just as the devilish thing was about to bounce onto the stage in the midst of the fight. Meanwhile Vulcan, who had been inventing lines to amuse the audience, gave Rose's cue again. She was still standing motionless, staring at the two men.

"Don't look at them!" Bordenave whispered to her furiously. "Get moving! There's nothing you can do about it! You're missing your cue!"

He gave her a push, forcing her to step over the two bodies, and she found herself on the stage, in the glare of the footlights, before the audience. She had not understood why they were fighting on the floor. She was trembling and there was a buzzing in her ears, but she stepped toward the footlights with Diana's amorous smile on her lips and began her duet in such a warm voice that the audience gave her an ovation. She could still hear the dull thuds of the fight going on backstage. They had now rolled nearly all the way to the stage. Fortunately the music covered the noise they made as they banged against the scenery flats.

"God damn it!" Bordenave cried in exasperation when he had finally succeeded in separating them. "Why couldn't you have fought at home? You know I don't like that! . . . Mignon, I want you to stay on this side of the theater; and you, Fauchery, I'll throw you out if you don't stay on the other side. Understand? Stay on opposite sides of the theater, or I won't let Rose bring you here."

When he returned to the Prince, the latter asked him what had been the trouble.

"Oh, it was nothing at all," Bordenave said calmly.

Nana, wrapped in a fur cloak, stood talking to the gentlemen while she waited for her cue. As Count Muffat was coming up to look at the stage between two scenery flats, he understood from a gesture made to him by the stage manager that he must walk softly. Everything was quiet overhead in the rigging loft. In the brightly colored wings, a few people were tiptoeing away, or staying to talk to each other in low voices. The gasman was at his post beside his complicated set of valves. A fireman was stretching his neck to get a view of the stage as he leaned against a scenery frame. On his bench high above, the curtain man sat with a look of resignation on his face, paying no attention to the performance, waiting for the bell that would signal him to begin maneuvering his ropes. And in that stifling air, amid the sound of whispering and soft footsteps, the voices of the actors on the stage seemed strangely muffled and surprisingly false. Further on, beyond the confused noises of the orchestra, the spectators seemed to be breathing in one vast respiration which occasionally swelled into murmurs, laughter, or applause. The invisible audience made its presence felt even during its silences.

"Something's open," Nana said suddenly, wrapping her fur cloak more tightly around her. "Go take a look, Barillot. I'll bet somebody just opened a window. . . . It's a wonder I haven't already caught my death of cold here!"

Barillot swore that he had shut all the windows himself. Maybe there were some broken panes. The actors were always complaining about drafts. In the heavy heat of the gaslights, the currents of cold air made the place a real pneumonia trap, as Fontan put it.

"I'd like to see *you* in a low-cut dress!" Nana said angrily.

"Sh!" replied Bordenave.

On the stage, Rose had just put so much expression into one of the phrases of her duet that the cheers of the audience drowned out the orchestra. Nana remained silent, with a serious look on her face. Meanwhile, as the Count was venturing into one of the slips, Barillot stopped him by warning him that he could be seen by the audience there. He saw the scenery at an angle from behind and noted that the backs of the flats had been strengthened with thick layers of old posters. Further on, he saw one corner of the stage: the grotto on Mount Etna, hollowed out of a silver mine, with Vulcan's forge in the background. Hanging stage-lights illuminated the patches of metallic paint that had been applied with broad brush strokes. Skillfully intermingled red and blue lights produced the effect of a blazing fire, while other lights had been placed along the floor at the back of the stage to make a row of black rocks stand out in sharp relief. And amid all those lights glowing like lanterns scattered across the grass on the night of a public celebration, old Madame Drouard, who played the part of Juno, was sitting on a gently sloping ramp, drowsy and half blinded by the glare, waiting for her entrance cue.

There was a slight commotion backstage. Simonne, who had been listening while Clarisse told her a story, exclaimed, "Look, there's Tricon!"

It was indeed old Tricon, still wearing her hair in ringlets and looking like a countess who haunted lawyers' offices. When she saw Nana, she walked straight toward her.

"No," said Nana after a quick exchange of words, "not now."

The old lady remained solemn. Prullière shook hands with her as he passed. Two little faces were watching her with emotion. She seemed to hesitate for a moment, then she beckoned to Simonne. There was another quick exchange of words.

"Yes," said Simonne. "In half an hour."

As she was going back to her dressing room, Madame Bron, who had again come down to deliver some letters, handed her one. Lowering his voice, Bordenave furiously reproached the concierge for having let Tricon into the theater. That woman! Why did she have to come at exactly the wrong time? He was indignant, because of His Highness. Madame Bron, who had been in the theater for thirty years, replied acrimoniously. How was she to know? Tricon did business with all the ladies; Monsieur Bordenave had seen her dozens of times before without ever saying a word. And while Bordenave was muttering a string of oaths, Tricon was calmly staring at the Prince, sizing him up with a practiced eye. A smile brightened her yellow face, and she slowly walked away, passing through a group of respectful women.

"You'll be on time, won't you?" she said, turning back to Simonne.

Simonne seemed to be upset. The letter was from a young man she had promised to meet after the performance. She gave Madame Bron a scribbled note: "Not tonight, darling, I'm busy." But she was still uneasy: the young man might wait for her anyway. Since she was not in the third act, she wanted to leave immediately, so she asked Clarisse to go and see. Clarisse did not have to go on stage until the end of the act. She went downstairs while Simonne returned for a moment to the dressing room they shared.

Downstairs in Madame Bron's little bar, the actor who had the minor role of Pluto was drinking alone, wearing a big red robe adorned with golden flames. The concierge's little business had apparently gone well, for the recess under the stairs was all damp from the rinsings of glasses. Clarisse raised the hem of the tunic she was wearing for her role of Iris, to prevent it from dragging on the slippery steps. She prudently stopped short of the last bend in the stairs, stretched her neck forward, and looked into the concierge's room. Her caution was justified: that idiot La Faloise was still there, sitting on the same chair, between the table and the stove! He had pretended to leave when Simonne saw him, then he had come back. The room was still full of fashionably dressed gentlemen looking docile and patient, gravely staring at one another as they waited. Only the dirty dishes were left on the table, for Madame Bron had just delivered the last of the bouquets. A rose had fallen on the floor and was withering near the black cat, who lay curled up while her kittens raced madly between the gentlemen's legs.

"Look out, he'll get you!" said Pluto, a practical joker, as he climbed the stairs, wiping his lips with the back of his hand.

Clarisse gave up the idea of making a scene with La Faloise. She had seen Madame Bron deliver Simonne's note to her young man. He had gone to read it under the gaslight in the vestibule. "Not tonight, darling, I'm busy." Then, apparently accustomed to reading these words, he had calmly left. There was one man, at least, who knew how to behave! He wasn't like the others, those who were still stubbornly waiting on Madame Bron's shabby straw-bottomed chairs, slowly baking in the heat of that foul-smelling room that glowed like a huge lantern through its glazed walls. Some men would stop at nothing when they wanted a woman! Clarisse went back upstairs, disgusted. She crossed over to the other side of the theater and ran up the three flights of stairs leading to the dressing rooms to report to Simonne.

In the wings, the Prince was standing to one side, talking to Nana. He had not left her, and he was now looking at her longingly with his eyes half closed. Without looking back at him, Nana was smiling and nodding her head. But suddenly Count Muffat obeyed an impulse that welled up from his whole being: he left Bordenave, who had been giving him some details about the operation of the windlasses, and went over to break up the conversation between Nana and the Prince. Nana raised her eyes, and smiled at him as she had been smiling at His Highness. At the same time, however, she continued to listen for her cue.

"The third act is the shortest, isn't it?" said the Prince, embarrassed by the Count's presence.

She did not answer: her face had abruptly changed expression and she was now concerned only with her work. She quickly slipped off her fur cloak, which Madame Jules, standing behind her, received in her arms. Then, after putting both hands to her hair as though to subdue it, she walked naked onto the stage.

"Quiet!" whispered Bordenave.

The Count and the Prince were surprised. In the midst of the silence there arose a deep sigh, the distant murmur of a crowd. The same effect was produced every night when Venus appeared in her goddess-like nudity. Then Muffat wanted to see; he put his eye to a hole. Beyond the dazzling semicircle of footlights, the house looked dark, as though filled with reddish smoke; and against this neutral background, on which the rows of faces cast a blurred pallor, Nana stood out in white. She seemed to have grown suddenly larger, so that she blotted out the boxes from the balcony to the ceiling. He saw her from behind, arching her back and opening her arms. On a level with her feet, the old prompter's head, with its humble, honest expression, looked as though it had been severed from his body. When she sang certain phrases of her entrance number, an undulating movement seemed to start from her neck, descend to her waist and finally expire at the trailing hem of her tunic.

When she had sung her last note she bowed amid a storm of cheers. Her gauze tunic fluttered and her hair touched the small of her back each time she straightened up. Seeing her move backward toward the hole through which he was looking, bending at the waist so that her hips were even broader, the Count stepped back, very pale. The scene vanished; he no longer saw anything except the back of the scenery, covered with multicolored old posters pasted in all directions. On the ramp, among the rows of gaslights, all the gods of Olympus had joined Madame Drouard, who was still dozing. They were waiting for the end of the act, Bosc and Fontan sitting on the floor with their chins on their knees, Prullière stretching and yawning before going on stage. They all looked weary; their eyes were red and they were eager to go to bed.

Then Fauchery, who had been roaming around the right-hand side of the theater ever since Bordenave had forbidden him to enter the other side, came up to the

Count, hoping to preserve his dignity by giving himself something to do, and offered to show him the dressing rooms. Muffat, drained of his will by a languor that had been growing inside him, finally went off with the journalist after looking around for the Marquis de Chouard, who was no longer there. He felt both relieved and anxious when he left the wings, from which he could hear Nana singing.

Fauchery was already preceding him up the staircase, which was closed by wooden revolving doors on the second and third floors. It was a staircase of a kind that Count Muffat had seen in some of the disreputable houses he had visited as a member of the charity committee: it had bare, dilapidated yellow walls, steps worn by the constant pounding of feet, and an iron rail polished by the rubbing of hands. On each landing, on a level with the floor, there was a low window set into a square recess like a cellar air-hole. Gaslights were burning in lanterns set into the wall, garishly illuminating that ugliness, giving off a heat which accumulated as it rose up the narrow spiral.

When he reached the foot of the stairs, the Count had again felt a hot breath descend on him, laden with the odor of women, coming down from the dressing rooms in a flood of light and sound. And now, with every upward step he took, the musky smell of face powder and the sharp scent of aromatic vinegar heated and dazed him still more. On the second floor there were two sharply turning corridors with yellow doors like those of an ill-famed hotel, bearing large white numerals. Some of the squares composing the floor had come loose, and the settling of the old building had caused them to rise. The Count ventured forward, glanced through a half-open door and saw a dirty room that reminded him of a barber's shop in a poor neighborhood. It was furnished with two chairs, a mirror, and a table with a drawer, blackened by the dirt of combs. A big, sweaty man, his shoulders steaming, was changing his linen in it. In a similar room next door, a woman was putting on her gloves, preparing to leave; her hair was wet and uncurled, as though she had just taken a bath. Fauchery called to the Count.

He had just reached the third floor when a furious "Damn it!" burst from the corridor on his right: Mathilde, a dirty little girl who played ingénue parts, had just broken her wash basin, and the soapy water had flowed out onto the landing. The door of a dressing room was slammed violently. Two women in corsets ran across the corridor; another, holding the hem of her chemise in her teeth, appeared briefly and hurried away. Then there was laughter, a quarrel, a song begun and suddenly stopped. All along the corridor, through the cracks of doors left ajar, there were glimpses of nudity, white skin, and pale underwear. Two girls were gaily showing each other their birthmarks; a third, very young, had lifted her petticoats above her knees and was mending her drawers. When the dressers saw the two men, they gently drew the curtains, out of decency. The great stir and bustle that always came with the end of a performance had already begun; women were removing their make-up, taking off their costumes and putting on their own clothes in a cloud of face powder, while the musky smell in the corridor was increased by the opening and closing of doors.

On the fourth floor, the Count abandoned himself to the intoxication that had been taking possession of him. The dressing room of the chorus girls was there: twenty women packed together amid a jumble of soaps and bottles of lavender water; it was like the common room of a brothel on the outskirts of Paris. As he was passing a closed door, he heard furious sounds of washing, a tempest in a basin. He was about to go up to the top floor when his curiosity prompted him to take one more look, through a peephole that had been left open: the room was empty and in the glare of a gaslight he saw only a chamber pot in the middle of some skirts lying in disorder on the floor. This room was the last vision he carried away with him.

When he reached the fifth floor he felt as though he were choking. All the odors and heat struck him there; the yellow ceiling seemed to have been baked, a lantern was burning in a reddish mist. For a moment he gripped the iron railing; it seemed to have a living warmth beneath his hand. He closed his eyes and breathed in that whole female sex of which he was still ignorant, but which was now pressing in upon him from all sides.

"Come on!" shouted Fauchery, who had disappeared a

few minutes earlier. "There's someone here who wants to see you."

At the end of the corridor was the dressing room occupied by Clarisse and Simonne. It was a long, badly constructed room directly under the roof, with sloping ceiling and walls. There were two skylights, but at this hour of the night it was lighted with gas. The wallpaper was of the kind that can be bought for seven sous a roll: pink flowers on green trellises. Two planks covered with oilcloth, darkened by the water that had been spilled on it, served as dressing tables. Under them there were battered zinc pitchers, buckets filled with dirty water, and coarse yellow earthenware jugs. There was a whole array of cheap articles deformed and dirtied by use: chipped basins, horn combs with missing teeth, and all the other clutter left by the haste and carelessness of two women who wash and undress in common, in a room they occupy only temporarily, and whose dirtiness has ceased to affect them.

"Come on," repeated Fauchery in that tone of comradeship which men adopt when they visit women together. "Clarisse wants to kiss you."

Muffat finally entered the room. He was astonished to see the Marquis de Chouard sitting on a chair between the two dressing tables. The Marquis had withdrawn there some time earlier. He sat with his feet apart because one of the buckets leaked and had made a big puddle of soapy water on the floor. He gave the impression that he was at ease, knowing the right spots, invigorated by the oppressive bathroom atmosphere, by the tranquil feminine immodesty that the dirty little room made natural and freer.

"Are you going to go with the old man?" Simonne whispered to Clarisse.

"Not on your life!" Clarisse replied loudly.

The dresser, a very ugly and very familiar young girl, who was helping Simonne put on her coat, was convulsed with laughter. The three of them egged one another on, murmuring words that redoubled their hilarity.

"Come, Clarisse, kiss the gentleman," said Fauchery. "You know he's loaded with money." He turned to the Count. "You'll see, she's very nice; she's going to kiss you."

But Clarisse was disgusted with men. She spoke vehemently of the dirty pigs who were waiting for her in the concierge's room. Besides, she was in a hurry to go down: they were going to make her miss her last scene. Then, when Fauchery blocked the door, she kissed Muffat's side whiskers and said, "It's not because of you, at least. It's because Fauchery is annoying me."

She slipped away. The Count was embarrassed in front of his father-in-law. The blood had rushed to his face. In Nana's dressing room, in that profusion of hangings and mirrors, he had not felt the acrid excitement he now felt in the shameful squalor of that garret room, filled with the two women's laxity. Meanwhile the Marquis had followed Simonne as she hurried out of the room; he whispered something to her and she shook her head. Fauchery walked after them, laughing. The Count found himself alone with the dresser, who was rinsing out the wash basins. He left. His legs were unsteady as he walked down the stairs, again startling women in their petticoats and causing doors to slam as he passed. But in the midst of those scurrying girls on all four floors, he saw nothing distinctly except a cat, the big red cat which, in that hothouse reeking with musk, was creeping down the stairs, rubbing its back against the balusters with its tail erect.

"I thought they were never going to let us go tonight!" said a woman's husky voice. "What a nuisance they are with their curtain calls!"

The performance was over, the curtain had just fallen. There was a veritable stampede on the staircase, which became filled with exclamations, for everyone was in a violent hurry to change clothes and leave. When Count Muffat reached the foot of the stairs he saw Nana and the Prince walking slowly along the corridor. She stopped, then smiled and said softly, "All right, in a little while."

The Prince went back to the stage, where Bordenave was waiting for him. Then, alone with Nana, Muffat yielded to a surge of anger and desire: he ran after her and, just as she was going into her dressing room, he kissed her roughly on the back of the neck, on the little curly hairs that extended down between her shoulders. It was as though he were returning the kiss he had received upstairs. Nana spun around furiously, raising her hand. When she saw the Count she smiled.

"Oh! You frightened me," she said simply.

And her smile was adorable; it was embarrassed and docile, as though she had given up hope of that kiss and was now happy to have received it at last. But she could not see him that night or the next day. They would have to wait. Even if she had been able to see him, she would have made him desire her a while longer. Her eyes spoke eloquently. Finally she said, "I'm a landowner now, you know. . . . Yes, I'm buying a country house near Orléans, in a region where you sometimes go. Baby told me that— little Georges Hugon; you know him, don't you? Come and see me there."

The Count, frightened by his own timid abruptness and ashamed of what he had done, bowed ceremoniously and accepted her invitation. Then he left her, walking in a dream.

He was on his way to rejoin the Prince when, as he was passing the greenroom, he heard Satin cry out, "What a dirty old man you are! Leave me alone!" These words were addressed to the Marquis de Chouard, who had begun laying siege to her, for lack of anything better. She had had enough of all those fashionable people. Nana had introduced her to Bordenave, but she had found it exasperating to keep her mouth shut all that time for fear of saying something foolish. She was eager to regain her freedom, especially since she had come across a former lover of hers in the wings: the man who played the part of Pluto, a pastry cook who had once given her a whole week of love and slaps. She was waiting for him, annoyed that the marquis was talking to her as though she were one of those ladies of the theater. She finally took on an expression of great dignity and said, "My husband's coming, you'll see!"

The actors, wearing their overcoats and looking weary, were leaving one by one. Groups of men and women were coming down the little spiral staircase. They wore battered hats and ragged shawls, and their faces had the pale ugliness of common actors who have taken off their make-up. On the stage, where the lights were being turned off, the Prince was listening to an anecdote that Bordenave was relating to him. He wanted to wait for Nana. When she finally appeared, the stage was dark and the fireman on

137

duty was making a tour of inspection with a lantern in his hand. So that His Highness would not have to make a detour through the Passage des Panoramas, Bordenave gave orders to open the corridor that went from the concierge's room to the lobby. There was immediately a rush of chorus girls who were glad to escape from the men waiting in the Passage. They jostled one another, glancing back over their shoulders, and did not breathe freely until they were outside. Fontan, Bosc, and Prullière walked out slowly, making jokes about the paying gentlemen who were pacing up and down the Galerie des Variétés while their women were fleeing across the boulevard with lovers they had freely chosen. Clarisse was especially sly. She was wary of La Faloise. And true enough, he was still there in the concierge's room, along with the other gentlemen who were stubbornly waiting on Madame Bron's chairs. They were all peering out the door. Clarisse walked by swiftly, hiding behind a friend. The gentlemen blinked their eyes, bewildered by the stream of swirling skirts at the foot of the little stairs, and in despair at having waited so long only to see all the women hurry away, without recognizing a single one of them. The litter of black kittens were sleeping on the oilcloth against the belly of their mother, who was blissfully stretching out her paws, while the big reddish cat sat on the other end of the table with his tail lying flat, watching the passing women with his yellow eyes.

"If Your Highness will be so good as to come this way," said Bordenave at the foot of the stairs, pointing to the corridor.

A few chorus girls were still crowding along it. The Prince followed Nana. Muffat and the marquis came behind them. It was a long passage running between the theater and the building next door, a kind of narrow alley covered with a sloping roof in which there were several skylights. Moisture was oozing from the walls. Footsteps resounded on the tiled floor as in an underground passage. It was filled with the disorder of an attic storeroom; there was a workbench on which the concierge's husband sometimes planed a piece of scenery, and a pile of wooden barriers that were set up outside the door in the evening to control the line of people. Nana had to raise her skirt as she passed by a leaking faucet that was flooding the floor. On reaching the lobby, they all bowed to one another. When Bordenave was alone, he summed up his opinion of the Prince with a shrug of his shoulders that was full of disdainful philosophy.

"Actually, he's a bit of a pig," he said without further explanation to Fauchery, whom Rose Mignon was taking home with her husband, in order to reconcile them there.

Muffat found himself alone on the sidewalk. His Highness had calmly helped Nana into his carriage. The Marquis had gone off behind Satin and her lover, excited, contenting himself with following those two personifications of vice with the vague hope that they might grant him some favor. Muffat's head was aflame. He decided to walk home. All struggle within him had ceased. The ideas and beliefs he had held for forty years were being drowned in a flood of new life. As he walked along the boulevard, the rumble of the last carriages seemed to deafen him with Nana's name, and he saw her nudity, her supple arms and white shoulders, dancing in the flames of the gaslights. He felt that she possessed him; he would have repudiated everything, sold everything, to have her for a single hour that very night. His youth was awakening at last; a lustful adolescent puberty had suddenly flared up in his Catholic coldness and mature dignity.

6

Count Muffat, accompanied by his wife and daughter, had arrived the previous evening at Les Fondettes, where Madame Hugon, who had been alone with her son Georges, had invited them to come and spend a week. The house, built toward the end of the seventeenth century, stood in the middle of an immense square enclosure, without a single ornament. But the garden had magnificent shade trees and a series of spring-fed fountains. It was like a wave of greenery along the road from Orléans to Paris, a bouquet of trees breaking the monotony of that flat countryside where cultivated fields stretched away as far as the eye could see.

At eleven o'clock, when the second ringing of the lunch bell had called everyone together, Madame Hugon, with her kindly maternal smile, kissed Sabine's cheeks and said, "You know it's my custom in the country. . . . It makes me feel twenty years younger to see you here. Did you sleep well in your old room?" Then, without waiting for a reply, she turned to Estelle: "And did this little girl get a good night's sleep too? . . . Give me a kiss, my child."

They were sitting in the spacious dining room, whose windows overlooked the garden. But they occupied only one end of the big table, because they had crowded close together for greater intimacy. Sabine spoke gaily of the childhood memories that were coming back to her: the months she had spent at Les Fondettes, the long walks, a fall into one of the fountains on a summer evening, an old novel of chivalry discovered on top of a cupboard and read in winter, in front of a fire of vine cuttings. Georges, who had not seen the Countess for several months, found her strange; something had changed in her face. That skinny Estelle, however, seemed more insignificant, silent, and awkward than ever.

140

While they were eating a simple meal of soft-boiled eggs and cutlets, Madame Hugon lamented like a housewife: the butchers were becoming impossible; she bought everything in Orléans, and she never received the pieces she asked for. Anyway, if her guests ate badly it was their own fault: they had come too late in the season.

"It's foolish," she said. "I've been waiting for you since June, and it's now the middle of September, so it's not nice outside any more, as you can see." She pointed to the trees on the lawn, which were beginning to turn yellow. It was a cloudy day; the horizon was shrouded in a bluish mist that gave an impression of soft, peaceful melancholy. "Oh, I'm expecting more company!" she went on. "Things will be gayer here when they come. First there will be two gentlemen whom Georges has invited: Monsieur Fauchery and Monsieur Daguenet. You know them, don't you? And then, Monsieur de Vandeuvres has been promising to come for the past five years; this year he may really do it."

"Ah!" exclaimed the Countess, laughing. "Let's not count on Monsieur de Vandeuvres! He's too busy."

"And Philippe?" asked Muffat.

"Philippe has asked for leave," replied the old lady, "but you'll probably be gone by the time he arrives."

Coffee was served. The conversation turned to Paris, and Steiner's name was mentioned. Madame Hugon uttered a little exclamation.

"That reminds me," she said; "Monsieur Steiner is that fat gentleman I met at your house one evening, a banker, isn't he? . . . He's a terrible man! Just imagine: he's bought a house for an actress two or three miles from here in the direction of Gumières, on the other side of the Choue! Everyone around here is scandalized. . . . Did you know that, my friend?"

"Not at all," replied Muffat. "So Steiner has bought an estate near here!"

On hearing his mother broach this subject, Georges had buried his nose in his cup, but he now raised his head and stared at the Count, astonished by his reply. Why had he told such an outright lie? The Count, having noticed the young man's movement, gave him a mistrustful glance. Madame Hugon went into detail: the estate was called La Mignotte; to reach it, one had to go along the bank of the Choue all the way to Gumières in order to cross the bridge there, otherwise one would get one's feet wet and run the risk of a ducking.

"And what's the actress's name?" asked the Countess.

"Let's see, now, I've heard it mentioned . . ." said the old lady. "Georges, you were there this morning when the gardener was talking to us . . ."

Georges appeared to be searching his memory. Muffat waited, turning a teaspoon between his fingers. The Countess addressed him: "Isn't Monsieur Steiner having an affair with that singer from the Variety Theater, that Nana?"

"Nana, that's it!" Madame Hugon cried out angrily. "She's a horror! And they're expecting her at La Mignotte! I was told all about it by the gardener. . . . Isn't that right, Georges? The gardener said they were expecting her this evening."

The Count started with surprise. But Georges hastily replied, "Oh, mama, the gardener was talking without knowing anything. . . . A little while ago the coachman said something quite different: they're not expecting anyone at La Mignotte until day after tomorrow."

He tried to maintain a natural manner, at the same time watching the Count out of the corner of his eye to see the effect of his words on him. The Count began toying with his teaspoon again, as though he felt reassured. The Countess, staring vaguely at the bluish mist in the distance with the shadow of a smile playing around her lips, had apparently withdrawn from the conversation entirely; she seemed to be pursuing a secret thought that had suddenly arisen within her. Estelle, sitting stiffly on her chair, had listened to everything that had been said about Nana without showing the slightest reaction on her white, virginal face.

"Well, after all," said Madame Hugon after a silence, recovering her good humor, "I'm wrong to get angry. Everyone has a right to live. . . . If we meet that lady on the road, we'll content ourselves with not greeting her, and let it go at that."

As they were leaving the table, she scolded Countess Sabine for having been so long in coming to see her that year. But the Countess defended herself and blamed her husband for their delays: twice when they were planning to leave the next day and had already packed their trunks, he had postponed their departure, saying that he had urgent business to attend to; and then, when the trip seemed to have been abandoned, he had suddenly decided to leave. The old lady said that Georges, too, had announced his arrival twice without coming, and had then turned up at Les Fondettes day before yesterday, when she was no longer expecting him. They had just gone out into the garden. The men walked on either side of the ladies, listening to them in solemn silence.

"In any case," said Madame Hugon, kissing her son's blond hair, "it's very nice of Zizi to come and bury himself in the country with his mother. . . . Zizi is a good boy; he doesn't forget me!"

In the afternoon she began to worry. Georges, who had complained of a slight pain in his head as soon as he left the table, seemed to be gradually overcome by a violent headache. Toward four o'clock he decided to go to bed; it was the only remedy; when he had slept till the next day, he would be perfectly all right again. His mother insisted on putting him to bed herself. As soon as she left his bedroom he locked the door, saying he was doing so because he did not want to be disturbed. He called out, "Good-night, little mother, I'll see you tomorrow!" in a loving tone, and promised to sleep straight through until the next morning. But he did not go back to bed. With flushed cheeks and shining eyes, he noiselessly put on his clothes again, then sat still on a chair, waiting. When the dinner bell rang, he listened for Count Muffat, who was walking toward the drawing room. Ten minutes later, certain of not being seen, he nimbly climbed out the window and slid down a drainpipe. His bedroom, on the second floor, faced the rear of the house. After alighting in a clump of bushes, he left the garden and began running across the fields in the direction of the Choue, his stomach empty, his heart pounding with emotion. It was getting dark and a fine rain had begun to fall.

It was indeed that evening that Nana was expected to arrive at La Mignotte. Ever since Steiner had bought her that country house in May, she had occasionally been seized with such a keen desire to go and stay in it that it made her burst into tears; but Bordenave had always told her she would have to wait till September because he had no intention of replacing her with an understudy, even for one evening, during the time of the Exposition. Toward the end of August, he spoke of October. Nana, furious, declared that she would be at La Mignotte on the fifteenth of September. And, to defy him, she had invited a number of people in his presence. One afternoon when Muffat, whom she was skillfully resisting, was begging her in her apartment, shaken by tremors, she finally promised to be nice to him, but not until she was at La Mignotte, and she also told him that she would be there on the fifteenth. Then, on the twelfth, she had a sudden impulse to go there immediately, alone with Zoé. If Bordenave knew, he might find some way of retaining her. She was delighted by the thought of simply walking out on him and sending him a doctor's certificate.

When she had conceived the idea of going to La Mignotte before anyone else and living there for two days without anyone's knowing it, she mercilessly hurried Zoé to pack their trunks, then pushed her into a cab, where she affectionately kissed her and asked her to forgive her. It was not until she was in the refreshment room of the station that she thought of sending Steiner a letter to notify him of her departure. She asked him to wait for two days before rejoining her, if he wanted to find her rested and in good spirits. Then, leaping to another plan, she wrote a second letter in which she begged her aunt to bring little Louis immediately. It would do the baby so much good! And what fun they would have together under the trees! She talked about nothing else during the train trip from Paris to Orléans; her eyes were moist and she mingled the flowers, the birds, and her child in a sudden surge of maternal love.

La Mignotte was more than seven miles from the station. Nana wasted an hour renting a carriage, a huge, dilapidated barouche that rolled slowly with a loud metallic clatter. She immediately took hold of the coachman, a taciturn little man, and overwhelmed him with questions. Had he often gone past La Mignotte? Was it behind that hill? There were probably trees everywhere, weren't there? And could the house be seen from far away? The little old man replied with grunts. In the carriage, Nana was consumed with impatience, while Zoé, annoyed at having had to leave Paris so soon, remained stiff and sullen. When the horse stopped short, Nana thought they had arrived. She put her head out the window and asked, "Are we there?"

The coachman's only answer was to whip his horse, which began laboriously climbing a slope. Nana was enraptured when she saw the vast plain beneath the gray sky in which big clouds were gathering.

"Oh, look, Zoé! Look at all that grass! Is all that wheat? . . . My God, it's so pretty!"

"I can see you're not from the country, Madame," Zoé said superciliously. "I got to know the country too well when I was working for my dentist. He had a house at Bougival. . . . And it's chilly this evening, too. The air is damp here."

They were passing beneath some trees. Nana sniffed the odor of the leaves like a puppy. Suddenly, at a bend in the road, she saw a corner of a house through the branches. Maybe this was it! She asked the coachman, who again shook his head. Then, as they were going down the other side of the hill, he contented himself with pointing his whip and saying, "There it is."

She stood up and leaned out the window.

"Where? Where?" she cried, pale, not yet seeing anything.

Finally she was able to see part of a wall. She cried out, hopped up and down, and showed all the other symptoms of a woman overflowing with keen emotion.

"Zoé, I see it, I see it! . . . Look out the other window. . . . Oh, there's a terrace with bricks on the roof! That's a greenhouse over there! It's a huge place! Oh, I'm so happy! Look, Zoé, look!"

The carriage stopped in front of the iron gates. A little door opened and the gardener, a tall, thin man, appeared with his cap in his hand. Nana tried to recover her dignity, for the coachman already seemed to be laughing inside, with his lips pressed tightly together. She restrained herself from running and listened to the gardener as he loquaciously begged her to forgive the disorder, since he had received her letter only that morning; but despite her efforts she seemed to be lifted from the ground: she walked so fast that Zoé could not keep up with her. At the end of the path she stopped for a moment to glance over the house. It was a large building in the Italian style, flanked by a smaller structure, which a rich Englishman had built after living for two years in Naples, and which he had immediately come to dislike.

"Let me show you around, Madame," said the gardener. But she had gone on ahead of him. She called back to him that there was no need for him to trouble himself, and that she would rather look over everything by herself anyway. Without taking off her hat, she began dashing from one room to another, calling Zoé, making comments to her from one end of the halls to the other, filling with her shouts and laughter the emptiness of the house that had remained vacant for many long months. First the entrance hall: a little damp, but it didn't matter, since no one would sleep in it. The drawing room was very elegant, with its windows overlooking the lawn; but its red furniture was terribly ugly: she would change that. As for the dining room, it was a beauty! What parties you could give in Paris if you had a dining room that size! As she was going up to the second floor, she remembered that she had not seen the kitchen; she went back down the stairs, uttering exclamations, and Zoé had to marvel at the beauty of the sink and the size of the fireplace, in which one could have roasted a sheep. When she went upstairs, she was particularly enthusiastic about the bedroom, which an upholsterer from Orléans had hung with pale pink Louis XVI cretonne. Ah, it must be good to sleep there! It was like a schoolgirl's dream! Next came four or five guest rooms, then some magnificent attic rooms: they would be very convenient for storing trunks. Zoé was still sullen; she cast a cold glance into each room and lingered behind Madame. She watched her disappear up the steep ladder leading to the attic. No, thanks, she had no desire to break her legs! Madame's voice sounded far away, as though it were coming down a chimney: "Zoé! Zoé! Where are you? Come on up! Oh, you can't imagine . . . It's like fairyland!"

Zoé went up, grumbling. She found Madame on the roof, leaning against the brick balustrade and looking at the valley spread out in the distance. The horizon was immense, but it was blurred by gray mist. A fierce wind was driving fine drops of rain before it. Nana had to hold her hat with both hands to keep it from being blown away, and her skirt billowed and flapped like a flag.

"Oh, no!" said Zoé, drawing back her head immediately. "You'll be blown away, Madame. . . . What terrible weather!"

Nana did not hear her. Leaning forward, she was looking at the grounds below her. There were seven or eight acres, all walled in. Then she was carried away by the sight of the vegetable garden. She rushed down, jostling Zoé on the stairs and exclaiming, "It's full of cabbages! . . . Oh, cabbages this big! . . . And lettuce, and sorrel, and onions, and everything! Hurry!"

The rain was falling more heavily. She opened her white silk parasol and ran along the paths.

"You'll catch a cold, Madame!" cried Zoé, who had calmly remained under the porch.

But Nana wanted to see. Each new discovery brought more exclamations.

"Zoé, there's spinach here! Come and see ! . . . Oh, artichokes! They look funny. I didn't know they had flowers. . . . What's this? I don't know what it is. . . . Come here, Zoé, maybe you'll know."

Zoé did not move. Madame must really be out of her mind. It was now raining in torrents. Madame's little white silk parasol was already soaked through, and it didn't even cover her: her skirt was sopping. But this did not bother her. Ignoring the rain, she continued to inspect the vegetable garden and the orchard, stopping at every tree, leaning over each bed of vegetables. Then she ran over to look down a well, lifted a wooden frame to see what was under it, became absorbed in contemplating an enormous pumpkin. She had a need to explore every path, to take immediate possession of the things she had dreamed of in the days when she had walked the streets of Paris in her working-girl's shoes. The rain was increasing, but she did not feel it; she only regretted that darkness was falling. Since she could no longer see clearly, she touched everything with her fingers to see what it was like. Suddenly, in the twilight, she caught sight of some strawberries. Her childhood burst forth in her.

"Strawberries! There are strawberries here, I can feel them! Zoé, bring a dish! Come and pick strawberries!"

Squatting in the mud, she put down her parasol and received the full force of the rain. She began picking strawberries with her wet hands among the leaves. Zoé did not bring a dish, however. When Nana stood up, she was seized with fear. She thought she had seen a shadow moving.

"An animal!" she cried. But then she stood rooted to the path in amazement. It was a man, and she had recognized him. "What! It's Baby! . . . What are you doing here, Baby?"

"I've come to see you, what else?" replied Georges.

She was still astonished.

"Did the gardener tell you I was coming? . . . Oh, poor boy! You're soaked!"

"Yes, I'll tell you about it. The rain caught me as I was coming here. I didn't want to go all the way to Gumières, so I waded across the Choue, and I fell into a deep hole while I was doing it."

Nana forgot her strawberries. She was overcome with pity. Poor Zizi had fallen into the water! She led him toward the house and spoke of making a big fire.

"I was hiding, you know," he said, stopping her in the semidarkness, "because I was afraid you'd scold me the way you do in Paris if I come to see you when you're not expecting me."

She laughed without answering and kissed him on the forehead. She had always treated him like a child, never taking his declarations seriously, amusing herself with him as though he were of no consequence whatever. She made a great fuss over him when they reached the house. She insisted that a fire be lighted in her bedroom; they would be more comfortable there. The sight of Georges had not surprised Zoé, who was used to all sorts of encounters. But when the gardener brought in the firewood he was dumbfounded on seeing a sopping-wet gentleman for whom he was certain he had not opened the gate. Nana sent him away; she no longer needed him. The room was lighted by a lamp and the fire began blazing brightly.

"He'll never get dry—he's going to catch a cold," said Nana, seeing Georges shiver.

And not one dry pair of trousers in the house! She was about to call the gardener back when she had an idea. Zoé, who had been unpacking the trunks in the dressing room, brought Madame some clean clothes: a chemise, some petticoats, and a negligee.

"Why, that's perfect!" cried Nana. "Zizi can wear those! You don't mind wearing my clothes, do you? As soon as yours are dry, you'll put them on and go home right away, so your mother won't scold you. . . . Hurry; I'm going to change my clothes in the dressing room."

When she reappeared in a negligee ten minutes later, she clasped her hands in delight.

"Oh, the darling! He looks so nice dressed as a woman!"

He had put on a long nightgown, a pair of embroidered drawers and a batiste negligee trimmed with lace. In these clothes he looked like a girl, with his bare young arms and his tawny hair, still wet, hanging down his neck.

"He's as thin as I am!" said Nana, putting her arm around his waist. "Zoé, come and see how well my clothes fit him. . . . They look as though they were made for him, except that they're too loose in the chest. . . . Poor Zizi, he doesn't have as much there as I do."

"Yes, I'm a little lacking in that department," said Georges, smiling.

All three of them were gay. Nana began buttoning the negligee from top to bottom, to make him decent. She turned him around like a doll, patted him, made his skirt billow in back. And she questioned him, asking him if he was comfortable, if he was warm. Oh, yes, he was quite comfortable! Nothing was warmer than a woman's nightgown; he would always wear one if he could. He moved around in it, delighted by the fine linen, by that sweet-smelling garment in which he seemed to find a little of Nana's warm life.

Meanwhile Zoé had taken his wet clothes down to the kitchen in order to dry them as quickly as possible in front of a fire of vine cuttings. Georges, stretched out in an armchair, ventured to make a confession: "Aren't you going to eat tonight? I'm starving. I haven't had any dinner."

Nana reproached him angrily: how foolish he had been to run away from his mother on an empty stomach and then fall into the water! But she was starving too. Of course they were going to eat! But they would have to eat whatever they could find. They pushed a little table in front of the fire and improvised an amusing dinner. Zoé hurried to the gardner's quarters: he had made some cabbage soup in case Madame did not dine at Orléans before she arrived; she had forgotten to tell him in her letter what he was to prepare. Fortunately the wine cellar was well stocked. And so they ate cabbage soup, with a piece of bacon. Then Nana rummaged in her bag and found some things she had put into it as a precaution: a little pâté de foie gras, a bag of bonbons, some oranges. They both ate like ogres, with young appetites, like two comrades perfectly at ease with each other. She called him "my dear girl"; it seemed more familiar and affectionate to her. For dessert they emptied a jar of jam they had found on top of a cupboard, taking turns eating with the same spoon, so as not to disturb Zoé.

"Ah, my dear girl, I haven't had such a good dinner in ten years!" said Nana, pushing back the table.

It was getting late, however, and she wanted to send him home to avoid making trouble for him. He said he had plenty of time. Anyway, his clothes weren't dry yet. Zoé said it would take at least another hour; and since she was so tired from the journey that she was almost falling asleep on her feet, they sent her off to bed. They were left alone together, in that silent house.

It was a very pleasant evening. The fire was dying down to embers and it became a little stuffy in that big blue bedroom, where Zoé had made the bed before going upstairs. Nana, feeling too warm, got up to open the window for a moment.

"My God, it's so beautiful!" she exclaimed. "Look!"

Georges went over to her. As though the railing in front of the window were not long enough for two, he put his arm around her waist and rested his head on her shoulder. The weather had changed abruptly: the sky was clear and a round moon was spreading a sheet of gold over the whole countryside. Everything was supremely peaceful; the valley widened into the vast plain, where trees made little islands of darkness in the motionless lake of light. Nana was deeply moved, and felt like a child again. She was sure she had dreamed of nights like this at some time in her life that she no longer remembered. Everything she had seen since getting off the train—the spacious countryside, the strong-smelling grass, the house, the vegetables—had overwhelmed her to such an extent that she seemed to have left Paris twenty years before. Her existence of the previous day was far away. She was feeling things that were unfamiliar to her. Meanwhile Georges was tenderly kissing her on the neck, and this increased her agitation. With a hesitant hand she pushed him away as though he were a child whose affection had become tiresome. She told him again that he must leave. He did not refuse; soon, he would leave soon.

A bird began to sing, then stopped. It was a robin, in an elder bush beneath the window.

"Just a minute," said Georges; "the lamp is frightening him: I'll put it out." And when he came back to take her by the waist again he added: "We'll light it again in a little while."

Then, listening to the robin while Georges pressed up against her, Nana remembered. Yes, it was while listening to love songs that she had dreamed of all this. She would once have given her heart to have a moon like that, and robins, and a young man filled with love. It all seemed so good and sweet to her that she nearly wept. Of course she was born to live virtuously. She again pushed Georges away, for he was becoming bolder.

"No, leave me alone, I don't want to. . . . It would be very wrong at your age. . . . Listen, I'll go on being a mother to you."

She felt modest. She was blushing, although no one could see her; the bedroom was filled with darkness behind them, while the countryside unfolded the silence and immobility of its solitude. Never before had she been so ashamed. Little by little, she felt her strength abandoning her, despite her embarrassment and her struggles. That disguise, that woman's nightgown and that negligee, made her laugh again. It was as though a girl friend were teasing her.

"Oh, it's wrong, it's wrong . . ." she stammered, after a last effort.

And she fell like a virgin into that child's arms, in the face of the beautiful night. The house was asleep.

When the lunch bell rang at Les Fondettes the next day,

the dining-room table was no longer too big. First a carriage had brought Fauchery and Daguenet, and behind them, having gotten off the following train, came Vandeuvres. Georges was the last to appear; he was rather pale and there were dark circles under his eyes when he came downstairs. He said he felt much better, but that he was still a little dazed by the violence of his attack. Madame Hugon looked into his eyes with an anxious smile and smoothed his hair, which he had combed badly that morning. He stepped back, as though embarrassed by her caress. At table she affectionately chided Vandeuvres, saying that she had been awaiting his visit for the past five years.

"Anyway, here you are. . . . How did you manage to come?"

Vandeuvres replied jokingly that he had lost an enormous sum of money at his club the night before and that he had left Paris with the idea of settling down in the country.

"Yes, if you can only find me an heiress in the vicinity. . . . There must be some delightful women around here."

The old lady was thanking Daguenet and Fauchery for having accepted her son's invitation when she had a happy surprise on seeing the Marquis de Chouard, who had just arrived in a third carriage, walk into the room.

"You must all have arranged to meet here this morning!" she exclaimed. "What's happening? For years I've been unable to bring you together, and now you all drop in on me at once. . . . But I'm not complaining, of course!"

Another place was laid. Fauchery was seated beside Countess Sabine. He was surprised by her sprightly gaiety, after having seen her so languid in her drawing room on the Rue Miromesnil. Daguenet, sitting on Estelle's left, seemed disturbed by the proximity of that tall, silent girl whose sharp elbows were disagreeable to him. Muffat and Chouard had exchanged a sly glance. Vandeuvres continued to joke about his forthcoming marriage.

"Speaking of ladies," Madame Hugon finally said, "I have a new neighbor whom you must know."

And she named Nana. Vandeuvres pretended to be greatly surprised.

"What! Nana's house is near here?"

Fauchery and Daguenet also uttered exclamations of

surprise. The Marquis de Chouard went on eating his chicken breast without seeming to understand. Not one of the men had smiled.

"Yes," said the old lady, "and she arrived at La Mignotte last night, as I said she would. I learned it through the gardener this morning."

This time the men could not hide a very genuine surprise. They all raised their heads. What! Nana had arrived? But they hadn't been expecting her until the next day, they thought they had arrived ahead of her! Only Georges kept his eyes lowered, looked wearily at his glass. Since the beginning of lunch he had seemed to be sleeping with his eyes open, smiling vaguely.

"Are you still in pain, Zizi?" asked his mother, who had been constantly looking at him.

He started and answered, blushing, that he was quite well again; and his face retained the exhausted yet greedy expression of a girl who had been dancing too much.

"What's that on your neck?" Madame Hugon asked in alarm. "It's all red."

He became so agitated that he could scarcely stammer out a reply. He didn't know; there was nothing wrong with his neck. Then, turning up his shirt collar: "Oh, yes, some kind of insect stung me."

The Marquis de Chouard had cast a sidelong glance at the little red spot. Muffat also looked at Georges. Lunch was nearly over. They began discussing plans for outings. Fauchery was becoming more and more affected by Countess Sabine's laughter. As he was passing her a dish of fruit, their hands touched. For a second she gave him such a deep look that he again thought about the secret that had been confided to him one drunken evening. And then she was no longer the same: something had become more pronounced in her; her gray silk dress, soft around her shoulders, gave a touch of abandon to her refined, sensitive elegance.

When the others left the table, Daguenet stayed behind with Fauchery to make crude jokes about Estelle: "A fine broomstick to shove into a man's arms!" He became serious, however, when the journalist told him the amount of her dowry: four hundred thousand francs.

"And her mother?" asked Fauchery. "She's an attractive woman!"

"Yes, I'd be glad to . . . But it can't be done, my friend."

"How do you know? I'd have to see. . . ."

The outings had to be called off that day: it was still raining intermittently. Georges had hastily disappeared and locked himself in his room. The gentlemen avoided giving one another any explanations, although none had any doubt about the others' reasons for being there. Vandeuvres, having lost heavily at gambling, really had conceived the idea of spending some time in the country, and he was counting on Nana's proximity to keep him from being too bored. Fauchery, taking advantage of the vacation given to him by Rose, who was greatly occupied for the moment, intended to discuss a second article with Nana, in case the country should inspire them both with tender feelings. Daguenet, who had severed relations with her when Steiner appeared on the scene, was thinking of resuming his affair with her, or of at least snatching a few moments of pleasure, if the opportunity arose. As for the Marquis de Chouard, he was waiting for his time to come. But among these men on the track of that Venus whose make-up was still only imperfectly removed, Muffat was the most ardent, the most tormented by the new sensations of desire, fear, and anger that were struggling within his disordered soul. He had a definite promise; Nana was expecting him. But then why had she left two days early? He resolved to go to La Mignotte after dinner.

That evening, when the Count left the garden, Georges followed him. He let him take the Gumières road, then waded across the Choue and burst into Nana's house out of breath, with tears of rage in his eyes. Ah, he understood! That old man who was on his way there had an appointment with her! Nana was surprised by this outburst of jealousy, and alarmed by the way things were turning out. She took him in her arms and comforted him as best she could. No, no, he was mistaken, she wasn't expecting anyone; if that gentleman was coming, it wasn't her fault. How silly Zizi was to get so upset over nothing! She swore by her own child that she loved only her Georges. She kissed him and dried his tears.

"Listen and you'll see that everything is for you," she

said when he was calmer. "Steiner has arrived, he's up-stairs now. You know I can't send *him* away, darling."

"Yes, I know, I'm not talking about him," murmured Georges.

"Well, I've put him in the room at the end of the hall, and I've told him I'm sick. He's unpacking his trunk. . . . Since no one saw you come in, run upstairs and hide in my bedroom, and wait for me there."

Georges threw his arms around her neck. Then it was true, she really did love him a little! It would be the same as the night before: they would put out the lamp and stay in the dark till daylight came. Hearing a bell ring, he quietly hurried away. Upstairs in Nana's bedroom, he took off his shoes to avoid making any noise, then hid on the floor behind a curtain and dutifully began waiting.

Nana was still somewhat shaken when she received Count Muffat, and she felt a certain embarrassment. She had given him her promise and she would have liked to keep it, for he seemed to be a serious man. But who could have foreseen what had happened the day before? That trip, that house she did not know, that boy who had come to her all wet; and how good it had seemed to her, and how sweet it would be to go on with it! So much the worse for the serious gentleman! For three months she had been making him wait, playing the part of a respectable woman in order to inflame him still more. Well, he would just have to wait some more, and if he didn't like it, he could leave. She would give up the whole thing if she had to, rather than deceive Georges.

The Count had sat down with the ceremonious air of a country neighbor paying a visit. Only his hands were trembling. Desire, stirred up by Nana's skillful tactics, had finally wrought terrible havoc in his sanguine though still virginal nature. That solemn man, that chamberlain who crossed the drawing rooms of the Tuileries with such a dignified step, had begun to bite his pillow at night, sobbing in exasperation, always evoking the same sensual image. But this time he was resolved to put an end to his suffering. As he walked along the road in the great peace of twilight, he had dreamed of brutalities. And as soon as he had exchanged a few words with Nana, he tried to seize her with both hands.

155

"No, no, be careful," she said simply, smiling without a trace of anger.

He caught hold of her again, clenching his teeth. When she began to struggle, he became vulgar: he crudely reminded her that he had come to go to bed with her. Still smiling, though embarrassed, she held his hands. She spoke to him lovingly, to soften her refusal: "Come, darling, be sensible. . . . Really, I can't. Steiner is upstairs."

But he was demented; never before had she seen a man in such a state. She was becoming frightened. She put her fingers over his mouth to stifle the cries that were escaping from him. Lowering her voice, she begged him to be quiet and let her go. Steiner was coming downstairs. The whole thing was stupid! When Steiner walked into the room, he saw Nana indolently stretched out in her armchair and heard her saying, "I love the country . . ." She stopped short and turned her head. "It's Count Muffat, darling. He saw a light in the house as he was taking a walk, so he came in to welcome us."

The two men shook hands. Muffat stood for a moment without speaking, his face in shadow. Steiner looked sullen. They talked about Paris; business was bad, abominable things had taken place in the stock market. A quarter of an hour later, Muffat left. As Nana was showing him to the door, he vainly asked for an appointment the following night. Steiner went upstairs to bed almost immediately, grumbling about the endless ailments of women. At last the two old men had been disposed of! When Nana went to rejoin Georges, she found him still waiting behind the curtain. The bedroom was dark. He drew her down on the floor beside him, and they played together, rolling, stopping, stifling their laughter with kisses whenever they accidentally kicked the furniture with their bare feet. Far away, on the Gumières road, Count Muffat was walking slowly, bathing his feverish head in the coolness and silence of the night.

During the days that followed, life was adorable. In Georges' arms, Nana felt as though she were once more a girl of fifteen. His youthful caresses made love bloom again in her, despite her monotonous experience and her disgust with men. She had sudden fits of blushing, emotions that left her quivering, impulses to laugh and cry, a whole apprehensive virginity permeated by desires of which she was ashamed. She had never felt that way before. The country filled her with tenderness. When she was a little girl, for a long time she had wanted to live in a meadow with a goat, because once, on the slope of the fortifications, she had seen a bleating goat tied to a stake. Her ambitions had now been so far surpassed by that estate, by all that land belonging to her, that she could scarcely contain her joy. She again experienced the fresh sensations of a child; and at night when, giddy from having spent a day in the open air and intoxicated by the smell of leaves, she went upstairs to rejoin her Zizi hiding behind the curtain, she felt like a schoolgirl on vacation having a love affair with a young cousin she would later marry, trembling at the slightest noise, dreading that her parents might hear, savoring the delightful experiments and voluptuous terrors of a first lapse from virtue.

She became subject to the fancies of a sentimental girl. She spent hours looking at the moon. One night she had a desire to go down into the garden with Georges, when the whole house was asleep. They strolled under the trees with their arms around each other's waists, then lay down on the grass and got soaked by the dew. Another time in the bedroom, after a silence, she sobbed on his neck and murmured that she was afraid of dying. Often she would softly sing a love song full of flowers and birds that she had learned from Madame Lerat, being moved to tears, stopping to clasp Georges in a passionate embrace and demand vows of eternal love from him. In short, she behaved foolishly, as she herself would acknowledge when they had become friends again and sat smoking a cigarette on the edge of the bed, their legs bare, tapping their heels against the wood.

But what caused her heart to melt completely was the arrival of Louiset. Her sudden surge of maternal love had the violence of a fit of madness. She often took her son out into the sunlight to watch him kicking and sprawling; she would roll in the grass with him, after having dressed him like a young prince. She immediately decided that he would have to sleep near her, in the room next door, where Madame Lerat, greatly affected by the country, began snoring as soon as she lay down. And Louiset did not in the least impair her feelings for Zizi. She said she had two children, and enveloped them both in the same capricious affection. Ten times a night she would leave Zizi to go and see if Louiset was breathing properly, but then she would come back to her Zizi and give him the remains of her maternal caresses. He took perverse pleasure in letting her act as though she were his mother; he liked to feel small in that big girl's arms as she lulled him like a baby being put to sleep. It was all so delightful that, charmed by this life, she seriously proposed to him that they should never leave the country. They would send everyone away and live alone together: he, she, and the baby. They made countless plans till dawn, without hearing Madame Lerat's loud snoring as she slept off the fatigue of having spent the day gathering wildflowers.

This charming life lasted for more than a week. Count Muffat came every evening and left with his face swollen and his hands burning. One evening he was not even received; since Steiner had been forced to make a trip to Paris, the Count was told that Madame was ill. Each day she rebelled more violently against the idea of deceiving Georges. He was such an innocent boy, and he believed in her! Anyway, it would have disgusted her. Zoé, who had been watching this affair with silent disdain, thought that Madame was becoming stupid.

On the sixth day, a group of visitors suddenly broke into this idyllic existence. Nana had invited a lot of people, thinking that none of them would come. So one afternoon she was amazed and very much annoyed to see an omnibus full of people stop in front of the gate of La Mignotte.

"It's us!" cried Mignon, the first to get out of the vehicle, from which he drew his sons, Henri and Charles.

Then Labordette appeared and helped an endless procession of ladies to descend: Lucy Stewart, Caroline Héquet, Tatan Néné, Maria Blond. Nana was hoping that this was the end, when La Faloise leapt out to receive Gaga and her daughter Amélie in his trembling arms. That made eleven people. Getting them installed was a laborious procedure. There were five guest rooms at La Mignotte, one of which was already occupied by Madame Lerat and Louiset. Gaga and La Faloise were given the largest one, and it was decided that Amélie would sleep on a cot in the adjoining dressing room. Mignon and his two sons were given the third bedroom, Labordette the fourth. The remaining room was turned into a dormitory, with four beds for Lucy, Caroline, Tatan, and Maria. As for Steiner, he would sleep on the sofa in the drawing room. By the time an hour had gone by and a place had been found for everyone, Nana, who had been furious at first, was enchanted by her role as lady of the manor. The ladies complimented her on La Mignotte: "It's a wonderful place, my dear!" And they brought her a breath of Paris air, along with all the gossip of the past week. They all talked at once, with laughter, exclamations, and little pats. And Bordenave, what had he said about her little escapade? Nothing much. After having shouted that he would have her brought back by the police, he had merely replaced her with her understudy, little Violaine, who had made quite a hit in *The Blond Venus*. This last piece of news made Nana serious.

It was only four o'clock. They spoke of going for a walk.

"I didn't tell you: I was about to go out and dig up some potatoes when you came."

They all wanted to dig potatoes, without even changing their clothes. They made it into a party. The gardener and two helpers were already in the field, at the far end of the property. The women knelt and began plunging their hands into the soil, leaving their rings on, crying out whenever they found an unusually large potato. It seemed so amusing to them! But Tatan Néné was triumphant: she had dug so many potatoes in her youth that she forgot herself and gave the others instructions, calling them stupid. The men worked with less enthusiasm. Mignon, looking like a solid citizen, took advantage of his stay in the country to complete his sons' education: he spoke to them about Parmentier.

Dinner that evening was wildly gay. They all ate ravenously. Nana, in a state of great excitement, quarreled with her butler, who had once served in the bishop's palace in Orléans. The ladies smoked with their coffee at the end of the meal. Loud sounds of revelry spilled out of the windows and died out far away in the serenity of the evening, while peasants going home late between the hedgerows turned their heads and looked at the house blazing with light.

"It's too bad you're leaving day after tomorrow," said Nana. "But we'll arrange something anyway."

It was decided that the next day, a Sunday, they would go to see the ruins of the old Abbey of Chamont, five miles away. Five carriages would come from Orléans for them after lunch and bring them back to La Mignotte for dinner at about seven o'clock. It would be delightful.

That evening, as usual, Count Muffat walked up the hill and rang the bell at the gate. But he was surprised by the lighted windows and the sound of laughter. When he recognized Mignon's voice he realized what had happened. He went away enraged by this new obstacle, at the end of his patience, determined to take violent action. Georges, who always went through a little door to which he had a key, calmly went up to Nana's bedroom, keeping close to the walls. This time, however, he had to wait until after midnight. She finally appeared, quite drunk and more maternal than ever; when she drank, it made her so amorous that she became clinging. And so she insisted that he accompany her to the Abbey of Chamont. He resisted, afraid of being seen; if he were seen in a carriage with her, it would cause a terrible scandal. But she burst into tears, seized with the noisy despair of a discarded woman. He comforted her and promised to come.

"Then you do love me," she stammered. "Tell me you love me. . . . Darling, if I died would you be very unhappy?"

At Les Fondettes, Nana's proximity had upset the whole household. Each day at lunch the good Madame Hugon talked about her in spite of herself, telling what her gardener had reported to her, experiencing the obsession that loose women arouse in the most dignified respectable ladies. Though usually very tolerant, she was now revolted and exasperated, with a vague presentiment of disaster that frightened her at night, as though she had learned that a wild animal had escaped from a zoo and was in the vicinity. She picked quarrels with her guests, accusing them all of going to Les Mignottes. Vandeuvres had been seen laughing on the highway with a bareheaded lady; but he defended himself, he denied that it was Nana, for he had actually been with Lucy, who had been telling him how she had just dismissed her third prince. The Marquis de Chouard also went out every night, but he spoke of his doctor's orders. As for Daguenet and Fauchery, Madame Hugon was unjust to them. Daguenet, particularly, never left Les Fondettes; he had given up his plan to resume his affair with Nana, and was now showering Estelle with respectful attention. Fauchery also remained with the Muffat ladies. On one occasion only, he had met Mignon on a path with his arms full of flowers, giving botany lessons to his sons. The two men had shaken hands and given each other news of Rose. She was in good health. They had each received a letter from her that morning in which she asked them to enjoy the country air a while longer. And so, of all her guests, the old lady spared only Count Muffat and Georges. The Count, who claimed to have serious business in Orléans, could not possibly be running after women; and as for Georges, the poor boy was worrying her, for every afternoon he had frightful headaches that forced him to go to bed before it was dark.

Meanwhile Fauchery had begun keeping Countess Sabine company every afternoon while the Count was absent. When they went to the far end of the garden he carried her parasol and folding chair. She was amused by his quaint journalistic mentality, and he soon led her into one of those sudden intimacies which the country makes permissible. She had apparently opened herself to him at once, awakened to a new youth in the company of that young man whose boisterous mockery seemed incapable of compromising her. And sometimes, when they found themselves alone together behind a bush, their eyes would meet and they would stop in the middle of a laugh, suddenly serious, looking at each other deeply, as though each had understood the other's innermost thoughts.

On Friday it was necessary to set another place for lunch. Monsieur Théophile Venot, whom Madame Hugon recalled having invited to the Muffats' the previous winter, had just arrived. He rounded his back and affected the good humor of an insignificant man, without appearing to notice the apprehensive deference with which he was treated. When he had succeeded in making the others forget his presence while he nibbled lumps of sugar during dessert, he examined Daguenet, who was handing some strawberries to Estelle, and listened to Fauchery as he told the Countess an anecdote which seemed to amuse her greatly. As soon as anyone looked at him, he would smile in his placid way. When the meal was over, he took the Count's arm and led him out into the garden. It was known that he had retained great influence over the Count since his mother's death. Strange stories were told about the former lawyer's domination over the household. Fauchery, no doubt hampered by his arrival, explained to Georges and Daguenet the source of his fortune: a big lawsuit which the Jesuits had once placed in his hands. According to Fauchery, Venot was a formidable man despite his fat, gentle face, and was now involved in all the intrigues of the clergy. Georges and Daguenet began joking, for the little old man looked idiotic to them. The idea of an unknown Venot, a gigantic Venot, acting on behalf of the clergy, struck them as a comical fantasy. But they fell silent when Count Muffat, still being led by the old gentleman, came back looking very pale, his eyes red, as though he had been weeping.

"They must have been talking about hell," Fauchery murmured sarcastically.

Countess Sabine overheard him. She slowly turned her head and their eyes met in one of those long looks with which they had been prudently sounding each other out before venturing anything further.

After lunch everyone usually went to the terrace overlooking the plain at the end of the flower bed. The Sunday afternoon was exquisitely mild. It had threatened to rain at about ten o'clock that morning, but the sky, without clearing, had melted into a milky fog, a kind of luminous dust, all golden with sunshine. Madame Hugon suggested that they go out through the little gate of the terrace and take a walk in the direction of Gumières, as far as the Choue. She liked walking, being still quite active despite her sixty years. Her guests all swore they had no need of a carriage. And so they arrived, somewhat disbanded, at the wooden bridge that crossed the river. Fauchery and Daguenet were in front of the Muffat ladies, then came the Count and the Marquis, on either side of Madame Hugon, while Vandeuvres, looking correct and bored on the highway, brought up the rear, smoking a cigar. Monsieur Venot, slowing or quickening his pace, went from one group to another, smiling, as though to be able to hear everything.

"And poor Georges is in Orléans!" said Madame Hugon. "He wanted to consult old Dr. Tavernier, who no longer goes out, about his headaches. . . . Yes, you weren't up yet, he left before seven o'clock. At least it will be a diversion for him." She stopped short and exclaimed, "Why are they standing still on the bridge?"

The ladies, Daguenet, and Fauchery were standing at the head of the bridge, hesitantly, as though some obstacle had made them uneasy. Yet the way was clear.

"Go ahead!" cried the Count.

They did not move; they were watching something coming toward them which the others could not yet see. There was a bend in the road, bordered by a thick line of poplars. A sound of rumbling wheels was gradually growing louder, mingled with laughter and the cracking of a whip. Suddenly five heavily laden carriages came into sight, following one another, bright with blue and pink dresses.

"What's that?" said Madame Hugon, surprised. Then she sensed who it was and became indignant at such an invasion of the road. "Oh, that woman!" she said. "Walk on, walk on. Pretend not to . . ."

But it was too late. The five carriages, which were taking Nana and her guests to the ruins of Chamont, had begun crossing the little wooden bridge. Fauchery, Daguenet, and the Muffat ladies had to step back, while Madame Hugon and the others also stopped, spaced out along the road. It was a superb procession. The laughter had ceased in the carriages; faces were turning with curiosity. Each group looked at the other amid a silence broken only by the regular trot of the horses. In the first carriage, Maria Blond and Tata Néné, reclining like duchesses with their skirts billowing over the wheels, looked disdainfully at those respectable women on foot. In the next was Gaga, occupying almost a whole seat to herself, crushing La Faloise, who was invisible except for his apprehensive nose. Then came Caroline Héquet with Labordette, Lucy Stewart with Mignon and his sons, and finally, in a victoria, Nana was sitting beside Steiner with poor little Zizi in front of her on a folding seat, pressing his knees against hers.

"That's the last one, isn't it?" the Countess calmly asked Fauchery, pretending not to recognize Nana.

The wheels of the victoria almost grazed her, but she did not step back. The two women had exchanged a profound look, one of those examinations which take only a second, yet are complete and definitive. As for the men, they behaved perfectly. Fauchery and Daguenet, very cool, recognized no one. The Marquis, anxious, afraid of some practical joke on the part of the women, had broken off a blade of grass and was rolling it between his fingers. Only Vandeuvres, standing at some distance from the others, greeted Lucy with a wink when she smiled at him as she passed.

"Be careful!" murmured Monsieur Venot, standing behind Count Muffat.

The Count, deeply perturbed, had been watching that vision of Nana passing in front of him. His wife slowly turned around and stared at him. He looked down at the ground, as though in order to escape from those galloping horses that were carrying away his flesh and his heart. He nearly cried out in his suffering: sudden understanding had just come to him when he saw Georges lost among Nana's skirts. A child! He was overwhelmed by the thought that she had preferred a child to him. Steiner didn't matter to him, but that child! . . .

Madame Hugon had not recognized Georges at first. As he was crossing the bridge, he would have jumped into the river if Nana's knees had not restrained him. Then, frozen, white as a sheet, he sat very stiffly, looking at no one. Perhaps he would not be seen.

"Oh! Good heavens!" suddenly exclaimed the old lady. "It's Georges who's with her!"

The carriages had passed in the midst of the uneasiness felt by people who know each other but give no sign of recognition. That quick, delicate encounter seemed to have lasted an eternity. And now the wheels were gaily carrying into the sunny countryside those carriages filled with girls stimulated by the open air. Brightly colored dresses were fluttering in the wind. The laughter began again, with jokes and backward glances at those respectable people standing beside the road, looking annoyed. Nana turned around and saw them hesitate, then go back

in the direction from which they had come, without crossing the bridge. Madame Hugon was leaning on Count
Muffat's arm. She was silent, and so sad that no one
dared to comfort her.

"Tell me," Nana shouted to Lucy, who was leaning out
of the carriage in front of hers, "did you see Fauchery, my
dear? What a dirty look he gave me! He'll pay for that. . . .
And Paul! I've been so good to him, but he acted as if
he'd never seen me before. . . . Oh, they're very polite!"

She made a terrible scene with Steiner when he stated
that he thought the gentlemen's attitude had been quite
correct. So she and her friends weren't even worth tipping
a hat to! They could be rudely insulted by anyone who
felt like it! That was very kind of him! He was just like
the others, that made it complete! No, a man should always bow to a woman.

"Who was the tall woman?" Lucy called out above the
noise of the wheels.

"Countess Muffat," replied Steiner.

"Ah, I thought so," said Nana. "Well, she may be a
countess, but she's not worth much. . . . That's right, she's
not worth much. I've got an eye for that kind of thing.
Now I know her as well as if I'd made her myself, your
Countess. . . . I'll bet you she's going to bed with that
viper Fauchery. . . . Yes, she's going to bed with him!
We women can sense that."

Steiner shrugged his shoulders. His ill temper had been
increasing since the day before. He had received some letters that would oblige him to leave the next morning; and
then, too, it wasn't very amusing to come to the country
just to sleep on a sofa in the drawing room.

"And poor Baby!" said Nana, suddenly moved to pity
when she noticed Georges' pallor. He was still rigid, and
scarcely able to breathe.

"Do you think my mother recognized me?" he said at
length.

"Oh yes, I'm sure she did. She cried out. . . . And it's
my fault, too. You didn't want to come and I made you.
. . . Listen, Zizi, do you want me to write to your mother?
She looked like a very decent woman. I'll tell her I'd never
seen you before, that Steiner brought you today for the
first time."

"No, no, don't write," Georges said anxiously. "I'll take care of it myself. . . . And if they bother me about it, I'll go away and never come back."

He sat lost in thought, trying to think of lies to tell that evening. The five carriages were rolling across the plain, along an endless straight road bordered by beautiful trees. The countryside was bathed in silvery-gray air. The women continued to shout from one carriage to another, behind the backs of the drivers, who laughed to themselves at that strange collection of people. Occasionally one of the women would stand up to get a better view and would stay on her feet, leaning against a companion's shoulders, until a sudden jolt brought her back down on the seat. Caroline Héquet was engaged in serious conversation with Labordette; they both agreed that Nana would sell her house within three months, and Caroline told Labordette to buy it for her in secret, for a ridiculously low price. In front of them, La Faloise, very amorous and unable to reach the back of Gaga's apoplectic neck, was kissing her spine through her dress, which was stretched so tightly that it was ready to split. Sitting stiffly on the edge of the folding seat in front of them, Amélie kept telling them to stop it; she was annoyed at having to sit there idly, watching her mother being kissed. In the next carriage, Mignon, to impress Lucy, was making each of his sons recite a fable by La Fontaine; Henri, especially, was prodigious: he could rattle it off without a single mistake. Maria Blond, at the head of the procession, was finally beginning to be bored, tired of fooling that simple-minded Tatan Néné, whom she had just told that Paris dairywomen made eggs out of paste and saffron. It was too far—weren't they ever going to get there? The question was passed from carriage to carriage until it reached Nana. After consulting her driver, she stood up and shouted, "Only fifteen minutes more! You see that church there, behind the trees . . ." Then she went on: "By the way, the owner of the Château de Chamont is an old woman who was a big success in the days of Napoleon. She had a fantastic life, wilder than anything that goes on nowadays. Joseph told me about her, and he heard the story from the servants in the bishop's palace. She's become very religious now."

"What's her name?" asked Lucy.

"Madame d'Anglars."

"Irma d'Anglars! I knew her!" cried Gaga.

Exclamations arose from all the carriages and were carried away by the more rapid trot of the horses. Women craned their necks in order to see Gaga; Maria Blond and Tatan Néné turned around, kneeling on the seat with their fists on the closed hood at the back of the carriage. There was a volley of questions, and malicious remarks tempered by secret admiration. Gaga had known her; this filled them all with respect for that distant past.

"I was very young then," said Gaga, "but I still remember seeing her pass by. . . . They used to say she was disgusting at home, but in her carriage she was magnificent. And what stories they told about her! You never heard of such dirty tricks! I'm not surprised she has a château: she could clean out a man as easy as looking at him. . . . Ah, so Irma d'Anglars is still alive! Well, I'll tell you this, girls: she must be close to ninety now."

The women suddenly became serious. Ninety years old! Not one of them, as Lucy cried out, had any chance of living to that age. They were all in bad shape already. Nana said she didn't want to live to be an old woman anyway; it wouldn't be any fun. They had nearly reached their destination. The conversation was interrupted by the cracking of whips as the drivers speeded up their horses. Despite the noise, however, Lucy went on talking; changing the subject, she urged Nana to leave with the rest of them the next day. The Exposition was about to close and they had to go back to Paris, where the season had been surpassing their hopes. But Nana stubbornly refused. She detested Paris; she had no intention of going back there so soon.

"We'll stay here, won't we, darling?" she said, pressing Georges' knees without troubling herself about Steiner.

The carriages stopped abruptly. Surprised, the company got out in a deserted spot at the foot of a hill. One of the drivers had to point his whip toward the ruins of the old Abbey of Chamont, lost among the trees. It was a great disappointment. The ladies found it stupid: nothing but a few piles of old stones covered with brambles, and half of a crumbling tower. It wasn't worth going five miles just to see that! The coachman then pointed out the château,

whose grounds began near the abbey, and advised them
to take a little path that followed the walls. They could
take a walk around it while the carriages waited for them
in the square of the village. It would be a delightful walk.
They all agreed to do it.

"My God, Irma has done all right for herself!" said Gaga,
stopping in front of a gate at one corner of the grounds
near the road.

They all looked in silence at the enormous thicket on
the other side of the gate. Then they began walking around
the wall of the grounds along the little path, looking up to
admire the trees, whose branches formed a thick green
canopy overhead. When they had walked for three minutes
they came to another gate; through this one they saw a
broad lawn on which two venerable oaks cast dark masses
of shade. And three minutes later still another gate showed
them a big tree-lined avenue, a tunnel of shadows at the
end of which the sunlight shone like a bright star. Their
amazement, silent at first, gradually burst into exclamations.
They had tried to joke about what they saw, with a touch
of envy, but they were now deeply impressed. What power
that Irma had! Things like that gave you a glorious idea
of women!

They went on; the trees were endless, and they constantly saw patches of ivy trailing over the wall, the roofs
of summer houses, screens of poplars, and deep clumps of
elms and aspens. Wasn't it ever going to end? Tired of
following the wall without seeing anything at each opening
except masses of greenery, they wished they could see the
château itself. They clutched the iron bars with both hands
and pressed their faces between them. A feeling of respect
came over them as they were thus kept at a distance,
dreaming of the invisible château that stood somewhere in
that immensity. Soon, since they were not used to walking,
they became tired. And still the wall went on: at every
turn in the deserted path, they saw the same line of gray
stones. Some of the women, despairing of ever reaching
the end, spoke of turning back. But the more their walk
tired them, the more respectful they became; with every
step they were increasingly overawed by the calm, regal
majesty of the domain.

"This is getting silly!" said Caroline Héquet, clenching her teeth.

Nana silenced her with a shrug of her shoulders. She had not said anything for some time; she was now a little pale, and very serious. Suddenly, at the last bend in the path, as they were approaching the square of the village, the wall stopped and the château appeared at the end of its vast courtyard. They all stood still, overwhelmed by the lofty grandeur of the broad front steps, the twenty windows of the façade and the great expanse of the three wings, whose brickwork was framed by stone. Henri IV had lived in that historic château, where his bedroom was still preserved, with its great bed hung with Genoa velvet. Nana gasped in amazement like a child. "Good God!" she murmured softly to herself.

They were all seized with excitement when Gaga suddenly said that Irma herself was standing over there in front of the church. She recognized her perfectly; she still held herself erect in spite of her age, the old rascal, and her eyes were still the same when she assumed her grand manner. Vespers were just over. Madame remained under the porch for a few moments. Wearing a brown silk dress, she looked tall and simple, with the venerable face of a marquise who had escaped the horrors of the Revolution. In her right hand, a big prayer book was gleaming in the sunlight. She slowly crossed the square, followed by a liveried footman who walked fifteen paces behind her. The church was emptying. The people of Chamont bowed deeply to her. An old man kissed her hand, a woman almost knelt before her. She was a powerful queen, laden with years and honors. She climbed the steps of her château and disappeared.

"There's an example of what good management can do," Mignon said in a tone of conviction, looking at his sons as though to give them a lesson.

Then everyone had his comment to make. Labordette thought she was wonderfully well-preserved. Maria Blond said something obscene and Lucy angrily told her that age ought to be respected. In short, they all agreed that she was fantastic. They got back into the carriages. Nana was silent all the way from Chamont to La Mignotte. She turned around twice to look at the château. Lulled by the sound of the wheels, she no longer felt Steiner beside her or saw Georges in front of her. A vision arose from the twilight: Madame d'Anglars was still passing by with the majesty of a powerful queen, laden with years and honors.

That evening, Georges returned to Les Fondettes for dinner. Nana, who had been growing increasingly distracted and odd, had sent him there to ask his mother to forgive him; it had to be done, she said sternly, seized with sudden respect for the family. She even made him swear not to come back later to spend the night with her. She was tired, and he would only be doing his duty in showing obedience. Georges was greatly annoyed by this display of morality. He appeared before his mother with a heavy heart, hanging his head. Fortunately his brother Philippe, a big, high-spirited soldier, had arrived. This cut short the scene he had been dreading. Madame Hugon merely looked at him with eyes full of tears, while Philippe, informed of what had happened, threatened to drag him back by the ears if he ever returned to that woman. Georges, feeling relieved, began secretly planning to slip away at two o'clock the next afternoon to arrange his meetings with Nana.

During dinner, the guests at Les Fondettes seemed ill at ease. Vandeuvres had announced his departure. He wanted to take Lucy back to Paris; he was amused by the idea of running off with that woman he had known for the past ten years without feeling any desire for her. The Marquis de Chouard, his nose buried in his plate, was thinking of Gaga's daughter. He remembered having bounced Lili on his knee. How quickly children grew up! She was becoming quite plump. Count Muffat remained silent; his face was red and he seemed to be lost in thought. He had given Georges a long look. When the meal was over he said he had a slight fever and went up to his room. Monsieur Venot hurried after him and there was a scene upstairs. The Count fell onto his bed, stifling convulsive sobs in his pillow, while Monsieur Venot gently called him his brother and advised him to implore divine mercy. Muffat did not hear him; he was moaning hoarsely. Suddenly he leapt from the bed and stammered, "I'm going there . . . I can no longer . . ."

As they went out, two shadows disappeared into a dark

lane. Fauchery and Countess Sabine now let Daguenet help Estelle to prepare the tea every evening. On the highway, the Count walked so swiftly that his companion had to run to keep up with him. Though out of breath, Monsieur Venot never ceased offering him the best arguments against the temptations of the flesh. The Count continued to hurry through the darkness without opening his mouth. When he reached the gate of La Mignotte he said simply, "I can no longer resist. Go away."

"God's will be done, then," murmured Monsieur Venot. "He uses all means to assure His triumph. Your sin will be one of His weapons."

At La Mignotte, there was quarreling during dinner. Nana had received a letter from Bordenave in which he advised her to take a rest and seemed to care nothing about her; little Violaine was being given two curtain calls every night. When Mignon again urged her to leave with them the next day, she angrily told him she didn't need his advice. Furthermore, she had been behaving in a ridiculously strait-laced manner at dinner. When Madame Lerat used a rather crude expression, she shouted that by God she wasn't going to let anybody, not even her aunt, say dirty things in her presence! Then, in a fit of stupid respectability, she bored everyone with her righteous sentiments; she presented her idea of a religious education for Louiset and a whole plan of good conduct for herself. When the others laughed, she made profound remarks and smugly nodded her head. She said that only order led to fortune, and that she did not want to die in poverty. The other women, irritated, cried out in protest: it was impossible; Nana had been changed! But she sat still, staring into space, and became absorbed in the vision of a very rich Nana whom everyone bowed to.

They were just going up to bed when Muffat arrived. It was Labordette who saw him in the garden. Understanding the situation immediately, he rendered him the service of getting Steiner out of the way and leading him by the hand along the dark hall to Nana's bedroom. In such matters Labordette was perfectly urbane and adroit, and he seemed delighted to make others happy. Nana showed no surprise; she was merely annoyed by Muffat's obsession with her. But after all, she had to be serious about her life. It was foolish to be in love, it led to nothing. Besides, she had scruples because of Zizi's youth. She had been behaving indecently. Well, she would get back on the right path: she was going to take an old man.

"Zoé," she said to her maid, who was overjoyed to be leaving the country, "pack the trunks as soon as you get up tomorrow morning. We're going back to Paris."

And she went to bed with Muffat, but without pleasure.

7

Three months later, on a December evening, Count Muffat was walking up and down the Passage des Panoramas. The weather was mild. A sudden shower had just filled the passage with people. There was a slow, laborious, tightly packed procession between the shops. Beneath the panes of glass brightened by reflections, there was a violent blaze of light: white globes, red lanterns, blue transparencies, rows of gas jets, gigantic watches and fans outlined in flame, burning in the air. The multicolored displays in the shop windows gleamed behind the clear glass, in the garish light of the reflectors: the gold of the jewelers, the bright silks of the milliners, the crystal vases of the confectioners. And among the chaos of gaudily painted signs, an enormous crimson glove looked like a bleeding hand that had been cut off and hung by a yellow cuff.

Count Muffat slowly walked to the boulevard. He glanced at the pavement, then returned at a leisurely pace, keeping close to the shop windows. The damp, heated air filled the narrow passage with a kind of luminous vapor. Along the flagstones, wet from the dripping of umbrellas, footsteps reverberated continuously, without the sound of a single voice. The passers-by, brushing against him at every turn, stared at his silent face made pale by the gaslights. To escape from their curiosity, he stopped in front of a stationer's shop and began attentively examining a display of paperweights in the form of glass balls containing landscapes and flowers.

He saw nothing; he was thinking of Nana. Why had she lied to him again? That morning she had written him a note telling him not to come that evening because Louiset was sick and she was going to stay with him all night at her aunt's house. But he had been suspicious: he had gone to her house, where the concierge had told him that Madame had just left for her theater. This surprised him, for she had no part in the new play. Why had she told that lie, and what could she be doing at the Variety Theater that evening.

Jostled by a passer-by, the Count unconsciously left the paperweights and found himself in front of a display of miscellaneous trinkets, staring with apparent interest at some notebooks and cigar cases which all had the same blue swallow painted on one corner. Yes, Nana had changed. At first, after her return from the country, she had driven him mad when she kissed him around the face and on the whiskers with kittenish affection, telling him he was her darling pet, the only man she adored. He was no longer afraid of Georges, whose mother had kept him at Les Fondettes. There was still Steiner; the Count was supposed to have replaced him, but he did not dare to question Nana specifically about him. He knew that Steiner was again in an extraordinary financial scrape, that he was about to be declared a defaulter on the stock market, and that he was beleaguering the stockholders of the Landes salt works, trying to get one last payment out of them. Whenever the Count saw him in Nana's apartment, she explained to him in a reasonable tone that she didn't want to throw him out like a dog, after what he had spent on her. Anyway, for the past three months the Count had been living in such a whirl of sensuality that he had no really clear impressions beyond the need to possess her. In that belated awakening of his flesh, he had a childish gluttony that left no room for vanity or jealousy. Only one precise realization was capable of striking him: Nana was becoming less nice to him, she no longer kissed him on the whiskers. This worried him and, being a man who knew nothing about women, he wondered how he had offended her. He thought he satisfied all her desires. He returned to the letter he had received that morning, to that complicated lie she had told him for the simple purpose of spending an evening at her theater. Pushed again by the crowd, he had crossed the Passage and was now racking his brain in front of a restaurant, his eyes fixed on some plucked larks and a big salmon laid out in the window.

Finally he seemed to tear himself away from this spec-

tacle. He shook his head, looked up and saw that it was
nearly nine o'clock. When Nana came out he would demand to know the truth. He began walking again, recalling
the other evenings he had spent in that place, when he
used to wait for her at the door of the theater. He knew
all the shops and he recognized their odors in the gas-laden
air: the strong smell of Russia leather, the fragrance of
vanilla rising from a confectioner's basement, the scent of
musk that floated from the open doors of perfume shops.
He no longer dared to stop in front of the pale faces of the
women behind the counters, who placidly looked on him
as an old acquaintance. For a moment he seemed to be
studying the row of little round windows above the shops,
as though he had just noticed them for the first time among
the jumble of signs. Then he walked to the boulevard
again and stood there a minute. The rain had turned into a
fine drizzle; its cold touch on his hands calmed him. He
now began thinking about his wife. She was in a château
near Mâcon, staying with her friend Madame de Chezelles,
who had been very ill since autumn. The carriages on the
boulevard were rolling through thick mud. The country
must be unbearable in such vile weather. Suddenly seized
with anxiety, he returned to the stifling heat of the Passage
and strode rapidly through the crowd: it had just occurred
to him that if Nana suspected he might be waiting for her,
she would leave by way of the Galerie Montmartre.

From then on, he watched for her at the stage door itself.
He did not like waiting in that little corridor. He was afraid
of being recognized. It was at the corner of the Galerie des
Variétés and the Galerie Saint-Marc, a sordid place with
dark shops: a cobbler who never had any customers, dusty
furniture stores, a smoky lending library whose shaded
lamps slept through the evening in a green glow; and there
was never anyone there except well-dressed, patient gentlemen wandering among the drunken stagehands and shabby
chorus girls who are always gathered around a stage door.
Outside the theater, the entrance was lighted only by a
single gas jet in a frosted globe. For a moment Muffat
thought of questioning Madame Bron, but then he was
afraid that Nana, informed of his presence, might escape
along the boulevard. He began walking again, determined
to wait, if necessary, until he was driven away when the

gates were closed for the night, as had already happened twice before. The idea of returning to his house and going to bed alone filled his heart with anguish. Each time hatless girls or men in dirty shirts came out and stared at him, he went back and stood in front of the lending library, where, between two posters pasted on a window pane, he always saw the same sight: a little old man sitting upright and alone at the immense table in the green light of a lamp, reading a green newspaper that he held with his green hands. A few minutes before ten o'clock, another gentleman, a tall, blond, handsome man wearing well-fitting gloves, began pacing back and forth outside the theater. Each time they passed each other, they exchanged a mistrustful sidelong glance. The Count walked to the corner of the two galleries, which was adorned with a tall mirror; and there, seeing himself with his solemn face and elegant attire, he felt a mixture of shame and fear.

Ten o'clock struck. Muffat suddenly realized that it would be easy for him to find out whether Nana was in her dressing room. He went up the three steps, passed through the little yellow hall and slipped into the courtyard through a door that was closed only with a latch. At that hour the narrow courtyard, damp as the bottom of a well, with its foul-smelling toilets, its fountain, the kitchen stove, and the plants with which the concierge littered it, was bathed in black mist; but the windows of the two walls that rose high above it were brightly lighted. On the ground floor were the property room and the firemen's station, to the left were the offices of the management, while the dressing rooms were to the right and upstairs. Along the sides of that dark pit, they looked like so many oven doors opening into the shadows. The Count immediately saw a light in the window of the dressing room on the second floor. Feeling relieved and happy, he continued looking at the window, standing there in the greasy mud and rancid stench of the courtyard of that old Paris building. Large drops were falling from a cracked drainpipe. A ray of yellow light from Madame Bron's window shone on a patch of moss-covered pavement, the base of a wall that had been eroded by the water from a sink, and a whole corner filled with rubbish and littered with old buckets and broken earthenware pans, where a scrawny spindle tree was growing in a pot. Hearing someone open a window, the Count hurried away.

Nana would surely come out before long. He went back to the lending library; in the sleeping shadows broken only by the dim glow of the lamp, the little old man had not moved: his face was still bent over his newspaper. The Count began walking again. He went further this time. He crossed the main passage and walked along the Galerie des Variétés until he came to the cold, deserted, gloomy Galerie Feydeau; then he came back, passed the theater, turned the corner of the Galerie Saint-Marc and ventured into the Galerie Montmartre, where he was interested by a machine sawing sugar in a grocer's shop.

But while he was making this little journey for the third time, the fear that Nana might escape behind his back made him lose all concern for what others might think. He went back and stood outside the theater with the blond gentleman. They gave each other a look of brotherly humility mixed with lingering mistrust with regard to the possibility of a rivalry. They were jostled by stagehands who came out to smoke a pipe during the intermission, but neither of them dared to complain. Three big girls with uncombed hair and dirty dresses appeared in the doorway, eating apples and throwing away the cores. The two men bowed their heads and submitted to the effrontery of their eyes and the coarseness of their words, spattered and dirtied by those wenches who found it amusing to push each other against them.

Finally Nana came down the three steps. She turned pale when she saw Muffat.

"Ah, it's you!" she stammered.

The chorus girls, who had been laughing, became frightened when they recognized her; they stood still in a row, looking stiff and serious, like servants caught doing something wrong by their mistress. The tall blond gentleman had moved some distance away, sad and reassured at the same time.

"Well, give me your arm," Nana said impatiently.

They slowly walked away. The Count had prepared a number of questions, but he was now unable to think of anything to say. Nana told him a story of her own accord: she had stayed at her aunt's house till eight o'clock, then, seeing that Louiset was feeling much better, she had decided to stop by the theater.

"For some important matter?" he asked.

"Yes, a new play," she replied after a slight hesitation. "They wanted my opinion."

He realized that she was lying. But the warm sensation of her arm, pressed strongly against his, left him without strength. The anger and rancor aroused in him by his long wait had vanished; his sole concern was to hang onto her, now that he had her with him. The next day he would try to find out what she had been doing in her dressing room. Nana, still hesitant, clearly trying to pull herself together and decide on a course of action, stopped in front of a fan-maker's window as soon as they had turned the corner of the Galerie des Variétés.

"Look at that one trimmed with mother-of-pearl and feathers," she said. "Isn't it pretty?" Then, in a tone of indifference: "You're taking me home?"

"Yes, of course," he said, astonished, "since your child is better now."

She regretted the story she had told him. She said that Louiset might be having another attack, and spoke of going back to Les Batignolles. But since he offered to go with her, she did not insist. For an instant she had the fierce rage of a woman who feels trapped, yet has to be sweet and docile. Finally she resigned herself and resolved to gain time; provided she could get rid of the Count by midnight, everything would work out as she wished.

"I'd forgotten that you're a bachelor tonight," she said. "Your wife won't be back till tomorrow morning, will she?"

"No," replied Muffat, slightly upset by hearing her speak familiarly of the Countess.

She continued to question him: she wanted to know what time the train arrived and whether he would meet her at the station. She had again slowed her pace, as though greatly interested by the shop windows.

"Oh, look!" she said, stopping in front of a jeweler's shop. "What an odd bracelet!"

She loved the Passage des Panoramas. Ever since her childhood she had had a passion for the gaudy articles sold in Paris: the imitation jewelry, the gilded zinc, the cardboard pretending to be leather. She never passed by without stopping to look at the windows, just as, when she was a ragged child, she used to stand staring at a confectioner's display, listening to the organ in a neighboring shop, especially fascinated by the flashy taste of cheap trinkets, such as nutshells made into sewing kits, miniature ragpicker's baskets for holding toothpicks, and Vendôme columns with thermometers embedded in them. But this evening she was too agitated; she looked without seeing. It was annoying not to be free! And in her inner revolt she felt a violent impulse to do something foolish. A lot of good it did her to have rich men! She had just cleaned out Steiner and the Prince with childish caprices, without knowing where the money had gone. Her apartment on the Boulevard Haussmann was not even completely furnished, except for the drawing room; it, however, was too full, and its red satin upholstery and excessive ornamentation clashed with the rest of the apartment. And her creditors were now tormenting her more than before, when she had no money at all. This constantly surprised her, for she considered herself a model of economy. For the past month, that thief Steiner had scarcely been able to get hold of a thousand francs on days when she threatened to throw him out unless he brought her at least that much. As for Muffat, he was a fool; he did not know how much a man ought to give a woman, so she could not hold his stinginess against him.

How quickly she would have dropped all those men if she had not repeated maxims of good conduct to herself a dozen times a day! She had to be sensible; Zoé told her so every morning, and she herself was still haunted by a religious memory: the regal sight she had seen at Chamont, constantly evoked and embellished. And that was why, despite a quiver of suppressed anger, she now forced herself to be submissive as she walked along, holding the Count's arm, from one shop window to another, in the thinning stream of passers-by. Outside, the pavement was drying. A cool wind was blowing along the gallery, driving out the warm air that had collected under the glass roof, alarming the colored lanterns, the rows of gas jets, and the gigantic fan blazing like a fireworks display. In front of the restaurant, a waiter was turning off the gas globes. The women behind the counters of the empty, brightly lit shops were standing motionless, apparently sleeping with their eyes open.

"Oh, how darling!" Nana said in front of the last shop window, coming back a few steps to admire a porcelain greyhound with its paw raised before a nest hidden among some roses.

They left the Passage at last. She did not want to take a cab. The weather was fine, she said, and besides, they were in no hurry. It would be nice to walk home. Then, when they were about to pass the Café Anglais, she had a sudden craving for oysters; she said she had not eaten anything since morning, because of Louiset's illness. Muffat did not dare to oppose her. He had not yet begun to show himself openly with her, so he asked for a private room and hurried along the halls. She followed him like a woman who was familiar with the establishment. They were about to enter their private room, whose door was being held open for them by a waiter, when a man suddenly came out of a nearby room from which a storm of shouts and laughter could be heard. It was Daguenet.

"Nana!" he exclaimed.

The Count had quickly disappeared into the private room, leaving the door ajar behind him. But when Daguenet caught a glimpse of his round back he winked and said jokingly, "My God, you're doing very well for yourself! You're taking them from the Tuileries now!"

Nana smiled and put her finger to her lips to silence him. She saw that he was quite tipsy, but she was glad to have met him there, for she still had a warm spot in her heart for him, despite his treachery in pretending not to recognize her that day when he was with respectable women.

"What have you been doing?" she asked in a friendly tone.

"I'm turning over a new leaf: I'm thinking of getting married."

She shrugged her shoulders with an expression of pity. He went on talking lightheartedly. He said he was tired of earning just enough on the stock market to enable him to give bouquets to the ladies, so that he would at least be a decent man. His three hundred thousand francs had lasted him eighteen months. He had decided to be practical: he would marry a girl with a big dowry and end up as a prefect, like his father. Nana smiled incredulously.

"Who's with you in there?" she asked, nodding toward the room from which he had come.

"Oh, a whole gang of people!" he said, forgetting his plans in a burst of drunkenness. "Léa has been telling us about her trip to Egypt. It's so funny! There's one story about a bath . . ."

And he told the story. Nana obligingly listened to it. They had leaned against the walls of the hall, facing each other. Gaslights were burning beneath the low ceiling and a vague odor of cooking lingered in the folds of the hangings. Now and then, when the noise from the next room increased, they had to move their faces close together in order to hear each other. Every twenty seconds or so they were disturbed by a waiter carrying dishes who found them blocking the hall. They would simply press up against the walls without interrupting their conversation, talking as though they were at home, amid the uproar of the customers and the jostling of the waiters.

"Look," murmured Daguenet, pointing to the door of the private room into which Muffat had disappeared.

They both looked. The door was quivering slightly, as though fluttering in a breath of air. Finally, with extreme slowness, it closed without a sound. They silently smiled at each other. The Count must be cutting a fine figure, all alone in there!

"By the way," she said, "have you read Fauchery's article about me?"

"Yes, 'The Golden Fly,' " replied Daguenet. "I didn't mention it because I was afraid it might upset you."

"Upset me? Why? It's a very long article."

She was flattered by having been written about in the *Figaro*. If it had not been for the explanations given to her by Francis, her hairdresser, who had brought her the newspaper, she would not have understood that the article was about her. Daguenet was furtively scrutinizing her, smiling ironically. Well, since she was pleased, everyone else ought to be.

"Excuse me!" cried a waiter who separated them, holding a dish of molded ice cream in both hands.

Nana took a step toward the private room in which Muffat was waiting for her.

"Well, good-by," said Daguenet. "Go back to your cuckold."

She stopped.

"Why do you call him a cuckold?"

"Because he's a cuckold, why else?"

She leaned against the wall again, deeply interested.

"Oh," she said simply.

"What! You didn't know? His wife goes to bed with Fauchery, my dear. . . . It must have started in the country. . . . Fauchery left me just before I came here, and I have an idea they're going to meet in his apartment tonight. I think they've invented some story about a trip."

Nana was dumbfounded.

"I thought so!" she said at last, slapping her thighs. "I guessed it just by looking at her on the road that day. . . . Think of it! A respectable woman deceiving her husband, and with a dirty pig like Fauchery! He'll teach her some fine things!"

"Oh, this isn't her first time," Daguenet said maliciously. "She may know as much as he does."

"What a nice bunch of people!" she exclaimed indignantly. "They're disgusting!"

"Excuse me!" cried a waiter laden with bottles, separating them.

Daguenet drew her forward and held her by the hand for a few moments. He assumed his crystalline voice, a voice with the tone of a harmonica, which was the cause of his success with the ladies: "Good-by, darling. . . . You know I still love you."

She withdrew her hand, smiling. "Don't be silly, it's all over now," she said, her voice scarcely audible above the shouts and cheers that shook the door of the room Daguenet had left. "But it doesn't matter—come to see me one of these days. We'll have a talk." Then, becoming very serious, in the tone of a scandalized matron: "So he's a cuckold! . . . I don't like that at all. Cuckolds have always disgusted me."

When she finally went into the private room, she saw Muffat sitting resignedly on the narrow sofa. His face was white and his hands were trembling nervously. He made no complaint. Deeply moved, she was divided between pity and contempt. Poor man! His nasty wife was deceiving him so shamefully! She felt like throwing her arms around his neck, to console him. But even so, it was only just: he was stupid with women, this would teach him a lesson. Her pity prevailed, however. She did not send him away after eating her oysters, as she had intended to do. They stayed in the Café Anglais no more than a quarter of an hour, then they went to her apartment together. It was eleven o'clock; by midnight she would find some gentle means of getting rid of him.

In the anteroom she took the precaution of giving Zoé an order: "Watch for him and tell him not to make any noise if the other one is still with me when he comes."

"But where shall I put him, Madame?"

"Keep him in the kitchen. That will be safer."

Muffat was already taking off his overcoat in the bedroom. There was a big fire in the fireplace. It was still the same bedroom, with its rosewood furniture and its hangings and upholstery of brocaded damask with big blue flowers against a gray background. Nana had twice thought of having it redone, the first time in black velvet, the second in white satin with pink bows; but as soon as Steiner had consented, she had squandered the money he gave her. She had added only a tiger-skin rug in front of the fireplace and a crystal night lamp that hung from the ceiling.

"I'm not sleepy, so I'm not going to bed yet," she said when they were alone in the bedroom together.

The Count obeyed her with the submissiveness of a man who is no longer afraid of being seen. His only concern was not to anger her.

"As you wish," he said softly.

However, he took off his boots before sitting down by the fire. One of Nana's pleasures was to undress in front of the mirror on the door of her wardrobe, in which she could see herself full length. She would take off everything, even her chemise, then stand naked and look at herself for a long time, oblivious to everything around her. She had a passion for her body, she was enraptured by the satin of her skin and the supple lines of her figure. She would remain serious, attentive, absorbed in self-love. The hairdresser often found her thus, without her even turning her head. Muffat would then become angry, and she would be surprised. What was the matter with him? It wasn't for others, it was for herself.

That evening, in order to see herself better, she lit the six candles attached to the wardrobe. But as she was taking off her chemise she stopped, preoccupied, with a question on the tip of her tongue.

"Have you read the article in the *Figaro?* . . . It's on the table." She recalled Daguenet's laughter and was torn by doubt. If Fauchery had slandered her, she would get even with him for it. "They say it's about me," she said with feigned indifference. "What do you think, darling?"

She slipped off her chemise and remained naked, waiting for Muffat to finish reading. He read slowly. Fauchery's article, "The Golden Fly," was the story of a girl descended from four or five generations of drunkards, her blood tainted by a long heredity of poverty and alcohol, which, in her case, was transformed into a derangement of her sexual nature. She had grown up on the pavements of a poor section of Paris, and now, tall, beautiful, with the superb physical development of a dunghill plant, she was avenging the beggars and outcasts from whom she sprang. With her, the putrefaction that was allowed to ferment among the common people had risen and was rotting the aristocracy. Without wishing it, she had become a force of nature, a ferment of destruction, corrupting and disrupting Paris between her snow-white thighs, turning it sour, as some women turn milk sour every month. It was at the end of the article that the comparison with the fly occurred: a sun-colored fly that had flown from a dunghill, a fly that gathered death from the carrion left on the streets, and then, buzzing, dancing, glittering like a precious stone, flew in through the windows of palaces and poisoned men merely by alighting on them.

Muffat raised his head and stared at the fire.

"Well?" said Nana.

He did not answer. He seemed to want to reread the article. A sensation of cold spread from his scalp to his shoulders. The article was written in a slapdash manner, with capering phrases and an excessive use of unexpected words and strange comparisons. It had affected him deeply, however, for it had suddenly aroused in him everything he had been trying not to stir up for the past few months.

He looked up. Nana was absorbed in enraptured contemplation of herself. She bent her neck and looked attentively in the mirror at a little brown mole above her right hip. She touched it with her fingertip and made it stand out by leaning back, apparently finding it odd and pretty. Then she studied other parts of her body with amusement and perverse, childish curiosity. It always surprised her to see herself; she had the amazed and fascinated look of a young girl discovering her puberty. She slowly spread her arms to display her plump, Venus-like torso, bent at the waist and examined herself front and back, lingering over the profile of her breasts and the curves of her thighs. Finally she abandoned herself to the strange amusement of standing with her knees apart, swinging the upper half of her body right and left, with the constant quivering motion of an Oriental dancing girl doing the belly dance.

Muffat was watching her. She frightened him. The newspaper had fallen from his hands. In that moment of clear vision, he despised himself. It was true: in three months she had corrupted his life, and he already felt himself tainted to the core by filth which he could never even have suspected before. Everything inside him would soon be rotten. For an instant he was conscious of the effects of his malady: he saw the disruption caused by that ferment, he saw himself poisoned, his family destroyed, a segment of society cracking and collapsing. And, unable to turn his eyes away, he stared at her, trying to fill himself with disgust for her nakedness.

She was no longer moving. With one arm behind her neck and one hand clasping the other, she was tilting her head back with her elbows wide apart. He had a foreshortened view of her half-closed eyes, her parted lips, and her amorous smile. Her yellow hair hung loosely down her back like the coat of a lioness. Bending thus, she showed the solid loins and firm breasts of an Amazon, with strong muscles beneath the satin texture of her skin. A delicate line, slightly undulated by her shoulder and her hip, went from one of her elbows to her foot. Muffat contemplated the soft profile, the golden luster of her flesh, the curves glowing like silk in the candlelight. He thought of his old horror of woman, the lascivious, musky-smelling monster of the Scriptures. Nana's whole body was covered with reddish down which gave her skin the appearance of velvet, and there was a strong animal quality in her sturdy buttocks and thighs, in the smooth swellings and deep hollows that gave her sex the provocative veil of their shadow. She was the Golden Beast, unconscious of her power, corrupting the world by her odor alone. Muffat continued to stare, obsessed, possessed, until finally, when he closed his eyes in order not to see, the animal appeared in the darkness, enlarged, terrible, exaggerating its posture. He knew it would remain there, before his eyes, in his flesh, forever.

Nana hunched her shoulders. A thrill of tenderness seemed to have passed through all her limbs. Her eyes were moist and she tried to make herself smaller, as though to feel herself better. Then she unclasped her hands and slid them down to her breasts, which she pressed in an ardent embrace. She threw back her head and melted into a caress of her whole body, fondly rubbing her cheeks against her shoulders. Her avid mouth breathed desire upon her. She put out her lips and gave herself a long kiss near the armpit, smiling at the other Nana who was also kissing herself in the mirror.

Muffat heaved a weary, prolonged sigh. Her solitary pleasure exasperated him. Suddenly everything within him was swept away as though by a great wind. In a surge of brutality he seized her around the waist and threw her down on the carpet.

"Let me go!" she cried. "You're hurting me!"

He was conscious of his defeat. He knew she was stupid, vile, and deceitful, yet he wanted her, however poisonous she might be.

"You fool!" she said furiously when he let her stand up.

She soon became calmer, however. Now he would go away. After putting on a lace-trimmed nightgown, she sat down on the floor in front of the fire. It was her favorite place. She again questioned him about Fauchery's article. He answered vaguely, wishing to avoid a scene. She said she couldn't stand Fauchery, then lapsed into a long silence, trying to think of a way to get rid of the Count. She wanted to do it pleasantly, for she was a good-natured girl and did not like to hurt anyone, especially Muffat, since he was a cuckold, which made her feel sorry for him.

"So you're expecting your wife tomorrow morning?" she said finally.

Muffat was stretched out in an armchair, looking drowsy and tired. He nodded. Nana looked at him seriously and thought deeply. Sitting on one thigh amid the rumpled lace of her nightgown, she held one of her bare feet with both hands, absent-mindedly turning it back and forth.

"How long have you been married?" she asked.

"Nineteen years," replied the Count.

"Ah! . . . And is your wife nice? Do you get along well with each other?"

He remained silent for a time, then said with embarrassment, "You know I've asked you never to talk about such things."

"And why not?" she cried, already beginning to lose her temper. "I won't hurt your wife just by talking about her. . . . All women are alike, my friend. . . ."

She stopped, for fear of saying too much. She assumed an air of superiority, however, because she considered that she was being very kind. She had to treat him gently, poor man! Then an amusing idea occurred to her and she smiled as she turned it over in her mind.

"I haven't told you the story Fauchery's been spreading about you," she said. "What a viper he is! I'm not angry with him, because his article seems to be all right, but he's a real viper anyway." She smiled more broadly, let go of her foot and crawled over to lean her chest against the Count's knees. "You know what he says? He says you were still a virgin when you married your wife! . . . Were you? . . . Is it true?"

Her eyes pressed him for an answer; she moved her hands up to his shoulders and shook him to make him confess.

"Yes, it's true," he finally said, in a solemn tone.

She sank down at his feet in a fit of wild laughter, stammering, giving him little pats.

"Oh, that's priceless! Only you could do that; you're fantastic! . . . How foolish you must have looked, my poor darling! It's always so funny when a man doesn't know how! I wish I could have seen you! . . . And did it go off all right? Tell me about it. Oh, please tell me about it!"

She overwhelmed him with questions, asking everything,

demanding details. She laughed so heartily, in abrupt outbursts that made her writhe while her nightgown slipped down from her shoulders and rose above her knees, and her skin looked so golden in the firelight, that the Count gradually told her the story of his wedding night. He no longer felt at all uneasy. He himself was finally amused as he told her how he had "lost his innocence," as he primly phrased it, for a last remnant of shame made him choose his words carefully. Nana, caught up in the story, questioned him about the Countess. She had a beautiful figure, he said, but she was a real icicle. "Oh, don't worry, you have no reason to be jealous!" he said shamelessly.

Nana had stopped laughing. She sat down again with her back to the fire and drew her knees under her chin with her clasped hands.

"It's a big mistake for a man to look foolish in front of his wife on their first night," she declared seriously.

"Why?" asked the Count, surprised.

"Because," she replied slowly and pompously. She nodded her head as though she had just revealed a great truth, but then she deigned to explain herself more clearly: "You see, I know all about those things. A woman doesn't like a man to be stupid. She won't say anything, because she has her modesty, you understand. . . . But you can be sure she'll think about it a lot. And if he doesn't know how to give her what she wants, sooner or later she'll go and look for it somewhere else. That's how it is, my friend."

He did not seem to understand, so she became more specific. She spoke maternally; she was giving him this lesson out of the goodness of her heart, as a friend. Ever since she had learned that he was a cuckold, the secret had weighed heavily on her mind, and she had a strong urge to discuss it with him.

"After all, though," she said, "I'm talking about things that are none of my business. . . . I'm telling you all this because everybody ought to be happy. We're just talking, aren't we? I want you to answer me frankly." But she interrupted herself to change her position. She was burning herself. "The fire's hot, isn't it? My back's roasted. . . . Just a minute, I'm going to cook my stomach a while. It's good for aches and pains!" Then, when she had turned around, with her breasts pointing toward the fire and her feet tucked under her thighs: "You don't go to bed with your wife any more?"

"No, I swear I don't," he said, fearing a scene.

"And you think she's a real icicle?"

He nodded, lowering his chin.

"And that's why you love me? . . . Answer me! I won't be angry."

He nodded again.

"I thought so!" she concluded. "Oh, my poor darling. . . . You know my aunt, Madame Lerat? When she comes, have her tell you the story of the grocer who lives across the street from her. He . . . My God but this fire is hot! I have to turn. I'm going to cook my left side now."

As she was presenting her hip to the flames, an amusing idea came to her and she good-naturedly made fun of herself, happy to see herself so plump and pink in the firelight: "I look like a goose, don't I? That's right, I'm a goose on a spit. . . . I keep turning and turning, I'm cooking in my own juice."

She was laughing again when there was a sound of voices and closing doors. Muffat, surprised, gave her a questioning look. She became serious again and her face took on an anxious expression. It must have been Zoé's cat—he was always breaking things. Twelve-thirty. Whatever had given her the idea of working for her cuckold's happiness? Now that the other one was there, she had to get rid of him, and quickly.

"What were you saying?" the Count asked obligingly, delighted to see her so amiable.

But in her desire to send him away, she changed her mood; she became impatient and spoke bluntly.

"Oh yes, the grocer and his wife . . . Well, they never touched each other, not one little bit! She was eager for it, but he was so stupid he didn't know how. . . . He thought she was made of wood, so he started going to whores who treated him to all kinds of filthy things, and she did the same with men who were smarter than her blockhead of a husband. . . . And that's how it always turns out when a man and a woman don't understand each other. I know what I'm talking about!"

Muffat turned pale; understanding her allusions at last, he tried to silence her. But she had not finished.

"No, keep quiet!" she said. "If you men weren't such pigs, you'd be as nice to your wives as you are to us, and if your wives weren't such fools, they'd take as much trouble to keep you as we do to get you. . . . It all depends on how you behave. . . . There, put that in your pipe and smoke it."

"Don't talk about respectable women," he said sternly. "You don't know anything about them."

Nana rose to her knees.

"I don't know anything about them! . . . Why, they're not even clean, your respectable women! No, they're not clean! I defy you to find one of them who'd dare to show herself the way I am now . . . You make me laugh with your respectable women! Don't push me too far, don't make me say things I'll regret later."

The Count's only answer was a muttered insult. Nana turned pale also. She looked at him for a few seconds without speaking, then said sharply, "What would you do if your wife deceived you?"

He made a threatening gesture.

"And what if I deceived you?"

"Oh, you . . ." he murmured, shrugging his shoulders.

Nana was certainly not spiteful. Ever since the first words, she had been resisting an impulse to throw his wife's unfaithfulness in his face. She would have liked to have a quiet talk with him about it. But now he was exasperating her; it had to end.

"Look," she said, "I don't know what you're doing here. You've been boring me for the last two hours. . . . Go find your wife—she's in bed with Fauchery. Yes, that's right, on the Rue Taitbout, at the corner of the Rue de Provence. . . . You see, I'm even giving you the address." Then, seeing Muffat rise to his feet, reeling like an ox that has been given a stunning blow, she said triumphantly, "If respectable women start taking our lovers away from us . . . Oh, yes, respectable women are very nice!"

But she was unable to continue. In a terrible surge of emotion, he threw her to the floor, raised his heel, and seemed determined to crush her head in order to silence her. For a moment she was horribly afraid. Then he began wandering blindly around the room, as though he had lost his reason. She was moved to tears by his choked silence

and the inner struggle that was shaking him. She felt
deadly regret. Curling up in front of the fire to cook her
right side, she tried to comfort him:

"I swear I thought you already knew, darling. Otherwise I wouldn't have said anything, of course. . . . Anyway, it may not be true. I don't know for sure. I was told
about it and people are talking about it, but what does
that prove? . . . Come, you shouldn't get so upset over it.
If I were a man, I wouldn't give a damn about any woman!
High or low, women are all the same: not one of them has
any morals."

She attacked women out of self-abnegation, hoping to
lessen the cruelty of the blow. But he did not listen to
her, he did not hear her. He had managed to put on his
boots and overcoat in the midst of his disorderly movements. He wandered around for a few more moments, and
then, as though he had finally succeeded in finding the
door, he rushed out of the room. Nana was greatly annoyed.

"All right, then, good-by!" she said aloud, although she
was now alone. "He's polite when somebody's talking to
him! And I was doing my best to make him feel better!
I was the first one to be friendly again. I even apologized!
. . . And he'd been getting on my nerves!"

She was disillusioned nevertheless. Then, scratching her
legs with both hands, she came to a decision: "To hell
with him! It's not my fault if he's a cuckold!"

Roasted on all sides, warm as toast, she crawled into
bed, after ringing for Zoé to bring in the other man, who
had been waiting in the kitchen.

Outside, Muffat was walking violently. Another shower
had just fallen. His feet slipped on the wet pavement.
When he distractedly looked up, he saw ragged black
clouds scudding in front of the moon. At that hour there
were few people on the Boulevard Haussmann. He walked
alongside the scaffolding of the new opera house, seeking
darkness, muttering incoherent words. Nana had lied. She
had invented that story out of stupidity and cruelty. He
should have crushed her head when he had it beneath his
heel. It was too shameful! He would never touch or see her
again; he would be a vile weakling if he did. He breathed
deeply, as though relieved. Ah, that stupid, naked monster,
cooking like a goose, sullying everything he had respected

for forty years! The moon had reappeared and was now bathing the deserted street in white light. He was seized with fear and burst into sobs, suddenly frantic and overwhelmed with despair, as though he had fallen into an immense void.

"My God, it's over," he mumbled, "there's nothing left!"

A few belated people were hurrying along the boulevards. He tried to calm himself. The story Nana had told him kept running through his fevered mind. He tried to examine the facts logically. The Countess was supposed to come back from Madame de Chezelles' château in the morning. To be sure, there was nothing to prevent her from returning to Paris the evening before and spending the night with Fauchery. He now recalled certain details of their stay at Les Fondettes. One evening he had come upon Sabine under the trees, so agitated that she was unable to speak. Fauchery had been there. Why couldn't she be in his apartment now? The more he thought about it, the more possible it seemed to him. He finally began to consider it natural and inevitable. While he was taking off his overcoat in a harlot's apartment, his wife had been undressing in her lover's bedroom; nothing could have been simpler or more logical. As he reasoned thus, he made every effort to remain cool-headed. He had a sensation of falling amid a madness of the flesh that was spreading all around him and sweeping away his whole world. Warm images pursued him. A naked Nana suddenly evoked a naked Sabine. At this vision, which brought the two women together in a kinship of immodesty, in the same breath of desire, he stumbled. A cab nearly ran over him on the pavement. Some women who had just left a café brushed against him, laughing. He gave way to tears again, despite his efforts. Not wishing to sob in front of others, he plunged into a dark, empty street, the Rue Rossini, and wept like a child as he walked past the silent houses.

"It's all over," he said in a hollow voice; "there's nothing left, nothing left."

He was weeping so violently that he leaned against a door and buried his face in his wet hands. The sound of footsteps drove him away. He felt a shame and a fear that made him flee from others with the apprehensive tread of a night prowler. Whenever anyone passed him on the sidewalk, he tried to assume a casual gait, imagining that his story could be read in the swing of his shoulders. He had followed the Rue de la Grange-Batelière as far as the Rue du Faubourg-Montmartre. The bright lights surprised him and he retraced his steps. He wandered around the neighborhood for over an hour, always choosing the darkest spots. He no doubt had a goal toward which his feet were patiently going of their own accord, by a winding, roundabout path.

Finally, at a bend in a street, he looked up. He had arrived. He was at the corner of the Rue Taitbout and the Rue de Provence. It had taken him an hour to go there, absorbed in the painful roaring of his brain, when he could have gone there in five minutes. He remembered going to Fauchery's apartment one morning during the previous month to thank him for an article on the ball at the Tuileries in which the journalist had mentioned his name. The apartment was on the second floor, with little square windows half hidden behind the colossal sign of a shop. The last window on the left was divided by a streak of lamplight passing between the partly opened curtains. He stared intently at that bright line, waiting for something.

The moon had disappeared in a black sky from which an icy drizzle was falling. The clock of La Trinité struck two. The gaslights along the Rue de Provence and the Rue Taitbout were swallowed up by a yellow mist in the distance. Muffat did not move. That was the bedroom; he remembered it now: red cotton hangings, with a Louis XIII bed at the back. The lamp must be to the right, on the mantelpiece. They were no doubt in bed, for no shadows passed across the window, and the streak of light was as motionless as the glow of a night lamp. Still looking up, he formed a plan: he would ring the doorbell, go upstairs despite the concierge's protests, break open the doors with his shoulder, and fall upon them in bed, without giving them time to disengage themselves from each other's arms. For a moment he was stopped by the thought that he had no weapon, then he decided that he would strangle them. He turned his plan over in his mind and perfected it, still waiting for something, some sort of sign that would make him certain. If a woman's shadow had appeared at that moment, he would have rung the doorbell. But he was frozen by the idea that he might be mistaken. What would he say? Doubt returned to him: his wife couldn't be in that man's apartment, it was monstrous and impossible. But he stayed on, gradually overcome by numbness, sinking into languor as he continued that long wait filled with hallucinations by the fixity of his stare.

It began to rain again. Two policemen approached and he had to leave the doorway in which he had taken shelter. When they had disappeared down the Rue de Provence, he came back, wet and shivering. The window was still divided by the streak of light. He was about to leave at last when he saw a shadow pass. It was so rapid that he thought he might have been mistaken. But then other shadows quickly crossed the window one after another, giving an impression of hectic movement in the bedroom. Rooted to the sidewalk again, he had an unbearable burning sensation in his stomach as he waited to understand what was taking place. Outlines of arms and legs flitted across the window; an enormous hand slowly passed with the silhouette of a water jug. He could distinguish nothing clearly, but he thought he recognized a woman's chignon. He argued with himself: it looked like Sabine's hair, yet the back of the neck was broader than hers. By now he was exhausted, he was no longer sure of anything. His stomach was making him suffer so much, in that terrible anguish of uncertainty, that he leaned against the door to calm himself, shivering like a homeless outcast. Then, as he kept his eyes on the window in spite of everything, his anger was transformed into a moralistic fantasy: he saw himself as a deputy speaking before an Assembly, inveighing against debauchery, prophesying catastrophes; he retraced Fauchery's article on the poisonous fly, and dramatically declared that society was no longer possible with such Byzantine morals. This made him feel better. But the shadows had disappeared. The couple had no doubt gone back to bed. He went on watching and waiting.

Three o'clock struck, then four. He could not leave. Whenever it began raining again he would squeeze into one corner of the doorway, getting his legs wet. There were no more passers-by now. Occasionally his eyes would close, as though burned by the streak of light at which he had been staring with idiotic persistence. Twice more the shadows began moving again, repeating the same gestures, carrying the silhouette of the same gigantic water jug; and twice more everything became calm again while the lamp continued to glow discreetly. These shadows increased his doubt. Furthermore, an idea had soothed him by deferring the time for action: he merely had to wait until the woman came out. He could easily recognize Sabine. Nothing could be simpler: there would be no scandal and he would be certain. All he had to do was to stay where he was. Of all the confused feelings that had agitated him, he now had only a stubborn desire to know. But the boredom of standing in that doorway was beginning to make him drowsy. To occupy his mind, he tried to calculate how much longer he would have to wait. Sabine was supposed to be at the station at about nine o'clock. That gave him nearly four and a half hours. He was full of patience. He had no inclination to move; he even found it charming to imagine that his wait in the night would be eternal.

Suddenly the streak of light vanished. This simple event was an unexpected catastrophe for him, something unpleasant and disquieting. They had obviously put out the lamp and were going to sleep. It was only natural at such an hour. But he was irritated, because that dark window no longer interested him. He looked at it for another quarter of an hour, then it tired him, so he left the doorway and took a few steps along the sidewalk. He walked back and forth until five o'clock, occasionally looking up. The window remained dead. Now and then he wondered whether he had not merely dreamed that he saw shadows moving across those panes. He was overwhelmed by an immense weariness. He sometimes felt so dazed that he forgot what he was waiting for on that street. He would stumble against a paving stone and awake with a start and the cold shiver of a man who no longer knows where he is. Nothing was worth tormenting himself about. Since those people were sleeping, why not let them sleep? What was the sense of meddling in their affairs? It was very dark; no one would ever know anything about those things. And everything within him, even his curiosity, was swept away by a desire to get it all over with and seek relief somewhere. The cold was increasing and the street was becoming unbearable to him. Twice he walked away and then returned, dragging his feet. Finally he went further away than before. It was over, there was nothing more. He walked to the boulevard and did not return.

He wandered forlornly through the streets. He walked slowly, never changing his pace, keeping close to the walls. He heard only the sound of his footsteps, saw nothing except his shadow, which turned, swelled, and then shrank each time he passed a streetlamp. This lulled him, and occupied him mechanically. Afterwards he never knew where he had gone; it seemed to him that he had dragged himself around in a circle for hours. He had only one clear recollection: somehow he had found himself with his face pressed against the grille of the Passage des Panoramas, holding the bars with both hands. He was not shaking them, he was merely trying to see into the Passage, seized with an emotion that filled his whole heart. But he could distinguish nothing; shadows were flowing along the deserted gallery, and the wind that came in from the Rue Saint-Marc blew against his face with the dampness of a cellar. He stubbornly remained. Then, as though awakening from a dream, he suddenly felt surprised and wondered what he was seeking at that hour, pressing against the grille so violently that the bars had left their mark on his face. He began walking again in despair, his heart swollen with an ultimate sadness, as though he had been betrayed and doomed to remain alone forever in all that darkness.

Day broke at last, the dirty dawn of winter nights which is so melancholy on the muddy pavement of Paris. Muffat had returned to the broad streets that were being constructed along with the new opera house. Soaked by the rain and rutted by wagons, the chalky soil had been transformed into a lake of mire. Without looking where he stepped, he walked on, constantly slipping and recovering his balance. The awakening of Paris, with the teams of street cleaners and the first groups of workmen, brought him new agitation as the daylight brightened. People looked at him in surprise, with his wet hat, dirty clothes, and bewildered expression. For a long time he took refuge against the wooden fences among the scaffolding. His mind was empty except for a single thought: he was very miserable.

Then he thought of God. This sudden idea of divine aid, of superhuman consolation, surprised him as though it were something extraordinary and unexpected. It aroused in him the image of Monsieur Venot; he saw his fat little face and rotten teeth. Surely Monsieur Venot, whom he had been grieving for several months by avoiding his presence, would be glad if he knocked on his door and wept in his arms. God had always been merciful to him in the past. Whenever he had the slightest sorrow or encountered any obstacle in his life, he would go into a church, kneel, and humble himself before the Supreme Power; and he had always come out strengthened by prayer, ready to abandon the things of this world, desiring only his everlasting salvation. But now he observed religious practices only sporadically, whenever the fear of hell overcame him; he had given in to all sorts of laxity, Nana had upset all his duties. The idea of God astonished him. Why had he not thought of God immediately, at the beginning of that fearful crisis in which his weak human nature was cracking and collapsing?

Walking laboriously, he began looking for a church. He was disoriented, for the streets no longer looked the same to him at that early hour. Then, as he turned a corner of the Rue de la Chaussée-d'Antin, he saw a tower vaguely outlined in the fog at the end of La Trinité. The white statues overlooking the bare garden seemed to be so many chilly Venuses among the yellow leaves of a park. He stopped under the porch for a moment to catch his breath, tired from having ascended the broad steps. Then he entered.

The church was cold, its furnace having been extinguished the night before. Its lofty arches were filled with fine mist that had filtered in through the windows. The aisles were deep in shadows. Not a soul was inside. Nothing could be heard in that ominous darkness except the shuffling footsteps of a verger who was not yet thoroughly awake. After bumping against some scattered chairs, he fell to his knees beside the grille of a little chapel, near a holy-water basin. He felt lost, and his heart was bursting with tears. He clasped his hands and tried to pray. He longed to pour out his whole being to God, but his lips only stammered empty words; his mind kept slipping away, moving along the streets again without repose, as though lashed on by some implacable necessity. And he repeated, "O God, help me! O God, do not abandon your creature, who abandons himself to your justice! O God, I adore you, do not let me perish beneath the blows of your enemies!" He received no answer; the darkness and the cold weighed down upon his shoulders, the footsteps in the distance prevented him from praying. He still heard nothing except that irritating sound in the deserted church, which was not even swept out before the first Masses had warmed the air a little. He supported himself on a chair and rose to his feet, making his knees crack. God was not yet there. Why should he go and weep in Monsieur Venot's arms? That man could do nothing.

Without thinking what he was doing, he began walking back toward Nana's apartment. His feet slipped on the sidewalk. He felt tears coming into his eyes. He had no anger against fate; he was simply weak and ill. He had finally become too tired, he had been out in the rain too long, he was suffering too much from the cold. He was chilled by the thought of returning to his dark house on the Rue Miromesnil. The front door of Nana's building was not yet open; he had to wait until the concierge came. As he walked up the stairs he smiled, already pervaded by the gentle warmth of that nest in which he would be able to lie down and sleep.

When Zoé opened the door she made a gesture of amazement and anxiety. Madame had been kept awake all night by a terrible headache. However, she would go and see whether she had finally fallen asleep. She slipped into the bedroom while he sank down on a chair in the drawing room. Nana appeared almost immediately. She had leapt out of bed, scarcely taking time to put on a petticoat. She was barefooted, her hair was disheveled, and her chemise was rumpled and torn, in the disorder of a night of love.

"What! You again!" she cried, her cheeks turning red. She rushed forward, goaded by anger, to push him out the door herself. But when she saw him in such a pitiful state she felt sorry for him again. "Well, you're a fine sight!" she said more gently. "What's the matter? Have you been watching for them and getting yourself all upset?"

He did not answer. He looked like a stunned animal. She gathered, however, that he had not yet obtained any proof. "You see, I was mistaken," she said, to comfort him. "Your wife hasn't deceived you, take my word for it! . . . And now you must go home and get some sleep. You need it." He did not move. "Come on, you have to leave now. I can't keep you here. . . . You don't think you're going to stay here at this time of day, do you?"

"Yes, let's go to bed," he stammered.

She restrained a violent gesture. Her patience was almost gone. Was he losing his mind?

"Look, you have to leave now," she said again.

"No."

She flared up in rebellious exasperation: "This is disgusting! . . . I'm sick of you, get that into your head once and for all! Go find your wife; she's probably still in bed with Fauchery. Yes, she's deceiving you, I'm not going to hide it from you any more. There, are you satisfied? Now will you leave me alone?"

Muffat's eyes filled with tears. He clasped his hands. "Let's go to bed."

Nana lost her head. She herself was choked by convulsive sobs. He was going too far! Was it her fault that his wife was deceiving him? She tried to break the news to him as gently as possible, because she felt sorry for him. And now he wanted her to pay the damages! No! She had a big heart, but not that big!

"I've had enough, by God!" she swore, striking the furniture with her fist. "And to think I did my best to please you, I wanted to be faithful! . . . I could be rich tomorrow if I wanted to! All I have to do is say the word!"

He looked up in surprise. He had never thought about the question of money. He told her that she had only to express a desire and he would gratify it at once. His whole fortune was hers.

"No, it's too late now," she replied angrily. "I like men who give without being asked. . . . No, if you offered me a million francs for just one night, I'd refuse. It's all over,

I've got something else. . . . Go away, or I don't know what will happen. I'll do something terrible.

She moved toward him threateningly, in the exasperation of a good-natured girl who has been pushed too far, convinced that she was in the right, confident of her superiority over the respectable people who had been tormenting her. But suddenly the door opened and Steiner appeared. This was the last straw. She cried out furiously:

"Here's the other one! That's all I need!"

Steiner stopped, taken aback by the loudness of her voice. Muffat's unexpected presence annoyed him, for he was afraid of a scene that he had been carefully avoiding for the past three months. Without looking at the Count, he stood blinking his eyes and uneasily shifting his weight from one foot to the other. He was out of breath, and he had the red, distorted features of a man who had hurried all the way across Paris to bring a piece of good news, only to find that he had fallen into a catastrophe.

"And what do *you* want?" Nana asked him roughly, ignoring the Count.

"I . . . I . . ." he stuttered, "I've brought you . . . you know . . ."

"What?"

He hesitated. Two days earlier she had told him that she would no longer receive him unless he brought her a thousand francs, which she needed to pay off a note. For two days he had been going all over Paris in search of the money, and he had completed the sum only that morning.

"The thousand francs," he finally said, taking an envelope from his pocket.

Nana had forgotten.

"The thousand francs!" she cried. "Am I asking you for charity? Look, this is what I think of your thousand francs!"

She took the envelope and threw it in his face. Being a prudent Jew, he laboriously picked it up. He looked at her in bewilderment. Muffat exchanged a despairing glance with him. She put her hands on her hips and shouted more loudly than ever:

"I've taken enough insults from both of you! . . . I'm glad you came too," she said to Steiner, "because now my cleaning-up is going to be complete. . . . Come on, get out!" Then, when they both continued to stand still, paralyzed: "You think I'm being foolish? Maybe so, but you've annoyed me too much! I've had enough of trying to be a lady! If I starve, it's my own business."

They tried to calm her; they pleaded with her.

"One . . . two . . . You refuse to go? All right, then, look: I have company."

She abruptly threw open the door of her bedroom. The two men saw Fontan in the middle of the unmade bed. He had not expected to be shown thus: his legs were bare beneath his shirttail and he was sprawling on the rumpled lace like a goat, with his swarthy skin. He was not at all embarrassed, however, for he was used to the surprises of the stage. After the first shock, he extricated himself from the situation with honor: he "made his rabbit face," as he called it, thrusting out his lips, wrinkling his nose, and rapidly moving the entire lower half of his face. Looking like a roguish satyr, he seemed to exude vice from every pore. Like many other women of her kind, Nana was strongly attracted by the grimacing ugliness of a comedian; it was Fontan whom she had been going to meet at the Variety Theater for the past week.

"There!" she said, pointing to him with a dramatic gesture.

Muffat, who had accepted everything till now, rebelled against this affront. "You whore!" he cried.

Nana, having already gone into her bedroom, came back to have the last word: "You think *I'm* a whore? What about your wife?"

She slammed the door and noisily bolted it. The two men, left alone, looked at each other in silence. Zoé came in, but she did not rush them. She talked to them quite reasonably. As a sensible woman, she felt that Madame had behaved rather foolishly. She defended her, however: her mania for her actor wouldn't last long; the best thing would be simply to wait till she got over it. The two men left. They had not said a word. On the sidewalk, moved by a feeling of fraternity, they silently shook hands, then walked off in opposite directions, dragging their feet.

When Muffat finally returned to his house on the Rue Miromesnil, his wife was just arriving. They met on the great staircase, whose walls exhaled an icy chill. They looked up and saw each other. The Count was still wearing his muddy clothes, and his pale face had the dazed look of a man returning from vice. The Countess seemed to be sleepy, as though exhausted from having spent a night on the train; her hair had been carelessly combed and there were dark rings around her eyes.

8

$\mathcal{N}$ana and Fontan were living in a little fifth-floor apartment on the Rue Véron, in Montmartre. They had invited a few friends to share their Twelfth-Night cake. They had been there for only three days, and this was to be their housewarming.

It had all been done suddenly, without any definite idea of living together, in the first glow of their honeymoon. On the day after her big flare-up, when she had so vigorously rid herself of the Count and the banker, Nana had felt everything collapsing around her. She quickly sized up the situation: her creditors would invade her anteroom, interfere in her love affairs, and threaten to have all her belongings sold if she was not reasonable; she would have to go through endless arguments and annoyances in order to keep what little furniture she had. She preferred to let everything go. Anyway, she was sick of her apartment on the Boulevard Haussmann. It was stupid, with its big gilded rooms. In her infatuation with Fontan, she dreamed of a bright, pretty room, returning to the ideals she had held in the days when she earned a living by making artificial flowers and longed for nothing more than a rosewood wardrobe with a mirror on the door and a bed hung with blue ribbed fabric. In two days she sold all the knickknacks and jewelry she could take out, then disappeared with nearly ten thousand francs, without saying a word to the concierge. She succeeded in slipping away without leaving a trace. That way, no men would come and hang onto her skirts.

Fontan was very nice. He was quite willing to let her do as she pleased. He even acted in a spirit of true comradeship: he had seven thousand francs of his own, which he consented to add to her ten thousand, despite the fact that he was often accused of stinginess. This seemed to them a thoroughly adequate sum with which to set up housekeeping. And so they began, each drawing from the common fund in order to rent and furnish the small apartment on the Rue Véron, sharing everything like old friends. At first it was really delightful.

On Twelfth Night, Madame Lerat arrived before any of the others, with Louiset. Since Fontan had not yet returned, she ventured to express her fears, for she trembled to see her niece renouncing fortune.

"Oh, aunt, I love him so much!" cried Nana, prettily pressing her hands against her chest.

These words had an extraordinary effect on Madame Lerat. Her eyes moistened and she said with conviction, "You're right: love comes before everything else."

And she exclaimed over the attractiveness of the rooms. Nana showed her the bedroom, dining room, and kitchen. No, it wasn't an enormous place, but it had new paint and wallpaper, and the sun shone in cheerfully.

Then Madame Lerat kept Nana in the bedroom while Louiset went into the kitchen and stood behind the housekeeper to watch a chicken being roasted. She said she was venturing to make a few comments only because Zoé had just come to see her. Zoé was gallantly remaining in the breach, out of devotion to Madame. Madame would pay her later, she wasn't worried about that. In the disaster of the apartment on the Boulevard Haussmann, she was dealing with the creditors, carrying out a dignified retreat, saving what she could from the wreckage, answering that Madame was traveling, without ever giving an address. But, for fear of being followed, she had deprived herself of the pleasure of visiting Madame. That morning, however, she had hurried to see Madame Lerat, because there had been a new development. The day before, some of the creditors—the upholsterer, the coal dealer, the linen-draper —had come to offer Madame time, and even a sizable loan, if she would come back to her apartment and act like an intelligent person. Her aunt repeated Zoé's words. There was no doubt a gentleman behind it.

"Never!" Nana declared indignantly. "What a fine bunch of people they are! Do they think I'm going to sell myself to pay their bills? I'd rather starve than deceive Fontan."

"That's what I said," replied Madame Lerat. "I said, 'My niece has too much honor for that.'"

Nana was greatly displeased, however, to learn that La Mignotte was being sold and that Labordette was buying it for Caroline Héquet at a ridiculous price. It made her angry with that whole clique: they were nothing but whores, despite the airs they gave themselves. Ah, yes, she was worth more than all of them put together!

"They can laugh," she said, "but money will never give them real happiness. . . . Anyway, I don't even know whether all those people are alive or not—I'm too happy to think about them."

Just then Madame Maloir came in, wearing one of those strange hats that only she could make. She said it was a pleasure to see Nana and her aunt again. She explained that luxury intimidated her; now she would come back occasionally to play a game of bezique. The apartment was inspected a second time, and in the kitchen, in front of the housekeeper, who was basting the chicken, Nana spoke of economy; she said that a maid would have been too expensive, and that she wanted to take care of her home herself. Louiset was still staring blissfully at the roasting chicken.

There was a sound of voices. It was Fontan, with Bosc and Prullière. Dinner could now be served. The soup was already on the table when Nana showed off the apartment for the third time.

"Ah, you've got a very nice place here!" said Bosc, only because he felt obliged to please the friends who were paying for his dinner; actually, he was totally indifferent to the question of living quarters. In the bedroom, he exaggerated his affability still more. He had a very low opinion of women, and the idea that a man could burden himself with one of those nasty bitches fired him with the only indignation he was capable of feeling in the drunken disdain in which he enveloped the world.

"They did it on the sly, the rascals!" he said, winking. "Well, you were right. It'll be charming, and we'll come to see you, by God!"

When Louiset came in, riding a broomstick, Prullière said with a malicious laugh, "What! You've had a baby already?"

They all thought it was very funny. Madame Lerat and Madame Maloir were convulsed with laughter. Far from becoming angry, Nana smiled tenderly and said that unfortunately it wasn't true. She wished it were, for the boy's sake as well as hers; but some day she and Fontan might really have a baby of their own. Fontan, affecting goodnatured simplicity, took Louiset in his arms and began playing with him.

"Just the same," he said childishly, "he loves his new papa . . . Call me papa, you little scoundrel!"

"Papa . . . papa . . ." stammered Louiset.

Everyone covered him with caresses. Bosc, bored, suggested that they sit down to table; nothing else was serious. Nana asked to be allowed to have Louiset next to her. The dinner was very gay, although Bosc was irritated by having to defend his plate against Louiset. Madame Lerat bothered him too. She became tender and softly told him mysterious things, stories about wealthy gentlemen who were still pursuing her; and twice he had to move his knee away when she pressed hers against it, looking at him with misty eyes. Prullière behaved discourteously toward Madame Maloir: he never served her anything. He was concerned solely with Nana, and seemed to resent seeing her with Fontan. Besides, the two lovebirds were kissing each other so much that they were becoming annoying. Against all the rules, they had insisted on sitting beside each other.

"Why can't you two stop that and eat your dinner?" said Bosc, with his mouth full. "You've got plenty of time! Wait till we're gone."

But Nana could not restrain herself. She was in a rapture of love, blushing like a virgin, with smiles and looks overflowing with tenderness. She kept her eyes on Fontan and constantly called him affectionate names. Whenever he passed her the water or the salt, she would lean toward him and kiss him at random, on his eyes, his nose, or his ear; then, if someone scolded her, she would humbly lean back again and, with skillful tactics and the litheness of a beaten cat, slyly hold his hand and kiss it. She had to be touching some part of him. He assumed an air of self-importance and condescendingly allowed her to adore him. His big nose quivered with sensual pleasure. His goatish face, with its comically monstrous ugliness, glowed in the devout adoration of that superb girl, so white and plump. Occasionally he would kiss her in return, like a man who has all the enjoyment for himself but is still willing to behave considerately.

"You two are getting on my nerves!" cried Prullière. "Get out of there, you!" He pulled Fontan out of his chair beside Nana and sat down in it himself, after transferring his plate. There were exclamations, cheers, and a few indecent remarks. Fontan pretended to be in despair, with his amusing expression of Vulcan weeping for Venus. Prullière immediately began making advances to Nana, seeking her foot under the table, but she gave him a kick to make him stop. No, she certainly wouldn't go to bed with him. A month or so earlier, she had begun to feel attracted to him because of his handsome face, but now she detested him. If he pinched her again while pretending to pick up his napkin, she would throw her glass in his face.

However, the evening went off well. They naturally began talking about the Variety Theater. Wasn't that miserable Bordenave ever going to die? His nasty ailments had come back and were making him suffer so much that you couldn't get anywhere near him. The day before, he had shouted at Simonne all through the rehearsal. Nobody in his theater would be sorry to see him go! Nana said that if he offered her another part she would tell him to go to the devil. Besides, she was thinking of giving up the theater altogether; her home meant much more to her. Fontan, who was in neither the current play nor the one that was being rehearsed, also exaggerated the joy of having his complete freedom, and of spending all his evenings in front of the fire with Nana. The others called them lucky and pretended to envy their happiness.

The Twelfth-Night cake was cut. The bean fell to Madame Lerat, who put it into Bosc's glass. There were the traditional shouts of "The king drinks! The king drinks!" Nana took advantage of this outburst of gaiety to kiss Fontan on the neck and whisper in his ear. But Prullière, with the offended smile of a handsome man whose advances have been rejected, cried out that it wasn't fair. Louiset was asleep on two chairs. The guests did not leave until one o'clock in the morning, when they called out their final good-bys from the stairs.

For three weeks the two lovers had led a truly delightful life. Nana felt as though she had returned to those early days when her first silk dress had given her such great pleasure. She seldom went out, for she was now an advocate of solitude and simplicity.

Early one morning, as she was on her way to the Rochefoucault market to buy some fish, she was suddenly startled to find herself face to face with Francis, her former hairdresser. He was dressed with his usual correctness: fine linen, impeccable frock coat. She was ashamed to be seen by him in the street, wearing a morning wrap and old shoes, with her hair in disorder. But he was tactful enough to exaggerate his politeness still more. He did not take the liberty of asking her any questions, and pretended to believe that she had been traveling. Ah, Madame had made many people unhappy by deciding to travel! It was a loss for everyone. She finally began to question him, however, for her curiosity made her forget her first embarrassment. Since the crowd was jostling them, she drew him into a doorway, where she stood in front of him, holding her basket in her hand. What was being said about her little escapade? Well, the ladies he saw said this, that, and the other thing; in short, it had caused a great commotion and was a real success. And Steiner? Monsieur Steiner's fortune was at a very low ebb, and he was going to be in serious trouble unless he found some new enterprise. And Daguenet? Oh, Monsieur Daguenet was doing very well; he was settling down. Nana, excited by her memories, opened her mouth to question him again, but she was reluctant to utter Muffat's name. Francis smiled and spoke without prompting: as for Count Muffat, it was heartbreaking to see how much he had suffered after Madame's departure; he had been like a lost soul, wandering around all the places where Madame might be. Then finally Monsieur Mignon had met him and taken him home with him. This news made Nana laugh a great deal, but in a constrained manner.

"So he's with Rose now!" she said. "Well, you know, Francis, I don't care. . . . Oh, what a hypocrite! He got so used to it that he can't even do without it for a week! And he used to swear he'd never have another woman after me!" She was raging inwardly. "Rose has taken my leavings," she went on. "Well, she's gotten herself a fine playmate! Oh, I understand! She wanted to get even with me for taking that brute of a Steiner away from her. . . . She can be very proud of herself for getting a man after I've thrown him out of my apartment!!"

"Monsieur Mignon tells a different story," said the hairdresser. "According to him, it was the Count who sent you away. . . . And in a disgusting way, too, with a kick in the behind."

Nana turned deathly pale.

"What!" she cried. "A kick in the behind? That's too much! I practically threw him down the stairs, the cuckold! Yes, he's a cuckold, you must know that already—his wife deceives him with everybody, even with that dirty Fauchery. . . . And Mignon is still walking the streets to find men for that ugly wife of his! He must have a hard time, because she's so skinny that nobody wants her. . . . What filthy people! What filthy people!"

She was choking. She stopped to catch her breath, then continued: "So that's what they're saying! . . . Well, Francis, I'm going to pay them a little visit. . . . Would you like to go with me right now? Yes, I'll go to them, and then we'll see if they still have the nerve to talk about kicks in the behind. . . . Kicks! I've never taken that from anybody. And nobody will ever beat me, either, because I'd kill any man who touched me."

She finally calmed down. After all, they could say whatever they liked, they meant no more to her than the mud on her shoes. It would have dirtied her to bother with such people. Her conscience was clear. Seeing her giving vent to her feelings as she stood there dressed like a housewife, Francis adopted a tone of familiarity with her; before leaving he took the liberty of giving her some advice. She was foolish to sacrifice everything to an infatuation. Infatuations could ruin one's life. She listened, keeping her head bowed, while he spoke to her with a pained expression, as a connoisseur who was sorry to see such a beautiful girl wasting herself like that.

"That's my business," she said at last, "but thanks anyway, my friend."

She shook his hand, which was always a little greasy in spite of his immaculate attire. Then she went off to buy her fish. She kept thinking about that story of the kick in the behind for the rest of the day. She even talked about it to Fontan, again presenting herself as a proud woman who would never allow anyone to lay a finger on her. Fontan declared loftily that all high-society men were vile and ought to be despised. From then on, Nana was filled with genuine disdain.

That evening they went to the Théâtre-Italien to see a girl whom Fontan knew make her debut in a ten-line role. It was nearly one o'clock in the morning when they walked back to Montmartre. They had stopped on the Rue de la Chaussée-d'Antin to buy a mocha cake. They ate it in bed, because the apartment was cold and they did not want to bother lighting a fire. Sitting side by side with the covers over their waists and the pillows piled up behind their backs, they ate their supper and talked about the girl who had made her debut. Nana said she thought she was ugly and without charm. Fontan rolled over on his stomach and handed her another piece of the cake, which he had set down on the edge of the bedside table, between the candle and the matches. But they finally began to quarrel.

"Oh! How can you say that?" exclaimed Nana. "She has beady eyes and washed-out hair."

"Shut up!" said Fontan. "She has beautiful hair and sparkling eyes. . . . It's funny the way you women always tear each other to pieces!"

He seemed greatly annoyed.

"All right, that's enough!" he finally said roughly. "You know I don't like to argue. . . . Let's go to sleep, or there's going to be trouble."

And he blew out the candle. Nana, furious, went on talking: she wasn't going to be spoken to in that tone of voice, she was used to being respected. Since he did not answer, she had to stop. But she was unable to sleep; she kept turning over.

"Damn it! Will you stop moving around?" he shouted, suddenly sitting up.

"It's not my fault if there are crumbs," she said sharply.

There were indeed crumbs in the bed. She felt them even under her thighs and she was itching everywhere. One crumb was enough to give her a burning sensation and make her scratch herself till she bled. Besides, anyone ought to have sense enough to shake the covers after eating a cake in bed. Fontan, in a cold rage, lit the candle. They both got up. Barefooted and in their night clothes, they swept the crumbs off the sheet with their hands. Shivering, he got back into bed and told her to go to hell when she asked him to wipe his feet. She returned to her place, but she began writhing again as soon as she had lain down. There were still some crumbs left.

"I knew it!" she said. "You brought them back in on your feet. . . . I can't sleep like this! I can't!"

She started to crawl over him to get out of bed again. Exasperated and wanting to go to sleep, he slapped her so violently that she found herself lying down again, with her head on the pillow. She felt dazed.

"Oh!" she said simply, with a big, childish sigh.

He threatened to slap her again if she moved around any more. Then, after blowing out the candle, he lay down on his back and almost immediately began to snore. She buried her face in the pillow and sobbed gently. It was cowardly of him to take advantage of her strength. But his usually comical face had looked so terrible that she had been frightened. And her anger died away, as though the slap had calmed it. She respected him; she pressed up against the wall to give him as much room as possible. With her cheek tingling and her eyes full of tears, she finally fell asleep in such delightful dejection, in such weary submission, that she no longer felt the crumbs. When she awoke in the morning, she was holding Fontan tightly against her breasts with her bare arms. He would never do that again, would he? She loved him too much; it was even good to be slapped by him.

From then on, their life was different. Fontan now slapped her at the drop of a hat. She became accustomed to it and submitted. Sometimes she would scream and threaten him; but then he would back her against the wall and talk of strangling her, and this always made her tractable. She would usually fall onto a chair and sob for five minutes. Then she would forget it and become cheerful, singing, laughing, and filling the apartment with the rustle of her skirts as she hurried busily from one room to another. The worst of it was that Fontan now disappeared all day and never came home before midnight. He had begun going to cafés, where he met his friends. Nana tolerated everything, trembling and affectionate, fearing only that he might not come back if she ever reproached him. But on certain days, when she had neither Madame Maloir nor her aunt and Louiset with her, she was terribly bored. And so one Sunday when she was haggling over some pigeons at the Rochefoucauld market, she was delighted to meet Satin, who was buying a bunch of radishes. They had not seen each other since the evening when the Prince had drunk Fontan's champagne.

"What! Are you living in this neighborhood?" said Satin, amazed to see her in the street, wearing slippers, at that hour. "Oh, you poor girl, you must have run into some bad luck!"

Nana silenced her with a frown, because there were other women there, in dressing gowns, without linen, their hair straggling and white with lint. In the morning all the prostitutes in the neighborhood came to do their shopping almost as soon as they had rid themselves of the men they had picked up the night before. Their eyes were heavy with sleep and they dragged their feet in the ill-humor and fatigue of a night of annoyances. They came in from all the streets leading into the market, some of them pale, still young, and charming in their abandon; others old, fat, and flabby, not minding at all being seen like that outside of their working hours. Not one of them deigned to smile at the passers-by who turned to look at them; they all had the disdainful look of housewives for whom men no longer existed. While Satin was paying for her radishes, a young man, some belated clerk, said "Good morning, darling" as he passed. She drew herself up with the dignity of an offended queen and said, "What's the matter with that pig?"

Then she thought she recognized him. Three days earlier, as she was walking along the boulevard alone at about midnight, she had had to talk to him for nearly half an hour at the corner of the Rue Labruyère before he would make up his mind. But this only disgusted her all the more.

"It's so rude of them to shout things like that at you in broad daylight!" she said. "When a girl goes out shopping, she expects to be respected."

Nana had finally bought her pigeons, even though she had doubts about their freshness. Satin wanted to show her where she lived; it was not far away, on the Rue La Rochefoucault. And as soon as they were alone, Nana told her about her passion for Fontan. When they arrived in front of her house, Satin stood still with her radishes under her arm, fascinated by one last detail being related to her by Nana, who was lying in her turn, swearing that it was she who had driven Count Muffat out of her apartment with a kick in the behind.

"Oh, that's wonderful!" said Satin. "You kicked him out the door! And he didn't say anything, did he? They're such cowards! I wish I could have seen his face. . . . You're right, my dear. To hell with money! When I fall in love with a man, I'm willing to starve for him. . . . Well, you'll come and see me, won't you? It's the door on the left. Knock three times, because there are all kinds of people who come to bother me."

From then on, whenever Nana felt too bored she would go to see Satin. She was always sure to find her in, since she never went out before ten o'clock. Satin lived in a two-room apartment that a pharmacist had furnished for her in order to save her from the police; but in less than thirteen months she had broken the furniture, caved in the bottoms of the chairs, soiled the curtains, and spread such dirt and disorder that the apartment looked as though it were inhabited by a pack of mad cats. On mornings when she became so disgusted that she decided to do some cleaning, she struggled so violently with the filth that she was left with chair legs and shreds of curtains in her hands. On those days, everything looked even dirtier than usual, and it was impossible to enter the rooms because there were things blocking the doors. She was therefore beginning to abandon housework altogether. In the lamplight, the wardrobe, the clock, and what was left of the curtains were still enough to satisfy the men who came there. Anyway, her landlord had been threatening to evict her for the past six months, so why should she take care of the furniture? For his sake? No, thanks! Whenever she got up in a good mood, she would yell "Giddap!" and kick the sides of the wardrobe and the dresser until she had made another crack in them.

Nana nearly always found her in bed. Even on days when Satin went out to do some shopping, she was so tired when she returned that she would go back to sleep on the edge of the bed. During the day she dragged herself around, dozing on chairs, and did not come out of her languor until evening, when the gaslights were lit. And Nana felt quite at ease in her apartment, sitting there doing nothing in the midst of the basins lying on the floor, the unmade bed, and the muddy skirts taken off the night before and now soiling the chairs on which they had been tossed. She would talk endlessly and confidentially while Satin listened to her, sprawling on the bed in her nightgown with her feet higher than her head, smoking cigarettes. Sometimes, on afternoons when they were feeling dejected, they would treat themselves to absinthe to forget their sorrows, they said; without going downstairs or even putting on a petticoat, Satin would lean over the railing and shout down her order to the concierge's daughter, a girl of ten, who glanced furtively at the lady's bare legs when she brought the absinthe in a glass.

All their conversations eventually turned to the subject of the vileness of men. Nana was unbearable with her Fontan; she could not say a dozen words without repeating some account of what he had said or done. But Satin listened tirelessly and good-naturedly to those everlasting stories about waits at the window, quarrels over a burned stew, and reconciliations in bed after hours of sulking. Nana had a need to talk about it; she told Satin about all the slaps she had received: last week he had given her a black eye, only last night he had knocked her against the bedside table because he couldn't find his slippers. And Satin showed no surprise; she went on smoking her cigarettes, pausing only to say that she always ducked, which made the man spin around with his slap. They would both settle down happily to exchanging stories of blows, lulled by the constant repetition of the same idiotic incidents, yielding to the warm lassitude of the ignoble beatings they were talking about. It was the enjoyment of discussing Fontan's blows again, of describing him, even to the way he took off his boots, that brought Nana back every day, especially since Satin always responded with stories of her own, some of them even more violent, such as that of a pastry cook who used to leave her unconscious on the floor, and whom she loved anyway.

Then there were days when Nana cried and said she couldn't stand it any longer. Satin would accompany her to her door and stay outside in the street for an hour or so to see that he did not murder her. And the next day the two women would enjoy the reconciliation all afternoon, although, without admitting it, they preferred days when there were beatings in the air, because that excited them more.

They became inseparable. Satin never went to see Nana, however, because Fontan had declared that he didn't want any whores in the apartment. They often went out together, and it was thus that Satin one day took her friend to see Madame Robert, a woman Nana had been thinking about with a certain respect ever since she had refused to come to her supper party. Madame Robert lived on the Rue Mosnier, a new and silent street in the Europe quarter, without a single shop, whose handsome houses, with their narrow little apartments, were inhabited by ladies. It was five o'clock; the broughams of merchants and stock-market speculators were parked alongside the nearly deserted sidewalks, in the aristocratic peace of the tall white houses, and men were hurrying past, looking up at the windows, where women in negligees seemed to be waiting.

At first Nana refused to go up, saying stiffly that she didn't know that lady. But Satin insisted. It was always permissible to bring a friend. She merely wanted to pay a social call: Madame Robert had been very nice to her when she had met her in a restaurant the day before and had made her swear that she would come to see her. Nana finally gave in. Upstairs, a sleepy little maid told them that Madame had not yet come back. She showed them into the drawing room, however, and left them there.

"My God, what a beautiful place!" said Satin. It was a severe, bourgeois apartment, hung with dark fabrics, in the conventional taste of a Parisian shopkeeper who has retired after making his fortune. Nana, impressed, made a joking remark, but Satin angrily answered for Madame Robert's virtue. She was always seen holding the arm of some solemn elderly gentleman. For the moment, she had a former confectioner, a serious-minded man. He was so delighted by the splendid appearance of the house that he always had himself announced when he came, and called her "my child."

"Look, there she is," said Satin, pointing to a photograph placed in front of the clock.

Nana studied the portrait for a few moments. It showed a very dark woman with a long face and a discreet smile. She looked like a fashionable lady, with more reserve than most.

"It's funny," Nana said, "I'm sure I've seen that face somewhere before. Where? I can't remember, but I don't think it was in a respectable place. . . . Oh, no, it wasn't in a respectable place!" She turned to her friend. "So she made you promise to come to see her? What does she want with you?"

"What does she want with me? Why, I suppose she just wants to talk. . . . It's only politeness."

Nana stared at Satin, then clicked her tongue. After all, what did it matter to her? However, since Madame Robert still had not come, she declared that she would not wait any longer. They left.

The next day, since Fontan had told her he would not be home for dinner, she went to see Satin early to take her out for a good meal in a restaurant. Choosing the restaurant involved a great deal of discussion. Satin suggested several that Nana thought were abominable. They finally decided to go to Laure's, a fixed-price restaurant on the Rue des Martyrs, where dinner cost three francs.

Tired of waiting until it was time for dinner, and not knowing what to do on the sidewalk, they went into Laure's twenty minutes early. The three rooms were still empty. They sat down at a table in the room where Laure Piedefer was enthroned on a high seat behind the counter. This Laure was a lady of fifty whose swelling contours were tightly held in check by belts and corsets. Women began arriving one after another, each one leaning over the saucers to kiss Laure on the mouth with tender familiarity, while the moist-eyed monster tried to divide her attentions in such a way as to make no one jealous. The waitress, however, was a tall, thin, pockmarked woman whose eyes, beneath their dark lids, flashed somber fire as she served the ladies.

The three rooms rapidly became full. There were nearly a hundred women seated wherever they could find a place for themselves. Most of them were somewhere around forty, with fat bodies, slack hips, and faces puffy with vice. And amid these bulging breasts and bellies, there were a few pretty, slender girls whose faces still looked guileless, despite the effrontery of their gestures. They were beginners who had been picked up in dance halls by some of Laure's customers and brought to her establishment, where a multitude of fat women, excited by the smell of their youth, crowded around them and anxiously paid court to them like old bachelors, buying them delicacies. As for the men, they were few in number: ten or fifteen at most. Except for four of them who had come to see the sight and were joking in a thoroughly relaxed manner, they all maintained a humble attitude in the overwhelming flood of skirts.

"The food is good here, isn't it?" said Satin.

Nana nodded, satisfied. It was the old-fashioned, solid dinner of a provincial hotel: meat pie, chicken with rice, beans with gravy, and vanilla cream with caramel sauce. The ladies were particularly fond of the chicken with rice; they ate until they almost burst their corsets, and slowly wiped their lips. At first Nana was afraid of meeting former friends who might ask her stupid questions, but she finally stopped worrying when she saw no one she knew among that motley crowd in which faded dresses and tattered hats were to be seen side by side with elegant costumes, in the fraternity of the same perversions. For a moment she was interested by a young man with blond, curly hair and an insolent face who was sitting at a table with a group of fat women, all breathlessly eager to satisfy his slightest whim. But when the young man laughed, his chest bulged. Nana could not hold back a little cry. "Why, it's a woman!" she exclaimed.

Satin, who was stuffing herself with chicken, looked up

and said, "Ah, yes, I know her. . . . She's very popular. They're all after her."

Nana grimaced in disgust. She couldn't understand that yet. However, she said in a reasonable tone that there was no use arguing about tastes, because you never knew what you might like some day. And she ate her vanilla cream with a philosophical air. She saw clearly that Satin, with her big, blue, virginal eyes, was causing a great stir among the women at the neighboring tables. There was, in particular, a buxom blond who was doing her best to be charming. She was aglow with excitement, and her behavior was so forward that Nana was on the point of intervening.

But then she was surprised by a woman who had just come in. She had recognized Madame Robert. The latter, with her dark, pretty, mouselike face, nodded familiarly to the tall, thin waitress, then leaned over Laure's counter. They kissed each other a long time. Nana found this very odd on the part of such a distinguished woman, especially since Madame Robert no longer had her modest air—quite the contrary. She glanced around the room, talking in a low voice. Laure sat down again with the majesty of an old idol of vice, her face worn and polished by the kisses of the faithful. Above the full plates, she reigned over her bloated clientele of fat women, monstrous in comparison with even the largest of them, enjoying the fortune that had rewarded forty years of labor.

Madame Robert noticed Satin. She left Laure and hurried over to Satin's table. She graciously told her how sorry she was that she had not been at home the day before. When Satin, charmed, insisted on making a little room for her, she swore she had already had her dinner. She had merely come to take a look around. As she stood behind her new friend, she leaned on her shoulders, smiling and affectionate. "When shall I see you?" she said. "If you were free . . ."

Unfortunately, Nana was not able to hear any more. The conversation annoyed her; she was dying to give that "respectable" woman a piece of her mind. But she was paralyzed by the sight of a group that had just entered. It was composed of fashionable women, wearing elegant dresses and diamonds, who all addressed Laure familiarly. Having relapsed into a perverse inclination, they had come there together, parading their three hundred thousand francs' worth of jewelry, to eat a three-franc dinner amid the jealous astonishment of poor, shabby prostitutes. When they had come in, talking and laughing loudly, giving the impression that they had brought in sunshine from the outside, Nana had quickly turned her head, greatly upset at having recognized Lucy Stewart and Maria Blond among them. For nearly five minutes, during the whole time when they were talking with Laure before going into the next room, she kept her head lowered, apparently absorbed in rolling bread crumbs across the tablecloth. Then, when she was finally able to turn around, she was stunned: the chair beside her was empty, Satin had disappeared. "Where could she be?" she said aloud.

The buxom blond, who had overwhelmed Satin with her attentions, laughed ill-humoredly. When Nana, irritated by her laughter, gave her a threatening look, she said indolently, "You can see *I* didn't run off with her—it was the other one."

Realizing that she would only be laughed at, Nana said nothing. She remained sitting for a few moments, not wanting to show her anger. From the next room she could hear Lucy Stewart talking loudly as she entertained a whole table of girls who had come from the dance halls of Montmartre and La Chapelle. It was hot. The waitress was taking away piles of dirty plates that smelled strongly of chicken and rice. The four gentlemen were pouring fine wine for half a dozen couples in the hope of getting them drunk and hearing some obscene stories. What now exasperated Nana was that she had to pay for Satin's dinner. What a bitch she was to let her take her out to dinner, then run off with the first woman who came along, without even saying thank you! It was only three francs, of course, but she hated to have to pay it after such a dirty trick. She threw the six francs to Laure, whom she now despised more than the mud in the gutters.

On the Rue des Martyrs, Nana felt her rancor growing still more intense. She certainly wasn't going to run after Satin—she wouldn't go anywhere near such a vile creature! But her evening was ruined. She slowly walked toward Montmartre, enraged above all against Madame Robert. That woman had her nerve to pretend to be a distinguished lady! She was about as distinguished as a garbage dump! Nana was now sure she had met her at the Papillon, a foul dance hall on the Rue des Poissonniers, where men could have her for thirty sous. And yet she hooked government officials with her modest ways, and refused to accept the honor of an invitation to supper because she wanted to give the impression that she was a model of virtue! Oh, she had her virtue all right! It was always those prudes who had wild orgies in sordid places that no one knew about.

Thinking over these things, Nana reached her apartment on the Rue Véron. She was amazed to see that there was a light burning inside. Fontan had come home in a bad humor, for he had also been abandoned by the friend who had taken him to dinner. He coldly listened to the explanations Nana gave him. Afraid of being beaten, and dismayed at having found him there when she had not expected him before one o'clock in the morning, she lied to him. She admitted having spent six francs, but she said she had been with Madame Maloir. He remained dignified and handed her a letter addressed to her, which he had calmly opened. It was from Georges, who was still a prisoner at Les Fondettes, relieving himself each week in burning pages.

Nana loved receiving letters, especially those which contained vows and impassioned declarations of love. She usually read them to everyone. Fontan knew Georges' style and appreciated it. But that evening she was so afraid of a scene that she pretended to be indifferent; she glanced over the letter with a gloomy expression and threw it aside. Fontan was drumming his fingers against a window pane, not wanting to go to bed so early and not knowing how to occupy his evening. Suddenly he turned to Nana and said, "Why don't we answer him right away?"

It was usually he who wrote. He took pride in his style. And he was always happy when Nana, enraptured by hearing his letter read aloud to her, kissed him and cried out that no one else could think up such things to say. It would finally excite them, and they would adore each other.

"As you like," she replied. "I'm going to make some tea. We can go to bed afterward."

Fontan sat down at the table after methodically laying out his pen, ink, and paper. He rounded his arm and thrust his chin forward. " 'My darling heart,' " he began, reading the words aloud.

And he worked diligently for over an hour, polishing his phrases, occasionally reflecting with his head between his hands, laughing to himself whenever he found a tender expression. Nana had drunk two cups of tea in silence. Finally he read the letter, as one reads in the theater, in a toneless voice, with gestures. He spoke, in five pages, of "the delightful hours spent at La Mignotte, those hours whose memory lingers like a subtle perfume," he swore "eternal fidelity to that springtime of live," and he ended by declaring that his sole desire was "to renew that happiness, if happiness can be renewed."

"I'm saying all that out of politeness," he explained. "As long as it's just for fun . . . Yes, I think I did a good job on this one!"

He gloated. But Nana, still wary, made the awkward mistake of not throwing her arms around his neck with an exclamation of joy. She said she thought the letter was very good, but that was all. He was offended. If she didn't like his letter, she could write one herself; and instead of kissing as they usually did, after stirring up words of love, they sat coldly on opposite sides of the table. Meanwhile she had poured him a cup of tea.

"What did you do to this stuff?" he cried when he had taken a sip of it. "You must have put salt in it!"

Nana had the misfortune to shrug her shoulders. He became furious.

"Ah, everything's going wrong tonight!"

And the quarrel started from there. It was a way of killing time, for it was only ten o'clock. He worked himself up, flinging all sorts of insults and accusations at Nana, without letting her defend herself. She was dirty, she was stupid, she had a disgusting past. Then he vehemently launched into the question of money. Did *he* spend six francs when he went out to dinner? No, unless somebody else paid for his dinner he ate at home. And for that old pimp Maloir, too! He was going to throw her out the next time she came around! Oh, they'd go far if they both threw six francs out the window like that every day!

"I'm going to find out how things stand now!" he

shouted. "Give me the money so I can see how much is left."

All his base miserliness came to the surface. Nana, subdued and terrified, hastened to bring the money from the desk drawer. Until then, the key had remained on the common cashbox, from which they had both drawn freely.

"What!" he exclaimed after counting the money. "There's less than seven thousand francs left out of the seventeen thousand, and we've been together only three months. . . . That's impossible!"

He rushed over to the desk, pulled out the drawer and examined it under the lamp. It was true: there was only six thousand eight hundred and some-odd francs. Then the storm burst.

"Ten thousand francs in three months!" he bellowed. "Good God, what did you do with it? Answer me! It all goes to that filthy aunt of yours, doesn't it? Or else you've been paying men to go to bed with you, that's clear. . . . Come on, answer me!"

"There's no use losing your temper," said Nana. "It's easy to figure out. You're forgetting about the furniture; and then I had to buy some linen. Money goes fast when you have to buy everything for a new apartment."

But although he demanded explanations, he would not listen to them.

"Yes, it goes too fast," he said more calmly. "Look, I'm tired of having everything in common. You know this seven thousand francs belongs to me. Well, since I've got it, I'm going to keep it. I don't want to be ruined. What's mine is mine, and what's yours is yours." He authoritatively put the money in his pocket. Nana stared at him, dumbfounded. He went on serenely: "I'm not stupid enough to support aunts and children that aren't mine. . . . You wanted to spend your money and that was your own business, but you're not going to touch *my* money! . . . Whenever you cook a roast, I'll pay for half of it. We'll settle up every night."

Nana was shocked. She could not prevent herself from crying out, "You had your share of my ten thousand francs! That's a dirty trick!"

But he did not waste any more time on discussion. He

leaned over the table, slapped her with all his might and said, "Let's hear that again!"

She repeated her statement in spite of his slap and he fell upon her, kicking her and hitting her with his fists. He soon put her into such a state that she ended, as usual, by undressing and going to bed, sobbing, while he caught his breath. He was about to go to bed also when he noticed the letter he had written to Georges lying on the table. He carefully folded it, facing the bed, and said theateningly. "It's a very good letter. I'm going to mail it myself, because I don't want you to get any funny ideas. . . . And stop whining, you're getting on my nerves."

Nana, who had been weeping with little sighs, held her breath. When he was lying beside her, she felt as though she were choking. She threw herself on his chest and began sobbing again. Their fights always ended this way; she trembled at the thought of losing him, she had an ignoble need to know that he belonged to her, in spite of everything. Twice he pushed her away with a haughty gesture. But finally a flame of desire was kindled in him by the warm embrace of that woman who was begging him with the big, tearful eyes of a faithful animal. He became magnanimous, though without lowering himself to the point of making any advances. He allowed himself to be caressed and taken by force, like a man whose forgiveness is worth earning. Then he was seized with anxiety: he was afraid Nana might be only putting on an act in order to get back the key to the cashbox. When he had blown out the candle, he felt a need to reassert his will.

"I meant what I said about the money. I'm going to keep it."

Nana, who was falling asleep with her arms around his neck, made a sublime reply: "Yes, don't worry . . . I'll work."

But from that evening on, their life together became more and more difficult. From one end of the week to the other, the sound of slaps seemed to regulate their existence like the ticking of a clock. The many beatings she received gave her the suppleness of fine linen. Her skin became still softer to touch, and took on such delicate shades of pink and white that she was more beautiful than ever. Prullière began ardently pursuing her. He came at times when

Fontan was not there, and pushed her into corners to kiss her. But she always resisted indignantly, blushing with shame; she found it disgusting that he should want to deceive a friend. Prullière would laugh resentfully. She was really becoming stupid! How could she stay with such a monkey? For Fontan was a real monkey, with that big nose of his always moving up and down. What an ugly face he had! And he was constantly beating her, too!

"Maybe so, but I love him the way he is," she answered one day, with the tranquillity of a woman admitting a revolting taste.

Bosc contented himself with having dinner there as often as possible. He shrugged his shoulders behind Prullière's back: a handsome man, but not at all serious. Bosc had witnessed several of the couple's quarrels. When Fontan slapped Nana during dessert, he would go on chewing gravely, finding it perfectly natural. To pay for his dinner, he always went into raptures over their good fortune. He proclaimed himself a philosopher; he had given up everything, even glory. Prullière and Fontan would sometimes lean back in their chairs before the cleared table and tell each other about their successes until two o'clock in the morning, with their stage voices and gestures, while Bosc sat lost in thought and silently finished the bottle of cognac, occasionally sniffing disdainfully. What was left of Talma*? Nothing, so why didn't they shut up? It was too stupid!

One evening he found Nana in tears. She took off her jacket to show him her bruised arms and back. He looked at her skin without being tempted to take advantage of the situation, as that idiot Prullière would have done, then said sententiously, "My girl, where there are women there are blows—I think it was Napoleon who said that. . . . Wash yourself with salt water, it's excellent for those little bruises. They won't be the last. As long as nothing gets broken, don't complain. . . . I'm inviting myself to dinner, you know; I saw a leg of mutton."

But Madame Lerat did not share his philosophy. Each time Nana showed her a new bruise on her white skin, she cried out in protest. Fontan was killing her niece; things

* François-Joseph Talma (1763–1826), famous French actor. (Translator's note.)

couldn't go on like that. He had put Madame Lerat out of his apartment and told her he never wanted to see her again; since that day, each time she was there when he came in, she had to leave by the kitchen door, which humiliated her terribly. And so she never stopped inveighing against that brutal man. She reproached him above all with having bad manners; and whenever she spoke of this she took on the expression of a respectable lady who knew all there was to know about good breeding.

"Oh, it's easy to see," she said to Nana. "He has no sense of what's proper. His mother must have been a common woman. No, don't try to deny it, it's obvious. . . . I'm not talking for myself, although a woman my age has a right to be respected. . . . But you, really, how can you put up with his bad conduct? I don't want to boast, but I always taught you how to behave, and you got the very best advice at home. We were all well-bred in our family, weren't we?"

Nana did not protest; she listened with her head bowed.

"And you knew only refined people," her aunt went on. "I was talking about that with Zoé only yesterday, at home. She doesn't understand either. She said to me, 'After Madame had a distinguished man like the Count under her thumb'—because, just between you and me, I hear you used to drive him crazy—'how can she let herself be beaten up by that ugly clown?' I told her it was possible to put up with slaps, but that I'd never have tolerated a lack of respect. . . . There's nothing good about him. I wouldn't have him in my bedroom for anything in the world! And you're ruining yourself for a miserable lout like that! Yes, you're ruining yourself, darling, you're at the end of your rope, and yet there are plenty of rich men around, and men high up in the government. . . . That's enough; I shouldn't be the one to tell you these things. But if I were you, the next time he tried one of his dirty tricks I'd cut the ground from under him by saying, 'Just who do you think I am?' in that haughty tone of yours, and then I'd walk out on him."

Nana burst into tears and sobbed, "Oh, aunt, I love him!"

The truth was that Madame Lerat was worried because Nana was now scarcely able to give her a one-franc coin now and then to pay for little Louis' board and lodging. She would go on sacrificing herself, of course; she would keep the child anyway and wait for better times. But the thought that Fontan was preventing her, Nana, and Louis from rolling in wealth enraged her so much that she denied love. And so she concluded with these stern words: "Listen, some day when he's taken the skin off your back, you'll come and knock on my door, and I'll let you in."

Money soon became Nana's great worry. Fontan had made the seven thousand francs disappear; he no doubt had it in a safe place, and she would never have dared to question him, for she was timid with that miserable lout, as Madame Lerat called him. She was afraid he might think her capable of staying with him because of his money. He had promised to provide for the needs of the household. At first he gave her three francs every morning. But as soon as he began to pay, he became exacting; he wanted everything for his three francs: butter, meat, early vegetables, and fruit. If she ventured to make a comment, if she insinuated that it was impossible to buy a whole market for three francs, he flew into a rage and called her a worthless, wasteful fool who let herself be cheated by all the tradesmen; and he was always ready to threaten to move out.

Then, after a month had gone by, there were mornings when he forgot to leave the three francs on the dresser. She had taken the liberty of asking for it, shyly and in a roundabout way, but there had been such violent quarrels, and he had made life so hard for her on the slightest pretext, that she had preferred not to count on him. Whenever he had not left the three francs and yet found food waiting for him when he came home, he became amorous and happy as a lark; he would kiss her and dance with the chairs. And this made her so happy that she began hoping not to find anything on the dresser, despite the difficulty she had in making both ends meet. One day she even gave him back his three francs, telling him that she still had the money he had given her the day before. Since he had given her nothing the day before, he hesitated for a moment, fearing she was trying to teach him a lesson. But she looked at him with eyes full of love and kissed him in an absolute gift of her whole person; he put the money in his pocket with the convulsive little quiver of a miser recovering a sum he has nearly lost. From then on he never worried, never asked where the money had come from. He looked glum when there were potatoes and laughed joyously when there was a turkey or a leg of mutton, although this did not prevent him from slapping her now and then, even in his happiness, just to keep himself in practice.

Nana had found a way of paying for everything. On certain days the apartment was packed with food. Bosc had indigestion twice a week. One afternoon when Madame Lerat was leaving, furious at seeing a copious dinner on the fire and knowing she would not eat any of it, she could not help asking bluntly who was paying for it. Nana, taken off guard, stared at her foolishly and began to cry.

"Well, that's a fine state of affairs!" said her aunt, who had understood.

Nana had resigned herself in order to enjoy peace in her home. And then it was the fault of old Tricon, whom she had met on the Rue de Laval one day when Fontan had gone off in a rage because of a dish of codfish. So she had said yes to Tricon, who happened to be in a difficulty at the time. Since Fontan never came home before six o'clock, she was free every afternoon, and she brought back forty to sixty francs, sometimes more. She could have been making many times that much if she had kept her former situation, but she was now glad simply to have enough to keep the pot boiling. At night she forgot everything when Bosc was stuffing himself with food, and Fontan, sitting with his elbows on the table, allowed himself to be kissed on the eyes with the superior air of a man who is loved for himself alone.

And so, while still adoring her darling Fontan with a passion that was all the more blind because she was now paying for everything, Nana fell back into the mire of her beginnings. She roamed the sidewalks as she had done in the days when she was a ragged little wench in search of a five-franc coin. One Sunday at the Rochefoucauld market she had made her peace with Satin, after rushing up to her and furiously reproaching her for having gone off with Madame Robert. Satin had merely replied that if one did not like something, that was no reason for trying to make others become disgusted with it. Nana, being broad-minded, and having accepted the philosophical idea that one never knew how one might end up, had forgiven her. Her curiosity was aroused and she even questioned her about some details of vice, amazed at learning something new at her age, after everything she knew already. She laughed and exclaimed, finding it funny, although at the same time she felt a certain repugnance, for at heart she had a bourgeois attitude toward anything to which she was not accustomed. She began eating at Laure's whenever Fontan went out for dinner. She was amused by the stories of love and jealousy that so greatly interested the other women there, though without ever making them miss a mouthful. Fat Laure, with her motherly tenderness, often invited her to spend a few days in her villa at Asnières, a country house in which there were bedrooms for seven ladies. Nana always refused, for she was afraid. But when Satin swore that she was mistaken, that gentlemen from Paris swung the women in swings there and played outdoor games with them, she promised to come later, as soon as she could get away.

At that time Nana was worried and in no mood for gay amusements. She had to get some money. When Tricon did not need her, which happened too often, she did not know where to go. She and Satin would then wander along those muddy Paris side streets where low vice prowls beneath the murky gaslights. Nana returned to the dance halls on the outskirts of Paris where she had first shaken her dirty petticoats; she again saw the dark corners of the outer boulevard, the posts against which men had kissed her when she was fifteen, while her father was looking for her to give her a hiding. The two women hurried along, stopping at all the dance halls and cafés in a neighborhood, climbing stairs damp with saliva and spilled beer; or else they walked quietly along the streets and stood in doorways. Satin, who had made her start in the Latin Quarter, took Nana to Bullier and the cafés along the Boulevard Saint-Michel. But vacation time was approaching and the quarter was too poor. They always returned to the main boulevards. It was there that they had the most luck. From the heights of Montmartre to the flat-lands of the Observatory, they covered the whole city.

Rainy evenings when their shoes wore down, warm evenings that made their dresses stick to their skin, long waits, endless walks, jostling and quarrels, the last brutalities of a passer-by who had been led into some wretched furnished room and came swearing down the slippery stairs.

Summer was drawing to a close; it had been a stormy summer, with hot nights. They would go off together after dinner, toward nine o'clock. Along the sidewalks of the Rue Notre-Dame de Lorette, two lines of women, keeping close to the shops, their petticoats tucked up and their faces turned down, were busily hurrying toward the boulevards without glancing at the window displays. It was the famished descent from the Bréda neighborhood, in the first glow of the gaslights. Nana and Satin passed by the church and always went along the Rue Le Peletier. Then, a hundred yards from the Café Riche, having reached the parade ground, they lowered their skirts, which they had been carefully holding up. From then on, disregarding the dust, sweeping the sidewalks with the hems of their dresses, they walked with little steps, swaying their hips, and they slowed down still more whenever they came into the flood of light from some large café. Holding their heads high, laughing loudly, and glancing back at the men who turned to look at them, they were in their element. In the shadows, their whitened faces, spotted by the red of their lips and the black of their eyebrows, took on the disquieting charm of a cheap Oriental bazaar in the open street. Until eleven o'clock, amid the jostling of the crowd, they remained cheerful, merely muttering "Stupid fool!" now and then behind the backs of the awkward men who stepped on their skirts; they exchanged familiar little greetings with the café waiters, stopped to talk in front of a table, accepted drinks which they sipped slowly, glad to sit down and wait until the people began coming out of the theaters.

But as the night advanced, if they had not made one or two trips to the Rue La Rochefoucauld, they became ill-tempered and more determined in their hunt for men. Beneath the trees along the boulevards, which were now becoming dark and deserted, they bargained fiercely, and sometimes there were angry oaths and blows, while respectable fathers with their wives and daughters, accustomed to such encounters, calmly walked past without quickening their pace. Then, after having gone back and forth a dozen times between the Opera and the Gymnase, when the men had begun to grow scarce and were walking more swiftly through the deepening darkness, Nana and Satin stuck to the sidewalks of the Rue du Faubourg-Montmartre. There, the lights of restaurants, beer houses, and delicatessens blazed until two o'clock, and swarms of women lingered around the doors of the cafés. It was the last lighted and living corner of nocturnal Paris, the last open market for one-night bargains, where business was transacted crudely among the groups, from one end of the street to the other, as in the open hall of a brothel. And on nights when they returned empty-handed, they quarreled with each other. The shadows of women moved slowly along the dark and deserted Rue Notre-Dame de Lorette; it was the belated return of the poor prostitutes of the neighborhood, exasperated by a night of fruitless wandering, refusing to give up yet, still arguing in hoarse voices with lost drunks whom they were detaining at the corner of the Rue Bréda or the Rue Fontaine.

However, there were occasional windfalls: twenty-franc coins given by elegant gentlemen who put their decorations in their pockets as they climbed the stairs. Satin, especially, had a keen nose. On humid nights when the wet city gave off the stale odor of a vast, dirty alcove, she knew that this muggy weather, this fetid smell of sordid corners, would drive the men into a frenzy of desire. She could see it in their pale eyes as she watched for the best-dressed ones. It was like a fit of carnal madness passing over the city. She was a little afraid, for those who seemed the most respectable were always the most filthy-minded. All the outer polish would vanish and the beast would appear, demanding in his monstrous tastes, refining his perversions. And so Satin, prostitute though she was, had little respect for anyone; she would burst into angry exclamations in front of men in carriages, saying that their coachmen were nicer, because they respected women and didn't half kill them with weird ideas.

The sight of fashionable people falling into the cesspool of vice still surprised Nana, who had retained certain prejudices that Satin was destroying. As she said when she talked seriously, there was no virtue left in the world. From the highest to the lowest, everyone was wallowing in sensuality. There must have been some fine things going on in Paris between nine in the evening and three in the morning! She laughed and said that if she could look into all the bedrooms she would see some funny sights: poor people going at it for all they were worth, and quite a few rich people sticking their noses into filth more deeply than the others. She was completing her education.

One evening when she came to call for Satin she saw the Marquis de Chouard coming down the stairs. His legs were so unsteady that he was leaning heavily on the railing, and his face was white. She pretended to blow her nose. Upstairs she found Satin amid her usual dirt and disorder: the apartment had not been touched for a week, the bed was soiled and there were pots lying around everywhere. She expressed surprise that Satin should know the Marquis. Oh yes, she knew him! He had made a terrible nuisance of himself when she and her pastry cook were together. Now he came back from time to time. But she couldn't stand him, he was always sniffing in dirty places, even in her slippers.

"That's right, in my slippers! . . . Oh, he's a filthy old man! He always asks for things. . . ."

What most disturbed Nana was the sincerity of this base debauchery. She recalled the comedies of pleasure she had engaged in while she was still enjoying her success; but she now saw the prostitutes around her slowly dying of it every day. And Satin made her horribly afraid of the police. She was full of stories about them. For a time she had gone to bed with a policeman of the vice squad in order to be left alone; he had twice saved her from being officially registered as a prostitute. She now trembled, for her case would be clear if she were arrested again. She talked endlessly on the subject. The police got a bonus for each woman they arrested, she said, so they arrested as many as they could. They grabbed every woman in sight and silenced them with slaps if they cried out, because they were sure of being upheld and rewarded, even if they had taken in a respectable girl along with the rest. In summer they made raids on the boulevard in groups of twelve or fifteen. They would surround a sidewalk and get as many as thirty women in one evening. Satin knew the places, however; as soon as she caught sight of the policemen she would run away in the middle of the wild rush of long skirts fleeing through the crowd. The terror of the law and the prefecture of police was so great that some of the women would stand as though paralyzed in the doorways of cafés while the raid swept down the street. But Satin was even more afraid of informers. Her pastry cook had been nasty enough to threaten to report her to the police when she left him. Yes, there were men who lived off their mistresses by that means, and then there were those dirty women who would turn you in out of sheer treachery, if you were prettier than they.

Nana listened to these stories with growing fear. She had always trembled before the law, that unknown power, the vengeance of men that could crush her without anyone in the world coming to her defense. She looked on the Saint-Lazare prison as a tomb, a black hole in which women were buried alive after having their hair cut off. She told herself that she could have protectors if she gave up Fontan, and Satin told her that the police were forbidden to touch certain women whose names and photographs were kept on file, but none of this reassured her: she was still afraid, she could still see herself being roughly dragged off to jail and forced to submit to a medical examination the next day; and the thought of that medical examination filled her with anguish and shame, despite the fact that she had so often cast all modesty to the winds.

One night toward the end of September when they were walking along the Boulevard Poissonnière, Satin suddenly began to run. When Nana questioned her she said breathlessly, "The police! Hurry!"

There was a wild rush through the crowd. Skirts flapped and were torn. There were blows and cries. One woman fell. The bystanders laughed as they watched the brutal onslaught of the policemen, who were rapidly narrowing their circle. Nana had lost sight of Satin. Her legs were failing her. She was about to be arrested when a man took her by the arm and led her past the furious policemen. It was Prullière, who had just recognized her. Without speaking, he guided her into the Rue Rougemont, which was now deserted, and there she was able to catch her breath. She felt so faint that he had to hold her up. She did not even thank him.

"Look, you'd better come up to my place for a while," he said at length.

He lived nearby, on the Rue Bergère. But she immediately drew herself up and said, "No, I won't."

"You go to bed with everyone else," he said coarsely, "so why not with me too?"

"Because."

To her mind, this said everything. She loved Fontan too much to betray him with one of his friends. The others didn't count, as long as it gave her no pleasure and she did it from necessity. In the face of this stupid obstinacy, Prullière reacted with the spitefulness of a handsome man whose vanity has been wounded.

"Well, do as you please," he said. "Only I'm not going your way, my dear. You're on your own."

And he abandoned her. Her fear returned. She made an enormous detour to return to Montmartre, walking swiftly past the shop windows, turning pale whenever a man approached her.

The next morning, still shaken by her terrors of the day before, Nana was on her way to see her aunt when she found herself face to face with Labordette at the end of a quiet little street in Les Batignolles. At first they both seemed embarrassed. Still as obliging as ever, he was on some errand that he did not reveal. He was the first to recover his composure, however. He expressed pleasure at having run into her, and told her that everyone was still amazed by her disappearance. People were always asking for her, her old friends were longing to see her again. He ended by giving her a fatherly little sermon:

"Frankly, my dear, you're making a fool of yourself. . . . I can understand an infatuation, but I can't see why any woman should let herself be robbed of all her money and get nothing but slaps in return! Are you trying to win a prize for virtue?"

She listened to him with an embarrassed expression. But when he spoke of Rose, who was triumphing in her conquest of Count Muffat, her eyes flashed and she murmured, "Oh, if I wanted to . . ."

He obligingly offered his services as a mediator. She refused. He then attacked her on another point: he informed her that Bordenave was going to produce a play written by Fauchery in which there was a magnificent part for her.

"What!" she exclaimed in surprise. "A play with a part in it for me? Why, he's in it and he's never said a word to me about it!"

She did not name Fontan. She immediately became calm, however. She would never return to the theater. Labordette was apparently not convinced, for he insisted with a smile:

"You know you have nothing to fear with me. I'll prepare your Muffat, you'll come back to the theater, and I'll lead him to you by the hand.

"No!" she said forcefully.

And she left him. She was deeply moved by her own heroism. No brute of a man would ever sacrifice himself like that, without making a big fuss about it. Yet she was struck by one thing: Labordette had just given her exactly the same advice as Francis. When Fontan came home that evening, she questioned him about Fauchery's play. He had been back at the Variety Theater for two months. Why hadn't he told her about the part?

"What part?" he said gruffly. "You're not talking about the part of the great lady, are you? Ah, you must think you have a lot of talent! That part is completely out of your class. . . . You make me laugh!"

Her feelings were terribly hurt. He made fun of her all evening, calling her "Mademoiselle Mars." And the more he attacked her, the more bravely she held firm, savoring a kind of bitter enjoyment in that heroism of her infatuation, which made her very great and very loving in her own eyes. Ever since she had begun selling herself to other men in order to feed him, she loved him all the more, with all the fatigue and disgust she brought back with her. He had become her vice, which she paid for and could not do without, beneath the goading of his slaps. Seeing her so docile, he had begun to abuse his power. She got on his nerves. He was seized with such a ferocious hatred of her that he forgot his own interests. Whenever Bosc made a remark to him he would cry out, with an exasperation that no one understood, that he didn't give a damn about her and her good dinners, that some day he would throw her out just so he could give his seven thousand francs to another woman. And that was how their affair ended.

One night when Nana came home at eleven o'clock, she found the door bolted. She knocked. No answer. She knocked again. Still no answer. But she saw light under the door and heard Fontan walking around inside. She went on knocking tirelessly, angrily calling to him. At last she heard him say slowly and deliberately, "Go to hell!"

She pounded on the door with both fists.

"Go to hell!"

She pounded still harder, with all her might.

"Go to hell!"

And for a quarter of an hour these same words answered her like a jeering echo of the blows with which she shook the door. Then, seeing that she would not give up, he suddenly opened the door, stood on the threshold with his arms crossed and said in the same coldly brutal tone, "Stop it, God damn it! What do you want? Go away and let us sleep! Can't you see I've got company?"

True enough, he was not alone. Nana saw the girl from the Théâtre-Italien, already in her nightgown, with her tousled, tow-colored hair and beady eyes, laughing in the midst of the furniture that she, Nana, had paid for. Fontan stepped forward with a terrifying look on his face, opening his big fingers like pincers.

"Get out of here or I'll strangle you!"

She sobbed convulsively, then became frightened and ran down the stairs. This time it was she who was being thrown out. In her rage, she suddenly recalled Muffat; but it certainly wasn't Fontan who should have done the same to her.

When she reached the sidewalk, her first thought was to go and spend the night with Satin, if there was no one with her. She met her in front of her house. She, too, had been thrown out: her landlord had just put a padlock on her door, against all legal right, for the furniture was hers. She swore, and spoke of having him taken before the commissary of police. In the meantime, since it was now midnight, she had to think of finding a bed. Judging it prudent not to involve the police in her affairs, she took Nana to a little hotel on the Rue de Laval. They were given a narrow room on the second floor with a window overlooking the courtyard.

"I could have gone to Madame Robert's," said Satin. "She always has room for me. . . . But with you it's out of the question. She's so jealous she's silly. The other night she beat me."

When they were in their room, Nana, who had not yet given vent to her feelings, burst into tears and told about Fontan's dirty trick again and again. Satin listened sympathetically and tried to console her. She finally became even more indignant than Nana, and began denouncing men.

"Oh, the pigs! The pigs! . . . You shouldn't have anything more to do with those pigs!"

She then helped Nana to undress, hovering around her like a considerate, submissive little woman. "Let's go to bed right now, darling," she said. "We'll be more comfortable. . . . Oh, you're so silly to be upset! They're all pigs! Don't think about them any more. . . . You know I like you. Stop crying, do that for your little darling."

As soon as they were in bed, she took Nana in her arms to calm her. She refused to hear Fontan's name; each time it came to Nana's lips she stopped it there with a kiss and a pretty little angry pout. Her hair hung loosely around her shoulders and she had a childish, tender beauty. Little by little, in that soft embrace, Nana dried her tears. She was touched; she began returning Satin's caresses. At two o'clock, the candle was still burning. They were both laughing softly and uttering words of love.

But suddenly there was an uproar in the hotel. Satin got up, half naked, and put her ear to the door.

"The police!" she said, turning pale. "What bad luck, damn it! We're done for!"

She had repeatedly told Nana about the raids the police made in hotels, yet neither of them had been wary that night when they took refuge on the Rue de Laval. On hearing the word "police," Nana lost her head. She leapt out of bed, ran across the room and opened the window like a madwoman about to jump out. But fortunately the little courtyard had a glass roof that was covered by a metal grating on a level with the floor of the room. She did not hesitate: she stepped out of the window and disappeared into the darkness with her chemise flying and her thighs exposed to the night air.

"Stop!" said Satin, alarmed. "You'll kill yourself!"

Then, since there was already a knock at the door, she good-naturedly closed the window and tossed her friend's clothes into a wardrobe. She resignedly told herself that, after all, if they registered her she would no longer have that miserable fear. Pretending to be half asleep, she yawned, parleyed, and finally opened the door to a big man with a dirty beard who said to her, "Let me see your hands. . . . You don't have any needle marks, so you don't work. Come on, get dressed."

"But I'm not a seamstress, I'm a burnisher," Satin declared boldly.

But she obediently got dressed, knowing that there was no use arguing. By now there were cries coming from all over the hotel. One girl was clutching the doors, refusing to walk; another, in bed with a lover who vouched for her respectability, was protesting indignantly and threatening to sue the prefect of police. For nearly an hour there were sounds of heavy shoes on the stairs, of doors shaken by hammering fists, of shrill quarrels suddenly stifled by sobs, of skirts rustling against the walls, of the whole abrupt awakening and frenzied departure of a troop of women brutally routed out by three policemen under the direction of a blond, very polite little commissary.

No one had betrayed Nana; she was safe. She groped her way back into the bedroom, shivering and almost dead with fright. Her bare feet were bleeding, torn by the iron grille. She sat on the edge of the bed for a long time, still listening. Toward morning, however, she fell asleep. When she awoke at eight o'clock she fled from the hotel and hurried to her aunt's house. Madame Lerat was having her coffee with Zoé. When she saw Nana at that hour, looking so bedraggled and upset, she understood immediately.

"Ah, so it's finally happened!" she said. "I told you he'd take the skin off your back. . . . Well, come in, you're always welcome here."

Zoé stood up and said with respectful familiarity, "You've come back to us at last, Madame . . . I was waiting for you."

Madame Lerat wanted Nana to go in and kiss Louiset

at once, because, she said, his mother's good sense was a great stroke of good luck for him. Louiset was still asleep, sickly and anemic. When Nana leaned over his pale, scrofulous face, all her troubles of the past few months took her by the throat and choked her.

"Oh, my poor baby, my poor baby!" she stammered in a final fit of sobbing.

9

The Little Duchess was being rehearsed at the Variety Theater. The first act had just been straightened out and they were about to begin working on the second. Sitting in old armchairs on the proscenium, Fauchery and Bordenave were discussing something while the prompter, old Cossard, a little hunchback, sat on a straw-bottomed chair, looking over the script with a pencil between his lips.

"Well, what are you waiting for?" Bordenave suddenly bellowed, furiously pounding the floor with his thick cane. "Barillot, why haven't they begun?"

"It's because of Monsieur Bosc: he's disappeared," replied Barillot, who was acting as assistant stage manager.

There was a storm of shouts: everyone called Bosc and Bordenave swore.

"God damn it! It's always the same! It doesn't do any good to ring the bell, they're never where they're supposed to be. . . . And then they grumble when they're kept after four o'clock!"

Bosc finally arrived with noble serenity.

"Yes? What do you want with me? Ah, it's time for me to make my entrance! Why didn't you say so? . . . All right, Simonne gives me my cue: 'The guests are arriving,' and I come in. . . . Where do I come in?"

"Through the door, of course," Fauchery said irritably.

"Yes, but where's the door?"

This time Bordenave directed his anger against Barillot, and once more began swearing and pounding the floor with his cane.

"God damn it! I told you to put a chair there to represent the door! The same things have to be done all over again every day. . . . Barillot? Where's Barillot? Another one! They all keep running away!"

Barillot brought in the chair, however, bowing beneath the tempest in silence. And the rehearsal began. Simonne, wearing a hat and a fur coat, made the movements of a maid arranging furniture. She interrupted herself to say, "I'm chilly, so I'm going to leave my hands in my muff." Then, changing her voice, she greeted Bosc with a little exclamation: "Ah! It's the Count! You're the first to arrive, Count. Madame will be very pleased."

Bosc was wearing a pair of muddy trousers, a big yellow overcoat, and an enormous scarf. With his hands in his pockets and an old hat on his head, he said slowly in a dull voice, not taking the trouble to act, "Don't disturb your mistress, Isabelle. I want to surprise her."

The rehearsal continued. Sprawling in his armchair, Bordenave scowled and listened wearily. Fauchery kept nervously changing his position, constantly tempted to interrupt but always controlling himself in time. He heard someone whispering in the dark, empty auditorium behind him.

"Is she here?" he asked, leaning toward Bordenave.

The producer nodded. Nana had wanted to see the play before accepting the role of Géraldine that had been offered to her, for she hesitated to play the part of a loose woman again. She had been dreaming of playing the part of an honest woman. She was hiding in the shadows of a box with Labordette, who had been acting as intermediary between her and Bordenave. Fauchery cast a glance in her direction, then turned his attention back to the rehearsal.

Only the proscenium was lighted. A gas jet on a support, fed by a pipe connected to the footlights, was burning in front of a reflector which directed all its light onto the front of the stage; it looked like a big yellow eye in the semidarkness, where it blazed with sordid sadness. Beside the slender support, Cossard was holding up the script to see it more clearly in the light, which made his hump stand out sharply. Bordenave and Fauchery were almost lost in the darkness. Only a small area in the middle of the enormous structure was lighted by a feeble glow like that of a lantern hung on a post in a railroad station. The actors looked like grotesque phantoms, with their shadows dancing behind them. The rest of the stage was filled with smoke, and suggested a house being torn down or a church nave fallen into ruin. It was littered with ladders, frames, and scenery flats whose faded paint gave them the appearance of piles of rubbish; and the backdrops hanging in the air were like tattered garments suspended from the rafters of some gigantic second-hand clothing store. Immediately under the ceiling, a sunbeam coming in through a window cut the darkness like a bar of gold.

At the back of the stage, some actors were talking while waiting for their cues. They had gradually raised their voices.

"Keep quiet back there!" howled Bordenave, angrily leaping up from his chair. "I can't hear a word! Go outside if you want to talk, the rest of us have work to do. . . . Barillot, if there's any more talking I'll fine everybody!"

They were silent for a time. They formed a little group, sitting on a bench and some rustic chairs in one corner of a garden, the first scene of the evening, which was waiting there, ready to be put into place. Fontan and Prullière had been listening to Rose Mignon, who had recently received a magnificent offer from the manager of the Folies-Dramatiques. A voice rang out:

"The Duchess! . . . Saint-Firmin! . . . Come on, the Duchess and Saint-Firmin!"

Only after the second call did Prullière remember that he was Saint-Firmin. Rose, who played the part of Duchess Hélène, was already waiting to make her entrance with him. Slowly, dragging his feet on the bare, resonant boards, old Bosc came back to sit down. Clarisse offered him half of the bench.

"Why is he yelling like that?" she said, referring to Bordenave. "He'll be unbearable before long. . . . He can't hold a rehearsal any more without having a nervous breakdown."

Bosc shrugged his shoulders. He was above all those storms. Fontan murmured, "He smells a fiasco already. This play seems idiotic to me." Then, addressing Clarisse, he returned to Rose's story: "Do you believe she really got that offer from the Folies-Dramatiques? Three hundred francs a night, with a guarantee of a hundred performances! Why not a country house into the bargain? If anyone offered his wife three hundred francs a night, Mignon would drop Bordenave like a hot potato!"

Clarisse believed in the three hundred francs. That Fontan was always running down his friends! But Simonne interruped them. She was shivering. With their coats buttoned up and scarves around their necks, they all looked at the sunbeam that shone without descending into the dismal cold of the stage. It was freezing outside, beneath a clear November sky.

"And there's no fire in the greenroom!" said Simonne. "He's getting to be so stingy it's disgusting. . . . I've got half a mind to leave: I don't want to catch a cold."

"Quiet!" thundered Bordenave.

For several minutes, nothing was heard but the confused recitation of the actors. They scarcely indicated their gestures, and spoke most of the time in even tones to avoid tiring themselves. Whenever they did emphasize a point, however, they glanced at the auditorium. It was filled with vague shadows that were like fine dust floating in a high, windowless barn. Lighted only by the dim glow from the stage, it seemed to be wrapped in melancholy, disquieting sleep. The paintings on the ceiling were drowned in opaque darkness. Broad pieces of gray canvas descended from the stage boxes on either side to protect the hangings. Strips of cloth were also draped over the velvet of the balustrades, girdling the galleries with a double shroud, staining the shadows with their pallid hues. In the general decolorization, the various levels of the auditorium were outlined only by the red velvet of the seats, which now looked black, and the dark recesses of the boxes. The great chandelier had been completely lowered. It filled the orchestra with its pendants and gave the impression that the auditorium had been deserted, that the public had gone off on a journey from which it would never return.

Rose, in her role as the little Duchess who had found herself in the house of a loose woman, walked toward the footlights. She raised her hands and pouted adorably at the dark, empty auditorium, which was as sad as a house in mourning.

"Good heavens, what strange people!" she said, stressing the phrase, certain of producing an effect.

From the back of the box in which she was hiding, Nana, wrapped in a big shawl, listened to the play and devoured Rose with her eyes. She turned to Labordette and said softly, "Are you sure he'll come?"

"Quite sure. He'll probably come with Mignon, to have a pretext. . . . As soon as he arrives, you'll go up to Mathilde's dressing room and I'll bring him to you there."

They were speaking of Count Muffat. Labordette had arranged for a meeting on neutral ground. He had had a serious talk with Bordenave, whose financial situation was very bad after two successive failures. Bordenave had therefore hastened to lend his theater and offer a part to Nana, wishing to get on good terms with the Count, for he was hoping to borrow money from him.

"And what do you think of the part of Géraldine?" asked Labordette.

Nana sat motionless and made no reply. In the first act, the author had established that the Duke de Beaurivage was receiving his wife with Géraldine, a blond musical-comedy star. In the second act, Duchess Hélène went to the actress's house, on a night when there was a masked ball, to find out by what power such women were able to capture and hold the husbands of virtuous ladies. A cousin of hers, the handsome Oscar de Saint-Firmin, had brought her there in the hope of debauching her. And, to her surprise, as a first lesson she heard Géraldine berating the Duke in coarse language while he listened with docility and apparent delight. This caused her to exclaim, "Ah, if that's the way men ought to be talked to! . . ." Géraldine had scarcely any other scene in the act. As for the Duchess, she was soon punished for her curiosity: an old rake, the Baron de Tardiveau, assuming that she was also a loose woman, began making vigorous advances to her while, on the other side, Beaurivage was making peace with Géraldine by kissing her, stretched out beside her on a chaise longue. Since the part of Géraldine had not yet been assigned, old Cossard was reading it. He was also acting it out against his will, for he had to represent Géraldine in Bosc's arms. They had reached this scene and the rehearsal was dragging along dully when Fauchery suddenly leapt up from his chair.

"You've got it all wrong!" he shouted.

The actors stopped, their arms hanging at their sides.

Fontan wrinkled his nose and asked in his sneering way, "Who's got it all wrong?"

"Everybody! You're not doing it right at all, not at all!" said Fauchery, gesticulating and pacing up and down the floor. Then he began acting out the scene himself. "Now, you, Fontan, you must understand Tardiveau's excitement; you lean forward like this, to take hold of the Duchess. . . . And you, Rose, that's when you make your move, quickly, like this. But not too soon, not till you hear the kiss . . ." He interrupted himself and cried out to Cossard in the heat of his explanations: "Géraldine, give the kiss. . . . Loud! It has to be heard clearly!"

Old Cossard turned to Bosc and smacked his lips energetically.

"Good, there's the kiss!" Fauchery said triumphantly. "Once again, the kiss . . . You see, Rose, I had time to make my move, and now I exclaim, 'Ah! He kissed her!' But, for that, Tardiveau must go upstage. . . . Do you hear, Fontan? You go upstage. . . . Now, let's try it again, and all together."

The actors went through the scene again; but Fontan played his part with such ill will that the whole thing was even worse than before. Fauchery had to repeat his instructions twice, demonstrating the motions more heatedly each time. They all listened to him glumly, looking at one another for an instant as though he had asked them to walk upside down. They awkwardly tried again, but stopped almost immediately, with the stiffness of puppets whose strings have been broken.

"It's too much for me, I can't understand it," Fontan finally said in his insolent tone.

Bordenave had not opened his mouth. He had slid so far down in his chair that only the top of his hat, pulled over his eyes, was visible in the murky glow of the gaslight. His cane lay across his stomach. He looked as though he might be asleep. Suddenly he sat up.

"My friend, it's stupid," he calmly said to Fauchery.

"What do you mean, it's stupid?" cried the author, turning pale. "You're stupid yourself, my friend!"

Bordenave began to lose his temper. He repeated the word "stupid," tried to think of something stronger, and hit upon "idiotic" and "asinine." The audience would hiss, the act would never be finished. Fauchery was exasperated, although he was not offended by the harsh language that was always used between them when they rehearsed a new play. He bluntly called Bordenave a fool. The producer lost all self-control. He swung his cane through the air, snorted like a bull, and shouted, "Shut up, God damn it! We've wasted a quarter of an hour on this stupidity! That's right, stupidity! It doesn't make sense. . . . And yet the whole thing is actually quite simple. You, Fontan, don't move. Rose, make a little movement like this, no more, then come forward. . . . Now, do it right this time. Give the kiss, Cossard."

Confusion followed. The scene went no better than before. Bordenave also began acting out the movements with the grace of an elephant, while Fauchery sneered and shrugged his shoulders disdainfully. Then Fontan tried to impose his opinion, and even Bosc ventured to give his advice. Rose, exhausted, had finally sat down on the chair that marked the location of the door. No one knew what he was doing any more. To make matters still worse, Simonne mistakenly thought she had heard her cue and made her entrance in the midst of the disorder. This so enraged Bordenave that he swung his cane in a wide arc and struck her on the behind with it. During rehearsals he often dealt out blows to the women with whom he had gone to bed. She ran away, pursued by this furious cry: "You had it coming, by God! And if anybody else annoys me I'll shut down the whole show!"

Fauchery had put on his hat as though he were about to leave the theater. He came back when he saw Bordenave sit down, streaming with perspiration. He, too, resumed his place in the other chair. They sat side by side for a time, without moving, while a heavy silence fell over the shadowy theater. The actors waited for nearly two minutes. They were all weak, as though they had just performed some overwhelming task.

"All right, let's go on," Bordenave finally said in his ordinary voice, perfectly calm.

"Yes, let's go on," said Fauchery. "We'll straighten out the scene tomorrow."

They stretched out in their chairs and the actors began rehearsing again with the same boredom and indifference.

During the quarrel between the producer and the author, Fontan and the others had enjoyed themselves at the back of the stage, sitting on the bench and the rustic chairs, laughing softly, grunting, and making ferocious remarks. But when Simonne came back, choked with tears, after Bordenave had struck her on the behind with his cane, they became dramatic and said that in her place they would have strangled the old pig. She wiped her eyes and nodded; she was going to walk out on him, especially since Steiner had offered to set her up only the day before. Clarisse was surprised: the banker no longer had a sou to his name; but Prullière laughed and reminded her of the way in which that clever Jew had displayed himself with Rose in order to get his Landes salt works going on the stock market. And he was now airing another project: a tunnel under the Bosporus. Simonne listened with great interest. As for Clarisse, she had been angry for the past week. That damned La Faloise, whom she had gotten rid of by pushing him into Gafa's venerable arms, was about to inherit the fortune of a very rich uncle! It was just her luck: she was always too early or too late. And then that dirty Bordenave had given her a miserable little part of no more than fifty lines, as though she couldn't have played Géraldine! She was still dreaming of the part, and hoping Nana would refuse it.

"And what about me?" Prullière said stiffly. "I have less than two hundred lines. I wanted to turn it down. . . . It's an insult to make me play that Saint-Firmin! And what a play, my friends! It's going to fall flat."

Simonne, who had been talking with old Barillot, came back and said breathlessly, "Nana's out front!"

"Where?" Clarisse asked quickly, standing up to see.

The news spread swiftly. Everyone leaned forward. For a moment the rehearsal almost came to a standstill. Then Bordenave emerged from his immobility and shouted, "What the matter with you? Finish the act! . . . And keep quiet back there, we can't go on with all that noise!"

Nana was still watching the play from her box. Labordette had tried to talk to her twice, but she had impatiently nudged him with her elbow to silence him. The second act was nearly over when two shadows appeared at the back of the theater. As they were tiptoeing toward the stage, Nana recognized Mignon and Count Muffat. They went up to Bordenave and greeted him silently.

"Ah, there they are!" she murmured with a sigh of relief.

Rose spoke the final words of the act. Bordenave said the whole second act would have to be repeated before they went on to the third. Abandoning the rehearsal, he welcomed the Count with exaggerated politeness while Fauchery pretended to give all his attention to the actors who were grouped around him. Mignon was whistling with his hands behind his back, looking tenderly at his wife, who seemed nervous.

"Well, shall we go upstairs?" Labordette asked Nana. "I'll take you to the dressing room, then I'll come back and get him."

Nana left her box immediately. She had to grope her way along the ground-floor corridor. But Bordenave caught sight of her as she was hurrying through the shadows. He caught up with her at the end of the corridor behind the stage, a narrow passage in which the gaslights were kept burning night and day. There, in order to settle the matter quickly, he began talking enthusiastically about the part of Géraldine.

"What a part! It has such style! It's made for you. . . . Why don't you come and rehearse tomorrow?"

Nana remained cold. She wanted to know what the third act was like.

"Oh, the third act is wonderful! The Duchess acts like a loose woman at home, and that disgusts Beaurivage and teaches him a lesson. Then there's a very funny mix-up when Tardiveau comes in, thinking he's at a dancer's house. . . ."

"And what does Géraldine do in all that?" interrupted Nana.

"Géraldine?" said Bordenave, a little embarrassed. "She has a scene; it's not very long, but it's excellent. . . . I tell you it's made for you! Will you sign?"

She stared at him. Finally she answered, "We'll see, later."

And she rejoined Labordette, who was waiting for her on the stairs. Everyone in the theater had recognized her. They were all whispering; Prullière was shocked by her return, Clarisse was worried about the part. As for Fontan, he pretended to be coldly indifferent; it would not have been proper for him to say anything against a woman he had loved. At the bottom of his heart, in his former infatuation that had turned to hatred, he still fiercely resented her devotion, her beauty, and the life together that he had finally come to detest through a perversion of his monstrous tastes.

When Labordette came back and approached the Count, Rose Mignon, alerted by Nana's presence, understood everything at once. Muffat bored her, but the thought of being abandoned like that was more than she could bear. She broke the silence she usually maintained with her husband concerning such things and said to him bluntly, "You see what's going on? If she tries the Steiner trick again, I'll scratch her eyes out!"

Mignon, calm and haughty, shrugged his shoulders like a man who sees everything.

"Be quiet!" he said. "Do me a favor and keep your mouth shut."

He knew what to expect. There was no use counting on Muffat any longer: he was obviously ready to lie down at Nana's feet whenever she said the word. It was impossible to fight against such a passion. And so, knowing what men were like, his only thought was to get as much as he could out of the situation. He would have to see. For the moment, he was waiting.

"Come on, Rose!" shouted Bordenave. "We're doing the second act again."

"Go on," said Mignon. "Leave it to me."

Then, still sarcastic in spite of everything, he found it amusing to compliment Fauchery on his play. It was a very good play, only why was the great lady so virtuous? It wasn't natural. He sneered and asked who had been the model for the Duke de Beaurivage, Géraldine's worn-out old lover. Far from becoming angry, Fauchery smiled. But Bordenave, glancing at Muffat, seemed annoyed. Mignon was struck by this and became serious again.

"Let's begin, for God's sake!" bellowed the producer. "Come on, Barillot. . . . What? Bosc isn't here? Is he trying to make a fool of me?"

Bosc, however, soon walked in calmly. The rehearsal began again just as Labordette was leading the Count away. Muffat was trembling at the idea of seeing Nana again. After their separation he had felt a great emptiness; he had let himself be taken to Rose, at a loss for anything better to do, thinking he was suffering only from the change in his habits. In his state of shock, he wanted to forget everything. He forbade himself to look for Nana, and avoided all discussion with the Countess. It seemed to him that his dignity required him to strive for this forgetfulness. But forces were still at work within him and Nana slowly reconquered him, by memories, by the weaknesses of his flesh, and by new feelings that were exclusive, tender, and almost paternal. The abominable scene faded away; he no longer saw Fontan, no longer heard Nana ordering him to leave, taunting him with his wife's adultery. All that was nothing but fleeting words, whereas he continued to feel something gripping his heart more and more tightly, causing him such pain that it nearly choked him. Foolish ideas came to him; he accusingly told himself that she would not have betrayed him if he had really loved her. His anguish became unbearable. He was utterly wretched. It was like the throbbing of an old wound, no longer the blind, immediate desire that accommodated itself to everything, but a jealous passion for Nana, a need for her alone, for her hair, her lips, her body. He was haunted by everything about her. Whenever he recalled the sound of her voice, a shiver ran through all his limbs. He desired her with infinite delicacy and the avidity of a miser. And that love had taken possession of him so painfully that, in an irresistible surge of emotion, he threw himself in Labordette's arms as soon as he began to speak of arranging a meeting with Nana. Immediately afterward he was ashamed of his abandon, which was so ridiculous in a man of his rank. But Labordette knew when to see and when not to. When he left the Count on the stairs he gave one more proof of his tact by softly uttering these simple words: "Third floor, right-hand corridor, the door isn't locked."

Muffat was now alone in that silent corner of the building. As he was passing the greenroom he had looked in through the open doors and seen the shabbiness of that spacious room, which looked shamefully stained and worn

249

in the daylight. After leaving the darkness and tumult of the stage, he was surprised by the white light and deep calm of the staircase that he had seen one evening filled with the smoke of gaslights and resounding with the footsteps of women hurrying up and down between the floors. He could sense the deserted dressing rooms and empty corridors. There was not a soul, not a sound. Through the square windows on a level with the steps, the pale November sunlight streamed in, making yellow patches in which little specks of dust were dancing, in the dead peace descending from above. He was glad of that calm and silence. He climbed the stairs slowly, trying to catch his breath. His heart was beating violently and he was afraid of acting like a child, with sighs and tears. On the second-floor landing, he leaned against the wall, certain of not being seen. Holding his handkerchief to his lips, he looked at the warped steps, the iron rail polished by the rubbing of hands, the scratched paint, all that squalor which gave the place the look of a brothel, crudely displayed at that pallid hour of the afternoon when all the prostitutes were asleep. When he reached the third floor he had to step over a big red cat that was lying curled up on the stairs. With half-closed eyes, the cat was guarding the building all alone, drowsing in the cold, stuffy odors that the women left there every night.

In the right-hand corridor he found that the door was indeed not locked. Nana had been waiting for him. That slovenly little Mathilde kept her room in a filthy state, with a clutter of chipped jars, a greasy dressing table, and a chair stained red, as though someone had bled on its straw bottom. The wallpaper had been spattered all the way to the ceiling with drops of soapy water. There was such a stench, such a strong smell of lavender turned sour, that Nana opened the window. She stood leaning her elbows on the crossbar for a minute, breathing the fresh air, putting her head out to see Madame Bron, whom she could hear sweeping the green flagstones of the dark, narrow courtyard below. A canary in a cage hung on a shutter was emitting piercing trills. She could not hear the carriages on the boulevards or the nearby streets. There was a provincial peacefulness, a broad space where the sun was asleep. When she looked up, she saw the little buildings and the gleaming glass of the galleries of the Passage, and further on, directly opposite her, the backs of the tall houses on the Rue Vivienne, which were so silent that they seemed empty. Terraces rose above one another. A photographer had perched a big blue glass cage on a roof. It looked very gay. Nana was becoming lost in contemplation when she heard a knock at the door. She turned around and called out, "Come in!"

When she saw the Count she closed the window. It was a cold day, and there was no need for that inquisitive Madame Bron to overhear their conversation. They looked at each other seriously. Then, as he stood there stiffly, looking as though he were choking, she laughed and said, "Well, so here you are, you silly fool!"

His emotion was so strong that he seemed frozen. He called her Madame, and said he considered himself fortunate to see her again. Then, in order to hurry things along, she became still more familiar.

"Stop being so dignified. You wanted to see me, and I don't think it was because you wanted us to stare at each other like a couple of statues, was it? We've both been in the wrong. . . . But I forgive you!"

And it was agreed that they would not talk about that again. He nodded his approval. He became calmer, although he was still unable to speak, despite the tumultuous flood that was rising to his lips. Surprised by his coldness, she adopted her grand manner.

"You're a sensible man," she said with a faint smile, "so now that we've made peace, let's shake hands and be good friends."

"Good friends?" he said, suddenly anxious.

"Yes, it may be stupid, but I wanted you to have a good opinion of me. I'm glad we've had this little talk, because at least we won't look foolish if we happen to meet each other again. . . ." He made a gesture to interrupt her. "Let me finish. I want you to know that no man could ever accuse me of playing a dirty trick on him, and it upset me to begin with you. Everybody has his own sense of honor. . . ."

"But that's not why I came!" he cried violently. "Sit down and listen to me."

As though he were afraid she might leave, he pushed

251

her into the only chair in the room, then began pacing back and forth with growing agitation. The little dressing room, tightly closed and filled with sunlight, was pleasantly warm. Its humid peace was disturbed by no outside sound except the canary's high-pitched singing, which was like the trill of a distant flute.

"Listen," he said, standing in front of her, "I've come to take you back. . . . Yes, I want to begin again. You know it very well, so why talk to me the way you've been doing? . . . Answer me: do you consent?"

She had lowered her head and was now scratching the red straw that was bleeding beneath her. Sensing his anxiety, she did not hurry. Finally she looked up. Her face had become serious, and she had managed to give her lovely eyes an expression of sadness.

"Oh, it's impossible, my friend. I'll never go back with you."

"Why?" he asked, his face contracted with inexpressible suffering.

"Why? Because . . . It's impossible, that's all. I don't want to."

He looked at her for a few more seconds, ardently. Then his legs gave way beneath him and he fell to the floor.

"Come, don't be childish," she said with a look of annoyance.

But he was already behaving childishly. He remained on the floor at her feet, took her by the waist, gripped her tightly, and pressed his face between her knees. When he felt her thus, when he again felt the velvety texture of her limbs beneath the thin cloth of her dress, he shook convulsively. Distraught, shivering with fever, he pressed still harder against her legs, as though he wanted to penetrate her. The old chair creaked. His sobs of desire were stifled beneath the low ceiling, in the sharp smell of stale perfume.

"What's the sense of all that?" said Nana, letting him do as he wished. "It won't do you any good. I've already told you it's impossible. . . . My God, you're so young!"

He became quieter, but he remained on the floor and did not let go of her.

"At least listen to what I came to offer you," he said in

a broken voice. "I've already looked at a house near the Parc Monceau. I'd satisfy all your wishes. I'd give my whole fortune to have you without sharing you. . . . Yes, that would be the only condition: without sharing you, do you understand? And if you consent to be mine alone, oh, I'll want you to be the richest and most beautiful woman in the world, with carriages, diamonds, dresses. . . ."

Nana haughtily shook her head at each offer. Then, as he went on, as he spoke of settling money on her, not knowing what else to lay at her feet, she appeared to lose patience:

"Stop pawing me, will you? I'm a good-natured girl, I don't mind putting up with it for a while, since you're so upset, but now I've had enough. . . . Let me get up, you're making me tired."

She pushed his arms away. When she was standing, she said, "No, no, no . . . I won't."

He stood up laboriously, then weakly fell into the chair and put his face between his hands. Nana began walking around the room. For a moment she looked at the stained wallpaper, the greasy dressing table, that dirty little hole bathed in pale sunlight. Then she stepped in front of the Count and spoke to him with calm directness.

"It's funny how rich men think they can get anything for their money. . . . But what if I'm not willing? . . . I don't care about your presents. If you gave me the whole city of Paris I'd still say no. . . . As you can see, this is a dirty little room. Well, I'd think it was beautiful if I was happy living in it with you, and I'd be miserable in a palace if my heart wasn't there. Ah, money! I don't give a damn about money! It means nothing to me, I spit on it!"

And her face took on an expression of disgust. Then, turning to sentiment, she said in a melancholy tone, "I know something that's worth more than money. . . . Ah, if only someone would give me what I want! . . ."

He slowly raised his head. There was a gleam of hope in his eyes.

"Oh, you can't give it to me," she said. "It doesn't depend on you, and that's why I mentioned it to you . . . I'm just talking . . . I wish I could play the part of the respectable woman in their play."

"What respectable woman?" he asked, surprised.

"Their Duchess Hélène, of course! If they think I'm going to play Géraldine, they'd better think again! It's a tiny little part—one scene, and not much even in that! I'm sick of playing loose women. That's the only kind of part I ever get, as though I couldn't do anything else! It's starting to get annoying, because I can see why it is: they think I'm vulgar. Well, they're wrong! When I want to be refined, I'm very good at it. . . . Just watch this."

She went over to the window, then came back, holding her head high and measuring her steps with the circumspect air of a big hen trying not to dirty her feet. He watched her with his eyes still full of tears, bewildered by the comedy scene that had just intruded on his suffering. She walked around for a few moments to show off her acting, smiling delicately, fluttering her eyelids, and swaying her skirt. Then she stood in front of him again and said, "Well, that should be good enough for anybody, shouldn't it?"

"Yes, yes, certainly," he said, still choking, his eyes still cloudy.

"I told you I could play the part of a respectable woman! I've practiced it at home. Nobody's as good as I am at looking like a duchess who doesn't care about men. Did you notice how I glanced at you when I walked past? It's something you have to have in your blood. . . . Anyway, I want to play the part of a respectable woman. I've been dreaming about it, it makes me unhappy. . . . I must have that part, do you hear?"

She had become serious; her voice was hard and she was deeply moved. Her foolish desire was causing her genuine suffering. Muffat, still heartbroken by her refusals, waited without understanding. There was a silence. Not even the buzzing of a fly troubled the quiet of the empty building.

"You know what?" she said abruptly. "You're going to get that part for me."

He was stupefied. Then, with a gesture of despair, he said, "But that's impossible! You told me yourself I couldn't give it to you!"

She interrupted him with a shrug of her shoulders: "You'll go downstairs and tell Bordenave you want me to have the part. Stop being so thick-headed! Bordenave needs money. Well, you're going to lend him some, since you've got so much of it!"

He continued to object. She became angry: "All right, I understand: you're afraid to make Rose angry! I didn't even mention her when you were crying on the floor; there's too much to say about her. . . . What do you think of a man who swears to love one woman forever, then takes up with another one the next day? Oh, the wound is still there, I haven't forgotten. . . . Besides, my friend, I'm not at all pleased by the idea of taking the Mignons' leavings! You should have broken off with that filthy pair before you came here to make a fool of yourself on my knees!"

He had been protesting; he was finally able to get in a few words: "Rose means nothing to me; I'll drop her right away."

Nana seemed satisfied on this point. She went on: "Then what's bothering you? Bordenave's the boss. . . . And of course, after Bordenave there's Fauchery. . . ."

She had begun speaking more slowly, for she had reached the delicate point of the matter. Muffat kept his eyes lowered and said nothing. He had remained in voluntary ignorance of Fauchery's attentions to the Countess, having eventually managed to soothe himself with the hope that he had been mistaken during the horrible night he had spent in a doorway on the Rue Taitbout. But inwardly he still thought of Fauchery with anger and repugnance.

"Look, Fauchery's not the devil," said Nana, feeling her way, trying to find out how things stood between the husband and the lover. "He won't be hard to deal with. He's really quite nice. . . . So you'll tell him it's for me, won't you?"

The thought of such an act was revolting to the Count. "No, no, never!" he cried.

She waited. She was tempted to say, "After all, Fauchery can't very well refuse you anything," but she realized that she would be going a little too far if she used that as an argument. She smiled in an odd way, however, and her smile said the words for her. Muffat, who had looked up at her, looked down again, embarrassed and pale.

"You're not very obliging!" she said at length.

255

"I can't!" he said, full of anguish. "I'll do anything you want, except that, my love. Oh, please, not that!"

She decided to waste no more time arguing. She pushed back his head with her little hands, leaned over him, and gave him a long kiss on the mouth. He quivered beneath her, overwhelmed, with his eyes closed. She pulled him to his feet.

"Go," she said simply.

He walked toward the door; but just as he was about to go out, she took him in her arms again and looked up at him, humble and affectionate, rubbing her chin on his vest like a cat.

"Where's the house?" she asked softly, with the laughing, embarrassed expression of a little girl coming back to something she had previously refused.

"On the Avenue de Villiers."

"And are there carriages?"

"Yes."

"Lace? Diamonds?"

"Yes."

"Oh, darling, you're so good to me! I acted the way I did at first only because I was jealous. . . . And this time I swear it won't be like it was before, because now you understand what a woman needs. You'll give me everything, so I won't need anyone else. . . . Look, it's all yours now: this, and this, and this!"

When she had pushed him out of the room, after stimulating him with a shower of kisses on his hands and face, she caught her breath for a moment. Good God, what a smell there was in that messy Mathilde's dressing room! It was pleasantly warm, like a room in Provence with the winter sun shining outside, but it smelled too strongly of stale lavender water, and other things that were not clean. She opened the window, leaned her elbows on the crossbar again and began examining the glass roof of the Passage to kill time.

Meanwhile Muffat was staggering down the stairs with a buzzing in his ears. What was he going to say? How was he going to bring up a matter that was none of his business? As he was approaching the stage he heard sounds of quarreling. The second act had just been finished. Prullière was furious because Fauchery had decided to take out one of his speeches.

"Take everything out, then!" he shouted. "You might as well. . . . I've got less than two hundred lines as it is, and now you want to shorten my part still more! No, I've had enough: I'm giving up the part."

He took a rumpled little notebook from his pocket, turned it over in his trembling hands, and prepared to toss it into Cossard's lap. His pale, contorted face, his compressed lips, and his inflamed eyes revealed his wounded vanity and inner turmoil. He, Prullière, the idol of the public, was expected to play a part of two hundred lines!

"Why not have me bring in letters on a tray?" he said bitterly.

"Come on, Prullière, be reasonable," said Bordenave, treating him gently because of his popularity with the people in the boxes. "Don't have one of your fits again. . . . We'll think of more things for you to do. Isn't that right, Fauchery? You'll add a few things, won't you? In the third act we might even lengthen one of the scenes."

"Then I want to have the last line," said Prullière. "You certainly owe me that."

Fauchery seemed to consent by his silence. Prullière put the script back into his pocket, although he was still agitated and dissatisfied. Bosc and Fontan had maintained a look of profound indifference during the argument: every man for himself, it was no concern of theirs, they were not interested. And all the actors gathered around Fauchery, questioning him, fishing for compliments, while Mignon listened to Prullière's final complaints without losing sight of Count Muffat, whose return he had been watching for.

The Count had stopped in the darkness at the back of the stage, reluctant to come in during the quarrel. But Bordenave saw him and hurried over to him.

"Oh, these people!" he said. "You can't imagine how much trouble I have with them, Count. They're all as vain as they can be, and lazy, and spiteful, always involved in some dirty business or other. They'd all be delighted if I broke my neck. . . . Excuse me, I'm losing my temper."

He stopped talking and there was a silence. Muffat tried to think of a transition, but failed; so, to get it over with, he said bluntly, "Nana wants to play the part of the Duchess."

Bordenave started and exclaimed, "What! That's ridiculous!" Then, when he looked at the Count and saw how pale and agitated he was, he became calm immediately. "Good God!" he said simply.

There was another silence. Actually, he didn't care. It might be funny to have that big Nana play the part of the Duchess. Besides, it would give him a solid hold on Muffat. He was therefore not long in coming to a decision. He turned around and called out, "Fauchery!"

The Count had made a gesture to stop him. Fauchery did not hear. Pushed up against the proscenium arch by Fontan, he was being forced to listen while the actor explained the way in which he envisaged the character of Tardiveau. In his opinion, Tardiveau ought to be from Marseilles, with an accent; and he recited whole speeches, imitating the accent. Was it better that way? He seemed to be only presenting ideas of which he himself was dubious. But he became resentful when Fauchery coldly raised objections. All right, then, since he didn't have the spirit of the part, it would be better for everybody if he didn't play it!

"Fauchery!" Bordenave shouted again.

Fauchery hurried away, glad to escape from the actor, who was offended by his abrupt departure.

"Let's not stay here," said Bordenave. "Come, gentlemen."

To be beyond the range of inquisitive ears, he led them into the property room behind the stage. Mignon, surprised, watched them disappear. They walked down a few steps. It was a square room whose windows overlooked a courtyard. Dim light came in through the dirty windows beneath the low ceiling. In the racks that cluttered the room there was a disorderly collection of all kinds of objects, like the display of a second-hand dealer on the Rue de Lappe who was selling out his stock, an indescribable jumble of plates, gilded cardboard cups, old red umbrellas, Italian pitchers, clocks in all styles, trays, inkstands, firearms, and syringes, all covered with an inch-thick coating of dust, unrecognizable, chipped, broken, and piled up. And an unbearable smell of old iron, rags, and damp cardboard rose from those piles on which the remains of plays had been collecting for the past fifty years.

"Go in," said Bordenave. "At least we'll be alone here."

The Count, greatly embarrassed, moved away a few steps to let the producer present the proposal by himself. Fauchery was mystified.

"Well?" he asked.

"An idea has occurred to us," said Bordenave. "Now don't jump, this is very serious. . . . What do you think of Nana in the role of the Duchess?"

The author was bewildered at first, then he exploded: "Oh, no! You must be joking! The audience would laugh!"

"Well, it's not so bad when they laugh. . . . Think it over, my friend. . . . The Count likes the idea very much."

To give himself something to do, Muffat had taken an object from a dusty shelf and was looking at it as though he did not know what it was. It was an eggcup whose base had been mended with plaster. He unconsciously kept it in his hand and came over to say, "Yes, yes, it would be very good."

Fauchery turned to him with a gesture of brusque impatience. The Count had nothing to do with his play. And he said sharply, "Never! As a loose woman, there's no one better than Nana, but as a fashionable lady, no, never!"

"You're mistaken, I assure you," said Muffat, growing bolder. "As a matter of fact, she was just showing me how well she could play the part of a fashionable lady."

"Where?" asked Fauchery, whose surprise was increasing.

"Upstairs, in a dressing room. . . . She did it perfectly. Such refinement! And she has a way of glancing at you as she walks past, like this. . . ."

With his eggcup in his hand, he tried to imitate Nana, forgetting himself in his passionate desire to convince the two men. Fauchery looked at him in amazement. He had understood; he was no longer angry. The Count felt his look, in which there was mockery and pity. He stopped, blushing slightly.

"Well, I suppose it's possible," Fauchery said amiably. "She might be very good in the part. But it's already been assigned. We can't take it away from Rose."

"Oh, if that's all that's bothering you, don't worry," said Bordenave, "I'll arrange it myself."

Fauchery now saw that they were both against him, and realized that Bordenave had a hidden interest. In order not to weaken, he refused still more forcefully, hoping to break off the conversation.

"No! No! Even if no one else had the part, I still wouldn't give it to her! There, is that clear? Leave me alone . . . I don't want to ruin my play."

There was an embarrassed silence. Bordenave, judging that he was in the way, walked to the other side of the room. The Count stood with his head bowed. He raised it with an effort and said in a faltering voice, "Suppose I were to ask you to do it for me as a favor?"

"I can't, I can't!" Fauchery said desperately.

Muffat's voice became harder: "Please . . . I insist!"

And he looked him straight in the eyes. Beneath that dark gaze, in which he sensed a threat, Fauchery yielded abruptly, stammering confusedly, "All right, go ahead. . . . After all, I don't care. . . . But you're taking unfair advantage of . . . You'll see, you'll see . . ."

The embarrassment then became greater. Fauchery had leaned against a shelf and was nervously tapping his foot. Muffat seemed to be attentively examining the eggcup, which he was still turning between his fingers. Bordenave came over to him and said obligingly, "That's an eggcup."

"Why, yes, so it is," said the Count.

"Excuse me, you've got dust all over you," Bordenave went on, putting the eggcup back on the shelf. "You understand, if we had to dust every day we'd never finish. . . . So it's not very clean in here. What a mess, eh? Well, believe it or not, it's still worth money. Look, look at all this."

In the greenish light that came in from the courtyard, he led Muffat in front of the racks, naming the various objects for him, trying to interest him in his ragpicker's inventory, as he laughingly called it. Then, when they had come back to Fauchery, he said casually, "Listen, since we're all in agreement, we'll settle this right now . . . Ah, here's Mignon."

Mignon had been prowling in the corridor for some time. He flared up as soon as Bordenave began speaking of altering their contract. It was an outrage, they were trying to ruin his wife's future, he would take it to court! Bordenave calmly stated reasons: he didn't think the part was worthy of Rose; he wanted to save her for a musical comedy he was going to produce after *The Little Duchess*. But when Mignon continued to protest loudly, he abruptly said he was willing to cancel the contract in view of the offer that had been made to Rose by the Folies-Dramatiques. Mignon was disconcerted for a moment; then, without denying the offer, he made a great show of disdain for money: his wife had been engaged to play the part of Duchess Hélène and he was going to make sure she played it, even if it cost him his whole fortune. It was a matter of dignity, of honor.

Once the discussion had taken this turn, it was endless. Bordenave kept coming back to this argument: since the Folies-Dramatiques had offered Rose three hundred francs a night for a hundred performances, whereas he was giving her only a hundred and fifty, she would be fifteen thousand francs ahead if he let her go. Mignon steadfastly viewed the matter from the standpoint of art. What would people say if the part were taken away from his wife? That she was incapable of handling it, that it had been necessary to replace her; and this would do great damage to her reputation as an artist. No, no, never! Glory before wealth! But then he suddenly suggested a compromise: according to the terms of her contract, Rose had to pay a forfeit of ten thousand francs if she withdrew from her role; well, Bordenave could give her ten thousand francs and she would go to the Folies-Dramatiques. The producer was dumbfounded. Mignon kept his eyes on the Count and waited calmly.

"Then everything's all right," said Muffat, relieved. "You can come to an agreement."

"Oh, no, that would be too stupid!" cried Bordenave, carried away by his business instincts. "Ten thousand francs to get rid of Rose! Everyone would laugh at me!"

But the Count nodded his head vigorously to tell him to accept the proposal. Bordenave still hesitated. Finally, grumbling, regretting the ten thousand francs, even though it would not come out of his pocket, he said gruffly, "After all, I'm willing. At least I'll be rid of you."

Fontan had been listening in the courtyard for the past quarter of an hour. Greatly intrigued, he had gone down and posted himself there. When he had understood what was taking place, he went back upstairs and gave himself the pleasure of telling Rose about it; they were having a big argument about her, she was in for some trouble. Rose ran to the property room. Everyone fell silent. She looked at the four men. Muffat bowed his head, Fauchery answered her questioning look with a hopeless shrug. As for Mignon, he soon went on discussing the terms of the contract with Bordenave.

"What's wrong?" she asked curtly.

"Nothing," replied her husband. "Bordenave is going to pay you ten thousand francs to give up your part."

She trembled, very pale, clenching her little fists. She glared at him for a moment in a revolt of her whole being, she who usually submitted to him obediently in all business matters, trusting him to work out all agreements with her producers and her lovers. She could think of nothing to say except these words, which struck him in the face like a whip: "Oh, you miserable coward!"

Then she ran away. Mignon, stupefied, hurried after her. What was the matter with her? Was she losing her mind? He explained to her in an undertone that ten thousand francs from one side and fifteen thousand from the other made twenty-five thousand. It was a wonderful deal! Muffat was going to drop her anyway, so it was a clever move to have pulled that last feather from his wing. But Rose was still enraged and did not answer. Mignon disdainfully left her to her feminine rancor. He said to Bordenave, who was going back to the stage with Fauchery and Mignon, "We'll sign tomorrow morning. Bring the money."

Just then Nana, having been informed by Labordette, came triumphantly down the stairs. She was still playing the part of a great lady, with refined mannerisms, to impress her spectators and prove to those idiots that, when she wanted to, she could be more distinguished than anyone else. But she nearly forgot herself. As soon as Rose saw her, she rushed up to her and said in a voice choked with rage, "I'll get even with you for this! You haven't seen the last of me, you hear!"

Taken off guard by this sudden attack, Nana was about

to put her hands on her hips and call Rose a dirty slut. She restrained herself, however. With the gesture of a marquise about to step on an orange peel, she exaggerated the fluty tone of her voice and said, "What's this? Why, you must be mad, my dear."

She continued giving herself airs while Rose left, followed by Mignon, who was shocked by her conduct. Clarisse was overjoyed: Bordenave had just given her the role of Géraldine. Fauchery, looking gloomy, was restlessly shuffling his feet, unable to make up his mind to leave the theater. His play was ruined; he was trying to think of some way to save it. Nana went over to him, took him by the wrists, drew him close to her, and asked him if he really thought she was so dreadful. After all, she wasn't going to eat his play! She made him laugh, and gave him to understand that he would be foolish to hold a grudge against her, in his position with regard to the Muffats. If she forgot her lines, the prompter would give them to her. They would pack the house. Besides, he was mistaken about her: he would see how she would hold the audience in the palm of her hand. It was then agreed that Fauchery would make some changes in the part of the Duchess in order to give Prullière more to do. The latter was delighted. In that joy which Nana naturally brought with her, only Fontan remained cold. His angular, goatlike profile was sharply outlined as he stood in the yellow glow of the gaslight, affecting a casual pose. Nana calmly walked up to him and shook his hand.

"How are you doing these days?"

"Pretty well. And you?"

"Very well, thank you."

That was all. It was as though they had left each other only the night before, at the door of the theater. Meanwhile the actors were waiting; but Bordenave said they would not rehearse the third act. Having arrived on time by accident, old Bosc went off grumbling: they were always being kept needlessly, so that they wasted whole afternoons. Everyone left. When they reached the sidewalk they blinked their eyes, blinded by the sunlight, with the bewilderment of people who had spent three hours quarreling in a cellar, in a constant state of nervous tension. The Count, exhausted in mind and body, got into a carriage with Nana, while Labordette accompanied Fauchery, trying to comfort him.

A month later, the first performance of *The Little Duchess* was a great disaster for Nana. She was atrociously bad in it. Her pretensions to high comedy aroused storms of laughter. The spectators were so amused that they did not hiss. Sitting in a stage box, Rose Mignon greeted each appearance of her rival with a shrill laugh which set off the whole house. This was her first vengeance.

After the performance, when Nana was alone with Muffat, who was greatly chagrined, she said to him furiously, "It was all a plot! They did it out of jealousy! Ah, if they only knew how little I care! I don't need them now! . . . I'll bet you a thousand francs that I'll make everybody who laughed at me tonight lick the ground in front of me! . . . I'll show your Paris what a great lady is like!"

10

$\mathcal{T}$hen Nana became a woman of fashion, a stockholder in the foolishness and depravity of men, a marquise of the streets. It was a sudden and decisive start, a rapid rise to amorous fame in the bright light of the follies of money and the wasteful audacities of beauty. She immediately established her reign among all those that were most expensive. Photographs of her were displayed in shop windows, she was mentioned in the newspapers. Whenever she passed along the boulevards in her carriage, the crowd turned to stare at her and spoke her name with the emotion of a people saluting its sovereign, while she sat casually in her flowing gown, smiling gaily beneath the little blond curls which framed the blue mascara of her eyes and the painted red of her lips. And the marvel was that this big girl, so awkward as an actress, so ludicrous in the role of a virtuous woman, was able to carry off the part of an enchantress with effortless ease as soon as she was off the stage. She wore exquisitely elegant negligees with skillful carelessness; she had the litheness of a serpent and the high-strung dignity of a pedigreed cat; she was an aristocrat of vice, haughty and defiant, trampling Paris underfoot like an all-powerful ruler. She set the fashion, and great ladies followed it.

Her house was on the Avenue de Villiers, at the corner of the Rue Cardinet, in the luxurious quarter that was growing up amid the vacant lots of the old Plaine Monceau. It had been built by a young painter who was intoxicated by a first success, and had then been forced to sell it almost as soon as the plaster was dry. It was in the Renaissance style, with the look of a palace, a whimsical interior arrangement, and modern conveniences in a setting of self-conscious originality. Count Muffat had bought it fully furnished, filled with all sorts of knickknacks, beautiful Oriental hangings, old sideboards, and big Louis XIII armchairs. Nana had thus come into a stock of well-chosen artistic furniture in a wide variety of styles and periods. But since the studio that occupied the center of the house was of no use to her, she had made extensive rearrangements. On the first floor she left a conservatory, a large drawing room, and the dining room, while on the second floor she had a small drawing room constructed near her bedroom and her dressing room. She surprised the architect by the ideas she gave him, for she was a daughter of the Paris pavements who instinctively knew about all kinds of elegance and instantly grasped the refinements of luxury. And so she did not spoil the house too much; she even added to the richness of the furniture, except for a few traces of tender foolishness and gaudy splendor which revealed the former working girl who had daydreamed in front of the shop windows in the Passages.

In the courtyard, a carpet ran up the front steps below the great porch. In the vestibule there was a smell of violets and warm air enclosed between thick hangings. A yellow and pink window, with the pallor of human flesh, lighted the broad staircase, at the foot of which a carved wooden Negro held a silver tray full of calling cards, and four white marble women with bare breasts supported lamps. Bronzes, enameled Chinese vases filled with flowers, sofas covered with ancient Persian carpets, and armchairs upholstered with old tapestries furnished the vestibule, adorned the landings and made the second floor a kind of anteroom in which men's hats and overcoats were always lying around. The fabrics deadened all sounds, and there was such peacefulness in the air that one might have imagined oneself entering a chapel traversed by a pious tremor, whose silence concealed a mystery behind the closed doors.

The large drawing room was done in overelaborate Louis XVI style. Nana opened it only on ceremonious evenings when she received visitors from the Tuileries or distinguished foreigners. She usually came downstairs only at mealtimes. She felt a little lost on days when she had lunch alone in the lofty dining room, which was adorned with Gobelin tapestries, contained a monumental sideboard, and was enlivened with old china and wonderful ancient silverware. She would go back upstairs immediately after the meal; she lived on the second floor in her three rooms: bedroom, dressing room, and small drawing room. She had already had the bedroom redone twice, the first time in mauve satin, the second in lace on blue silk. She was still not satisfied; she found it dull, but had not yet been able to decide what she would prefer. There was twenty thousand francs' worth of Venetian lace on the padded bed, which was as low as a sofa. The furniture was in white and blue lacquer, inlaid with silver fillets. There were white bearskins everywhere, so numerous that they covered the carpet; this was a whim, a refinement on Nana's part, for she had not been able to give up her habit of sitting on the floor to take off her stockings. Beside the bedroom, the small drawing room offered an amusing and exquisitely artistic jumble. Against the pale hangings of faded pink Turkish silk brocaded in gold, one could see a multitude of objects of all countries and all styles: Spanish and Portuguese chests, Chinese statues, a Japanese screen of superb workmanship, china, bronzes, embroidered silks, and delicate tapestries. Armchairs as broad as beds and sofas as deep as alcoves gave an impression of soft indolence and suggested the somnolent life of a seraglio. The room kept a tone of old gold blended with green and red, and, except for the voluptuousness of the seats, nothing in it indicated too strongly that it belonged to a loose woman; two porcelain statuettes, however—one of a woman in her chemise looking for fleas, the other of a completely naked woman walking on her hands, with her legs in the air— were enough to add a stain of primordial stupidity. And through a door that was nearly always open, one could see the dressing room, all in marble and glass, with its white bathtub, its silver pitchers and basins, and its crystal and ivory fittings. A closed curtain filled the room with a wan light that seemed to be sleeping in the odor of violets, that provocative perfume of Nana's, with which the whole house and even the courtyard were permeated.

Establishing the household was the greatest undertaking. Nana still had Zoé, the maid who was so devoted to her fortune, and who had calmly waited for this sudden rise to glory, confident of her instinct. Zoé was now triumphant:

she was mistress of the household, and she was feathering her nest, while at the same time serving Madame as honestly as possible. But one maid was no longer sufficient. Nana needed a butler, a coachman, a concierge, and a cook. Furthermore, the stables had to be equipped. Labordette made himself very useful by dealing with matters that were distasteful to the Count. He bargained over the purchase of the horses, called on the carriage makers, and guided Nana's choice in everything. She was seen on his arm in the establishments of the various tradesmen. He even engaged the servants: Charles, a tall coachman who had been in the service of the Duke de Corbreuse; Julien, a smiling, curly-haired little butler; and a married couple: Victorine, the cook, and her husband François, who assumed the duties of concierge and footman. The latter, with powdered hair, wearing knee breeches and Nana's livery, which was light blue with silver braid, received the visitors in the vestibule in regal style.

By the second month the household was in working order. The expenses exceeded three hundred thousand francs. There were eight horses in the stables and five carriages in the coach houses, one of which, a landau with silver trimmings, was the talk of Paris for a time. And in the midst of this fortune, Nana began settling down, making her own niche. She had left the theater after the second performance of *The Little Duchess,* leaving Bordenave in danger of bankruptcy, despite the Count's money. She was still bitter about her failure, however. It added to the lesson Fontan had given her, a dirty trick for which she held all men responsible. She now claimed to have an unshakable resistance to all infatuations. But thoughts of vengeance did not remain long in her flighty brain. What did remain beyond her hours of anger was an insatiable appetite for spending money, a natural disdain for the man who paid, a continuous series of wasteful and destructive caprices, a pride in the ruin of her lovers.

At first, Nana placed the Count on a satisfactory footing. She clearly set forth the conditions of their relationship. He gave her twelve thousand francs a month, not counting presents, and asked only for absolute faithfulness in return. She swore to be faithful. But she demanded consideration, unrestricted freedom as mistress of her own house, and complete respect for her wishes. Thus, for example, she would receive her friends every day and he would come only at predetermined hours; in short, he was to trust her blindly in everything. Whenever he hesitated, seized with jealous anxiety, she either stood on her dignity and threatened to give everything back to him, or swore by the head of her little Louis. That ought to be enough for him. There could be no love without esteem. By the end of the first month, Muffat respected her.

But she wanted and obtained more. She soon acquired still greater influence over him through her good-natured sympathy. When he arrived in a gloomy state of mind, she would cheer him up, then give him advice, after making him tell her what was bothering him. She gradually began to concern herself with his worries about his home, his wife, and his daughter, with all his emotional problems and financial affairs. She was very sensible, and full of justice and honesty. Only once did she allow herself to be carried away by passion, on the day when he told her that Daguenet was no doubt going to ask for his daughter's hand in marriage. When the Count had ceased hiding his affair with Nana, Daguenet had decided that it would be clever of him to stop seeing her; he now called her an unscrupulous wench and swore he would rescue his future father-in-law from that creature's clutches. She therefore painted a charming picture of her old friend Mimi: he was a libertine who had squandered his whole fortune on vile women; he had no moral sense, for while he did not make women give him money, he did take advantage of their money and repaid them only with a bouquet or a dinner at rare intervals. When the Count seemed to excuse these weaknesses, she told him crudely that Daguenet had been her lover, and she added a few disgusting details. Muffat turned very pale and never mentioned Daguenet again. That would teach him to be ungrateful!

However, the house had scarcely been furnished when one night, after she had profusely sworn to be faithful to Muffat, Nana allowed Count Xavier de Vandeuvres to stay with her. For the past two weeks he had been assiduously paying court to her with visits and flowers. She yielded to him not from infatuation, but in order to prove to herself that she was free. The idea of self-interest came later, the next day, when Vandeuvres helped her to pay a bill which she had not wanted to mention to Muffat. She would be able to get nine or ten thousand francs a month from him; it would be useful pocket money. He was in the process of finished off his fortune in a fever of extravagance. His horses and Lucy had cost him three farms, and Nana was about to swallow his last château, near Amiens, in a single mouthful. It was as though he were in a hurry to get rid of everything, even the remains of the old tower built by a Vandeuvres during the reign of Philip Augustus. He had a frenzied appetite for ruin, and felt it was a fine gesture to leave the last gold bezants of his coat-of-arms in the hands of that courtesan who was desired by every man in Paris. He, too, accepted Nana's conditions—complete freedom, love at regularly scheduled times—without being so naively impassioned as to demand a vow of faithfulness. Muffat suspected nothing. As for Vandeuvres, he was quite certain of what was going on, but he never made the slightest allusion to it. He pretended not to know, with the subtle smile of a skeptical man about town who does not ask for the impossible as long as he has his hour and all Paris knows it.

From then on, Nana's household was really well established. The staff was complete, in the stable, the kitchen, and Madame's bedroom. Zoé managed everything and was able to cope with the most unexpected complications. The functioning of the household was as carefully organized as a theatrical performance, as closely regulated as a great administration, and it took place with such precision that nothing went wrong for the first few months. But Madame gave Zoé a great deal of trouble with her recklessness, her whims, and her wild bravado. And so Zoé finally began to relax her vigilance a little; she had noticed, moreover, that she made her greatest profits when things were in a mess, when Madame had made some foolish mistake that had to be corrected. At those times she was showered with presents, and fished gold coins from the troubled waters.

One morning when Muffat was still in the bedroom, Zoé showed a trembling gentleman into the dressing room, where Nana was changing her linen.

"Why, it's Zizi!" Nana exclaimed in amazement.

It was indeed Georges. When he saw her in her chemise,

with her golden hair hanging over her bare shoulders, he threw his arms around her neck and began kissing her everywhere. She struggled with him, frightened, and said in a muffled voice, "Stop it, he's here! It's stupid. . . . And you, Zoé, are you out of your mind? Take him away! Keep him downstairs, I'll try to come there in a little while."

Zoé had to push him out of the room. Downstairs in the dining room, when Nana was able to rejoin them, she scolded them both. Zoé pinched her lips and left with a look of resentment, saying that she had thought Madame would be pleased. Georges looked at Nana, so happy to see her again that his beautiful eyes filled with tears. The bad days were now over: his mother, believing he had become sensible again, had allowed him to leave Les Fondettes. As soon as he had gotten off the train, he had taken a cab to come and kiss his darling Nana as quickly as possible. He spoke of living with her as he had done at La Mignotte, in the days when he used to wait for her, barefooted, in her bedroom every night. And as he told her his story, he put out his fingers, longing to touch her after that cruel year of separation. He took hold of her hands, then began fondling her arms inside the wide sleeves of her negligee until he reached her shoulders.

"Do you still love your Baby?" he asked in his childish voice.

"Of course!" replied Nana, abruptly drawing away from him. "But you just popped in on me without any warning. . . . You know I'm not free. You must be sensible."

Having gotten out of the cab in the blind excitement of a long desire about to be satisfied, Georges had not even seen the house he was entering. Only now did he become aware of a change in his surroundings. He examined the luxurious dining room, with its high decorated ceiling, its Gobelin tapestries, and its sideboard gleaming with silverware.

"Ah, yes," he said sadly.

And she gave him to understand that he was never to come in the morning. He could come any afternoon between four and six o'clock; this was her usual time for receiving visitors. Then, when he gave her a beseeching, questioning look without asking anything, she kissed him on the forehead and said benevolently, "Behave yourself and I'll do my best."

But the truth was that she no longer had any desire for him. She still thought he was very nice and she was willing to have him as a friend, but that was all. However, when he began arriving every day at four o'clock he seemed so unhappy that she often yielded to him, hiding him in her closets, constantly letting him pick up the crumbs of her beauty. Before long he was spending nearly all his time in the house, as much at home there as the little dog Bijou; they both trailed after their mistress's skirts, keeping something of her even when she was with another, getting occasional windfalls of sugar and caresses when she was alone and bored.

Madame Hugon eventually learned that her son had fallen back into the arms of that wicked woman. She hurried to Paris and sought the aid of her other son, Lieutenant Philippe Hugon, who was then stationed at Vincennes. Georges, who had been hiding from his older brother, was seized with despair, fearing some sort of forceful action. Since he could keep nothing to himself in the anxious expansiveness of his love, he was soon constantly talking to Nana about his big brother, a strong, daring man who would stop at nothing.

"You see," he explained, "my mother won't come here, but she can send my brother. . . . Yes, I'm sure she's going to send Philippe to get me."

The first time he said this, Nana was offended. She said sharply, "Just let him try! I don't care if he's a lieutenant or not, I'll have François throw him out before he knows what's happened!"

Then, since Georges went on talking about his brother, she finally began taking an interest in Philippe. Within a week she knew what he was like from head to toe: he was very tall, very strong, lighthearted, and a little brutal; and she even became acquainted with such intimate details as the hairs on his arms and the birthmark on his shoulder. One day, full of the image of the man whom she planned to have thrown out of her house, she exclaimed, "Well, your brother still hasn't come, Zizi! He must be snubbing us!"

The next day, while Georges was alone with Nana, François came in to ask if Madame would receive Lieutenant Philippe Hugon. Georges turned pale and said, "I've been expecting it. My mother talked to me about it this morning." And he begged Nana to send word that she was not receiving visitors. But she had already stood up, highly incensed.

"Why should I?" she said. "He'd think I was afraid. We're going to have a good laugh. . . . François, let that gentleman wait in the drawing room for a quarter of an hour, then bring him to me."

She did not sit down again. She began pacing feverishly back and forth between the mirror on the mantlepiece and a Venetian mirror that hung above an Italian chest; and each time she came to one of them she glanced at herself and tried out a smile, while Georges, sitting limply on a sofa, trembled at the thought of the scene that was about to take place. She kept uttering short sentences as she walked:

"It'll calm him down to wait for a quarter of an hour. . . . And if he thinks he's coming to a low-class woman's house, the drawing room will make him think again. Yes, take a good look, my friend. It's the real thing. That'll teach you to respect the lady who lives here. Men have to have respect. . . . Has the quarter of an hour gone by? No, only ten minues. Oh, we've got plenty of time!"

She could not stand still. When the time was up, she sent Georges away after making him promise not to listen at the door, because that would look bad if the servants saw him. As he walked toward the bedroom, he ventured to say in a choked voice, "Remember, he's my brother. . . ."

"Don't worry," she said with dignity; "if he's polite to me, I'll be polite to him."

François ushered in Philippe Hugon, who was wearing a frock coat. At first Georges tiptoed across the bedroom, to obey Nana. But the sound of voices held him; he hesitated, so full of anguish that his legs almost gave way beneath him. He imagined catastrophes, slaps, something abominable that would separate him from Nana forever. He was therefore unable to resist the temptation to come back and put his ear to the door. He heard very indistinctly, for the thickness of the hangings muffled the sounds. However, he was able to catch a few things said by Philippe, harsh phrases containing such words as "child," "family,"

and "honor." In his anxiety over what his darling Nana
would reply, his heart pounded and he was almost deaf-
ened by a confused buzzing in his ears. He was sure she
was going to say something like "You dirty pig!" or "Get
out! This is my house!" But nothing came from her,
not a word; it was as though she were dead in there. Soon
even his brother's voice grew softer. He could no longer
understand anything he was saying. Then a strange sound
completed his bewilderment: Nana was sobbing. For a
moment he was torn between two conflicting impulses: to
run away, and to attack Philippe. But just then Zoé came
into the bedroom and he moved away from the door,
ashamed at having been caught.

She calmly put some linen into a cupboard while he
stood silent and motionless with his forehead pressed
against a windowpane, consumed with uncertainty.

"Is it your brother who's with Madame?"

"Yes," he replied in a broken voice.

"And you're worried about it, aren't you, Monsieur
Georges?"

"Yes," he repeated with the same painful difficulty.

Zoé took her time. She folded some lace and said slowly,
"There's no reason to worry. . . . Madame will arrange
everything."

And that was all; they did not speak again. But she did
not leave. She bustled around the bedroom for a good
quarter of an hour, without appearing to notice Georges'
growing exasperation. He was pale from constraint and
doubt. He kept glancing furtively toward the drawing
room. What could they be doing in there for so long?
Maybe Nana was still crying. That brutal Philippe must
have slapped her. When Zoé left at last, he rushed back to
the door and put his ear to it. He was more bewildered
than ever and was afraid he must be losing his head
entirely, for he heard a sudden burst of gaiety, tender
voices whispering, and laughter like that of a woman
being tickled. Then, almost immediately afterward, Nana
accompanied Philippe to the stairs and exchanged a few
cordial and familiar words with him.

When Georges dared to enter the drawing room, Nana
was standing in front of the mirror, looking at herself.

"Well?" he asked, thoroughly confused.

"Well what?" she said without turning around. Then, casually: "Why did you tell me all those things about your brother? He's very nice!"

"Then it's all settled?"

"Of course it's settled. . . . What's the matter with you? You sound as though you thought we were going to fight!"

Georges still did not understand. He stammered, "It seemed to me I heard. . . . Weren't you crying?"

"Crying?" she said, staring at him. "You must have been dreaming! Why should I have cried?"

And he became greatly agitated when she angrily reprimanded him for having disobeyed her by spying on her behind the door. She sulkily walked away from him. He followed her with coaxing submissiveness, wanting to know.

"So my brother . . ."

"Your brother saw where he was right away. . . . I might have been a low-class woman, and in that case he'd have been right to interfere, because of your age and your family's honor. I can understand his feelings very well. . . . But one glance was enough for him, and he behaved like a gentleman. . . . So don't worry, it's all over now. He'll put your mother's mind at rest." And she added, laughing, "Anyway, you'll see your brother here. . . . I've invited him . . . he'll come back."

"Ah, he'll come back. . . ." said Georges, turning pale.

He said nothing more and they stopped talking about Philippe. She was getting dressed to go out. He looked at her with his big, sad eyes. He was glad things had worked out so smoothly, for he would rather die than give up Nana; but at the bottom of his heart there was a secret anxiety and a deep sorrow that he did not recognize, and of which he did not dare to speak.

He never knew how Philippe reassured their mother. Three days later she went back to Les Fondettes, apparently satisfied. That evening at Nana's house, he started when François announced Lieutenant Hugon. Philippe came in gaily, joked with him, and called him a young rascal; he said he had helped him in his escapade because he knew it was of no consequence. Georges, heavy-hearted, not daring to move, blushed like a girl at the slightest word. He was ten years younger than Philippe and was not used to being treated by him as a comrade. He feared him as a father, from whom one hides adventures with women. He therefore felt ashamed and uneasy when he saw him behaving so freely with Nana, laughing loudly, enjoying himself wholeheartedly, with his magnificent health. However, since his brother soon began coming every day, Georges became somewhat accustomed to seeing him there. Nana was radiant. It was as though she were having an insolent housewarming in a mansion already overflowing with men and furniture, a final installation in the riotous disorder of the life of a courtesan.

One afternoon when the Hugon brothers were there, Count Muffat came outside of his regular hours. When Zoé told him that Madame was with some friends, he withdrew without going inside, affecting the discretion of a gallant man. When he came back that evening, Nana received him with the cold anger of an outraged woman.

"Monsieur," she said, "I've given you no reason to insult me. . . . Listen to me: when I'm at home, I want you to come in like anyone else."

The Count stared at her with his mouth open.

"But darling . . ." he tried to explain.

"You went away because I had company, didn't you? Yes, there were men here. What do you think I was doing with them? . . . Acting like a discreet lover is the best way to make a woman notorious, and I don't want to be notorious!"

He obtained forgiveness only with difficulty. At heart he was delighted. It was by such scenes that she kept him pliant and trusting. She had long since succeeded in making him accept Georges, a child who amused her, she said. She made him have dinner with Philippe, and the Count behaved quite graciously. When they left the table, he took the young man aside and asked about his mother. From then on, the Hugon brothers, Vandeuvres, and Muffat were openly acknowledged as regular visitors in Nana's house, where they shook hands like close friends. It was more convenient that way. Only Muffat was still careful not to come more often. He always maintained the formal manner of a stranger paying his first call. At night, when Nana was sitting on her bearskins, taking off her stockings, he would talk in a friendly tone about the other men, particularly Philippe, who was uprightness personified.

"Yes, it's true they're all nice," said Nana, remaining on the floor while she put on her nightgown. "But they know who I am. They know I'd throw them out if they ever said anything disrespectful."

And yet, in the midst of all that luxury, surrounded by that court, Nana was bored to tears. She had men for every minute of the night, and money everywhere, even in the drawers of her dressing table, mingled with her combs and brushes; but this did not satisfy her; she felt an emptiness somewhere, a hollowness that made her yawn. Her life dragged along, unoccupied, always bringing back the same monotonous hours. The future did not exist; she lived like a bird, sure of being able to eat, ready to sleep on the nearest branch. In this certainty that she would be fed, she remained lying down all day long without making an effort of any kind, drowsing in the depths of that convent-like idleness and submission, as though a prisoner of her trade. Since she went out only in a carriage, she began to lose the use of her legs. She reverted to childish tastes, kissing Bijou from morning till night, killing time in stupid amusements while waiting for the man to whom she would submit with an air of obliging weariness. In this self-abandon, she was concerned only with her beauty. She was constantly examining herself, washing and perfuming herself all over, taking pride in being able to appear naked before anyone at any time without having to feel ashamed.

She usually got up at ten o'clock in the morning. Bijou, her Scottish terrier, would awaken her by licking her face. She would then play with him for five minutes while he scampered over her arms and thighs. This always offended Count Muffat. Bijou was the first male of whom he was jealous. It was indecent to let an animal put its nose under the covers like that! Then Nana would go into her dressing room and take a bath. Toward eleven o'clock, Francis would come and put up her hair in a simple style, leaving the more elaborate arrangement for the afternoon. At lunch, since she hated to eat alone, she nearly always had Madame Maloir, who arrived in the morning from parts unknown, wearing one of her absurd hats, and returned at night to the mystery of her life, which no one troubled himself about. But the worst time was the two or three hours between lunch and her afternoon toilet. She usually suggested a game of bezique with her old friend; sometimes she read the *Figaro*, in which the theatrical and society news interested her; occasionally she even opened a book, for she had pretensions to literary taste. Her toilet occupied her until nearly five o'clock. Only then did she awaken from her long somnolence, going out in her carriage or receiving a whole crowd of men at home, often dining out, going to bed very late; then the next morning she would get up with the same fatigue and begin another day like the one before.

Her great diversion was to go to Les Batignolles to see her little Louis at her aunt's house. She would forget him for two weeks at a time, then suddenly have an imperious need to see him. She would hurry there on foot, full of modesty and maternal tenderness, bring hospital presents: snuff for her aunt, oranges and cakes for Louis; or else she would arrive in her landau on her way back from the Bois, wearing a dress whose gaudy splendor caused a sensation all along the quiet street. Madame Lerat had been puffed up with vanity ever since her niece had risen to greatness. She seldom went to Nana's house on the Avenue de Villiers, claiming that she was out of place there, but she triumphed on her own street, happy when Nana came to see her in dresses costing four or five thousand francs, busy all the next day showing off her presents and quoting figures that dumbfounded her neighbors.

Nana usually reserved Sundays for her family; if Muffat offered to take her somewhere on one of those days, she would refuse with the smile of a humble housewife: she couldn't, she was going to see her baby and have dinner with her aunt. And poor little Louiset was always ill. He was nearly three years old now; he was getting to be quite a little man. But he had had eczema on the back of his neck, and now there were abscesses in his ears, which gave rise to the fear that there might be caries of the bones of the skull. When she saw him so pale, with his poor blood and his soft flesh spotted with yellow, she became serious; and above all she was astonished: what could be the matter with the little darling to make him so sick all the time? She, his mother, was in such good health!

On days when she was not occupied by her child, Nana

relapsed into the noisy monotony of her existence: rides in the Bois, first nights, dinners and suppers at the Maison-d'Or or the Café Anglais, then all the public places, all the spectacles to which the crowd rushed, the Bal Mabille, reviews, races. And she still had the hollow feeling of stupid idleness that almost gave her pains in her stomach. Despite the constant infatuations that passed through her heart, as soon as she was alone she would stretch her arms in a gesture of immense fatigue. Solitude made her sad immediately, for she again became conscious of her emptiness and her boredom with herself. Although very gay by trade and by nature, she would then become gloomy, summing up her life in this cry, which always returned, between two yawns: "Oh, how men annoy me!"

One afternoon as she was coming home from a concert, Nana saw a woman hurrying along a sidewalk of the Rue Montmartre with worn shoes, dirty skirts, and a rain-soaked hat. Suddenly she recognized her.

"Stop, Charles!" she shouted to the coachman. Then she called out: "Satin! Satin!"

The passers-by turned their heads; everyone on the street looked. Satin came over to the carriage and dirtied herself still more on its wheels.

"Get in," Nana said calmly, ignoring the onlookers.

And she took her away, disgustingly dirty, in her light blue landau, beside her pearl-gray silk dress trimmed with Chantilly lace, while the people along the street smiled at the lofty dignity of the coachman.

From then on, Nana had a passion that occupied her. Satin was her vice. When she had been washed, dressed, and installed in Nana's house on the Avenue de Villiers, she spent three days telling about the Saint-Lazare prison, her troubles with the nuns, and those damned policemen who had registered her as a prostitute. Nana became indignant, consoled her, and swore she would get her name taken off the list, even if she had to go to the minister herself. In the meantime there was no hurry: they certainly wouldn't come for her there. And afternoons of tenderness began between the two women, with caressing words and kisses mingled with laughter. They were resuming, in a joking way, the little game that had been interrupted by the arrival of the police in the hotel on the Rue de Laval. Then one fine night it became serious. Nana, who had been so disgusted by what she saw in Laure's restaurant, now understood. She was greatly perturbed and excited, especially since Satin disappeared on the morning of the fourth day. No one had seen her leave. She had run away in her new dress, seized with a need for open air, homesick for her sidewalks.

On that day there was such a violent storm in the house that all the servants bowed their heads without breathing a word. Nana almost beat François for not having blocked the door to prevent Satin from leaving. She tried to restrain herself, however; she called Satin a dirty whore. This would teach her to pick up such garbage from the gutter! In the afternoon, when Madame locked herself in her bedroom, Zoé heard her sobbing. That evening she suddenly asked for her carriage and had herself driven to Laure's. It had occurred to her that she might find Satin in the restaurant on the Rue des Martyrs. She was going there not to get her back, but to slap her face. True enough, Satin was eating at a little table with Madame Robert. When she saw Nana, she began to laugh. Though cut to the quick, Nana did not make a scene; on the contrary, she was gentle and docile. She bought enough champagne to intoxicate all the women at five or six nearby tables, then took Satin away while Madame Robert was in the bathroom. Only when they were in the carriage did she bite her and threaten to kill her if she ran away again.

But the same thing happened again and again. A dozen times, tragic in the fury of a deceived woman, Nana went off in pursuit of that little tramp who kept running away on a sudden impulse, bored by the comfort of the luxurious house. She spoke of slapping Madame Robert. One day she even considered a duel: there was one woman too many. She now wore her diamonds whenever she had dinner at Laure's, and sometimes she took Louise Violaine, Maria Blond, and Tatan Néné, all resplendent in their finery. Beneath the yellow gaslights, in the smell of burnt fat that pervaded the three rooms, they would display their luxury in those sordid surroundings, happy to be able to impress the young neighborhood prostitutes they took away with them when they had finished their meal. On those days, Laure, sleek and tightly laced, kissed her customers with more expansive maternity. In the midst of all this, Satin remained calm, with her blue eyes and her pure, virginal face; bitten, slapped, and pulled back and forth between the two women, she merely said that it was funny, and that it would be more sensible for them to come to an understanding with each other. It did no good to slap her; she couldn't cut herself in two, despite her willingness to be nice to everyone. In the end it was Nana who won out, by overwhelming Satin with tenderness and presents. To avenge herself, Madame Robert wrote abominable anonymous letters to her rival's lovers.

Count Muffat had seemed worried for some time. One morning, greatly agitated, he showed Nana an anonymous letter. In the first few lines she saw that she was accused of deceiving the Count with Vandeuvres and the Hugon brothers.

"It's a lie! It's a lie!" she cried forcefully, in a tone of extraordinary candor.

"Do you swear it's not true?" asked Muffat, already relieved.

"Oh, I'll swear by anything you like! . . . Yes, I swear it by my own son!"

But the letter was long. Next, her relations with Satin were described in crude, obscene terms. When she had finished reading, she smiled and said simply, "Now I know where this came from."

In response to Muffat's request for a denial, she said calmly, "It's something that doesn't concern you. . . . What difference does it make to you?"

She did not deny it. He expressed shocked indignation. She shrugged her shoulders. Where had he been all his life? It was something that was done everywhere; she named her friends and swore that ladies in high society went in for it as much as anyone else. In short, according to her, nothing was more common or more natural. But a lie was a lie, and so he had seen how angry she was when she read the accusation about Vandeuvres and the Hugon brothers. Ah, if that were true, he would be right to strangle her! But what was the use lying to him about something that had no importance? And she repeated her question: "What difference does it make to you?"

Then, when he continued to complain, she cut him short

by saying to him roughly, "Look, if you don't like it, you know what to do: the doors are unlocked. . . . You'll have to take me as I am or leave me alone."

He bowed his head. Actually, her vows had made him happy. Seeing her power, she ceased to consider his feelings. From then on, Satin was openly installed in the house, on the same footing as the gentlemen. Vandeuvres had not needed an anonymous letter to make him understand the situation; he jested about it and picked jealous quarrels with Satin. Philippe and Georges treated her as a comrade, with handshakes and coarse jokes.

Nana had an adventure one night when she had been abandoned by that little tramp and had gone to have dinner at Laure's without being able to get her hands on her. As she was eating alone, Daguenet appeared. Although he was now leading a respectable life, he occasionally returned to his old haunts, yielding to a need for vice, hoping he would not meet anyone he knew in those dark corners of Parisian depravity. At first, therefore, Nana's presence seemed to make him uneasy. But he was not a man to run away. He walked up to her with a smile and asked if Madame would be so kind as allow him to dine at her table. Seeing that he was joking, Nana assumed a cold, dignified air and said sharply, "Sit wherever you like, Monsieur. This is a public place."

Having begun in this way, the conversation was odd. But during dessert Nana became bored with it. Eager to triumph, she put her elbows on the table and said familiarly, "Tell me, how are your plans to get married coming along?"

"Not too well," confessed Daguenet.

As a matter of fact, when he had gone to the Muffats' to ask for their daughter's hand, he had felt such coldness on the Count's part that he had prudently refrained from making his request. He felt that he might as well give up. Nana stared at him with her bright eyes, resting her chin on her hand, an ironic smile on her lips.

"So I'm an unscrupulous wench!" she said slowly. "So you'll have to rescue your future father-in-law from my clutches! . . . Really, for such an intelligent man, you're terribly stupid! Whatever gave you the idea of saying nasty things about me to a man who adores me and repeats everything to me? Listen, my boy, you'll get married only if I want you to."

He had realized this a few moments before, and he was already working out a plan of submission. He continued to joke, however, not wishing to let the matter sink into seriousness. After putting on his gloves, he asked her with strict formality for the hand of Mademoiselle Estelle de Beuville. She finally began to laugh as though she were being tickled. Oh, that Mimi! It was impossible to hold a grudge against him! Daguenet's great success with women was due to the softness of his voice, a voice of musical purity and flexibility that had earned him the nickname of "Velvet Mouth" among the loose women of Paris. They all yielded to the sonorous caresses in which he enveloped them. Conscious of this power, he lulled Nana with an endless flow of words, telling her idiotic stories. When they left the restaurant, she was pink, trembling on his arm, reconquered. Since the weather was mild, she sent her carriage away. She walked to his apartment with him and went inside without hesitation. Two hours later she said to him as she was getting dressed again, "So you really want to marry her, do you, Mimi?"

"Can you think of anything better for me to do? You know I'm broke."

She called him over to button her shoes; then, after a silence: "Well, it's all right with me . . . I'll use my influence. . . . That girl is as skinny as a rail, but since it suits everybody . . . Oh, you can't say I'm not obliging! I'll take care of it for you." She laughed, with her breasts still bare. "But what will you give me?"

He had seized her and was now kissing her shoulders in an outburst of gratitude. She gaily struggled with him, quivering, throwing back her head.

"Oh, I know!" she cried, excited by this game. "Listen, this is what I want as my commission: on your wedding day, you'll make me a present of your innocence! Before you touch your wife, you understand?"

"Yes, that's it, that's it!" he said, laughing more loudly than she.

This bargain amused them. They considered it a good joke.

There was a dinner at Nana's house the next day, the

usual Thursday gathering: Muffat, Vandeuvres, the Hugon brothers, and Satin. The Count arrived early. He needed eighty thousand francs to rid Nana of two or three debts and buy her a set of sapphires she was dying to have. Since he had already spent a considerable portion of his fortune and did not yet dare to sell one of his estates, he wanted to find someone who would lend him money. Following the advice given to him by Nana herself, he had addressed himself to Labordette; but the latter, finding it too heavy an undertaking, had offered to speak about it to Francis the hairdresser, who was always glad to oblige his customers. The Count placed himself in the hands of these two gentlemen on the express condition that his name was to remain secret. They both agreed not to show anyone the note for a hundred thousand francs which he would sign, and they apologized for the twenty thousand francs interest, loudly denouncing the vile usurers with whom, they said, they had been forced to deal.

When Muffat arrived, Francis was just finishing Nana's hair. Labordette was also in the dressing room, with the familiarity of an inconsequential friend. When he saw the Count, he discreetly placed a thick bundle of banknotes among the powders and the pomades, and the note was signed on the marble top of the dressing table. Nana invited Labordette to stay for dinner. He declined: he was showing a rich foreigner around Paris. However, when Muffat took him aside and begged him to hurry to Becker, the jeweler, and bring back the set of sapphires, with which he wanted to surprise Nana that same evening, Labordette gladly agreed to run the errand. Half an hour later, Julien secretly handed the Count a jewel case.

Nana was nervous during dinner. She had been agitated by the sight of the eighty thousand francs. To think that all that money was going to be paid to tradesmen! It disgusted her. When the soup was served in that superb dining room, brightened by the reflections of silverware and crystal, she became sentimental and began extolling the joys of poverty. The men were wearing evening coats, she herself was wearing an embroidered white satin dress, while Satin, more modest, was dressed in black silk, with a golden heart, a present from her dear friend, hanging from a chain around her neck. And the guests were served by

Julien and François, aided by Zoé, all three looking very dignified.

"I had a lot more fun when I had no money at all," said Nana.

She had placed Muffat on her right and Vandeuvres on her left, but she scarcely even glanced at them, for she was entirely occupied with Satin, who sat across the table from her, between Philippe and Georges. "Isn't that right, darling?" she kept saying to her. "How we used to laugh in the days we went to Mother Josse's school on the Rue Polonceau!"

The roast was being served. The two women plunged into their memories. They were occasionally seized by a need to talk about them, to stir up the mud of their youth; and it was always when there were men present, as though they were yielding to an urge to impose on them the dunghill from which they had sprung. The men turned pale and looked embarrassed. The Hugon brothers tried to laugh, while Vandeuvres nervously curled his beard and Muffat redoubled his solemnity.

"Do you remember Victor?" said Nana. "What a perverted boy he was! He used to take little girls into cellars . . ."

"That's right," said Satin. "And I remember the big courtyard at your house. There was a concierge with a broom . . ."

"Yes, old Madame Boche. She's dead now."

"And I can still see your place. . . . Your mother was very fat. One night when we were playing, your father came home drunk, and I really mean drunk!"

At this point, Vandeuvres tried to divert the two women from their recollections: "I'd like some more of those truffles," he said to Nana; "they're excellent. Yesterday, at the Duke de Corbreuse's, I ate some that weren't nearly so good."

"Julien, the truffles!" Nana said curtly. Then she resumed: "Yes, papa overdid it. . . . And it really made things hard for us, too! You can't imagine how poor we were! I can say I've been through everything, and it's a wonder it didn't kill me the way it did my parents."

This time Muffat, who had been irritably toying with a

knife, ventured to intervene: "What you're saying isn't very cheerful."

"Not cheerful!" she cried, giving him a withering look. "You bet it's not cheerful! You should have brought us some bread, my friend. . . . I'm perfectly frank, I don't try to hide anything: my mother was a washerwoman, my father was a drunk and he died of it. There! If that doesn't suit any of you, if you're ashamed of my family . . ."

They all protested. She was being ridiculous! They respected her family. But she continued: "If you're ashamed of my family, leave me, because I'm not one of those women who disown their parents. . . . You have to take me with them, you understand?"

They took her, they were willing to accept her father, her past, anything she wanted. All four of them humbly bowed their heads while she held them beneath the muddy old shoes she had worn on the Rue de la Goutte-d'Or, with the passion of her omnipotence. And she was not yet ready to lay down her arms: men could give her fortunes and build palaces for her, but she would always miss the days when she used to eat apples in the street. Their stupid money meant nothing to her! It was made only for tradesmen! Then her outburst ended in a sentimental longing for a simple, open-hearted life in the midst of universal kindness.

But then she noticed Julien waiting with his arms hanging at his sides.

"Go on, serve the champagne!" she said to him. "Don't just stand there staring at me like an idiot!"

The servants had not smiled during the entire scene. They seemed not to hear, and the more Madame let herself go, the more majestic they became. As he was passing the fruit around, François had the misfortune to tilt the dish too much and the apples, pears, and grapes rolled across the table.

"Clumsy fool!" cried Nana.

The footman was ungracious enough to explain that the fruit had not been solidly piled up because Zoé had loosened it by taking out some oranges.

"Then it's Zoé who's a fool," said Nana.

"But Madame . . ." murmured the maid, offended.

Nana stood up and said curtly, with a gesture of regal

authority, "Enough! Leave, all of you! We don't need you any more."

This decisive act calmed her. She immediately became gentle and amiable. During dessert, the gentlemen were greatly amused by having to serve themselves. Satin, who had peeled a pear, came to eat it behind her darling, leaning on her shoulders and whispering things to her which made her laugh loudly. Then, wishing to share the last of her pear, she presented it to Nana between her teeth; they playfully bit each other's lips and finished the pear in a kiss. There was then a comical protest from the gentlemen. Philippe told them to go ahead. Vandeuvres asked them if they wanted the men to leave the room. Georges put his arm around Satin's waist and led her back to her seat.

"Stop being so silly, you're making her blush, poor girl!" said Nana. "Never mind, darling, let them joke. It's our business." She turned to Muffat, who was looking at her with his serious expression. "Isn't that right, my friend?"

"Yes, of course," he replied, nodding slowly.

There were no more protests. In the midst of those gentlemen, of those great names and ancient integrities, the two women faced each other and exchanged a tender look, imposing themselves and reigning with the tranquil abuse of their sex and their avowed contempt for men. The gentlemen applauded.

They went up to the little drawing room for coffee. Two lamps cast a soft glow on the pink hangings and the knicknacks in lacquer and old gold. At that hour of the night, amid the chests, bronzes, and porcelains, the light discreetly illuminated the silver and ivory inlays, heightened the gloss of a carved stick, gleamed on a panel with silky reflections. The afternoon fire had died down to embers. There was a languid warmth in the still air beneath the curtains and the hangings. And in that room filled with Nana's intimate life, where her gloves, a handkerchief, and an open book lay scattered about, she was present in all her simplicity, with her odor of violets and that good-natured disorder which produced such a charming effect among all that wealth, while armchairs as broad as beds and sofas as deep as alcoves invited one to somnolences forgetful of time, to laughing, tender words whispered in dark corners.

Satin stretched out on a sofa in front of the fireplace. She had lighted a cigarette. Vandeuvres amused himself by pretending to be fiercely jealous of her; he threatened to challenge her to a duel if she persisted in turning Nana away from her duties. Philippe and Georges joined in, teasing her and pinching her so hard that she finally cried out, "Darling, make them leave me alone! They're bothering me again."

"All right, stop it," Nana said seriously. "I won't have her being tormented, you know that. . . . And you, darling, why are you always with them, since they're so silly?"

Satin, red in the face, stuck out her tongue at them and went into the dressing room, whose open door revealed the pallor of marble illuminated by a gas flame burning inside a frosted glass globe. Nana began talking with the four men like a charming hostess. During the day she had read a novel that was causing quite a sensation, the story of a prostitute. She was disgusted, she said it was all false; and she expressed indignant repugnance for that filthy kind of literature which claimed to depict nature—as though one could show everything, as though a novel shouldn't be written in order to provide a few pleasant hours of reading! She was very definite opinions with regard to books and plays: she wanted tender and noble works that would nourish her daydreams and elevate her soul.

Then the conversation turned to the disturbances that were agitating Paris, the incendiary articles, the incipient riots which followed the calls to arms that were issued every night at public meetings. She angrily denounced the republicans. What did they want, those dirty men who never washed? Wasn't the country prospering? Hadn't the Emperor done everything for the common people? Oh, the common people were a bunch of pigs! She knew them well, so she could talk about them! And, forgetting the respect she had demanded during dinner for her family and friends of the Rue de la Goutte-d'Or, she began assailing her own class with all the disgust and fear of a woman who has fought her way to the top. Only that afternoon she had read in the *Figaro* a comical article about a public meeting. It still made her laugh, because of the slang words that were used, and a description of the ugly face of a drunk who had been expelled.

"Oh, those drunks!" she said with a look of repugnance. "No, it would be a disaster for everybody if they got their republic. . . . May God keep the Emperor with us as long as possible!"

"God will hear you, my dear," Muffat said gravely. "Don't worry, the Emperor is strong."

He was glad to see such good sentiments in her. They agreed with each other in political matters. Vandeuvres and Captain Hugon made endless jokes about the revolutionary rabble—they were all loud-mouthed cowards who ran away as soon as they saw a bayonet. Georges was pale and gloomy. .

"What's the matter, Baby?" Nana asked when she noticed his uneasiness.

"Nothing, I'm listening," he said softly.

But he was suffering. As they were leaving the dining room, he had heard Philippe jesting with Nana, and now it was Philippe, not he, who was sitting beside her. For some reason that he did not understand, his chest felt as though it were ready to burst. He could not bear to see them beside each other; such vile ideas came into his mind that he had a choking sensation, and he felt ashamed in his anguish. He laughed at Satin, he had accepted Steiner, then Muffat, then all the others, but he rebelled, he saw red at the thought that Philippe might some day touch her.

"Here, take Bijou," she said to console him, handing him the little dog that had fallen asleep on her skirt.

And Georges became cheerful again, for the animal, full of the warmth of her knees, made him feel that he was holding part of her.

The conversation had turned to a serious gambling loss that Vandeuvres had suffered the night before at the Cercle Impérial. Muffat, who was not a gambler, expressed surprise. Vandeuvres, smiling, alluded to his approaching ruin, about which all Paris was talking already; the kind of death one had did not matter, what counted was to die well. For some time now, Nana had noticed that Vandeuvres was nervous, with a sharp bend at the corners of his mouth and an unsteady glow in his bright eyes. He still had his aristocratic haughtiness and the refined elegance of his impoverished race; so far, his decline had been manifested only by short spells of dizziness whirling in his skull, which had been emptied by gambling and women. One night as he lay beside her, he had frightened her with a horrible idea: he was thinking of locking himself in his stable with his horses and setting fire to it, when he had spent the last of his fortune. His only hope was now a horse, Lusignan, which he was preparing for the Prix de Paris. He was living on that horse; his whole shaky financial position depended on it. Whenever Nana demanded money from him, he told her he would give it to her in June, if Lusignan won.

"He can afford to lose at cards," Nana said jokingly, "because he's going to clean everybody out at the races."

He replied only with a faint, mysterious smile. Then he said casually, "By the way, I've taken the liberty of giving your name to my outsider, a filly. . . . Nana, Nana . . . It sounds good. . . . You don't mind?"

"Why should I mind?" she said, inwardly delighted.

The conversation continued. They were talking about a forthcoming execution, which Nana was eager to see, when Satin appeared in the doorway of the dressing room and called her in a supplicating tone. She stood up at once and left the gentlemen lolling in their chairs, finishing their cigars and discussing the grave question of the degree of responsibility that ought to be attributed to a murderer who was a chronic alcoholic. In the dressing room, Zoé was sitting limply on a chair, crying bitterly, while Satin vainly tried to comfort her.

"What's the matter?" asked Nana, surprised.

"Oh, darling, talk to her!" said Satin. "I've been trying to make her listen to reason for the past twenty minutes. . . . She's crying because you called her a fool."

"Yes, Madame, it's hard . . . very hard . . ." stammered Zoé, choked by a fit of sobbing.

Nana was deeply moved by the sight. She said a few kind words; then, since Zoé still did not calm down, she squatted in front of her and took her by the waist in a gesture of affectionate familiarity.

"Look, silly, I didn't mean anything when I called you a fool. I just said it the same as I might have said anything else. I was angry. . . . I was wrong. There! Now please be calm."

"I love Madame so much!" said Zoé. "After all I've done for Madame . . ."

Nana kissed her. Then, wishing to show that she was not angry, she gave her a dress that she had worn only three times. Their quarrels always ended with presents. Zoé dried her eyes with her handkerchief. Before carrying the dress away on her arm, she said that everyone was very sad in the kitchen, and that Julien and François had not been able to eat, because Madame's anger had taken away their appetite. She sent them twenty francs as a token of reconciliation. She could not bear to have sorrow around her.

She was about to go back to the drawing room, happy to have patched up that quarrel, which had been making her secretly apprehensive for the next day, when Satin began whispering excitedly in her ear. She complained and threatened to leave if those men teased her any more. And she demanded that Nana send them all away that night. It would teach them a lesson! Besides, it would be so nice to be alone together, just the two of them! Nana became anxious again, and swore it was impossible. Satin bullied her like a bad-tempered child, imposing her authority: "I won't stay with them, you hear! Either they go or I do!" And she went into the drawing room. She lay down on a sofa near the window and stared at Nana with her big eyes, silent and motionless, waiting.

The gentlemen were condemning the new theories of criminology: with that wonderful invention of irresponsibility in certain pathological cases, there were no more criminals, there were only sick men. Nana nodded approvingly and tried to think of how she could get rid of the Count. The others would soon be going, but he was sure to stay. When Philippe stood up to go, Georges followed him immediately, for his sole concern was not to leave his brother behind him. Vandeuvres stayed a few minutes longer, trying to find out whether Muffat might not happen to have some important business to attend to that would force him to yield his place; but when he saw him settled down for the night he gave up and took his leave like a tactful man. As he was walking toward the door he noticed Satin's fixed stare. Amused and apparently understanding the situation, he went over and shook her hand.

"You're not angry with me, are you?" he said. "Forgive me. . . . You're the nicest of all, really."

She did not deign to answer. She went on staring at Nana and the Count, who were now left to themselves. No longer feeling any constraint, Muffat sat down beside Nana, took her fingers and kissed them. Seeking a transition, she asked him if his daughter Estelle was feeling better. He had complained about her sadness the day before; he could not spend a happy day at home, with his wife always gone and his daughter wrapped in icy silence. Nana was always full of good advice with regard to these family matters. As Muffat's mind and body relaxed, he resumed his lamentations.

"Why don't you arrange a marriage for her?" she said, recalling the promise she had made.

She immediately dared to speak of Daguenet. The Count rebelled as soon as he heard his name. No, never, not after what she had told him!

She pretended to be surprised, then laughed and put her arms around his neck.

"Oh, how can you be so jealous? Be reasonable for a minute. . . ."

Just then, however, she looked over Muffat's shoulder and her eyes met Satin's. Feeling uneasy, she let go of him and continued seriously: "My friend, your daughter must marry Daguenet. I don't want to prevent her from being happy. He's a very nice young man; you couldn't find a better husband for her."

And she launched into extraordinary praise of Daguenet. The Count had taken her hands again. He no longer said no; he would see, they would talk it over again. Then, when he spoke of going to bed, she lowered her voice and made objections. It was impossible, she was indisposed; if he loved her at all, he would not insist. But he stubbornly refused to leave, and she was beginning to weaken when her eyes again met Satin's. She then became inflexible. No, he couldn't stay. The Count, pained and greatly perturbed, stood up and got his hat. When he reached the door he felt the jewel case in his pocket and remembered the set of sapphires. He had wanted to hide it in the bed so that she would find it with her legs when she got in; he had been thinking about this childish plan ever since dinner. In his agitation, in his anguish over being sent away like that, he abruptly handed her the case.

"What's this?" she asked. "Look, sapphires! Ah, yes, it's the set. You're so kind! . . . Tell me, darling, are you sure it's the same one? It looked more impressive in the shop window."

That was all the thanks he got. She did not detain him. He glanced at Satin waiting silently on the sofa. He looked at the two women and submissively left. The door of the vestibule had not yet closed when Satin took Nana by the waist and began dancing and singing. Then she ran over to the window and said, "Let's see how he looks when he gets outside!"

The two women leaned their elbows on the iron railing, in the shadow of the curtains. It was one o'clock in the morning. The Avenue de Villiers, deserted, stretched its double row of gaslights into the damp March night, which was swept by gusts of rain-laden wind. Vacant lots formed pits of darkness; the scaffolding of houses under construction rose toward the black sky. They laughed wildly when they saw Muffat's round back as he walked off along the wet sidewalk, with the tearful reflection of his shadow, across that cold, empty plain of the new Paris. But then Nana silenced Satin: "Look out, the police!"

They stifled their laughter and looked fearfully at two black figures walking in step on the other side of the avenue. In all her luxury, in her royalty as a woman obeyed by everyone, Nana still had a terror of the police; she did not like to hear them mentioned any more than death. She felt uneasy when one of the policemen looked up at her house. You never knew with them: they might take them for prostitutes if they had heard them laughing at that hour of the night. Satin pressed up against Nana with a little shudder. Then they were interested by the approach of a lantern whose light danced on the puddles in the street. It was an old ragpicker who was searching the gutters. Satin recognized her: "It's Queen Pomaré with her wicker shawl!"

And while the wind lashed their faces with little drops

of rain, she told Nana the story of Queen Pomaré. She had once been a magnificent woman whose beauty was the talk of Paris. She was famous for her flamboyance and insolent charm. She had led men by the nose, and often had great personages weeping on her stairs. Now she was a drunkard. The women of the neighborhood amused themselves by giving her absinthe, and urchins threw stones at her on the sidewalk. In short, she had hit bottom, she was a queen who had fallen into the mud!

Nana had listened coldly. "Watch this," said Satin. She whistled like a man. The ragpicker, who was now under the window, looked up and showed herself in the yellow glow of the lantern. In that bundle of rags, beneath a tattered scarf, they saw a scarred, bluish face with a toothless mouth and red eyes. Seeing this horrible old age of a prostitute drowned in wine, Nana had a sudden recollection. She again saw, in the shadows, the vision she had seen at Chamont: Irma d'Anglars, the former courtesan now laden with years and honors, ascending the steps of her château amid a reverent crowd of villagers. When Satin whistled again, laughing at the old woman, who could not see them, Nana said in a changed voice, "Stop it, here come the policemen again! Quick, darling, inside!"

The rhythmic footsteps were returning. Nana closed the window; then, when she turned around, shivering beneath her wet hair, she was astonished for a moment by the sight of her drawing room, as though she had never seen it before and had entered some unknown place. She was pleasantly surprised by the warm, fragrant air. The piled-up wealth, the antique furniture, the fabrics of silk and gold, the ivories and the bronzes were sleeping in the pink light of the lamps. From all over the silent house rose a sensation of great luxury: the solemnity of the large drawing room, the comfortable spaciousness of the dining room, the calm of the vast staircase, the softness of the carpets and seats. It was like a sudden expansion of herself, of her needs for domination and pleasure, of her desire to have everything in order to destroy everything. Never before had she felt so deeply the power of her sex. She looked around slowly, then said in a gravely philosophical tone, "Ah, I'm right to get everything I can while I'm young!"

294

Satin was already rolling on the bearskins in the bedroom. "Come on!" she called out.

Nana took off her clothes in the dressing room. To finish more quickly, she took her thick blond hair in both hands and shook it above the silver basin while long pins fell out of it, ringing a chime on the bright metal.

11

On that Sunday, beneath the cloudy sky of one of the first warms days of June, the race for the Grand Prix de Paris was to be run in the Bois de Boulogne. The sun had risen in a reddish mist that morning, but toward eleven o'clock, when the carriages were beginning to arrive at the Longchamps racetrack, a south wind had swept away the clouds. There were long, ragged trails of gray vapor, and bright, broadening patches of blue from one end of the horizon to the other. And in the bursts of sunlight that shone through breaks in the clouds, everything sparkled abruptly: the grass, which was gradually being covered by a throng of vehicles, riders, and pedestrians, the judge's box, the winning post, the indicator-boards, and, on the other side, in the middle of the enclosure, the five symmetrical stands with their galleries of brick and wood. And the vast plain lay stretched out beyond in the midday sun, bordered by little trees, cut off to the west by the wooded hills of Saint-Cloud and Suresnes, which were dominated by the stern profile of Mont-Valérien.

Nana was as excited as if the Grand Prix were going to decide her own fortune. She insisted on having a place against the railing beside the winning post. She had been one of the first to arrive, in her silver-trimmed landau drawn by four magnificent white horses, which had been given to her by Count Muffat. When she appeared at the entrance to the field with two postillions riding the left-hand horses and two footmen looking like statues at the back of her carriage, she stirred up as great a commotion in the crowd as if she had been a queen. She was wearing the blue and white colors of the Vandeuvres stable in a remarkable way: a tight-fitting blue silk bodice and tunic raised in back by a bustle, which outlined her thighs in a manner that was quite daring in those days of voluminous skirts; and a white satin dress with a white satin scarf over the shoulder, adorned with silver lace that glittered in the sun. And in order to look all the more like a jockey, she had boldly placed a blue cap with a white plume over her hair, which hung down the middle of her back like a long blond tail.

It was noon. Three more hours to wait for the Grand Prix. When the landau had drawn up beside the railing, Nana put herself at ease, as though she were at home. Acting on a sudden whim, she had brought Bijou and Louiset with her. The dog, lying on her skirt, was shivering with cold, despite the warmth of the day. Louiset was decked out in ribbons and lace. His poor little waxen face looked still paler in the open air. Oblivious to everyone around her, Nana was talking very loudly with Georges and Philippe, who sat on the seat opposite her, buried up to their shoulders in bouquets of white roses and forget-me-nots.

"He was getting on my nerves," she said, "so I showed him to the door. He's been sulking for two days now."

She was speaking of Muffat, but she did not tell the young men the real cause of this first quarrel. One night he had found a man's hat in her bedroom. She had indulged a foolish caprice by bringing in a passer-by from the street, out of boredom.

"You can't imagine how funny he is," she went on, amusing herself by the details she was giving. "He's really a pious prude. He says his prayers every night. Yes, that's right! He thinks I don't see him because I always go to bed before he does, to keep from bothering him. But I watch him out of the corner of my eye. He mumbles his prayers, then he turns away from me to cross himself when he crawls over me to get to the other side of the bed."

"That's pretty clever of him," said Philippe. "He probably does it before and after."

She laughed melodiously.

"Yes, that's it: before and after! When I go to sleep I hear his mumbling again. . . . What annoys me is that we can't have an argument any more without him bringing religion into it. I've always been religious myself. You can laugh if you want to; I still believe what I believe. But he overdoes it, he's always sobbing and talking about his remorse. Day before yesterday, when we had our quarrel, he got himself so worked up that I was starting to worry . . ."

She interrupted herself to say, "Here come the Mignons! And they've brought their children! Just look how they've dressed them up!"

The Mignons were in a landau whose austere colors suggested the solid luxury of a middle-class couple who have made their fortune. Rose was wearing a gray silk dress adorned with red bows and puffs. She was smiling, happy to see the joy of Henri and Charles, who were sitting on the front seat, looking awkward in their loose schoolboy tunics. But when the landau had drawn up alongside the railing and she saw Nana triumphing in the midst of her bouquets, with her four horses and her liveried servants, she pinched her lips and stiffly turned her head away. Mignon, however, looking lively and gay, waved to her. He made it a rule to remain aloof from women's quarrels.

"By the way," said Nana, "do you know a well-dressed little old man with bad teeth, by the name of Venot? He came to see me this morning."

"Monsieur Venot!" exclaimed Georges, astonished. "It can't be! He's a Jesuit!"

"Yes, I could tell that right away. Oh, you can't imagine the conversation we had! It was so funny! . . . He talked to me about Muffat and his broken marriage, and begged me to make his family happy again. He was very polite, and he kept smiling. . . . I told him I'd like nothing better. I promised to make Muffat go back to his wife. . . . And I meant it, too—I'd be delighted to see all those people happy! Besides, it would be a relief to me, because there are days when he annoys me so much I can't stand it!"

Her weariness of the past few months escaped from her in this heartfelt cry. Besides, the Count seemed to be having great financial problems. He was worried; it looked as though he might not be able to pay back the money he had borrowed from Labordette.

"There's the Countess," said Georges, who had been looking over the stands.

"Where?" cried Nana. "What sharp eyes that Baby has! Hold my parasol, Philippe."

But Georges moved more quickly than his brother; he was overjoyed to be able to hold the blue silk parasol with its silver fringe. Nana began looking through an enormous pair of binoculars.

"Ah, yes, I see her," she said at length. "That's her in the stand on the right, near a pillar, isn't it? She's wearing a purple dress and her daughter is beside her, in white. . . . Oh! There's Daguenet going up to them!"

Philippe then spoke of the approaching marriage between Daguenet and that bean-pole Estelle. It was all settled, the banns were about to be published. The Countess had resisted at first, but the Count, it was said, had finally imposed his will. Nana smiled.

"I know, I know," she said. "I'm glad for Paul's sake. He's a nice boy, he deserves it."

Then, turning toward Louiset: "Are you enjoying yourself? Oh, what a serious face!"

Louiset was watching all the people without smiling, looking very old, as though filled with sad reflections on what he saw. Bijou, driven from Nana's skirts by her animated movements, had gone to shiver against the boy.

Meanwhile the field was filling up. Vehicles were pouring in through the Cascade Gate in a dense, endless stream. There were big omnibuses, such as the *Pauline,* which had left from the Boulevard des Italiens with its fifty passengers and was now drawing up to the right of the stands; and then there were dogcarts, victorias, and superbly elegant landaus mingled with rickety cabs drawn by swaybacked nags; and four-in-hands with their owners sitting on benches in the open air, leaving their servants inside to guard the baskets filled with bottles of champagne; and buggies with immense, glittering steel wheels; and light tandems, as delicate as clockwork, which glided along with a jingling of little bells. Now and then a man on horseback rode by and there was a rush of startled pedestrians among the vehicles. The distant rumble that came from the roads of the Bois was suddenly turned into a dull rustling sound on the grass; nothing was heard except the hubbub of the growing crowd, shouts, calls, and the cracking of whips in the open air. And each time the sun shone through the clouds scattered by the wind, a streak of gold lit up the harnesses and varnished panels and set the women's dresses ablaze, while, in that dusty radiance, the coachmen, on their high seats, with their big whips, were bathed in a fiery glow.

Labordette got out of a barouche in which Gaga, Clarisse, and Blanche de Sivry had reserved a place for him. As he was hurrying to cross the track and enter the enclosure, Nana had Georges call him. When he came up to her she asked him, laughing, "What are the odds on me?"

She was referring to Nana the filly, that Nana who had let herself be shamefully beaten in the race for the Prix de Diane, and who, in April and May, had finished out of the money in the Prix des Cars and the Prix de la Grande Poule des Produits, both of which had been won by Lusignan, the other horse of the Vandeuvres stable. Lusignan was therefore the favorite; since the day before, the usual odds given on him had been two to one.

"Still fifty to one," replied Labordette.

"My God, I'm not worth much!" said Nana, amused by this joke. "In that case, I won't bet on myself. . . . No, I won't bet a single franc on myself!"

Labordette, in a great hurry, walked away; but she called him back. She wanted some advice. Since he maintained relations in the world of trainers and jockeys, he had special information about the various stables. His predictions had come true at least a score of times already. He was known as "the king of tipsters."

"Tell me what horses I should bet on," she said. "What are the odds on the English horse?"

"Spirit? Three to one . . . Valerio II the same. . . . Then all the others: Cosinus at twenty-five to one, Hasard at forty, Boum at thirty, Pichenette at thirty-five, Frangipane at ten. . . ."

"No, I won't bet on the English horse; I'm a patriot. . . . How about Valerio II? The Duke de Corbreuse looked very happy just now. . . . No! A thousand francs on Lusignan—what do you think of that?"

Labordette gave her a strange look. She leaned forward and questioned him in a low voice, for she knew that Vandeuvres had him place bets for him with bookmakers, in order to be able to bet more freely. If he had found out anything, he could tell her about it. But Labordette, without explaining himself, persuaded her to rely on his instinct: he would bet her thousand francs as he thought best, and she would not regret it.

"Bet on any horses you like," she said gaily, letting him leave, "except Nana—she's a nag!"

There was a burst of laughter in the carriage. The young men thought her remark was very funny. Louiset, without understanding, raised his pale eyes to his mother, whose loud exclamations surprised him. Labordette was still unable to get away: Rose Mignon had beckoned to him and was now giving him orders while he wrote figures in a little notebook. Then Clarisse and Gaga called him over to change their bets; having overheard certain things in the crowd, they no longer wanted Valerio II and had decided to bet on Lusignan instead. Labordette impassively wrote in his notebook. Finally he managed to escape, and he was seen disappearing between two stands on the other side of the track.

Carriages were still arriving. There were now five rows of them lined up along the railing in a deep mass broken here and there by the bright spots formed by white horses. Then, further on, there was a disorderly collection of other vehicles which looked as though they had been stranded on the grass, a jumble of wheels and teams turned in all directions, side by side, slantwise, crosswise, and head to head. And on the patches of grass that had remained clear, riders were trotting and pedestrians were moving in tight little clusters. Above this fairground, amid the motley confusion of the crowd, rose the gray canvas refreshment tents, turned white by the sunlight. But the greatest commotion, with tightly packed throngs and eddies of hats, took place around the bookmakers, who stood in open carriages, gesticulating like dentists, with their odds posted on high boards beside them.

"It's stupid not to know which horse to bet on," said Nana. "I'll have to risk some money myself."

She stood up to select a bookmaker whose face appealed to her. But she forgot her intention when she saw a whole crowd of acquaintances on either side, in the middle of the mass of carriages that now imprisoned her landau. Besides the Mignons, Gaga, Clarisse, and Blanche, there were

Tatan Néné and Maria Blond in a victoria; Caroline Héquet with her mother and two gentlemen in a barouche; Louise Violaine, all alone, driving a little basket carriage adorned with orange and green ribbons, the colors of the Méchain stable; and Léa de Horn sitting on one of the high seats of a four-in-hand in which a group of young men were making an uproar. Further on, in an aristocratic-looking carriage with eight springs, Lucy Stewart, wearing a simple black silk dress, was giving herself distinguished airs beside a tall young man in a midshipman's uniform. But Nana was dumbfounded to see Simonne arrive in a tandem driven by Steiner while a footman sat motionless behind them with folded arms. Simonne was dazzling, all in white satin striped with yellow, covered with diamonds from her belt to her hat. The banker, wielding an immense whip, urged on the two horses, one of them a little chestnut with a dainty trot, the other a big, high-stepping bay.

"So that thief Steiner has cleaned out the stock market again!" said Nana. "And look at the way Simonne is dressed! It's too much; she's going to get herself in trouble."

However, she exchanged greetings with them, from a distance. She waved her hand, smiling and turning, forgetting no one in order to make sure she was seen by everyone. And she went on talking: "Why, that's Lucy's son who's with her! He looks nice in his uniform. . . . That's why she's trying to be so elegant! She's afraid of him, you know; she makes him think she's an actress. . . . Poor young man! He doesn't seem to suspect anything."

"Oh, she'll find him a provincial heiress whenever she wants to," said Philippe, laughing.

Nana made no reply. She had just caught sight of old Tricon in the thick of the vehicles. Having arrived in a cab from which she could see nothing, Tricon had calmly climbed up onto the driver's seat. There, with her tall figure, noble face, and long curls, she towered above the crowd and seemed to reign over her female subjects. They all smiled at her discreetly. She loftily pretended not to know them. She was not there to work, she was watching the races for pleasure. She was an ardent gambler, with a passion for horses.

"Look, there's that idiot La Faloise!" Georges said suddenly.

This was a surprise to them all. Nana no longer recognized her La Faloise. Since inheriting from his uncle, he had become extraordinarily fashionable. He had his hair parted in the middle and he was wearing a turned-down collar and a light-colored suit that clung to his narrow shoulders. He affected a weary swagger, a languid voice, slang words, and sentences that he did not take the trouble to finish.

"Why, he looks very good!" declared Nana, enchanted.

Gaga and Clarisse had called La Faloise over and were throwing themselves at him, trying to get him back. He left them immediately, swaying his hips with mocking disdain. Nana dazzled him and he hurried over to stand on the step of her carriage. When she made a joking reference to Gaga, he said, "Oh, no, I'm through with the old guard! I don't want to hear about that any more! Besides, you know, you're my Juliet now. . . ."

He had put his hand over his heart. Nana laughed heartily at that sudden declaration in the open air.

"Never mind that," she said; "you're making me forget that I want to bet some money. . . . Georges, you see that bookmaker over there, the big, red-faced one, with curly hair? I like that rough, vulgar face of his. I want you to go to him and place a bet on . . . What horse shall I bet on?"

"I'm no patriot, not at all!" said La Faloise. "All my money's on the English horse. It'll be wonderful if the Englishman wins! To hell with the French!"

Nana was scandalized. Then they discussed the merits of the various horses. To give the impression that he was very well informed, La Faloise called them all sorry nags. Baron Verdier's Frangipane, by The Truth out of Lenore, was a big bay who would have had a chance if they hadn't foundered him during training. As for Valerio II, of the Corbreuse stable, he wasn't ready yet: he'd had a bad case of colic in April. Oh, they were keeping it quiet, but he was sure of it, on his word of honor! And he finally recommended Hasard, of the Méchain stable, the most defective of all, a horse no one wanted to bet on. Yes, Hasard—what form, what style! There was a horse that was going to surprise everybody!

"No," said Nana, "I'm going to put two hundred francs on Lusignan and a hundred on Boum."

"But Boum is hopeless, my dear!" cried La Faloise. "Don't bet on him! Even Gasc isn't backing his own horse. . . . And your Lusignan—never! It's ridiculous! He's my Lamb out of Princess, just think of it! By Lamb out of Princess! They're all too short-legged!"

He was almost choking. Philippe pointed out that Lusignan had nevertheless won the Prix des Cars and the Prix de la Grande Poule des Produits. But La Faloise brushed aside the objection. What did that prove? Nothing at all. On the contrary, it meant that one ought to be suspicious. Besides, Gresham was riding Lusignan, so there was no use talking about it! Gresham was jinxed, he never won.

And the discussion which had started in Nana's landau seemed to spread from one end of the field to the other. Voices rose shrilly, the passion for gambling passed over the crowd, making faces flushed and gestures erratic. The bookmakers, perched on their carriages, were furiously shouting out odds and writing down figures. They were dealing only with the small fry of the bettors; the big bets were being made inside the enclosure. Here reigned the avidity of those who risked five francs in the hope of winning a few louis. The great battle was between Spirit and Lusignan. Englishmen, recognizable as such, were strolling among the groups, their faces red with excitement, triumphant already. Bramah, a horse belonging to Lord Reading, had won the Grand Prix the year before, a defeat for the French from which hearts were still bleeding. It would be a disaster if France were beaten again this year. The ladies were therefore passionately interested in the race, out of national pride. The Vandeuvres stable was the rampart of French honor. Lusignan was upheld, defended, and acclaimed. Lucy abstained, because of her son; but there was a rumor that Rose Mignon had given Labordette four thousand francs to bet for her. Tricon sat beside her coachman, waiting until the last minute, remaining aloof from the quarrels, dominating the uproar in which the names of horses kept recurring, along with lively Parisian phrases and guttural English exclamations; she listened and took notes with a majestic air.

"And what about Nana?" said Georges. "Isn't anyone betting on her?"

No, no one was betting on her; no one had even mentioned her. The outsider of the Vandeuvres stable had been overshadowed by Lusignan's popularity. But La Faloise raised his arms and said, "I've just had an inspiration: I'm putting twenty francs on Nana."

"Bravo!" said Georges. "I'll put forty on her!"

"And I'll bet sixty!" said Philippe.

They all raised their bets, paying court to Nana, calling out figures as though they were bidding for her at an auction. La Faloise spoke of covering her with gold. Furthermore, everyone ought to bet on her. They would go and solicit backers. But as the three young men were going off to propagandize, Nana called out to them, "I'm not betting on her, you know! Not for anything in the world! . . . Georges, put two hundred francs on Lusignan for me, and a hundred on Valerio II."

They hurried away. Highly amused, she watched them slipping between wheels, ducking under horses' heads, moving all over the whole field. As soon as they recognized anyone in a carriage, they rushed up and began urging them to bet on Nana. Loud laughter ran through the crowd when they occasionally turned around and triumphantly indicated numbers by holding up their fingers, while Nana stood waving her parasol to them. They made rather poor progress, however. A few men let themselves be convinced: Steiner, for example, who was stirred by the sight of Nana, risked sixty francs. But the women flatly refused. No, thanks, they didn't want to bet on a sure loser! Besides, they were not eager to work for the success of a vile girl who put them all to shame with her four white horses, her postillions, and her look of swallowing the whole world. Gaga and Clarisse stiffly asked La Faloise if he was making fun of them. When Georges boldly went up to the Mignons' landau, Rose, outraged, turned her head away without answering. A woman had to be pretty low to let her name be given to a horse! Mignon, however, accepted the suggestion, looking amused and saying that women always brought good luck.

"Well?" said Nana when the young men came back after a long visit to the bookmakers.

"The odds on you are forty to one," said La Faloise.

"Forty!" she exclaimed in amazement. "They were fifty to one. . . . What's happened?"

Just then Labordette returned. The track was being closed and a bell was announcing the first race. Amid the expectant clamor, she questioned him about that sudden drop in the odds. He answered evasively; there had no doubt been a few sizable bets. She had to content herself with this explanation. Looking preoccupied, Labordette told her that Vandeuvres was going to come if he could manage to slip away.

The first race was ending, almost unnoticed in the impatient wait for the Grand Prix, when a cloud burst over the race track. The sun had vanished some time before, and a dull light darkened the crowd. The wind rose; huge raindrops fell in a sudden deluge. There was a minute of confusion, with shouting, joking, and swearing, as the people who were on foot scurried under the canvas refreshment tents. In the carriages, the women tried to shelter themselves, holding their parasols with both hands, while footmen frantically hastened to raise the tops. But the shower was already ceasing. The sun rose through the fine drops of rain that were still falling. A patch of blue opened behind the cloud as it was swept away above the Bois. Then the whole sky brightened, bringing laughter to the lips of the reassured women; and while the horses snorted and the soaked, agitated crowd shook itself, a flood of golden sunshine lit up the wet grass sparkling with drops of crystal.

"Oh, poor Louiset!" said Nana. "Did you get very wet, darling?"

Without speaking, the boy let her wipe his hands. She had taken out her handkerchief. She then dried Bijou, who was shivering more violently than ever. No damage had been done, only a few spots on her white satin dress, but she didn't care. The freshened bouquets glittered like snow. She smelled one happily, wetting her lips as though in dew.

Meanwhile the shower had abruptly filled the stands. Nana looked through her binoculars. At that distance one could distinguish only a compact, confused mass heaped up on the seats, a dark background dotted with pale faces. The sun slipped in through the corners of the roof, cutting the seated crowd with an angle of light and making the women's dresses look faded. Nana was especially amused by the ladies whom the shower had driven away from the rows of chairs lined up on the gravel in front of the stands. Since courtesans were strictly forbidden to enter the enclosure, she made bitter remarks about all those respectable women; she found their clothes ugly and their faces ridiculous.

There was a rumor that the Empress was entering the little center stand, a pavilion in the form of a chalet whose broad balcony was furnished with red armchairs.

"Look who's there!" said Georges. "I didn't think he was on duty this week."

Count Muffat's stiff, solemn face had appeared behind the Empress. The young men began to joke, regretting that Nana was not there to give him a pat on the stomach. But then Nana, still looking through her binoculars, saw the Prince of Scotland in the imperial stand.

"Why, it's Charles!" she cried. She thought he had put on weight. He seemed to have grown broader in eighteen months. And she gave details. Oh, he was solidly built!

The women in the carriages around her were whispering that the Count had abandoned her. There was a whole story about it. The Tuileries had been shocked by the chamberlain's conduct ever since he had been openly displaying his relationship with her, so, to keep his position, he had just broken off with her. La Faloise bluntly repeated this story to her, offering himself to her again, and calling her "his Juliet." She laughed and said, "That idiot . . . You don't know him: all I have to do is whistle and he'll give everything up for me."

For the past few moments she had been examining Countess Sabine and Estelle. Daguenet was still with them. Fauchery arrived and disturbed everyone to go and greet them; then he, too, remained there, smiling. Nana pointed to the stands with a disdainful gesture. "Those people don't impress me any more," she said. "I know them too well. You ought to see what they're like underneath! No more respect, that's all over now. There's filth at the bottom, and filth at the top, and filth everywhere you go. . . . That's why I'm not going to let anybody annoy me."

And she broadened her gesture to include them all, from the grooms leading the horses onto the track to the sovereign herself, who was talking with Charles, a prince, but a dirty pig just the same.

"Bravo, Nana!" La Faloise cried enthusiastically. "You're wonderful, Nana!"

The sounds of the bell were lost in the wind. The races continued. Berlingot, a horse from the Méchain stable, had just won the Prix d'Ispahan. Nana called Labordette to ask about her two thousand francs. He laughed and refused to tell her which horses he had put her money on, in order not to change her luck, he said. Her money was well placed, she would soon see. When she told him the bets she had made herself—two hundred francs on Lusignan and a hundred on Valerio II—he shrugged his shoulders as though to say that women were always doing foolish things. This surprised her; she no longer understood anything.

The field was now becoming more animated than ever. People were preparing to have lunch in the open air while waiting for the Grand Prix. There was much eating and more drinking, everywhere—on the grass, on the high seats of four-in-hands, in the victorias, the broughams, the landaus. There was a vast display of cold meats and champagne, which footmen had taken from box seats. Corks were pulled out with sharp little pops that were carried away by the wind. Jokes were exchanged from one carriage to the next. The sound of breaking glasses added a harsh note to the nervous gaiety. Gaga, Clarisse, and Blanche were having a serious meal, eating sandwiches on a blanket they had spread over their knees. Louise Violaine had left her basket carriage to rejoin Caroline Héquet. On the grass at their feet, some gentlemen had set up a little bar, at which Tatan, Maria, Simonne, and the others came to drink. Nearby, high up on Léa de Horn's four-in-hand, a group of people were emptying bottles, getting drunk in the sunlight, posing and blustering above the crowd. But soon the largest group of all was pressing around Nana's landau. She was standing up, filling glasses of champagne for the men who came to greet her. One of the footmen, François, passed the bottles while La Faloise called out, imitating a sideshow barker, "Step right up, gentlemen, step right up! It's all free! There's plenty for everyone!"

"Stop it, will you?" Nana finally said. "You're making us look like a traveling circus."

She was greatly amused, however, and thought he was very funny. For a moment she had the idea of sending a glass of champagne to Rose Mignon, who was ostentatiously refraining from drinking. Henri and Charles were bored to tears; the poor little boys would surely like some champagne. But Georges drank the glass, fearing a quarrel. Then Nana remembered Louiset, whom she had forgotten behind her. Perhaps he was thirsty; and she forced him to drink a few drops of champagne, which made him cough terribly.

"Step right up, gentlemen, step right up!" repeated La Faloise. "It doesn't cost two sous, it doesn't cost one—we're giving it away . . ."

Nana interrupted him with an exclamation: "Look! There's Bordenave! Call him. Run over to him, please!"

It was indeed Bordenave, walking along with his hands behind his back, wearing a hat that looked reddish in the sunlight and a greasy frock coat faded at the seams; a Bordenave battered by bankruptcy but still defiant, displaying his poverty in the midst of the fashionable world with the boldness of a man who is always ready to take fortune by storm.

"My God, what style!" he said when Nana amiably held out her hand to him. Then, after emptying a glass of champagne, he said with deep regret, "Ah, if only I were a woman! . . . But it doesn't matter, by God! Will you come back to the theater? I've got an idea. I'll rent the Gaîté and we'll have the whole town at our feet in no time at all! What do you say? You at least owe me that. . . ."

And he stayed with her, grumbling even though he was glad to see her again, for, as he said, it made him feel good just to see her living. She was his daughter, his real blood.

The circle was growing larger. La Faloise was now pouring the champagne, while Philippe and Georges were recruiting more friends. A slow movement was gradually bringing in all the people on the field. Nana had a smile and an amusing remark for everyone. Groups of drinkers were coming closer, all the scattered champaign was moving toward her; soon there was a single dense crowd around her landau, and she reigned amid the uproar and the outstretched glasses, with her yellow hair floating in the breeze and her snow-white face bathed in sunshine. Then, to deal the final blow to the other women who were enraged by her triumph, she raised a full glass in her old pose as Venus victorious.

But someone touched her from behind, and when she turned around she was surprised to see Mignon on the seat. She disappeared for a moment and sat down beside him, for he had come to tell her something serious. He had been saying everywhere that his wife was ridiculous to hold a grudge against Nana; he found it foolish and useless.

"Listen, my dear," he said, "be careful: don't make Rose too angry. . . . I think I'd better warn you, you understand. . . . Yes, she has a weapon, and she's never forgiven you for that business of *The Little Duchess* . . ."

"A weapon!" said Nana. "What do I care about that?"

"Look, it's a letter she must have found in that miserable Fauchery's pocket, a letter written to him by Countess Muffat. The whole story's in it, clearly spelled out. . . . Rose wants to send the letter to the Count, to get even with him and you."

"What do I care about that?" repeated Nana. "It's funny. . . . So she knows about Fauchery! Well, so much the better, she was getting on my nerves. We'll have a good laugh."

"No, no, I don't want that to happen," Mignon said quickly. "What a scandal it would cause! And we have nothing to gain from it . . ."

He stopped short, afraid of saying too much. She cried out that she had no desire to save a respectable woman's reputation. When he continued to insist, she stared at him. He was no doubt afraid that Fauchery would resume his affair with Rose if he broke off with the Countess; that was what Rose wanted, despite her thirst for vengeance, because she still had a warm spot in her heart for the journalist. Nana became thoughtful, recalling Monsieur Venot's visit. She began forming a plan while Mignon tried to convince her:

"Let's say Rose sends the letter. There's a scandal. You're involved in it, everyone will say it's all your fault. . . . First of all, the Count will separate from his wife . . ."

"Why should he?" she said. "In fact . . ."

She, too, stopped short. There was no need for her to think aloud. Finally she pretended to agree with Mignon, to get rid of him; and when he advised her to give in to Rose a little, to pay her a short visit right there, for example, in front of everyone, she replied that she would see, that she would think it over.

A tumult made her stand up again. On the track, horses were flashing across the finish line. Cornemuse had just won the Prix de la Ville de Paris. It would soon be time for the Grand Prix. The excitement increased; the impatient crowd shifted restlessly, trying to make the time pass more quickly. And at the last minute the bettors were surprised and bewildered by the constant drop in the odds on Nana, the outsider of the Vandeuvres stable. Gentlemen kept coming back with new figures: Nana was at thirty to one, then twenty-five, then twenty, then fifteen. No one could understand it. A filly that had been beaten at every track, a filly that no one had been willing to bet on that morning at fifty to one! What was the meaning of that sudden frenzy? Some laughed, and spoke of all the money that was going to be lost by the fools who had let themselves be taken in by that joke; others, serious and worried, were afraid something might be wrong. Maybe the race was "fixed." Stories were told about past racing scandals; but this time the great name of Vandeuvres silenced the accusations, and the general opinion finally sided with the skeptics who predicted that Nana would come in last.

"Who's riding Nana?" asked La Faloise.

Just then the original Nana returned; the gentlemen gave the question an indecent meaning and burst into exaggerated laughter. Nana bowed.

"Price," she replied.

And the discussion began again. Price was a famous English jockey who had never ridden in France before. Why had Vandeuvres brought him over, when it was usually Gresham who rode Nana? Furthermore, they were surprised that he had in turn entrusted Lusignan to Gresham, who never won, according to La Faloise. But all these remarks were swallowed up in a loud confusion of jokes, denials, and contradictory opinions. They began emptying bottles of champagne again, to kill time. Then a whisper ran through the crowd and several groups stepped aside to make way for Vandeuvres. Nana pretended to be angry.

"It's very nice of you to come so late! I was dying to see the enclosure."

"Then come on," said Vandeuvres, "there's still time. I'll show you around. I just happen to have a lady's pass on me."

And he led her away on his arm. She enjoyed the jealous expressions with which Lucy, Caroline, and the others watched her. Behind her, La Faloise and the Hugon brothers remained in her landau and continued to pour out her champagne. She shouted to them that she would be back soon.

Vandeuvres caught sight of Labordette, called him over, and exchanged a few words with him.

"Have you picked up everything?"

"Yes."

"How much?"

"Thirty thousand francs, all over the place."

Seeing that Nana was listening curiously, they fell silent. Vandeuvres was very nervous. His eyes were alight with the same little flames that had frightened her on the night when he had talked of burning himself up with his horses. As they were crossing the track she lowered her voice and said to him familiarly, "Listen, I want you to explain to me why the odds on your filly are falling. It's causing a sensation!"

He started and exclaimed, "Ah, so they're talking about it! What a breed those bettors are! Whenever I have a favorite they all jump on him, so there's nothing left for me. Then when there's some betting on an outsider they start howling as though they were being skinned alive."

"You ought to let me know," she said, "because I've already made some bets. Does she have a chance?"

He had an abrupt, irrational surge of anger: "Stop hounding me, will you? Every horse has a chance! The odds are falling because bets are being made on her; that's simple enough, isn't it? What else do you expect me to know? I'd rather leave you right now if you intend to go on annoying me with your idiotic questions!"

This tone was not in accordance with either his temperament or his habits. Nana was more astonished than offended. Moreover, he immediately felt ashamed of himself, and when she curtly asked him to be polite, he apologized. For some time past he had been subject to such sudden fits of ill-humor. Everyone in the fashionable and pleasure-seeking world of Paris knew that he was playing his last card that day. If neither of his horses won, if he lost the great sums he had bet on them, it would be a disaster for him, a complete collapse; the whole structure of his credit, and the lofty appearances which his existence still maintained, even though it had been undermined and almost emptied by disorder and debt, would come tumbling down in a resounding ruin.

And everyone also knew that Nana was the voracious woman who had finished him off; she had been the last to attack his tottering fortune, and she had made a clean sweep of everything that was left of it. Stories were told of wild caprices, of money thrown to the winds, of a trip to Baden, where she had not left him enough to pay the hotel bill, of a handful of diamonds thrown into the fire one drunken night, to see if they would burn like coal. Little by little, with her plump limbs and her coarse, vulgar laughter, she had taken complete possession of that impoverished and subtly intelligent scion of an ancient family. He was now staking everything on his horses, so thoroughly in the grip of his taste for filth and foolishness that he had lost even the strength of his skepticism. A week earlier, Nana had made him promise to buy her a château on the Normandy coast between Le Havre and Trouville, and he still placed all his honor on keeping his word. But she now irritated him, and she seemed so stupid to him that he felt like beating her.

The gatekeeper had allowed them to enter the enclosure, not daring to stop the woman on the Count's arm. Swelling with pride at having at last set foot on that forbidden ground, Nana walked slowly, with studied composure, before the ladies seated at the bottom of the stands. Spread over ten rows of chairs, there was a deep mass of dresses mingling their colors in the gaiety of the open air. Some of the chairs had been shifted to form intimate circles, as in a public park, among friends and acquaintances who happened to be sitting near one another. Children were running freely among the groups. Further up, the stands rose in crowded tiers until the bright colors of the women's dresses faded into the shadows under the roof. Nana examined all those ladies. She pointedly stared at Countess Sabine. Then, as she was passing in front of the imperial stand, she was amused by the sight of Muffat standing beside the Empress with all his official stiffness.

"Oh, how silly he looks!" she said loudly to Vandeuvres.

She wanted to see everything. The little park, with its grass and its clumps of trees, did not interest her. A vendor of ices had set up a large counter near the gates. Beneath a round, rustic thatched roof, a dense crowd was shouting and gesticulating; this was the betting ring. Nearby were some empty stalls, and she was disappointed to see only a gendarme's horse in one of them. Then there was the paddock, with a track no more than a hundred yards in circumference, on which Valerio II, arching his neck, was being walked by a stableboy. And that was all, except for a lot of men walking along the gravel paths with orange cards attached to their buttonholes, and a constant parade of people along the open galleries of the stands, which interested her for a moment. Really, it wasn't worth getting upset because they wouldn't let you go in!

Daguenet and Fauchery greeted her as they were passing by. She beckoned to them and they had to come over to her. She was expressing her contempt for the enclosure when she stopped short and exclaimed, "Look, there's the Marquis de Chouard! How he's aged! He's killing himself, the old lecher! Is he still as wild as ever?"

Daguenet told her about the old man's latest exploit, something that had happened only two days before and was not yet widely known: after hovering around for months, he had bought Gaga's daughter Amélie, for thirty thousand francs, it was said.

"That's disgusting!" Nana cried indignantly. "What a fine way for a mother to treat her daughter! . . . Come to think of it, that must be Lili over there in a brougham with a lady. I thought I recognized her face. . . . The old man must have brought her."

Vandeuvres was not listening; he was impatient and eager to get rid of her. As Fauchery was leaving, however, he said that if she had not seen the bookmakers she had not seen anything; and the Count had to take her to see them, despite his obvious reluctance. This time she was happy: it was really very interesting.

In a round area between lawns bordered by young chestnut trees, shaded by light green leaves, the bookmakers were lined up side by side in a wide circle, waiting for bettors, as though at a fair. Their odds were posted on trees beside them. Their eyes were constantly alert, and they wrote down bets in response to gestures and winks, so rapidly that curious bystanders gaped at them without understanding. There was a loud confusion of shouted figures, and a tumult greeted each unexpected change of odds. Occasionally the uproar was increased still more by a messenger who came running up to the edge of the circle and bellowed out the news of a start or a finish, which gave rise to a long clamor in the gambling fever pulsing in the sunlight.

"They're very funny!" said Nana, highly amused. "What crooked faces they have! . . . You see that tall one over there? I'd hate to meet *him* in a dark alley!"

Vandeuvres showed her a bookmaker, once a clerk in a dry-goods shop, who had made three million francs in two years. He was a frail, blond little man. He was surrounded by respect; people smiled as they talked to him, while others stood nearby to look at him.

They were about to leave when Vandeuvres nodded to another bookmaker, who then ventured to call him. He was a former coachman of the Count's, an enormous man with bulky shoulders and a ruddy face. Now that he was trying his luck at the track, with a capital of dubious origin, Vandeuvres was doing his best to get him started by allowing him to handle all his secret bets, still treating him as a servant from whom he hid nothing. Despite this assistance, he had suffered a series of very heavy losses, and he, too, was playing his last card that day, with bloodshot eyes and an apoplectic face.

"Well, Maréchal, how much have you covered?" Vandeuvres asked him in a low voice.

"A hundred thousand francs, Monsieur," replied the bookmaker, also lowering his voice. "That's pretty good, isn't it? I admit I raised the odds to three to one."

Vandeuvres looked annoyed.

"No, I won't have that. Put them back down to two to

one immediately. . . . I won't tell you anything more, Maréchal."

"Oh, what difference can it make to you now, Monsieur?" asked Maréchal with the humble smile of an accomplice. "I had to attract people to take your forty thousand francs."

Vandeuvres silenced him. But as he was walking away, Maréchal suddenly regretted that he had forgotten to question him about the drop in the odds on his filly. He would be in a fine mess if she had a chance, because he had taken four thousand francs' worth of bets on her at fifty to one.

Although she had understood nothing of what Vandeuvres had been whispering, Nana did not dare to ask him for any more explanations, for he seemed more nervous than ever. He abruptly handed her over to Labordette, whom they encountered in front of the weighing-in room.

"You can take her back," he said. "I have things to do. Good-by."

And he entered the room, which was narrow and low. With its big scales, it looked like the baggage room of a provincial railroad station. Nana had another disappointment, for she had been imagining something enormous, a monumental machine for weighing the horses. What! They only weighed the jockeys? Then it wasn't worth making such a fuss about their weighing! A stupid-looking jockey was sitting on the scales with his harness on his lap, waiting for a fat man in a frock coat to check his weight, while at the door a stableboy held the horse, Cosinus, around which a silent, attentive crowd was gathering.

The track was about to be closed. Labordette hurried Nana away, but then he turned back to show her a little man talking with Vandeuvres, off to one side.

"That's Price," he said.

"Ah, yes, the jockey who's riding me!" she replied, laughing.

She thought he was terribly ugly. All the jockeys looked ugly to her; probably, she said, because they had been prevented from growing up. This one, a man in his early forties, was like an old, shriveled-up child, with a long, thin, wrinkled face that looked hard and dead. His body was so knotty and small that his blue jacket with white sleeves seemed to have been placed on a piece of wood.

"No," she said as they walked away, "he's not the man of my dreams."

There was still a mob of people on the track, whose wet, trampled grass had become black. They thronged around the tall iron pillars of the two indicator boards, looking up and clamoring each time an electric wire, connected with the weighing-in room, made the number of a horse appear. Gentlemen were checking their racing cards. There was a slight commotion when Pichenette was scratched. Nana, however, walked straight across, holding Labordette's arm. The bell hanging from the flagstaff was ringing persistently as a signal to clear the track.

"Ah, let me tell you," Nana said as she got back into her landau, "their enclosure is nothing at all!"

Everyone around her began applauding and cheering: "Bravo, Nana! . . . Our Nana has come back to us!" They were so silly! Had they thought she was going to abandon them? She had returned in time. Attention! It was about to begin. And the champagne was forgotten, they all stopped drinking.

But Nana was surprised to find Gaga in her carriage, with Bijou and Louiset on her lap. Gaga had decided to go there in order to be near La Faloise, although she had said that she had come to give the baby a kiss. She adored children.

"By the way, what about Lili?" asked Nana. "That's her over there in that old man's brougham, isn't it? . . . I've just been told something disgusting . . ."

Gaga assumed a tearful expression. "My dear, it's made me ill," she said sorrowfully. "Yesterday I cried so much I had to stay in bed, and today I didn't think I'd be able to come here. . . . You know my way of thinking. I didn't want her to . . . I had her brought up in a convent, so she could get a good husband. I gave her strict advice, and always kept an eye on her. Well, she's the one who wanted to do it! She made a scene, she cried and said nasty things till I finally slapped her. She was too bored, she wanted to go through with it. Then when she said, 'After all, *you* don't have any right to stop me,' I said to her, 'You're a worthless girl and you're dishonoring us—get out.' And so it happened. I agreed to arrange it . . . Now my last hope is gone. I'd been dreaming of such nice things!"

The sound of a quarrel made them stand up. Georges was defending Vandeuvres against the vague rumors that had been circulating among the various groups.

"How can you say he's not backing his own horse?" he shouted. "Yesterday, at the Salon des Courses, he put twenty thousand francs on Lusignan."

"Yes, I was there," affirmed Philippe. "And he didn't put a single franc on Nana. . . . If the odds on Nana are ten to one, he has nothing to do with it. It's ridiculous to attribute such calculating maneuvers to people. What would he have to gain by it?"

Labordette had been listening calmly. He shrugged his shoulders and said, "Never mind, people are always talking. . . . The Count just put at least another ten thousand francs on Lusignan, and if he put two thousand on Nana it's only because an owner should always act as though he believes in his horses."

"Anyway, what does it matter to us?" said La Faloise, waving his arms. "Spirit is going to win. France is done for, hurrah for England!"

A long tremor ran through the crowd while the bell announced that the horses were on the track. In order to see better, Nana stood up on the seat of her landau, trampling the bouquets of forget-me-nots and roses. She glanced around the immense horizon. At this final moment of excitement the track was empty, closed by gray barriers, with policemen standing at every other post. The strip of grass, muddy in front of her, grew greener as it stretched away, until it finally turned into a bright, velvety carpet in the distance. Then, when she lowered her eyes, she saw the field swarming with people standing on tiptoe or perched on carriages, raised and stirred by a wave of passion. Horses were neighing, tent flaps were fluttering in the wind, riders were urging their mounts through the people on foot rushing to lean against the barriers. When she looked at the stands on the other side of the track, the faces seemed smaller, the heads formed a motley mass that filled the passages, tiers, and balconies with dark profiles outlined against the sky. And she saw the surrounding plain beyond. Past the ivy-covered mill to her right, there were shady meadows; in front of her, all the way to the Seine, which was flowing at the foot of the hill, the intersecting roads were lined with waiting carriages; then, in the direction of Boulogne, to her left, the landscape widened again, opening into the bluish, faraway expanse of Meudon, crossed by a road lined with paulownias, whose pink, leafless tops made a strip of bright color. People were still arriving, looking like a long procession of ants as they moved along the thin ribbon of a road that stretched across the fields. Far away, toward Paris, the non-paying spectators formed a line of dark, moving points beneath the trees at the edge of the Bois.

Suddenly a surge of gaiety swept through the hundred thousand people covering the field like a host of scurrying insects beneath the vast sky. The sun, which had been hidden for the past quarter of an hour, reappeared and poured out a flood of light. Everything sparkled again. The women's parasols were like countless golden shields above the crowd. The sun was greeted with applause and laughter; arms reached up to push away the clouds.

A solitary police officer was walking along the middle of the track. Further on, to the left, a man appeared with a red flag in his hand.

"That's the starter, Baron de Mauriac," said Labordette in answer to a question from Nana.

Among the men who were pressing all around her, even on the steps of her landau, there were exclamations and disconnected remarks uttered under the immediate influence of first impressions. Philippe, Georges, Bordenave, and La Faloise could not keep silent.

"Stop shoving! . . . Let me see! . . . Ah, the judge is going into his box. . . . You say it's Monsieur de Souvigney? . . . It must take good eyes to decide a close finish from a place like that! . . . Be quiet, the flag is going up. . . . Here they come! . . . The first one is Cosinus."

A red and yellow flag was waving in the air at the top of its staff. Stableboys were leading out the horses one by one. The jockeys sat in their saddles with their arms motionless, making bright spots in the sunlight. Then a murmur greeted Spirit, a superb big bay whose harsh colors, yellow and black, had a British sadness. Valerio II was loudly cheered when he appeared, small and lively, in pale green bordered with pink. The two Vandeuvres horses were among the last to arrive. Finally, behind Frangipane, the blue and white colors were seen. But Lusignan, a dark bay of irreproachable form, was almost forgotten in the surprise caused by Nana. The chestnut filly had never been seen like this before: the sunshine gave her a reddish-blond hue; she glittered in the light like a new gold coin. Her chest was deep, her head and neck were slender, her back was long, high-strung, and delicate.

"Look, her hair's the same color as mine!" cried Nana, overjoyed. "Oh, I'm proud of her!"

Several of the men climbed up on the landau. Bordenave nearly stepped on Louiset, who had been forgotten by his mother. He picked him up with paternal grunts, lifted him to his shoulder, and said, "Poor little fellow, he wants to see too. . . . Just a minute, I'll show you your mother. . . . Look, over there—see the pretty horse?"

And when Bijou began scratching his leg, he picked him up too. Nana, delighted with the horse that bore her name, glanced at the other women to see their expressions. They were all enraged. Tricon, who had remained motionless on her cab until then, waved her hands above the crowd and called out instructions to a bookmaker. Her instinct had just spoken: she was betting on Nana.

La Faloise was chattering unbearably. He had taken a violent fancy to Frangipane.

"I've got an inspiration," he said. "Just look at Frangipane! What form! I'll take Frangipane at eight to one. Who wants to bet?"

"Calm down," Labordette finally said to him, "or you'll be sorry later."

"Frangipane is a second-rate nag," declared Philippe. "He's already wet all over. . . . Wait till you see him canter."

The horses had gone up the track to the right. They now started the preliminary canter, passing in front of the stands in a disorderly group. There was an outburst of excited remarks, with everyone talking at once:

"Lusignan is too long in the back, but he's in good condition. . . . Not one franc on Valerio II! He's nervous, he canters with his head high: that's a bad sign. . . . Look! It's Burne who's riding Spirit. . . . I tell you he has no shoulders! Well-built shoulders, that's what counts. . . . No, Spirit is much too calm. . . . Listen, I saw Nana after the

Grande Poule des Produits. She was soaking wet, her coat was dull, and her flanks were heaving as though she were about to die. I'll bet four hundred francs she's not even in the money! . . . Enough! You're getting on our nerves with your Frangipane! Anyway, it's too late: they're about to start."

Almost in tears, La Faloise was making frantic efforts to find a bookmaker. The others had to reason with him. They all stretched their necks forward, but the first start was not good: the starter, who looked like a thin streak of black in the distance, had not lowered his red flag. The horses came back after galloping for a short time. There were two more false starts. Finally the starter reassembled the horses and sent them off with a skill which aroused shouts of admiration.

"Wonderful! . . . No, it was only luck. . . . Never mind, they're off!"

The clamor was stifled by the anxiety that gripped every heart. The betting was over now; everything was being decided on the broad track. There was silence at first, as though everyone were holding his breath. White, quivering faces were raised. Hasard and Cosinus had taken the lead; they were closely followed by Valerio II, with the others in a confused mass behind. By the time they passed in front of the stands, shaking the ground and raising a stormy wind by their speed, the group had stretched out to forty lengths. Frangipane was last, Nana was a little behind Lusignan and Spirit.

"My God, look at the way that English horse is gaining!" said Labordette.

There were comments and exclamations from everyone in the landau. They all stood on tiptoe and watched the bright colors of the jockeys flashing in the sunlight. When they came to the rise, Valerio II took the lead, Cosinus and Hasard began to lose ground, and Nana was still behind Lusignan and Spirit, who were running neck and neck.

"The English horse is going to win, it's obvious," said Bordenave. "Lusignan is tiring and Valerio II can't hold out."

"It'll be disgraceful if the English horse wins!" cried Philippe in a fit of patriotic grief.

A feeling of anguish began to settle over the whole

tightly packed crowd. Another defeat! They wished ardently, almost religiously, for Lusignan's victory, and
roundly abused Spirit and his funereal-looking jockey. A
wind of excitement sent groups of people running across
the grass while riders galloped furiously among them. And
Nana, slowly turning around, saw at her feet that wave of
animals and people, that sea of heads churned and swept
along in the whirlpool of the race, which was streaking
the horizon with the lightning of the jockeys. She had
watched the horses speed past, and seen their legs dwindle
to the thinness of hairs as they swiftly moved away from
her. She now saw them from the side as they rounded
the far turn, looking small and delicate against the distant
green background of the Bois. Then suddenly they
vanished behind a large clump of trees.

"Don't give up!" cried Georges, still hopeful. "It's not
over yet. . . . The English horse is tiring too."

But La Faloise, again filled with disdain for his native
land, became scandalous by cheering Spirit. Bravo! It
served them right! France needed that! Spirit first and
Frangipane second, that would annoy his country! Labordette, exasperated, seriously threatened to throw him out
of the landau.

"Let's see how long they take," Bordenave said calmly;
still holding Louiset, he had taken out his watch.

One by one, the horses were reappearing from behind
the clump of trees. The crowd gasped in amazement.
Valerio II was still in the lead, but Spirit was gaining on
him, Lusignan had fallen back and another horse had
taken his place. At first the spectators could not make out
the colors, but then there were loud exclamations:

"Why, it's Nana! . . . Don't be silly, it's still Lusignan!
. . . No, it's Nana! You can easily recognize her by her
golden color. . . . Just look at her! She's on fire! . . . Come
on, Nana! . . . She's putting up a good fight! . . . That
doesn't mean anything. Lusignan is just saving his
strength."

This was the general opinion for several seconds. But
the filly continued to gain slowly, with a sustained effort.
Then there was a burst of feverish excitement. There was
no longer any interest in the trailing horses. A supreme
struggle had begun among Spirit, Nana, Lusignan, and

Valerio II. Their names were shouted, there were stammered, disconnected comments whenever one of them moved ahead or fell back. Nana, who had just climbed up on the driver's seat as though lifted by her emotion, was pale, trembling, and so deeply moved that she was speechless. Beside her, Labordette had begun to smile again.

"The English horse is having trouble!" Philippe said joyfully. "He's not doing so well!"

"In any case, Lusignan is done for," said La Faloise. "It's Valerio II who's coming up. . . . Look the four of them are all together!"

The same words came from every mouth.

"Look at them go! My God, just look at them go!"

The horses were now coming toward Nana's landau with a distant rumble that grew louder every second. The whole crowd impetuously rushed to the railing, and a deep clamor, like the roar of a surf, preceded the horses as they approached. It was the last fierce outburst of a colossal contest, a hundred thousand spectators with a single fixed idea, burning with the same lust for luck as they watched those horses on whose speed millions of francs depended. They shoved and crushed one another, with clenched fists and open mouths, each one for himself, each one urging on his horse with shouts and gestures. And the cry of that whole multitude, an animal cry despite the dresses and frock coats, became more and more distinct:

"Here they come! Here they come! Here they come!"

Nana was still gaining. Valerio II was now outdistanced. Only Spirit was ahead of her now, by two or three necks. The thunderous rumble had grown louder. They were coming down the homestretch. A storm of oaths greeted them from the landau.

"Come on, Lusignan, you coward, you dirty nag! . . . Good going, Spirit, keep it up, keep it up! . . . That Valerio is disgusting! Oh, the miserable beast! I can kiss my two hundred francs good-by! . . . Only Nana's left now! Come on, Nana, come on, you little slut!"

And on the driver's seat, Nana was unconsciously moving her hips and thighs, as though she herself were running. She kept throwing her belly forward, feeling that this helped the filly, and each time she did so she heaved a sigh of fatigue and said in a low, anguished voice, "Go! Go! Go!"

Then something superb happened. Price stood up in the stirrups, raised his whip and began lashing Nana with an iron hand. That old, shriveled-up child, with his long, hard, dead face, was now flashing fire. In a burst of reckless fury and triumphant will, he breathed his own spirit into the filly and drove her forward. She was covered with foam and her eyes were red. The whole cluster of horses thundered past, sweeping the air away and cutting short the breath of the crowd, while the judge coolly waited, looking straight ahead. Then an immense cheer rang out. In a supreme effort, Price had just flung Nana across the finish line, beating Spirit by a head.

There was a clamor like the roar of a rising tide. Nana! Nana! Nana! The cry rolled and swelled with the violence of a tempest, filling the horizon from the depths of the Bois to Mont-Valérien, from the meadows of Longchamp to the plain of Boulogne. Wild enthusiasm had broken out all over the field. Long live Nana! Long live France! Down with England! The women waved their parasols. Some of the men leapt and spun around as they shouted, while others threw their hats in the air with unrestrained laughter. And on the other side of the track, the crowd in the enclosure responded. The stands were shaken by a violent agitation, although nothing could be seen distinctly except a quivering in the air, like the invisible flame of a bed of live coals, above that living heap of flailing arms and faces with little black dots for eyes and mouths. The uproar grew still louder; it was echoed from the distant roads by the people under the trees, it was augmented in the excitement of the imperial stand, where the Empress had applauded. Nana! Nana! Nana! The cry rose in the glory of the sunlight, whose golden rays stimulated the delirium of the crowd.

Standing up straight on the seat of her landau, Nana felt as though it were she who was being acclaimed. For a moment she had remained motionless, stupefied by her triumph, staring at the track, which was now so tightly packed with people that the grass was entirely covered and nothing could be seen except a sea of black hats. Then, when they pressed up against the railings to make way for the filly, cheering her again as she walked toward the exit with Price hanging over her neck as though lifeless and empty, Nana slapped her thighs, forgot everything, and triumphed in crude exclamations.

"Ah, it's *me*, by God! . . . Yes, by God! What luck!"

Not knowing how to express the joy that was overwhelming her, she seized and kissed Louiset, whom she had just noticed on Bordenave's shoulder.

"Three minutes and fourteen seconds," said Bordenave, putting his watch back into his pocket.

Nana was still listening to her name, with which the whole plain was resounding. It was her people who were applauding her, while she dominated them, erect in the sunlight, with her hair shining like a star, and her white and sky-blue dress. Before leaving her, Labordette had told her that she had won forty thousand francs, for he had bet her thousand francs on Nana at forty to one. But the money affected her less than that unexpected victory, whose splendor had made her the queen of Paris. The other women had all lost. Rose Mignon had broken her parasol in a fit of rage. Caroline Héquet, Clarisse, Simonne, and even Lucy Stewart, despite her son, were swearing under their breath, exasperated by that big girl's luck. Tricon, however, who had crossed herself at the start and finish of the race, towered above them with her tall figure, delighted by her instinct, cursing Nana affectionately like an experienced matron.

The crush of men around the landau was increasing still more. The little group had been uttering ferocious cries. Only Georges was still shouting now, however, in a choked, cracked voice. Since the champagne had run out, Philippe had gone off to the refreshment tents, taking the footmen with him. And Nana's court continued to grow. Her triumph had decided the laggards. The movement that had made her landau the center of the field was now ending in a grand finale: Queen Venus surrounded by her delirious subjects. Bordenave, behind her, was muttering oaths with fatherly affection. Even Steiner, reconquered, had abandoned Simonne and was now standing on one of the carriage steps. When the champagne had arrived and she had raised her full glass, the applause was so great and the shouts of "Nana! Nana! Nana!" were so loud that the surprised crowd looked around for the filly, and no one knew any longer whether it was the horse or the woman that was filling the men's hearts.

Meanwhile, Mignon came hurrying up, despite Rose's black looks. That damned girl was driving him mad; he had to give her a kiss! After kissing her paternally on both cheeks he said to her, "What bothers me is that Rose is sure to send the letter now. . . . She's too angry."

"Good! That's just what I want!" Nana said without thinking. But when she saw that he was dumbfounded she hastened to add, "No, no, what am I saying? Really, I don't know what I'm saying any more! I'm drunk."

And she was indeed drunk with joy and sunlight. Still holding up her glass, she acclaimed herself: "To Nana! To Nana!" she cried, in the midst of the growing uproar of shouts and laughter that had gradually spread over the whole track.

The races were nearly over. The Prix Vaublanc was being run. Carriages were leaving one by one. Vandeuvres' name kept recurring in quarrels. It was now clear: Vandeuvres had been preparing this stroke for the past two years by having Gresham hold Nana back, and he had produced Lusignan only to cover up for his filly. The losers were angry, the winners shrugged their shoulders. What of it? Wasn't it permissible? An owner could run his stable as he saw fit. This was nothing compared to some of the other things that had been done! The majority considered Vandeuvres very clever to have had some friends of his bet as much money as possible for him on Nana, which explained the sudden drop in the odds. They spoke of forty thousand francs bet at average odds of thirty to one, making a gain of a million two hundred thousand francs, a figure that commanded respect and excused everything.

But other rumors, very serious ones, were being whispered in the enclosure. The men who returned from there brought details. Voices were raised and a terrible scandal was loudly related. Poor Vandeuvres was finished. He had ruined his superb stroke by a piece of stupidity, an idiotic theft. He had commissioned Maréchal, a shady bookmaker, to take forty thousand francs in bets for him against Lusignan, in order to recover the twenty thousand or so that he had bet openly, a mere trifle; and this proved that he had already cracked in the final collapse of his fortune. The bookmaker, informed that the favorite was not going to win, had taken bets on him amounting to over sixty thousand francs. But Labordette, not having been given precise and detailed instructions, had placed a four-thousand-franc bet on Nana with him, at the fifty-to-one odds that, in his ignorance of Vandeuvres' real plans, the bookmaker was still giving. Having lost hundreds of thousands of francs on the filly, with a net loss of forty thousand, Maréchal had felt everything crumbling beneath his feet. Then, on seeing Labordette and Vandeuvres talking together in front of the weighing-in room after the race, he had suddenly understood what had taken place. With the fury of a former coachman and the savagery of a man who has been robbed, he had publicly made a frightful scene, telling the story in atrocious terms and gathering a mob around him. It was said that the board of stewards was about to make an inquiry.

As Philippe and Georges were relating all this to Nana, she made comments without ceasing to laugh and drink. After all, it was possible; she remembered certain things; and besides, that Maréchal had a nasty face. She was still doubtful, however, when Labordette appeared. He was very pale.

"Well?" she asked in a low voice.

"He's done for," he replied simply.

And he shrugged his shoulders. That Vandeuvres was a child! She made a gesture of annoyance.

That night at the Bal Mabille, Nana met with a colossal success. When she arrived at about ten o'clock, the uproar was already formidable. This classic night of madness had assembled all the pleasure-loving young people in Paris, and the members of this fashionable gathering were disporting themselves with plebeian coarseness and stupidity. There was a crush beneath the garlands of gaslights. Men in black suits and women in outrageously low-cut old dresses, which they did not mind soiling, were milling around and shouting, agitated by drinking on an enormous scale. The brasses of the orchestra could not be heard from thirty paces away. No one was dancing. Idiotic remarks, repeated no one knew why, circulated among the groups. Everyone was making strained and unsuccessful efforts to be amusing. Seven women who had been locked in the cloakroom were weeping and demanding to be released. Forty francs had just been bid for a scallion which had been found and put up for auction. It was then that Nana arrived, still wearing the blue and white dress she had worn at the races. She was given the scallion amid thunderous cheers. She was seized against her will, and three gentlemen carried her triumphantly into the garden, across ravaged lawns and disemboweled masses of greenery. Since the orchestra was in the way, they took it by assault, and smashed the chairs and music stands. Paternal policemen organized the disorder.

It was not until Tuesday that Nana recovered from the agitation of her victory. She was talking that morning with Madame Lerat. Her aunt had come to give her news of Louiset, who had been made ill by the open air. She was fascinated by a story that everyone in Paris was talking about. After being excluded from the race tracks and expelled from the Cercle Impérial that same evening, Vandeuvres had burned himself and his horses in his stable the next day.

"He told me he'd do it!" said Nana. "He was a real madman! . . . It gave me the shivers when I heard about it yesterday—he might have murdered me some night! . . . He should have told me about his horse. I'd have made my fortune at least! He told Labordette that if I knew about it I'd immediately tell my hairdresser and a lot of other men. Wasn't that polite of him? No, really, I can't be very sorry he's gone."

On thinking it over, she became furious. Then Labordette came in. He had collected her bets for her and was bringing her forty thousand francs. This only increased her ill-humor, for she should have won a million. Labordette, who claimed innocence in the whole matter, flatly repudiated Vandeuvres. Those old families were worn out and always came to a stupid end.

"No," said Nana, "it's not stupid to burn yourself up like that in a stable. I think he ended in real style. . . . Oh, I'm not defending what he did to Maréchal. That was idiotic. When I think that Blanche had the nerve to blame *me* for it! I said to her, 'Did I tell him to steal?' You can ask a man for money without making him commit a crime. If he'd said to me, 'I have nothing left,' I'd have said,

'All right, then, let's part company,' and that would have been the end of it."

"Of course," her aunt said gravely. "When men are stubborn, it's their own fault!"

"Yes, but I still think his closing scene was wonderful," said Nana. "They say it was terrible, enough to give you gooseflesh! He sent everybody away, then locked himself in the stable with some kerosene. . . . It made a tremendous blaze. Just think of it: a big building made mostly of wood, full of straw and hay! The flames went up as high as steeples. And the most sensational part of it was the horses—they didn't want to be roasted, and they were heard kicking and banging against the doors, screaming like human beings. . . . Some of the people who saw it still haven't gotten over it."

Labordette gave a little hiss of incredulity. He didn't believe Vandeuvres was dead. There was one man who swore he had seen him go out through a window. He had set fire to his stable in a fit of madness, but he must have come back to his senses as soon as it started to get hot. A man so worn out and so foolish with women could not have died so gallantly.

Nana listened to him, disillusioned. She made only one comment: "Oh, the miserable coward! It was such a beautiful idea!"

12

$\mathcal{T}$oward one o'clock in the morning, in the great bed draped with Venetian lace, Nana and the Count were still awake. He had come back that evening, after sulking for three days. The bedroom, dimly lighted by a lamp, seemed to be sleeping in a warm, moist smell of love, with the vague pallor of its white lacquer furniture inlaid with silver. A drawn curtain flooded the bed with shadows. There was a sigh; then a kiss broke the silence. Nana slipped out from under the covers and sat on the edge of the bed with her legs bare. The Count let his head fall back on the pillow and remained in darkness.

"Darling, do you believe in God?" she asked after a moment of reflection. Her face was serious; she had been seized with religious terror after leaving her lover's arms.

She had been feeling uncomfortable ever since morning, and all her stupid ideas, as she called them—ideas of death and hell—had been inwardly tormenting her. There were nights when she had childish fears and imagined horrible things that gave her waking nightmares.

"Tell me, do you think I'll go to heaven?"

And she shuddered. The Count, surprised by such strange questions at such a time, felt his Catholic remorse coming back to him. Then, with her nightgown slipped down from her shoulders and her hair hanging loosely, she fell on his chest and clung to him, sobbing: "I'm afraid to die. . . . I'm afraid to die. . . ."

He had great difficulty in freeing himself from her. He himself was afraid of yielding to her madness as she pressed her body to his in the contagious fear of the invisible. He reasoned with her: she was in perfect health, and all she had to do was to behave well in order to deserve forgiveness later. She shook her head. No doubt she wasn't harming anyone, and she even wore a medal of the Virgin, which she showed him, hanging by a red string between her breasts; but it was settled in advance: all unmarried women who had anything to do with men would go to hell. Fragments of her catechism returned to her. Ah, if only she could know for certain! But that was the whole trouble: nobody had ever come back to tell about the next world, and it would be foolish to worry about such things if the priests were talking nonsense. Yet she devoutly kissed the medal, still warm from her skin, as a conjuration against death, the thought of which filled her with cold horror.

Muffat had to go into the dressing room with her, for she was afraid to be alone there, even with the door open. When he was back in bed, she wandered around the bedroom, looking into all the corners, starting at the slightest sound. A mirror stopped her and, as in the past, she became lost in contemplation of her nakedness. But the sight of her breasts, hips, and thighs redoubled her fear. For a long time she felt the bones of her face with both hands.

"People are ugly when they're dead," she said slowly.

She drew in her cheeks, opened her eyes wide, and lowered her jaw to see how she would look. Thus disfigured, she turned to the Count and said, "Look. See how little my head will be?"

He became angry: "You're insane; come to bed."

He saw her in a grave, with fleshlessness of a century of sleep. He joined his hands and stammered a prayer. Religion had reconquered him some time ago; every day his attacks of faith took on the violence of apoplectic fits and left him as though stunned. His fingers would crack and he would repeat these words over and over: "My God . . . my God . . . my God . . ." It was the cry of his impotence, the cry of his sin, against which he was without strength, despite his certainty of damnation. When Nana came back, she found him under the covers, haggard, his fingernails sunk into his chest, his eyes turned upward as though seeking heaven. She began crying again. They kissed each other, chattering their teeth without knowing why, rolling in the depths of the same idiotic obsession. They had already spent a similar night together, only this time it was completely stupid, as Nana declared when she was no longer afraid. A suspicion made her question him prudently: perhaps Rose Mignon had sent that famous letter. But it was not that, it was only fright, nothing more, for he was still not clearly aware that he was a cuckold.

Two days later, after another disappearance, Muffat came in the morning, which was highly unusual for him. His face was livid, his eyes were red, and he was still shaken by a great inner struggle. But Zoé herself was so alarmed that she did not notice his agitation. She ran toward him and cried out, "Oh, Monsieur, come! Madame nearly died last night." And when he asked for details: "It's something unbelievable, Monsieur: a miscarriage!"

Nana had been three months pregnant. For a long time she had thought she was merely indisposed. Even Dr. Boutarel had had his doubts. But when he made a definite pronouncement she was so upset that she did everything she could to hide her pregnancy. Her nervous fears and gloomy moods had come to some extent from this mishap, which she had kept secret with the shame of an unmarried mother forced to conceal her plight. It seemed to her a ridiculous accident, something that degraded her and would have made others laugh at her. What a bad joke! Just her luck! She had gotten caught just when she thought the danger was over. She felt constantly surprised, as though her sexuality had been thrown out of order. So it still made children even when you didn't want them any more and were using it for other things! Nature exasperated her: this solemn maternity that had arisen in her pleasure, this life given in the midst of all the deaths she was sowing around her. Shouldn't a woman be able to do as she pleased without having to be bothered by all that? And where had the baby come from? She had no idea. Well, the man who had made it would have done much better to keep it to himself, because no one wanted it, it was in everyone's way, and it would surely not have a very happy life.

Zoé related the catastrophe. "Madame began having sharp pains in her stomach at about four o'clock. She went into her dressing room. When I didn't see her come back, I went in and found her lying on the floor, unconscious.

Yes, Monsieur, she was lying on the floor in a pool of blood, as if she'd been murdered. . . . Then I understood. I was furious, because she could have told me about her misfortune. . . . Monsieur Georges happened to be there. He helped me pick her up, but as soon as he heard the word 'miscarriage,' he fainted too! . . . I've been terribly worried ever since yesterday."

Indeed, the whole house seemed upset. Georges had spent the night on a chair in the drawing room. It was he who had told Nana's friends the news when they had come to visit her that evening. He had been pale as he told the story with stunned emotion. Steiner, La Faloise, Philippe, and others had come. At the first words, they had uttered exclamations. Impossible! It must be a joke! Then they had become serious, staring at the bedroom door, looking chagrined, shaking their heads, and feeling deep concern. Until midnight, a dozen gentlemen had talked softly in front of the fireplace, all friends, all tormented by the same idea of paternity. They seemed to be apologizing to one another, with embarrassed, awkward expressions. Then they had assumed a more casual attitude. That Nana was amazing, wasn't she? Who would ever have thought she'd do a thing like that? And they had gone away one by one, on tiptoe, as though in the presence of death, where one cannot laugh.

"Come on upstairs, Monsieur," Zoé said to Muffat. "Madame is feeling much better now, she's going to receive you. . . . We're expecting the doctor. He promised to come back this morning."

Zoé had persuaded Georges to go home and get some sleep. Upstairs in the drawing room, there was no one left but Satin. She was lying on a sofa, smoking a cigarette and looking up at the ceiling. Since the accident, amid the alarm of the household, she had shown only cold rage, shrugging her shoulders and making venomous remarks. When Zoé passed in front of her, repeating to the Count that poor Madame had suffered greatly, Satin said sharply, "It serves her right! It'll teach her a lesson!"

They turned around, surprised. Satin had not moved; her eyes were still on the ceiling, her cigarette was still pinched nervously between her lips.

"What a thing to say!" exclaimed Zoé.

But Satin sat up, gave the Count a furious look, and threw her words in his face again: "It serves her right! It'll teach her a lesson!" Then she lay down again and blew out a thin trail of smoke, as though disinterested and determined not to become involved in anything. No, it was too stupid!

Zoé showed Muffat into Nana's bedroom. There was a smell of ether, and a warm silence that was scarcely broken by the dull rumble of the few carriages passing along the Avenue de Villiers. Nana was awake, looking very white against her pillow. Her big eyes were open and dreamy. When she saw the Count, she smiled without moving.

"Ah, my friend," she murmured slowly, "I thought I'd never see you again."

Then, when he leaned down to kiss her hair, she spoke to him of the child, in good faith, as though he were the father. "I was afraid to tell you. . . . I felt so happy! I made all kinds of plans, I wanted him to be worthy of you. But now it's all over. . . . Well, maybe it's better that way. I don't want to do anything that will make trouble for you."

Surprised by this paternity, he uttered a few vague sentences. He had taken a chair and sat down next to the bed, resting one arm on the covers. Then Nana noticed his agitated expression, his bloodshot eyes, and the feverish quivering of his lips.

"What's wrong?" she asked. "Are you sick too?"

"No," he said painfully.

She gave him a penetrating look. With a gesture, she dismissed Zoé, who had been lingering in the room, arranging the medicine bottles. When they were alone, she drew him toward her and said, "What's the matter, darling? Tears are about to come into your eyes, I can see it. . . . Come on, tell me about it, you came here to tell me something."

"No, no, I swear I didn't," he said. But, choking with pain, moved all the more deeply by that sickroom in which he had unexpectedly found himself, he burst out sobbing and buried his face in the sheets to smother the explosion of his grief. Nana understood. Rose Mignon had finally made up her mind to send the letter. She let him go on sobbing, so convulsively that he shook her in her bed.

Finally she said in a tone of maternal compassion, "Do you have worries at home?"

He nodded. She paused, then asked, "So you know everything?"

He nodded again. And silence fell, a heavy silence in the sorrowful bedroom. It was the night before, on returning from a reception given by the Empress, that he had received the letter written by Sabine to her lover. After spending a horrible night dreaming of vengeance, he had gone out that morning to resist the temptation to kill his wife. Outside, seized by the softness of a beautiful June morning, he had been unable to collect his thoughts. He had gone to Nana as he always went to her at times of stress. Only with her did he abandon himself to his misery, with the base joy of being consoled.

"Now, now, be calm," she said with great kindness. "I've known about it for a long time, but I'd never have opened your eyes. You were suspicious last year; then, thanks to my carefulness, the whole thing was smoothed over. You didn't have any proof. . . . Well, if you have proof now, it's hard to take; I can understand that. But you've got to make the best of it. It doesn't dishonor you."

He was no longer weeping. He felt ashamed, even though he had long since begun confiding the most intimate details of his married life to her. She had to encourage him. After all, she was a woman, he could tell her everything.

"You're ill," he said dully. "What's the use of tiring you? It was foolish of me to come. I'll leave now."

"No, stay," she said quickly. "Maybe I'll give you some good advice. Only don't make me talk too much, the doctor told me I mustn't."

He had stood up at last, and was now walking around the room.

"What are you going to do now?" she asked.

"Challenge that man to a duel, of course!"

She pouted disapprovingly.

"That's not a good idea. . . . And what about your wife?"

"I'll go to court; I have proof."

"Not a good idea at all, my friend. In fact, it's stupid. . . . I'd never let you do that."

And in her weak voice she calmly pointed out the useless

scandal of a duel and a lawsuit. There would be sensational stories about him in all the newspapers for a week. He would be gambling with his whole life, his peace of mind, his high position at court, the honor of his name. And what would he accomplish? He would only get himself laughed at.

"What does it matter?" he cried. "I'll have my revenge!"

"My friend," she said, "in things like that, if a man doesn't get his revenge right away, he never gets it at all."

He stopped short, stammering. He was certainly not a coward, but he felt that she was right; a kind of uneasiness was growing in him, something impoverished and shameful that had just enervated him in the heat of his anger. Then, in her frank determination to say everything, she dealt him another blow.

"Do you want to know what's bothering you, darling? It's that you're deceiving your wife, too. You don't stay away from home all night to twiddle your thumbs, do you? Your wife must have a pretty good idea of what you're doing. So how can you accuse her? She'd answer that she's only following your example, and that would shut you up. . . . That's why you're walking the floor in my bedroom instead of going off to kill them both."

Muffat sank into a chair, overwhelmed by the bluntness of her words. She remained silent for a moment, catching her breath, then she said softly, "Oh, I'm exhausted. . . . Help me move up a little. I keep slipping down . . . my head is too low."

When he had helped her, she sighed and felt better. And she returned to the subject of the spectacle he would make of himself by asking for a separation. Couldn't he just see his wife's lawyer amusing everyone in Paris by talking about Nana? He would bring up everything: her fiasco at the Variety Theater, her house, her life. Ah, no, she didn't want all that publicity! There were certain vile women who, in her place, might have urged him to go through with it so that they could attract a lot of attention to themselves, but she placed his happiness above everything else.

She had drawn him to her and put her arm around his neck. His head was now on the pillow beside hers. "Listen, darling," she said gently, "you must make up with your wife."

He rebelled. Never! His heart would burst, it would be too shameful. But she insisted affectionately: "You must make up with your wife. . . . You don't want everybody to say I took you away from your wife and family, do you? It would give me too bad a reputation. What would people think of me? . . . But swear you'll always love me, because when you're with another woman . . ."

She was choked by tears. He interrupted her with kisses and said, "You've lost your reason! It's impossible!"

"No, you must," she said. "I'll make myself accept it. After all, she's your wife. It's not as if you were going to deceive me with the first woman who came along."

And she continued thus, giving him the best advice. She even spoke of God. He felt as though he were listening to one of the sermons Monsieur Venot had preached to him in his efforts to tear him away from his sin. She was not telling him to break off with her, however; she was preaching indulgence, a good-natured sharing of himself between his wife and his mistress, a life of tranquillity, without annoyances for anyone, something like a happy sleep in the inevitable nastiness of existence. It would change nothing in their life; he would still be her favorite little man, only he would come less often and would give his wife the nights he did not spend with her. Her strength was failing her; she concluded in a whisper: "And I'll feel I've done a good deed. . . . You'll love me more."

There was a silence. She closed her eyes, looking still paler on the pillow. Muffat said nothing, giving himself the pretext that he did not wish to tire her. After a long minute she opened her eyes and murmured, "And what about money, too? Where will you get enough money if you separate from your wife? Labordette came yesterday about the note. . . . As for me, I need everything, I don't even have anything to wear."

Then, closing her eyes again, she appeared to be dead. A shadow of deep anxiety had passed over Muffat's face. Since the night before, in the agitation that had taken possession of him, he had forgotten about his financial difficulties, from which he did not know how to extricate himself. Despite strict promises to the contrary, the note he had signed for a hundred thousand francs had just been put into circulation after having been renewed once.

Labordette pretended to be in despair and blamed it all on Francis, saying that he would never again compromise himself by dealing with an ill-bred man. The note had to be paid, for the Count would never allow his signature to be protested.

And in addition to Nana's new demands, he had a profusion of extraordinary expenses at home. On returning from Les Fondettes, the Countess had shown a taste for luxury and an appetite for worldly enjoyments that were devouring their fortune. People were beginning to talk about her ruinous caprices, a radical change in the household, half a million francs wasted on remodeling the old house on the Rue Miromesnil, extravagant clothes, and large sums that had been squandered, or given away perhaps, without her even bothering to account for them. Muffat had twice ventured to make comments, wanting to know what was happening to the money; but she had smiled and given him such a strange look that he had not dared to question her any further, for fear of receiving too direct an answer. If he was about to allow Nana to give him Daguenet as a son-in-law, it was chiefly because he thought he would be able to reduce Estelle's dowry to two hundred thousand francs and make some sort of arrangement for the rest of it with the young man, who was still delighted by the prospect of such an unhoped-for marriage.

For the past week, however, under the immediate necessity of finding Labordette's hundred thousand francs, Muffat had been able to think of only one expedient, from which he recoiled. It was to sell Les Bordes, a magnificent estate valued at half a million francs, which the Countess had just inherited from an uncle. He would require her signature, however, just as, according to the deed, she could not transfer the estate without his authorization. The day before, he had finally decided to talk to her about that signature. But he had abandoned the idea, for now he would never accept such a compromise. This thought made the blow of his wife's adultery all the harder. He clearly understood what Nana was asking, for in the increasing abandon that prompted him to confide everything to her, he had complained of his situation and told her about his anxiety with regard to the Countess's signature.

Nana did not appear to insist, however. She had not

opened her eyes. Seeing her so pale, he became frightened. He made her take a little ether. She sighed and questioned him, without naming Daguenet: "When will the wedding be?"

"The contract will be signed on Tuesday, five days from now," he replied.

"Well, see what you've got to do," she said with her eyes still closed, as though she were talking in the night of her thoughts. "I want everybody to be happy."

He took her hand to calm her. Yes, he would see, but the main thing was for her to rest now. And he no longer rebelled; that sickroom, so warm and sleepy, smelling of ether, had finally lulled him into a need for happy peace. All his virility, maddened by insult, had been drained out of him by the warmth of the bed as he lay beside that suffering woman whom he was nursing, with the excitement of his fever and the memory of their sensual pleasures. He leaned over her and clasped her in his arms. Although her face was motionless, there was a faint smile of victory on her lips. Just then Dr. Boutarel arrived.

"Well, how's this dear girl coming along?" he said familiarly to Muffat, whom he treated as her husband. "Oh, I see you've been making her talk!"

The doctor was a handsome man, still young, who had a splendid practice in the pleasure-seeking world. He was very cheerful, and laughed like a comrade with the courtesans he treated, but never went to bed with them. He charged enormous fees and demanded prompt payment. He was always willing to come for any reason whatever. Nana had been sending for him two or three times a week, constantly trembling at the thought of death, anxiously consulting him about little ailments, which he cured while amusing her with gossip and funny stories. The ladies all adored him. But this time the ailment was serious.

Muffat withdrew, deeply moved. He now felt only tender pity at seeing his poor Nana so weak. As he was leaving, she motioned him back, presented her forehead to him, and said softly, in a playfully threatening tone, "You know what I've allowed you to do. . . . Make up with your wife or I'll be angry and you'll get nothing more!"

Countess Sabine had wanted her daughter's marriage

contract to be signed on a Tuesday so that she could give a big party to inaugurate the remodeled house, whose paint was scarcely dry. Five hundred invitations had been sent out to people in nearly all the various social circles. On Tuesday morning the upholsterers were still putting up some of the hangings, and when the chandeliers were lighted, toward nine o'clock, the architect was giving his final orders, accompanied by the Countess, who was passionately interested in everything.

It was one of those springtime parties that have such a delicate charm. The warmth of the June evening had made it possible to open both doors of the main drawing room and extend the ball out onto the gravel of the garden. When the first guests arrived, greeted at the door by the Count and the Countess, they were dazzled. It was difficult to recall the former drawing room, haunted by the icy memory of Countess Muffat, that ancient room filled with devout severity, with its solid mahogany Empire furniture, its yellow velvet hangings, and its damp, greenish ceiling. Now, in the entrance hall, mosaics set off with gold shone beneath tall candelabra, while the marble staircase unrolled its finely carved balustrade. The drawing room itself was resplendent; it now had Genoa velvet hangings, and its ceiling was adorned with a vast decorative painting by Boucher, for which the architect had paid a hundred thousand francs at the sale of the Château de Dampierre. The crystal sconces and chandeliers illuminated a wealth of mirrors and costly furniture. It was as though Sabine's red silk chaise longue, whose softness seemed so greatly out of place in the past, had multiplied and spread until it had filled the whole house with voluptuous indolence and keen enjoyment that burned with the intensity of a slow fire.

Couples were already dancing. The orchestra, placed in the garden in front of one of the open windows, was playing a waltz whose supple rhythm came in softened by the open air. And the garden stretched out in transparent shadow, lighted by Venetian lanterns, with a crimson refreshment tent erected at the edge of a lawn. The waltz, which happened to be the roguish waltz from *The Blond Venus*, with its ribald little laughter, penetrated the old house in a sonorous wave, a tremor that warmed its walls.

It seemed to be some carnal wind from the street, sweeping a dead age out of the haughty building, carrying away the past of the Muffats, a century of honor and faith sleeping under the ceilings.

The old friends of the Count's mother had taken refuge in their usual places near the fireplace, feeling lost and bewildered. They formed a little group in the middle of the gradually swelling crowd. Madame Du Joncquoy, no longer recognizing any of the rooms, had walked through the dining room. Madame Chantereau was looking in amazement at the garden, which seemed immense to her. The ladies soon began making bitter, low-voiced comments in their corner.

"Suppose the Countess were to come back now," said Madame Chantereau. "Can't you imagine her making her entrance in the middle of this crowd? And all that gold, and the uproar . . . It's scandalous!"

"Sabine has lost her senses," said Madame Du Joncquoy. "Did you see her at the door? Look, you can see her from here. She's wearing all her diamonds."

They stood up for a moment to examine the Countess and the Count from a distance. Sabine, wearing a white dress trimmed with magnificent English lace, was triumphant in her beauty, youthful, gay, with a touch of intoxication in her constant smile. Beside her, Muffat, looking older and rather pale, was also smiling, with his air of calm dignity.

"And to think that he was once the master of this house!" said Madame Chantereau. "Not one chair would have been brought in without his permission. Well, she's changed that: he's in *her* house now. . . . Do you remember when she wouldn't redecorate the drawing room? Now she's renovated the whole house!"

They fell silent, for Madame de Chezelles had just come in, followed by a group of young gentlemen, going into ecstasies, expressing her approval with little exclamations: "Oh, wonderful! . . . Exquisite! . . . Such taste!" And she called out to them from a distance: "I told you so! There's nothing like these old buildings when they're redecorated. They become so elegant The house is worthy of Louis XIV now. . . . At last she can receive."

The two old ladies sat down again. Lowering their

voices, they began talking about the forthcoming marriage, which was surprising many people. Estelle had just passed by in a pink silk dress, still thin and flat, with her dull, virginal face. She had placidly accepted Daguenet, showing neither joy nor sadness; she was as cold and white as she had been during those winter evenings when she put logs on the fire. That whole party given for her, those lights, those flowers, that music, left her unmoved.

"An adventurer," said Madame Du Joncquoy. "I've never seen him."

"Careful, here he comes," murmured Madame Chantereau.

Daguenet, having seen Madame Hugon with her sons, had hastened to offer her his arm; he was laughing and showering her with affection, as though she had contributed something to his stroke of good fortune.

"Thank you," she said, sitting down near the fireplace. "This is my old corner."

"Do you know him?" asked Madame Du Joncquoy when Daguenet was gone.

"Of course. He's a charming young man. Georges likes him very much. . . . Oh, he comes from a most honorable family!"

And the good lady defended him against an unexpressed hostility that she sensed in the others. His father, highly esteemed by Louise-Philippe, had been a prefect until his death. The young man had perhaps been a bit frivolous. He was said to be ruined. In any case, one of his uncles, a great landowner, was going to bequeath his fortune to him. The ladies nodded their heads while Madame Hugon, embarrassed, kept returning to the honorableness of his family. She was very tired and complained of her legs. For the past month she had been living in her house on the Rue Richelieu, in order to deal with all sorts of business matters, she said. A shadow of sadness veiled her maternal smile.

"Just the same," concluded Madame Chantereau, "Estelle could have made a much better match."

There was a fanfare. A quadrille was about to begin. The crowd moved to the sides of the drawing room to leave an open space. Light-colored dresses passed by and mingled with dark coats. The bright light shining on the sea of heads illuminated sparkling gems, quivering white plumes, and a profusion of lilacs and roses. The room was already quite warm. A pungent scent rose from those light tulles and rumpled satins and silks among which the bare shoulders looked pale. The orchestra was now playing loudly. Through the open doors one could see women sitting in rows at the far ends of the adjoining rooms, with the discreet flash of their smiles, the glow of their eyes, and the occasional pout that appeared on their lips as they gently fanned themselves. And guests were still arriving. A footman called out their names while, amid the various groups, gentlemen were trying to find places for the ladies who clung uneasily to their arms, craning their necks in search of an empty chair. The house was filling up; skirts were being pressed against one another with little rustling sounds, and there were places so tightly packed with lace, bows, and bustles that it was impossible to get through. The ladies, accustomed to such dazzling throngs, kept their grace and maintained a polite resignation. Couples were escaping from the stifling air of the drawing room to go out into the garden, beneath the pink glow of the Venetian lanterns. The shadows of dresses passed swiftly along the edge of the lawn, as though keeping time to the music of the quadrille, which sounded soft and faraway behind the trees.

Steiner had just met Foucarmont and La Faloise there, drinking a glass of champagne at the refreshment tent.

"Very impressive!" said La Faloise, examining the crimson tent held up by gilded lances. "It's like a gingerbread fair. . . . Yes, that's it, a gingerbread fair!"

He now affected a constant bantering tone, posing as a young man who had overindulged in everything and could no longer find anything worthy of being taken seriously.

"Poor Vandeuvres would be surprised if he came back now," said Foucarmont. "Do you remember how bored he used to be over there in front of the fireplace? Ah, you weren't supposed to laugh in those days!"

"Don't mention Vandeuvres; he was a miserable failure!" La Faloise said disdainfully. "He was sadly mistaken if he thought he was going to bowl us over with his roasting! No one even talks about it any more. He's dead, buried, and forgotten. Let's talk about something else." Then, when Steiner shook hands with him: "Nana just came, you know. . . . Oh, what an entrance she made! It was phenomenal! First she kissed the Countess, then when Estelle and Daguenet came up to her she congratulated them and said to Daguenet, 'Listen, Paul, if you deceive her you'll have to answer for it to me. . . .' What! You didn't see it? Oh, she was magnificent! What a success!"

The others listened to him, gaping. Finally they laughed. La Faloise was delighted, and felt proud of his wit.

"You thought it really happened, didn't you? . . . Well, it's true that Nana arranged the marriage. After all, she's one of the family."

The Hugon brothers came up and Philippe silenced him. The group of men then began discussing the marriage. Georges became angry with La Faloise for telling the story. It was true that Nana had saddled Muffat with one of her former lovers as a son-in-law, but it was false that she had gone to bed with Daguenet the night before. Foucarmont shrugged his shoulders. Did anyone ever know when Nana had gone to bed with someone? Georges, carried away, replied with a "Yes, Monsieur, *I* know!" which made them all laugh. In any case, as Steiner said, it was still a peculiar situation.

The refreshment tent was gradually becoming crowded. They moved away without separating from one another. La Faloise looked at the women brazenly, as though he thought he was at the Bal Mabille. At the end of a path they were surprised to see Monsieur Venot in serious conversation with Daguenet. The sight gave rise to facile jokes: Venot was confessing Daguenet; he was giving him advice about his wedding night. Then they went back inside and stood at one of the doors of the drawing room, where couples were dancing a polka, leaving a wake among the men who had remained standing. The candles were burning high in the breeze coming from outside. Whenever a dress passed by, swirling in time to the music, it made a little puff of wind that relieved the intense heat that was descending from the chandeliers.

"My God, they're not cold in there!" said La Faloise.

They blinked their eyes on returning from the mysterious shadows of the garden. Then they called each other's attention to the Marquis de Chouard, who was standing alone, his tall figure towering above the bare shoulders that surrounded him. His face was pale and stern, with an air of haughty dignity, beneath his crown of sparse white hair. Shocked by Count Muffat's conduct, he had publicly broken off with him and said he would never again set foot in his house. He had consented to come that evening only because of the earnest entreaties of his grand-daughter, although he disapproved of her marriage and had spoken indignantly against the disruption of the ruling classes by the shameful compromises of modern de-bauchery.

"Ah, it's the end!" Madame Du Joncquoy whispered to Madame Chantereau as they sat near the fireplace. "That woman has bewitched the poor man. . . . And he used to be so religious, so noble!"

"They say he's ruining himself," said Madame Chanter-eau. "My husband has seen a note signed by him. . . . He now spends all his time in that house on the Avenue de Villiers. Everyone in Paris is talking about it. . . . Oh, I don't excuse Sabine either, although I must admit he gives her great cause for complaint, and if she throws money away—"

"That's not the only thing she's throwing away," inter-rupted Madame Du Joncquoy. "Between the two of them, they'll go all the faster. . . . They're rapidly sinking into the mud, my dear."

Just then a gentle voice broke into their conversation. It was Monsieur Venot. He had sat down behind them, as though wishing to disappear. He leaned toward them and said, "Why give up hope? God manifests Himself just when everything seems lost."

He was calmly watching the downfall of the house that he had once ruled. Since his stay at Les Fondettes, he had simply allowed the turmoil to increase, clearly aware that he was powerless to stop it. He had accepted everything: the Count's mad passion for Nana, the Countess's relation-ship with Fauchery, even Estelle's marriage to Daguenet. What did those things matter? And he became more supple and mysterious, harboring the idea of gaining ascendancy over the young couple as well as the disunited one, knowing that great disorder leads to great piety. Providence would have its hour.

"Our friend," he continued in a low voice, "is still animated by the best religious sentiments. He's given me touching proof of it."

"Then first he should go back to his wife," said Madame Du Joncquoy.

"Yes, of course, and I have hopes that their reconciliation will soon take place."

The two ladies questioned him, but he became very humble again; they would have to let heaven act in its own way. His only desire in bringing the Count and the Countess together again was to avoid a public scandal. Religion would tolerate many weaknesses as long as one kept up appearances.

"You should have prevented that marriage with an adventurer," said Madame Du Joncquoy.

The little old man took on a look of profound astonishment.

"You're mistaken: Monsieur Daguenet is a young man of great merit. I know his way of thinking. He wants to make others forget his youthful errors. Estelle will bring him back to the right path, you may be sure of it."

"Oh, Estelle!" Madame Chantereau said disdainfully. "I think the dear child has no will at all. She's so insignificant!"

This opinion made Monsieur Venot smile. However, he said nothing more about the bride. Closing his eyes as though to disclaim any further interest in the matter, he again hid himself in his corner, behind the skirts. Madame Hugon had overheard a few words in the midst of her distracted weariness. She joined in the conversation, and concluded with her tolerant expression, addressing the Marquis de Chouard, who had come over to greet her: "These ladies are very stern. Life is so hard for everyone. . . . Isn't it true, my friend, that we ought to forgive a great deal in others if we ourselves wish to be worthy of forgiveness?"

The Marquis was uneasy for a few seconds, fearing that she might be alluding to his own conduct. But the good lady had such a sad smile that he was quickly reassured. "No, there are certain things that shouldn't be forgiven," he said. "Such indulgence can make a society sink into ruin."

346

The ball had become more animated than ever. Another quadrille was making the floor of the drawing room sway slightly, as though the old house were giving way beneath the commotion of the festivities. Now and then, in the confused pallor of heads, a woman's face stood out briefly, swept away by the dance, with sparkling eyes and parted lips, while the light of the chandelier shone on her white skin. Madame Du Joncquoy declared that the whole thing was absurd. It was senseless to squeeze five hundred people into a room that could scarcely hold two hundred. Why not have the marriage contract signed on the Place du Carrousel? It was one more example of the new ways of doing things, said Madame Chantereau. In the past, such solemn ceremonies took place within the family; nowadays there had to be a mob, everyone in the street had to be allowed to enter freely, and the house had to be packed, otherwise the evening seemed dull. People showed off their wealth, and invited the scum of Paris into their houses; it was inevitable that such promiscuity should eventually corrupt the home.

The two ladies complained that they recognized no more than fifty people. Where had that crowd come from? Young girls in low-cut dresses were displaying their shoulders. One woman had a gold dagger stuck in her chignon and wore a dress covered with little black beads, which looked like a coat of mail. Another woman had such an extraordinary appearance in her tight-fitting skirt that she was followed around the room by smiling men. All the luxury of the close of the winter season was there, the world of pleasure with its tolerance, everything the mistress of a household could gather from her one-day relationships, a society in which great names and great shames were mingled in the same appetite for enjoyment. The heat was increasing, the quadrille was unrolling the rhythmic symmetry of its figures in the overcrowded rooms.

"The Countess is magnificent!" said La Faloise, standing at the door to the garden. "She looks ten years younger than her daughter. . . . By the way, Foucarmont, you can settle this for us: Vandeuvres used to bet that she had no thighs worth talking about."

The other men were annoyed by this cynical pose.

Foucarmont contented himself with replying, "Ask your cousin about it, my friend. Here he comes now."

"Yes, that's an ideal" cried La Faloise. "I'll bet two hundred francs she has good thighs."

Fauchery was indeed coming toward them. Being intimately acquainted with the house, he had come around by way of the dining room to avoid the crush at the doors. Rose had taken him back at the beginning of winter, and he was now dividing himself between her and the Countess, extremely weary, not knowing how to get rid of one of them. Sabine flattered his vanity, but Rose amused him more. Furthermore, Rose loved him with genuine passion, great tenderness, and conjugal fidelity, which drove Mignon to despair.

"Listen, give us some information," said La Faloise, gripping his cousin's arm. "You see that lady in the white silk dress?" Ever since his inheritance had given him insolent self-assurance, he had affected a bantering attitude toward Fauchery, having an old rancor to satisfy, wishing to be avenged for the fun that had been poked at him in the days when he had just arrived from the provinces. "Yes, that lady wearing lace."

The journalist stood on tiptoe to see better, not yet understanding. "You mean the Countess?" he finally said.

"That's right, my boy. . . . I've bet two hundred francs. Does she have good thighs?"

And he laughed, delighted at having taken Fauchery down a peg, still recalling how disconcerted he had once been when his cousin had asked him if the Countess went to bed with anyone.

But Fauchery merely stared at him without showing the least surprise. "Idiot!" he said at length, shrugging his shoulders. He then shook hands with the other men, while La Faloise, abashed, was no longer sure he had said something funny. They all talked together. Since the races, Steiner and Foucarmont had been part of the regular company at the house on the Avenue de Villiers. Nana was much better now. The Count paid a visit every evening to see how she was progressing. Fauchery listened, apparently preoccupied. That morning, during a quarrel, Rose had bluntly admitted having sent the letter; yes, he could go to his fashionable lady's house, he would be given a warm welcome. After hesitating for a long time, he had decided to come anyway, to prove his courage. But beneath his outer calm he had been greatly upset by La Faloise's stupid joke.

"What's wrong?" Philippe asked him. "You look as though you don't feel well."

"No, I'm all right. . . . I've been working, that's why I came so late." Then, coolly, in one of those unknown acts of heroism that resolve the commonplace dramas of life: "I haven't greeted our hosts yet. I must be polite." He even dared to jest, turning to La Faloise: "Isn't that right, idiot?"

And he made his way through the crowd. The footman's loud voice was no longer calling out names, but the Count and the Countess were still talking near the door, held there by ladies who were coming in. He finally joined them while the men he had left on the steps leading to the garden craned their necks to see the scene. Nana must have talked.

"The Count hasn't seen him yet," said Georges. "Ah, he's turning around! . . . There!"

The orchestra was again playing the waltz from *The Blond Venus*. Fauchery had first greeted the Countess, who was still smiling with blissful serenity. Then he had stood for a few moments behind the Count's back, waiting calmly. The Count was maintaining his lofty gravity that night, the official bearing of a great dignitary. When he finally lowered his eyes to the journalist, he exaggerated his majestic posture still more. The two men looked at each other for several seconds. And it was Fauchery who first held out his hand. Muffat took it. They shook hands while the Countess smiled in front of them with her eyes lowered. The waltz continued to unfold its mockingly ribald rhythm.

"Why, it's going off without a hitch!" exclaimed Steiner.

"Are their hands stuck together?" said Foucarmont, surprised by the duration of their clasp.

An ineradicable memory brought a pink glow to Fauchery's pale cheeks. He again saw the property room, with its greenish light and dusty odds and ends, and Muffat holding the eggcup, taking advantage of his suspicions. Now, Muffat no longer had any doubts; the last vestige of his dignity was crumbling. Relieved of his fear and seeing the Countess's bright gaiety, Fauchery felt like laughing. It struck him as comical.

"Ah, this time she's really here!" cried La Faloise, who did not abandon a joke when he thought it was a good one. "There's Nana, don't you see her coming in?"

"Quiet, you idiot," said Philippe.

"I tell you it's Nana! They're playing her waltz for her. She's coming! . . . What! You don't see her? She's embracing all three of them—my cousin Fauchery, my cousin Sabine, and her husband—and calling them her little darlings. These family scenes always have a strong effect on me."

Estelle had come up, and Fauchery congratulated her while she stood stiffly in her pink dress, silently looking at him with her surprised, childish expression and casting occasional glances at her parents. Daguenet also exchanged a warm handshake with the journalist. They formed a smiling group; and Monsieur Venot slipped behind them, looking at them tenderly, enveloping them in his pious gentleness, glad of those final abandonments that were preparing the ways of Providence.

The waltz was still beating out its laughing, voluptuous measure, accentuating the waves of pleasure that were pounding against the old house like a rising tide. The orchestra swelled the trills of its little flutes and the enraptured sighs of its violins. Beneath the Genoa velvet, the gildings, and the paintings, the chandeliers gave off a living heat, a mist of sunlight. The crowd of guests, multiplied by the mirrors, seemed to spread out with the louder hum of their voices. Around the drawing room, the shaking of the floor was increased by the couples passing by with arms around waists, among the smiles of the seated women. In the garden, the glowing Venetian lanterns cast a distant fiery reflection on the strollers seeking a little fresh air on the paths. And that quivering of the walls and that red cloud were like a final blaze which was consuming the ancient honor burning all over the house. The timid gaieties, then scarcely beginning, which Fauchery had heard ringing out with the sound of breaking glass one April evening, had gradually become bolder and more frenzied until they had burst into the brilliance of these festivities. Now the crack was growing; it was splitting

the house, announcing impending collapse. Among drunkards in the slums it is in bleak poverty—the cupboard
without bread, the madness of alcohol draining the last
resources—that tainted families reach their end. Here, on
the ruins of those riches, heaped up and ignited all at
once, the waltz sounded the death knell of an ancient
race, while Nana, invisible, hovered above the ball with
her lithe limbs, decomposing that society, permeating it
with the ferment of her odor floating in the warm air and in
the roguish rhythm of the music.

On the night after the church wedding, Count Muffat
came into his wife's bedroom for the first time in two
years. The Countess, greatly surprised, stepped back at
first. She kept her smile, however, the intoxicated smile
that was now always on her lips. He stammered in great
embarrassment. She then gave him a little lecture. But
neither of them dared to bring things into the open. It was
religion that required their mutual forgiveness; and it was
tacitly agreed that each would keep his freedom. Before
going to bed, since the Countess still seemed to be a little
hesitant, they talked business. He spoke of selling Les
Bordes. She consented immediately. They both had great
need of money; they would share the proceeds of the sale.
This completed their reconciliation. Muffat felt genuine
relief, despite his remorse.

Toward two o'clock that afternoon, while Nana was
dozing, Zoé had taken the liberty of knocking on the door
of her bedroom. The curtains were drawn and warm air
was coming in through the window, in the silent coolness
of the semidarkness. Nana was by now able to be out of
bed part of the time, although she was still rather weak.
She opened her eyes and asked, "Who is it?"

Zoé was about to answer, but Daguenet forced his way
past her and announced himself. Nana propped herself up
on her elbow and sent Zoé away.

"What! It's you! On your wedding day! . . . What's
the matter?"

He stood still for a moment, surprised by the darkness.
Then, when his eyes had become accustomed to it, he
walked over to the bed. He was wearing a dress suit, with
white tie and gloves.

351

"Yes, of course it's me. . . . Don't you remember?"

No, she didn't remember anything. He had to offer himself to her bluntly, in his joking tone: "It's time to collect your commission . . . I've come to make you a present of my innocence."

Since he was standing at the edge of the bed, she took him in her bare arms, shaking with laughter and almost weeping because it was so nice of him.

"Ah, Mimi, you're so funny! . . . I'd forgotten all about it, but you remembered! . . . So you've slipped away, you've just left the church? Yes, I can smell the incense on you. . . . Well, go on, kiss me! . . . Oh, more than that, Mimi! It may be the last time."

In the dark bedroom, where there was still a vague smell of ether in the air, their tender laughter died away. The curtains billowed in the warm breeze, the voices of children could be heard coming from the avenue. Then they joked with each other, pressed for time. Daguenet was to leave with his bride immediately after the luncheon.

13

One day toward the end of September, Count Muffat, who was to have dinner at Nana's house that evening, came at dusk to tell her that he had suddenly received an order to be at the Tuileries. The house was not yet lighted. The servants were laughing loudly in the kitchen. He slowly walked up the staircase, whose windows glowed in the warm shadows. Upstairs, the door of the drawing room made no noise when he opened it. Pink daylight was fading on the ceiling; the red hangings, the deep sofas, the lacquered furniture, and the jumble of bronzes, porcelains, and embroidered fabrics were already asleep beneath the slowly descending flood of shadows that filled the corners, blotting out the gleam of ivory and the glitter of gold. And there, in that semidarkness, he saw Nana reclining in Georges' arms, clearly visible by her outspread white petticoat. All denial was impossible. He uttered a stifled cry and stood gaping at them.

Nana sprang to her feet and pushed him into the bedroom, to give Georges time to get away.

"Go in," she said, her mind in a whirl, "and I'll tell you . . ."

She was exasperated at having been taken by surprise. Never before had she yielded like that in her own house, in the drawing room, with the door unlocked. And she would not have done it if she had not had a quarrel with Georges, who was wildly jealous of Philippe; he had sobbed so bitterly, with his arms around her neck, that she had given in to him, feeling sorry for him and not knowing how else to calm him. And when, for once in her life, she had been foolish enough to forget herself with a boy whose mother held him in such close check that he could not even bring her a bouquet of violets, the Count had picked that very moment to come in and catch them together. Just her luck! That was what you got for being tender-hearted!

The bedroom into which she had pushed Muffat was completely dark. She groped her way to the bell cord and rang furiously to ask for a lamp. Actually, it was Julien's fault! If there had been a lamp in the drawing room the whole thing would not have happened. That damned darkness had weakened her heart!

"Please, darling, be reasonable," she said when Zoé had brought a lamp.

The Count was sitting with his hands on his knees, staring at the floor, still dazed by what he had seen. He could not cry out in anger. He was quivering, as though overcome by chilling horror. Nana was touched by his silent grief. She tried to comfort him.

"Yes, I was wrong. What I did was very bad. . . . You see: I'm sorry. I'm very sad about it, because it's upset you so much. . . . Come, be nice to me too and forgive me."

She had crouched at his feet, trying to look into his eyes with an expression of submissive tenderness, in order to see whether he was very angry with her. Then, when he heaved a long sigh and seemed to be recovering, she became still more affectionate and gave him a final reason, in a tone of grave kindness: "You have to understand, darling—I can't refuse that to my friends who have no money."

The Count let himself be swayed by her entreaties. He merely demanded that she never see Georges again. But all illusion was dead; he no longer believed in her sworn fidelity. She would deceive him again the next day. He remained in the torment of his passion only out of cowardly necessity, out of a fear of life, of the idea of living without her.

It was during this period of her life that Nana illuminated Paris with redoubled splendor. She loomed still larger on the horizon of vice, she dominated the city with the insolent display of her luxury, of her contempt for money, which made her openly squander fortunes. Her house gave the impression of a glowing furnace: her desires blazed constantly there, and the slightest breath from her lips changed gold into fine ashes, which the wind swept away at every moment. Never before had such a mania for spending money been seen. The house seemed to have been built over an abyss that swallowed up men, their property, their bodies, and even their names, without leaving so much as a little dust behind. Nana ate like a parrot, nibbling radishes and pralines and pecking at her meat, yet her food bills amounted to five thousand francs a month. In the servants' quarters there was unbridled waste, a turbulent leakage that emptied casks of wine and ran up bills swollen by three or four successive hands. Victorine and François reigned over the kitchen, where they invited company, in addition to the whole tribe of cousins they fed at home on cold meat and soup. Julien exacted commissions from the tradesmen; the glaziers never put in a thirty-sou pane of glass without his making them add twenty sous for himself. Charles made a handsome profit on the oats for the horses; he doubled the amounts of all the supplies he ordered, and resold at the back door what came in at the front. And in the midst of this general pillage, this sack of a town taken by assault, Zoé cleverly managed to save appearances, covering up everyone else's thefts in order the better to dissimulate and secure her own.

But what was wasted was still worse: the discarded food of the day before, the litter of provisions for which the servants had lost their taste, the thick deposits of sugar at the bottoms of dirty glasses, the gaslights left blazing until the rooms seemed ready to burst; and neglect, and spitefulness, and accidents—everything that could hasten the ruin of a house being devoured by all those mouths. And upstairs, in Madame's rooms, the devastation went on at an even greater pace: dresses costing ten thousand francs were sold by Zoé after they had been worn only twice; jewelry vanished as if it had crumbled in the drawers; there were foolish purchases, novelties that were forgotten and thrown away the next day. Nana could not see anything expensive without wanting to have it; she was thus constantly surrounded by a profusion of flowers and costly trinkets, and her momentary caprices made her happy in proportion to the amount they cost. Nothing remained in her hands; everything broke, withered, or became soiled between her little white fingers. Her path was strewn with nameless wreckage, twisted shreds, and muddy rags.

Then, amid this reckless squandering of pocket money, big bills began to crop up: she owed twenty thousand francs to the milliner, thirty thousand to the linen-draper, twelve thousand to the shoemaker; her stable cost her fifty thousand; in six months she ran up a bill for a hundred and twenty thousand francs with her dressmaker. Without making any changes in her household, whose annual expenses had been estimated by Labordette at four hundred thousand francs, she spent a million that year. She herself was amazed by this figure, and she had no idea where such a sum could have gone. Men piled on top of one another and gold poured in by the bucketful were unable to fill the hole that grew deeper and deeper beneath her house, in the disruption of her luxury.

Meanwhile she was contemplating her latest caprice. Agitated once more by the idea of redecorating her bedroom, she felt she had finally hit upon what she wanted: a bedroom hung with tea-rose velvet reaching up to the ceiling in the form of a tent, decorated with little silver buttons, tassels, and gold lace. It seemed to her that this would be both rich and tender, and a superb background for her fair skin. The bedroom, however, was merely to serve as a setting for the bed, which would be a dazzling wonder. She was dreaming of a bed such as had never been seen before, a throne, an altar, to which all Paris would come to worship her sovereign nakedness. It would be all in chased gold and silver, like an immense piece of jewelry, with gold roses scattered over a silver trellis; on the headboard, among the flowers, a group of laughing cupids would be looking down, watching the voluptuous pleasures in the shadows of the curtains. She had consulted Labordette, who had brought two goldsmiths to see her. They were already making sketches. The bed would cost fifty thousand francs, and Muffat was to give it to her as her New Year's present.

What surprised her was that, in that river of gold which flowed between her limbs, she was constantly short of money. There were days when she was hard pressed for ridiculous sums of less than a hundred francs. She had to borrow from Zoé, or raise funds as best she could. But before resigning herself to extreme measures, she would sound out her friends and take whatever the men had on them, even their small change, treating it as a joke. For the past three months she had thus been emptying Philippe's pockets. He never came at times of crisis without leaving all his cash behind when he left. She had soon become bolder and had begun asking him for loans of two or three hundred francs, never more, with which to pay bills or pressing debts; and Philippe, who had been made a paymaster in July, always brought the money the next day, apologizing for not being rich, for the good Madame Hugon was now treating her sons with extraordinary severity. At the end of three months these little loans, often renewed, amounted to over ten thousand francs. Although the captain still had his hearty laugh, he was losing weight and sometimes seemed distracted, with a shadow of suffering on his face. But one look from Nana was enough to transfigure him in a kind of sensual ecstasy. She was very affectionate to him, intoxicating him with kisses behind doors, bewitching him with sudden abandonments of herself that kept him tied to her skirts whenever he was able to get away from his military duties.

One evening, after Nana had mentioned that her name was also Thérèse and that her name day was October 15, the gentlemen all sent her presents. Captain Philippe brought his in person; it was an antique Dresden china candy box. He found her alone in her dressing room, having just taken a bath, wearing only a white and red flannel bathrobe. She was busily examining the presents spread out on the table. She had already broken a rock-crystal perfume bottle in trying to get the stopper out.

"Oh, you're too nice!" she said. "What is it? Let's see. . . . How childish of you to spend your money on little things like that!"

She scolded him, because he was not rich; but at heart she was glad to see him spend everything for her, the only proof of love which touched her. She handled the candy box, opening and closing it, wanting to see how it was made.

"Be careful," he said, "it's fragile."

She shrugged her shoulders. Did he think she had the hands of a stevedore? And suddenly the hinge remained

357

between her fingers while the lid fell to the floor and broke. She stared at the pieces in astonishment.

"Oh, it's broken!" she said. Then she began to laugh. The pieces on the floor seemed funny to her. It was a nervous gaiety; she had the stupid, malicious laugh of a child who is amused by destruction. Philippe was indignant for a moment: that wretched girl didn't know how much anguish that knickknack had cost him. When she saw that he was upset, she tried to restrain herself.

"It wasn't my fault. . . . It was cracked. Those antiques don't hold together. . . . It was the lid! Did you see the way it fell off?"

And she laughed wildly. But when tears came into his eyes despite his efforts, she tenderly put her arms around his neck and said, "Don't be silly! I love you just the same. If nothing was ever broken, the shopkeepers would never sell anything. All those things are made to be broken. . . . Look at this fan, for example, it's only glued together."

She picked up a fan and pulled on it. The silk ripped in half. This seemed to excite her. To show that she cared nothing about the other presents, since she had broken his, she treated herself to a general massacre, pounding the objects and proving that not one of them was solid by destroying them all. A glow lighted up her vacant eyes, a slight curl of her upper lip displayed her white teeth. When everything had been broken to pieces, she laughed again. Her cheeks were flushed. She struck the table with her outspread hands and said in a childish voice, "All gone! All gone!"

Philippe finally cheered up, overcome by the same intoxication. He took her in his arms, tilted her back, and kissed her throat and breasts. She abandoned herself, holding onto his shoulders, so happy that she could not remember having enjoyed herself so much for a long time. Without letting go of him, she said to him in a caressing tone, "Listen, darling, I wish you'd bring me two hundred francs tomorrow. . . . My baker has been tormenting me about his bill."

He turned pale; then, giving her one last kiss on the forehead, he said simply, "I'll try."

There was a silence. She began getting dressed. He

stood leaning his forehead against a window pane. A minute later he came back to her and said slowly, "Nana, you ought to marry me."

This idea struck her as so hilarious that she could not finish fastening her petticoat.

"You must be sick, my poor darling! Are you offering me your hand just because I asked you for two hundred francs? . . . Never. I love you too much. What a stupid mistake that would be!"

Just then Zoé came in to put on Nana's shoes, so they said no more about it. Zoé immediately stared at the fragments of the presents on the table. She asked if she should put them away. When Nana told her to throw them away instead, she gathered them into her skirt and carried them out. In the kitchen, the servants picked through the wreckage of Madame's presents and shared whatever could be salvaged.

Although Nana had forbidden him to come, Georges had slipped into the house that day. François had seen him, but by now the servants merely laughed among themselves at Madame's embarrassing predicaments. He was just entering the little drawing room when he was stopped by the sound of his brother's voice. With his ear glued to the door, he heard the whole scene, including the kisses and the proposal of marriage. He was chilled with horror. He went away, stupefied, with a feeling of emptiness in his head. It was not until he was in his room above his mother's apartment on the Rue de Richelieu that his heart burst into furious sobs. This time he could have no doubt. An abominable vision kept appearing before his eyes: Nana in Philippe's arms. It seemed like incest to him. Each time he thought he had recovered his calm, a new fit of jealous rage threw him onto his bed, where he bit the sheets and cried out infamous words that inflamed him still more.

He spent the rest of the day in this manner. He stayed in his room on the pretext that he had a headache. But the night was even more terrible; he was shaken by a murderous fever and had constant nightmares. If his brother had lived in the house, he would have gone to stab him. When daylight came he tried to reason. It was he who had to die; he would jump out the window in front of an omnibus. However, he left the house at ten o'clock. He wandered all over Paris, lingered on a bridge and at the last moment felt an irresistible need to see Nana again. Perhaps she would save him with a word. At three o'clock he entered her house on the Avenue de Villiers.

Toward noon, Madame Hugon had been overwhelmed by a horrible piece of news. Philippe had been in prison since the night before, accused of having stolen twelve thousand francs from the treasury of his regiment. For the past three months he had been embezzling small sums, hoping to repay them, covering up the deficit with false accounts; and thanks to the negligence of the administrative committee, this fraud had always been successful.

Madame Hugon, crushed by her son's crime, uttered a first cry of anger against Nana. She knew about his affair with her, and her sadness came from this misfortune, which had been keeping her in Paris, fearing a catastrophe; but she had never anticipated such a disgrace, and she now reproached herself for having refused money to him, as though she were an accomplice. She sank into a chair, her legs paralyzed, feeling useless, incapable of any action, rooted there to die. Then the sudden thought of Georges consoled her; she still had Georges, he would be able to act and perhaps to save them. Without asking for help from anyone, for she wished to keep the whole matter hidden between herself and Georges, she dragged herself out of the room and climbed the stairs, sustained by the thought that one of her loving sons was still with her. But she found his room empty. The concierge told her that Monsieur Georges had gone out some time ago. A second misfortune was evident in the room: the bed, with its bitten sheets, bore witness to a long anguish; a chair, overturned among some scattered clothes, seemed dead. Georges must be with that woman. And Madame Hugon, her eyes dry, her legs strong now, went down the stairs. She wanted her sons, and she was going off to demand their return.

Nana had been having annoyances ever since morning. First it was that baker, who had come at nine o'clock with his bill for a hundred and thirty-three francs' worth of bread. It was a mere trifle, and yet, in her regal style of living, she had not been able to pay it. He had come a dozen times before, angry because he had been replaced by another baker as soon as he had refused to extend any further credit. And the servants espoused his cause. François said that Madame would never pay him unless he made a big scene. Charles spoke of going upstairs to get an old bill for straw settled. Victorine said it would be better to wait till a gentleman was with Madame, and then get the money out of him by breaking into the conversation. They discussed the matter heatedly and kept the tradesmen informed. There were sessions of gossip lasting three or four hours; Madame was stripped, plucked, and analyzed with all the ferocity of idle servants bursting with prosperity. Only Julien, the butler, defended her: after all, she was nice; and when the others accused him of going to bed with her, he laughed in a conceited way that enraged the cook, for such women disgusted her so much that she wished she were a man so that she could spit on their behinds. François had maliciously posted the baker in the vestibule without telling Madame. She found him in front of her when she came downstairs for lunch. She took his bill and told him to come back at three o'clock. After muttering a few foul words he left, swearing that he would be on time and that he would make sure he was paid in one way or another.

Irritated by this scene, Nana did not enjoy her lunch. This time she had to get rid of that man. She had set the money aside for him at least ten times, but it had never stayed long enough for him to get it; one day she had spent it for flowers, another day she had put it into a collection that was being taken up for an old gendarme. She was now counting on Philippe, although she was beginning to be surprised that she had not yet seen him with his two hundred francs. It was bad luck, because two days before she had bought Satin a whole new outfit, twelve hundred francs' worth of dresses and linen, so she had no money left at all.

Toward two o'clock, when Nana was beginning to worry, Labordette came. He had brought the sketches for the bed. This was a diversion, a joy that made her forget everything else. She clapped her hands and danced. Then, bursting with curiosity, she leaned over a table in the drawing room and examined the sketches while Labordette explained them to her: "You see, this is the body of the bed. In the middle there's a bunch of roses in full bloom, then a garland of flowers and buds. The leaves will be in green gold and the roses in red gold. . . . And here's the main design for the headboard: a circle of cupids on a silver trellis . . ."

Nana interrupted him, carried away by rapture: "Oh, that little one is so funny, the one in the corner with his behind in the air! . . . And that sly smile! They've all got lecherous eyes! . . . I'll never be able to do anything immodest in front of them!"

She was in an extraordinary state of satisfied pride. The goldsmiths had said that no queen had ever slept in such a bed. There was one complication, however. Labordette showed her two sketches for the footboard; one of them reproduced the motif of the sides, the other was entirely different: a female figure representing Night wrapped in her veils, with a faun uncovering her magnificent nudity. He said that if she chose the latter, the goldsmiths intended to make the figure of Night look like her. This rather daring idea made her turn pale with delight. She saw herself as a silver statuette, the symbol of the warm, sensual pleasures of darkness.

"Of course you'd only pose for the head and shoulders," said Labordette.

She looked at him calmly.

"Why? As long as it's for a work of art, I don't care about the sculptor who copies me!"

It was settled: she would take the second design. But he stopped her: "Just a minute, it will cost six thousand francs more."

"It makes no difference to me!" she cried, laughing. "My little muff is rich!"

This was what she now called Muffat when speaking to her close friends, and those gentlemen always referred to him in the same way: "Did you see your little muff last night?" "I thought your little muff would be here now." It was merely a familiar nickname, although she did not yet allow herself to use it in his presence.

Labordette rolled up the sketches and gave her some final information: the goldsmiths had promised to deliver the bed in two months, around December 25; a sculptor would come the next week to make a clay model for the figure of Night. As she was showing him to the door, she remembered the baker. "By the way," she said abruptly, "do you have two hundred francs on you?"

One of Labordette's principles, which served him well, was never to lend money to women. He always gave the same answer.

"No, my dear, I'm broke. . . . But I can go to see your little muff if you want me to."

She declined, saying it was unnecessary. She had already gotten five thousand francs out of the Count two days before. She soon regretted her discretion, however. As soon as Labordette was gone, the baker returned, even though it was only two-thirty. He roughly sat down on a bench in the vestibule and began swearing loudly. Nana listened to him from the second floor. She turned pale, suffering especially from hearing the servants' secret joy: they were dying of laughter in the kitchen. The coachman looked in from the courtyard. François walked through the vestibule without any necessity, then hastened to report to the others, after giving the baker a knowing smile. They were all making fun of Madame, the walls were bursting; she felt all alone, surrounded by the contempt of her servants, who were spying on her and spattering her with their filthy jokes. For a moment she thought of borrowing the hundred and thirty-three francs from Zoé, but she quickly abandoned the idea; she owed her money already, and she was too proud to risk a refusal. She was so overcome with emotion that she went back to her bedroom, talking aloud: "Don't count on anyone but yourself, my girl. . . . Your body belongs to you, and it's better to use it than to put up with an insult."

And without even calling Zoé, she feverishly got dressed to hurry to Tricon. This was her ultimate resource at times of great distress. Eagerly sought after and always solicited by the old lady, she either refused or resigned herself, according to her needs. On those increasingly frequent days when she encountered difficulties in her regal style of living, she was sure to find five hundred francs waiting for her there. She would go to Tricon's with the ease born of habit, as poor people go to a pawnshop.

But when she left her bedroom she ran into Georges,

who was standing in the middle of the drawing room. She did not notice his waxy pallor or the somber fire in his widened eyes. She sighed with relief.

"Ah, your brother sent you?"

"No," he said, turning still whiter.

She made a gesture of despair. What did he want? Why was he standing in front of her? She was in a hurry! Then she came back to him and said, "Do you have any money?"

"No."

"Of course, how stupid of me! You never have anything, not even the six sous for the omnibus. Your mother won't let you. . . . Oh, what men!"

She tried to leave, but he held her back. He wanted to talk to her. She struggled and said she had no time. He stopped her by saying, "Listen, I know you're going to marry my brother."

That was a good one! She sank into a chair to laugh at ease.

"Yes," continued Georges, "and I won't let you do it. You're going to marry me instead. That's why I've come."

"What!" she cried. "You too? It must be a family disease! . . . No, never! What an idea! Have I ever asked either of you to do a dirty thing like that? No, neither of you, never!"

Georges' face brightened. Perhaps he was mistaken. . . .

"Then swear to me that you don't go to bed with my brother."

"Oh, you're getting on my nerves!" said Nana, standing up. All her impatience returned. "It's funny for a little while, but I've already told you I'm in a hurry! . . . I'll go to bed with your brother if I feel like it. I don't owe you anything! Do you support me, do you pay for everything here? . . . Yes, I go to bed with your brother. . . ."

He gripped her arm, squeezed it almost hard enough to break it, and stammered, "Don't say that. . . . Don't say that. . . ."

She gave him a little slap and freed herself from him.

"Are you trying to beat me now? What a rough little boy! Get out of here, right now! I kept you because I have a kind heart. That's right, go ahead and stare at me! You didn't expect me to go on being your mother till I died, did you? I've got better things to do than bring up children."

He listened to her with an anguish that stiffened him without rousing him to revolt. Each word stabbed him so painfully in the heart that he felt he was dying. She did not even notice his suffering; she went on, glad of the chance to take out on him all the annoyances she had had that morning:

"You're just like your brother! Ah, there's another fine one! He promised to bring me two hundred francs, and I'm still waiting. . . . Not that his money means anything to me—it's hardly enough to buy my pomade. But he's left me in a mess. . . . Would you like to know something? Because of your brother, I'm about to go out and earn five hundred francs with another man."

Georges frantically blocked the door, sobbing, begging her with his hands clasped, moaning, "Oh, no! Oh, no!"

"Well, I'm willing," she said. "Have you got the money?"

No, he didn't have the money. He would have given his life to have it. Never before had he felt so miserable, so useless, such a little boy. His whole wretched being, shaken by tears, expressed such overwhelming grief that she finally noticed it and felt sorry for him. She gently pushed him aside.

"Look, darling, let me go, I must. . . . Be reasonable. You're only a baby; it was nice for a week or so, but now I have to take care of my business. Think about it a little. . . . Your brother's a man, I'm not talking about him. . . . Please do me a favor and don't tell him about this. He doesn't need to know where I'm going. I always say too much when I get angry." She laughed. Then she took hold of him, kissed him on the forehead, and said, "Good-by, my little Baby. It's all over now, it's all over, you understand? . . . I'm going."

And she left him. He was standing in the middle of the drawing room. Her words rang like a knell in his ears: "It's all over now." He felt as though the earth were opening up beneath his feet. In the emptiness of his brain, the man who was waiting for Nana had disappeared; only Philippe remained, constantly in her bare arms. She had not denied it; she was in love with him, since she wanted to spare him the grief of knowing she was unfaithful. It was over now, all over. He breathed heavily and looked around the room, smothered by the weight that was crushing him. Memories came back to him one by one: the lighthearted nights at La Mignotte, the hours of love during which he had felt like her child, then the voluptuous pleasures he had stolen in that very room. And never, never again! He was too young, he had not grown up quickly enough; Philippe had replaced him because he had a beard. It was the end, he could not go on living. His vice had become tempered with infinite tenderness, with a sensual adoration that absorbed his whole being. And how could he forget, when his brother would still be there? His brother, his own blood, another self whose pleasure drove him mad with jealousy! It was the end, he wanted to die.

All the doors had been left open when the servants had noisily scurried around the house after seeing Madame walk out. Downstairs, on the bench in the vestibule, the baker was laughing with Charles and François. As Zoé was running across the drawing room, she was surprised to see Georges. She asked him if he was waiting for Madame. Yes, he was waiting for her, he had forgotten to tell her something. As soon as he was alone again he began looking around. In the dressing room, unable to find anything else, he took a pair of very sharp-pointed scissors that Nana often used for clipping hairs all over her body. Then for an hour he waited with his hand in his pocket and his fingers nervously clutching the scissors.

"Here comes Madame," said Zoé, returning. She had apparently been watching for her from the bedroom window.

There was a sound of running in the house; the laughter died away, the doors were closed. Georges heard Nana say a few curt words to the baker as she paid him. Then she came upstairs.

"What! Are you still here?" she said when she saw him. "We're going to be angry, my friend!"

He followed her while she walked toward the bedroom.

"Nana, will you marry me?"

She shrugged her shoulders. It was too stupid, she was not even going to answer him again. She intended to slam the door in his face.

"Nana, will you marry me?"

She slammed the door. He opened it with one hand and took the other from his pocket, holding the scissors. And, simply, with one great blow, he sank them into his chest.

Nana, meanwhile, had had a feeling that something terrible was about to happen. She had turned around. When she saw him stab himself, she was seized with indignation.

"Oh, what a fool you are! What a fool! And with my scissors, too! Stop it, you nasty child! . . . Oh, my God, my God!"

She was panic-stricken. Georges, fallen to his knees, had just stabbed himself a second time and was now lying on the carpet, blocking the bedroom doorway. She then lost her head completely, screaming at the top of her lungs, not daring to step over that body, which shut her in and prevented her from running off to bring help.

"Zoé! Zoé! Hurry! . . . Make him stop! It's stupid, a child like that! . . . Now he's killing himself, and in my house! Who ever heard of such a thing?"

He frightened her. He was deathly pale and his eyes were closed. His wounds were hardly bleeding, only a thin trickle of blood that was soaked up by his vest. She was about to gather her courage to step over the body when an apparition made her draw back. An old lady was walking toward her through the open door of the drawing room. Terrified, she recognized Madame Hugon. She was unable to account for her presence there. She stepped back further, still wearing her gloves and hat. Her terror became so great that she began defending herself in a faltering voice:

"I didn't do it, Madame, I swear I didn't. . . . He asked me to marry him, I said no, and he killed himself."

Madame Hugon slowly approached, dressed in black, her face pale, with her white hair. In the carriage, the thought of Georges had left her and her mind had been entirely occupied by Philippe's crime. Perhaps that woman could give the judges explanations that would touch them; and she conceived the plan of begging her to testify in her son's favor. Downstairs, the doors of the house were open. She was hesitating on the stairs, with her weak legs, when horrified screams directed her steps. Then, upstairs, she saw a man lying on the floor, his shirt stained with blood. It was Georges, her other son.

Nana repeated in a stupefied tone, "He asked me to marry him, I said no, and he killed himself."

Without a cry, Madame Hugon bent down. Yes, it was her other son, it was Georges. One was dishonored, the other had been murdered. It did not surprise her, in the collapse of her whole life. Kneeling on the carpet, not knowing where she was, not seeing anyone, she stared at Georges' face and listened with her hand over his heart. Then she uttered a faint sigh. She had felt his heart beating. She looked up, examined the bedroom and the woman before her, and seemed to remember. A flame was kindled in her empty eyes. She was so great and terrible in her silence that Nana trembled and continued to defend herself, above the body that separated them.

"I give you my word, Madame. . . . If his brother were here, he could explain to you. . . ."

"His brother has stolen some money and is now in prison," Madame Hugon said harshly.

Nana felt as though she were choking. Why, why was all this happening? Now his brother had stolen money? The whole family was insane! She stopped struggling; she no longer seemed to be in her own house, she let Madame Hugon give the orders. Some of the servants had finally come. The old lady insisted that they carry Georges, who was unconscious, downstairs to her carriage. She wanted to get him out of that house even if it meant causing his death. With her dazed eyes, Nana watched the servants who were holding poor Zizi by the shoulders and legs. His mother walked behind, exhausted now, leaning on the furniture, as though she were being annihilated along with everything she loved. When she reached the landing, she sobbed, turned around, and said, "Ah, you've done us great harm! . . . You've done us great harm!"

That was all. In her stupor, Nana had sat down, with her gloves still on her hands and her hat still on her head. Heavy silence settled over the house. The carriage left. Nana remained motionless, unable to think, her head buzzing from what had just happened. A quarter of an hour later, Count Muffat found her in the same place. She then relieved herself with a flow of words, telling him all about the disaster, returning a dozen times to the same details, picking up the bloodstained scissors to show how Zizi had stabbed himself. She was especially eager to prove her innocence.

"Look, darling, was it my fault? If you were a judge, would you convict me? I didn't tell Philippe to steal, and I didn't tell poor Georges to kill himself. . . . I've had worse luck than anyone else. They come and do stupid things in my house, they make me miserable, they treat me like an evil woman. . . ."

And she began to cry. A slight relaxation of her nervous tension left her limp and plaintive, with an enormous grief.

"You look dissatisfied too. . . . Just ask Zoé if I had anything to do with it. . . . Zoé, talk to Monsieur, explain to him. . . ."

Zoé had taken a towel and a basin of water from the dressing room and was trying to wash the blood out of the carpet while it was still fresh.

"Oh, Monsieur," she said, "Madame is heartbroken enough already!"

Muffat was stunned, chilled by that tragedy, his mind filled with the thought of that mother weeping for her sons. He knew her great heart; he saw her in her mourning clothes, withering away all alone at Les Fondettes. But Nana's despair was becoming more violent. She was thrown into a frenzy by the image of Zizi stretched out on the floor with a red hole in his shirt.

"He was so handsome, so gentle, so affectionate. . . . You know, darling, I loved that baby! I can't help saying it, even if it upsets you. . . . Anyway, it shouldn't matter to you now: he's not here any more. You've got what you wanted, you can be sure you'll never catch us together again. . . ."

And this last idea choked her with such regret that he tried to comfort her. She had to get a grip on herself; she was right, it wasn't her fault. But she stopped crying of her own accord and said, "Listen, I want you to go and find out how he is. Hurry! You must!"

He took his hat and went off to ask about Georges. When he returned three-quarters of an hour later, he saw Nana leaning anxiously from a window. He shouted up to

369

her from the sidewalk that Georges was not dead and that there was great hope for his recovery. She was immediately filled with extreme joy. She sang and danced; life was beautiful again. Zoé, however, was not satisfied with her washing: she kept looking at the bloodstain each time she passed.

"It's still there, you know, Madame."

The spot was reappearing, pale red on one of the white rosettes of the carpet. It was like a line of blood barring the bedroom door.

"Oh, it'll be worn away by footsteps," said Nana, happy.

By the next day, Count Muffat had also forgotten the incident. While he was in a cab on his way to the Rue Richelieu, he had sworn never to go back to that woman's house. Heaven had given him a warning; he looked on the disaster that had befallen Philippe and Georges as an announcement of his own ruin. But the sight of Madame Hugon in tears, and of her son burning with fever, had not had the power to make him keep his vow. The horror aroused in him by the tragedy had given way to a secret delight at being rid of a rival whose charming youthfulness had always exasperated him. His passion had become exclusive, the passion of a man who has had no youth. He loved Nana with a need to know that she belonged to him alone, to hear her, to touch her, to be in her breath. His tenderness had gone beyond the senses and into the realm of pure feeling. It was an anxious affection, jealous of the past.

He sometimes dreamed of redemption, of forgiveness bestowed on them both while they knelt before God the Father. Religion was regaining its hold on him more strongly each day. He had resumed his religious practices, he now went to confession and took Communion. He was constantly struggling within himself; his remorse was mingled with the joy of sin and penitence. Then, when his confessor had enabled him to wear out his passion, he had made a habit of that daily damnation, redeeming it with bursts of faith that were full of devout humility. He guilelessly offered heaven, as an expiatory suffering, the abominable torments he endured. These torments were growing still greater. He was climbing his Calvary with the profound and solemn heart of a believer ensnared by the frenzied sensuality of a harlot. It was her constant infidelities that caused him the most agony. He could not accustom himself to sharing her, he could not understand her idiotic caprices. He longed for an eternal love, always the same. She had sworn to give it to him, and he was paying her for it, but he knew she lied to him, that she was unable to restrain herself, that she gave herself to friends and passers-by, like a docile animal born to live naked.

One morning when he had seen Foucarmont leaving her house at an unusual hour, he made a scene with her. She immediately became angry. She was tired of his jealousy. She had already been nice to him several times. On the night when he had caught her with Georges, for example, she had been the first to try to make it up, she had admitted she was wrong and had showered him with caresses and kind words to help him get over it. But now she had had enough of his stubborn refusal to understand women.

"All right, yes, I've been to bed with Foucarmont," she said roughly. "What of it? That takes the wind out of your sails, doesn't it, my little muff?"

This was the first time she had ever called him "my little muff" to his face. He was dumbfounded by the bluntness of her admission. As he was clenching his fists, she walked up to him, looked him straight in the eye and said, "I've had enough of this, you understand? If you don't like it, you can get out. I won't have you yelling in my house. Get it into your head that I intend to do as I please. When I like a man, I go to bed with him. You heard me, that's how it is. . . . And you've got to make up your mind right away: yes or no. You can leave if you want to."

She opened the door. He did not leave. This was now her way of attaching him to her all the more: for any trifle, at the slightest quarrel, she would put the choice to him, with odious remarks. She could always find better men! There were so many she wouldn't know where to start! She could pick up men on the sidewalk, as many as she wanted, and less simple-minded ones, too, men who had blood in their veins! He would bow his head and wait for her to be gentler, when she needed money. At those times she became affectionate and he forgot; a night of tenderness compensated him for a whole week of torture.

His reconciliation with his wife had made his home unbearable to him. The Countess, abandoned by Faucbery, who had again fallen under Rose's domination, had begun pursuing other love affairs with the anxiety of a woman approaching forty. She was always nervous, and she filled the house with the irritating whirl of her life. Since her marriage, Estelle had stopped seeing her father. That dull, insignificant girl had been abruptly transformed into a woman so iron-willed and autocratic that Daguenet trembled before her. He now accompanied her to Mass, converted. He was furious with his father-in-law for ruining them with a vile creature. Only Monsieur Venot remained affectionate toward the Count, biding his time. He had even succeeded in placing himself on friendly terms with Nana. He now frequented both houses, where his constant smile was often seen behind the doors. And Muffat, miserable at home, driven away by boredom and shame, preferred to spend his time at Nana's house despite the insults he had to endure.

Soon there was only one question left between Nana and the Count: money. One day, after promising to bring her ten thousand francs, he dared to come empty-handed at the time they had agreed upon. She had been warming him with caresses for the past two days. She was thrown into an abusive rage by this lack of good faith, and by the thought of all the endearing efforts she had wasted. Her face turned white.

"What! You don't have the money? In that case, my little muff, go back where you came from, right now! And you expected to kiss me after a dirty trick like that? No money, no nothing, understand?"

He gave her explanations; he would have the money the next day. But she interrupted him violently: "And what about my bills? My creditors will take all my belongings while you're coming here free! . . . Just take a look at yourself! Do you think I love you for your good looks? When a man has a face like yours, he has to pay women who are willing to put up with him. By God, if you don't bring me that ten thousand francs tonight, I won't even let you suck the tip of my little finger! I mean it! I'll send you back to your wife!"

That night he brought the ten thousand francs. Nana

held out her lips and he gave her a long kiss which consoled him for his whole day of anguish. What annoyed her
was having him constantly trailing around behind her. She
complained about it to Monsieur Venot, and begged him
to take her little muff back to the Countess. Hadn't their
reconciliation done any good? She was sorry she had taken
a hand in it, since she was still burdened with him anyway. On days when she became so angry that she forgot
her own interests, she swore she would do something so
nasty that he would never set foot in her house again. But,
as she herself shouted, slapping her thighs, she could have
spat in his face and he would still have stayed, thanking
her. She made constant scenes about money. She brutally
demanded it of him. She quarreled with him over trifling
sums and was odiously greedy at every moment. She
cruelly repeated to him that she went to bed with him
only for his money, that she didn't enjoy it, that she was in
love with another man, and that she was very unlucky to
have to put up with an idiot like him! They didn't even
want him at court any more, and there was talk of forcing
him to resign. The Empress had said, "He's too disgusting." And she was right. Nana repeated the words to end
all their quarrels, "Oh, you're too disgusting!"

She had ceased to restrain herself in any way; her freedom was complete. Every day she took a drive around the
lake, making acquaintances that reached a climax elsewhere. There, in the sunlight and open air, she joined the
illustrious prostitutes who plied their trade in the smiling
tolerance and dazzling luxury of Paris. Duchesses pointed
her out to one another with a glance, her hats were copied
by middle-class women whose husbands had become rich.
Sometimes her landau, in passing, would stop a whole line
of great carriages containing financiers who held all of
Europe in their coffers, or cabinet members whose fat
fingers gripped France by the throat. She was part of the
world of the Bois de Boulogne, she occupied a prominent
place in it; she was known by men in all the capitals of
Europe, and was sought after by all the foreigners who
came to Paris. To the splendors of that crowd she added
the wanton madness of her debauchery, like the glory and
keen enjoyment of a nation. And her one-night affairs and
brief amorous encounters, which she herself forgot every

morning, brought her to the great restaurants, often to the Madrid, when the weather was good. The staffs of all the embassies appeared there; she had dinner with Lucy Stewart, Caroline Héquet, and Maria Blond, in the company of gentlemen who murdered the French language and paid to be entertained. These men hired women by the evening, with orders to be amusing, but they were so jaded and worn out that they did not even touch them. The women called this "going on a spree." They would come home, happy with their disdain, and finish the night in the arms of a lover of their choice.

Count Muffat pretended to be ignorant of all this, whenever she did not throw men in his face. He suffered a great deal from the little indignities of his daily life. Nana's house was becoming an inferno, a madhouse in which wild caprices constantly gave rise to odious scenes. She had even begun quarreling with her servants. For a time she was very good to Charles the coachman. Whenever she went to a restaurant she would have a waiter take out glasses of beer to him; she gaily talked to him from inside her landau, highly amused by the way he shouted at the cab drivers when traffic became blocked. Then, for no apparent reason, she began calling him an idiot and bickering with him about the straw, the bran, and the oats; despite her love for animals, she thought the horses were eating too much. Finally, one day when she was looking over his accounts, she accused him of stealing. He flew into a rage and called her a whore. He said her horses were better than she was—they didn't go to bed with everybody! She answered in the same vein. The Count had to separate them and dismiss the coachman.

But this was only the beginning of a general stampede among the servants. Victorine and François left after some diamonds had been stolen. Even Julien disappeared; and there was a rumor that the Count had given him a large sum of money and begged him to leave, because he was going to bed with Madame. Every week there were new faces in the servants' quarters. Never before had there been such waste; the house was like a passage through which the scum of the employment agencies galloped, pillaging everything in sight. Zoé remained, with her prim air and her concern for organizing the disorder, until she had enough money to set herself up independently, a plan she had been nurturing for a long time.

And these were only the avowable cares. The Count put up with Madame Maloir's stupidity, playing bezique with her despite her rancid smell; he put up with Madame Lerat and her gossip, with little Louis and his sad complaints of a child devoured by disease, some putrefaction bequeathed to him by an unknown father. But he spent worse hours. One night, behind a door, he had heard Nana furiously telling Zoé that a man who claimed to be rich had just cheated her; yes, he was a handsome man who said he was an American and that he owned gold mines in his country, but he was actually nothing but a dirty swindler, because he had slipped away while she was asleep, without leaving her a sou, and had even taken a packet of cigarette papers from her. And the Count, very pale, had tiptoed down the stairs, in order not to know any more.

On another occasion, however, he was forced to know everything. Nana had become infatuated with a music-hall baritone. When he left her, she had a fit of gloomy sentimentality and decided to commit suicide. She drank a glass of water in which she had soaked a handful of matches. It made her horribly sick, but did not kill her. The Count had to nurse her and listen to the story of her passion, intermingled with tears and oaths never to become attached to any man again. In her contempt for those pigs, as she called them, she was nevertheless unable to keep her heart free: she always had some chosen lover around her, and the perverse tastes of her weary body made her indulge in all sorts of inexplicable caprices. Since Zoé had deliberately begun to relax her vigilance, the functioning of the household had deteriorated to such a point that Muffat no longer dared to open a door, pull back a curtain, or look into a closet. The tricks no longer worked: there were men all over the house, and they kept running into each other at every moment. The Count now coughed before entering a room, having once almost found Nana with her arms around Francis' neck one night when he had left the dressing room for a few minutes to tell the coachman to put the horses to the carriage, while the hairdresser was giving the finishing touches to her hair. She often abandoned herself abruptly behind his back, took brief pleasures in all sorts of corners, hurriedly, in her nightgown or in an elegant dress, with the first man who came along. She would then rejoin the Count with her face still red, delighted by the theft. With him, it was nothing but boring drudgery.

In his jealous anguish, the wretched man had reached the point of feeling at ease when he left Nana and Satin alone together. He would even have urged this vice upon her, if necessary, in order to keep men away. But in this direction, too, things were going wrong. Nana deceived Satin just as she deceived the Count, plunging into monstrous infatuations, picking up girls in the street. When she was on her way home in her carriage she would occasionally become enamored of some little slut she saw on the sidewalk. With her senses inflamed and her imagination running wild, she would take the girl with her, then later pay her and send her away. At other times, disguised as a man, she would go to infamous houses and witness spectacles of debauchery that relieved her boredom. And Satin, annoyed at being constantly forsaken, often upset the whole house with terrible scenes; she had finally acquired absolute dominion over Nana, who respected her. Muffat even thought of allying himself with her. When he was afraid to say anything, he turned Satin loose on Nana. She had twice forced her to take him back. For his part, he was most obliging to her, kept her informed, and went away at the slightest sign from her. But this understanding did not last long, for Satin, too, was unbalanced. There were days when she smashed everything, half dead, exhausting herself in fits of anger or tenderness, looking pretty in spite of it all. Zoé apparently worked on her feelings, for she took her in corners, as though she were trying to recruit her for her great undertaking, that plan of which she had not yet spoken to anyone.

Count Muffat was still roused to strange revolts, however. He had been tolerating Satin for months, he had finally come to accept those strangers, that whole troop of men who streamed in and out of Nana's bedroom, and yet he was enraged by the idea of her deceiving him with one of his friends, or even one of his acquaintances. When she confessed her intimacy with Foucarmont, he suffered so acutely, and found the young man's treachery so outrageous, that he decided to challenge him to a duel. Since he did not know where to find seconds for such an affair, he addressed himself to Labordette. The latter was astounded, and could not help laughing.

"A duel over Nana! . . . But my dear Count, everyone in Paris would make fun of you! One doesn't fight a duel over Nana, it's ridiculous."

The Count turned very pale and made a violent gesture. "Then I'll slap his face in the street."

Labordette had to reason with him for an hour. A slap would make the affair odious; by evening, everyone would know the real cause of the duel and he would be the laughingstock of the newspapers. And Labordette kept returning to this conclusion: "Impossible; it's ridiculous."

Each time Muffat heard these words they stabbed him like a knife. He could not even fight for the woman he loved: everyone would have laughed. Never before had he so painfully felt the misery of his love, the seriousness of his heart lost in that joke of pleasure. This was his last revolt; he let himself be convinced, and from then on he watched the procession of friends, of all the men who lived there in the intimacy of Nana's house.

Nana gradually devoured them one after another in a few months. The growing needs of her luxury whetted her appetite; she could finish off a man at a single bite. First she had Foucarmont, who lasted only a few days. He had been dreaming of leaving the navy. In ten years of seafaring, he had saved some thirty thousand francs, which he wanted to risk in the United States. His instincts of prudence, even avarice, were swept away: he gave everything, and even placed his signature on accommodation bills that involved his future. When Nana turned him out of her house, he had been stripped clean. She showed kindness toward him, however, and advised him to go back to his ship. What was the use of being stubborn? Since he had no more money, it was no longer possible. He must understand and be reasonable. A ruined man fell from her hands like a ripe fruit, to rot on the ground.

Next she took up with Steiner again, without disgust but also without affection. She called him a dirty Jew, apparently gratifying an old hatred of which she was not clearly

conscious. He was fat, he was stupid; and she hurried him,
taking double mouthfuls, wanting to finish with that Prussian as quickly as possible. He had abandoned Simonne.
His Bosporus scheme was in danger of collapsing. Nana
precipitated his downfall by her insane demands. He went
on struggling for another month, performing miracles; he
covered Europe with a colossal publicity campaign—posters, newspaper advertisements, prospectuses—and drew
money from the most distant countries. All that capital, the
louis of speculators as well as the sous of poor people, was
swallowed up in the house on the Avenue de Villiers. He
had also gone into partnership with an iron manufacturer
in Alsace, where there were workers blackened by coal
dust and soaked with sweat who, night and day, stiffened
their muscles and heard their bones cracking in order to
provide for Nana's pleasures. She consumed everything
like a great fire: the thefts of speculation and the earnings
of labor. This time she finished Steiner; she put him out
into the street, so thoroughly cleaned out that he was not
even capable of inventing another swindle. In the collapse
of his banking house, he stammered and trembled at the
idea of the police. He had just been declared bankrupt;
and the man who had handled millions was flustered and
thrown into childish embarrassment by the mere mention
of money. One night in Nana's house he began weeping
and asked her to lend him a hundred francs so that he
could pay his maid. And Nana, touched and amused by
this end of the terrible man who had been squeezing the
Paris market for the past twenty years, brought him the
money and said to him, "I'm giving it to you because it's
funny. But listen, my friend: you're too old to be supported by me. You'll have to find another occupation."

Then she immediately started on La Faloise. For a long
time he had been seeking the honor of being ruined by
her, so that he could be perfectly fashionable. It was the
only thing he still lacked; he needed a woman to launch
him into complete success. In two months he would be
known to everyone in Paris, and he would read his name in
the newspapers. It took only six weeks. His inheritance was
in land: fields, meadows, woods, and farms. He had to sell
them rapidly, one after the other. Nana devoured an acre
with each mouthful. The foliage quivering in the sunlight,

378

the tall, ripe grain, the vines golden in September, the high grass in which cows sank up to their bellies—everything was engulfed as in an abyss. There were even three mills, a waterway, and a gypsum quarry that disappeared. Nana passed like an invading army, like one of those swarms of grasshoppers whose flaming flight razes a whole province. She scorched the earth on which she placed her little foot. Farm by farm, meadow by meadow, she ate up the inheritance, looking amiable all the while, not even noticing what she was doing, just as she would eat between meals a bag of pralines placed on her lap. It was a matter of no consequence, they were only tidbits. But one evening there was nothing left except a small forest. She swallowed it disdainfully, for it was really not worth the trouble of opening her mouth. La Faloise laughed idiotically, sucking the knob of his cane. He was crushed by debt, he no longer had a hundred francs of income. He saw himself forced to go back to the country and live with a lunatic uncle, but it didn't matter: he was fashionable, his name had appeared twice in the *Figaro*. With his skinny neck imprisoned in his turned-down collar and his chest squeezed into a vest that was too short, he swayed back and forth, exclaimed like a parrot, and affected the lassitude of a wooden puppet that had never had an emotion. He irritated Nana so much that she finally slapped him.

Meanwhile Fauchery had returned, brought by his cousin. Poor Fauchery was now as good as married. After breaking off with the Countess, he had found himself in Rose's hands, and she treated him like a real husband. Mignon was merely her major-domo. Having been installed as master of the household, the journalist lied to Rose and took all sorts of precautions when he deceived her. He was filled with the scruples of a good husband who wishes to settle down at last. Nana's triumph was to take possession of him and make him liquidate a newspaper he had started with a friend's money. She did not openly display her conquest; on the contrary, it pleased her to treat him like a gentleman who had to conceal his affair with her. And whenever she spoke of Rose she called her "that poor Rose." The newspaper kept her in flowers for two months. She had subscribers in the provinces, she took everything, from the front-page stories to the theatrical column. Then, after she had broken down the editorial staff and disrupted the management, she satisfied a big whim, a winter garden in one corner of her house, which swept away the printing plant. And it was only for fun. When Mignon, delighted by what was taking place, came to her to see if he could get her to take over Fauchery completely, she asked if he was joking: a man who had no money and lived from his articles and plays—no, thanks! Such foolishness was all right for a talented woman like that poor Rose, but not for her. Mistrustful and afraid of treachery on Mignon's part, for he was capable of denouncing them to his wife, she dismissed Fauchery, who had recently been paying her only in publicity.

But she kept fond memories of him; they had had a great deal of amusement together at the expense of that idiot La Faloise. They might never have even thought of seeing each other again if they had not been stimulated by the pleasure of making fun of such an imbecile. They enjoyed themselves immensely; they kissed each other under his nose, and went on riotous sprees with his money. They would send him to the other end of Paris on some errand or other in order to be alone, and then when he came back they would make jokes and allusions which he could not understand. One day, egged on by Fauchery, she bet that she would slap La Faloise. She did so that evening, and she continued it afterward. It amused her, and she was glad to show how cowardly men were. She called him her "slapping machine." She would tell him to step forward and get his slap, which reddened her hand because she was not yet accustomed to it. La Faloise would laugh in his foppish way, with tears in his eyes. This familiarity delighted him, he thought it was magnificent.

"You know," he said one night, excited by having received several slaps, "you ought to marry me. . . . What a couple we'd make, eh?"

These were not empty words. He had been secretly planning this marriage, seized with a need to astonish Paris. Nana's husband—what an impressive title! It would be a splendid climax for his career. But Nana quickly put him in his place:

"What an idea! Listen, if I wanted to get married I'd have found a husband long ago, and it would have been a man worth ten times as much as you, my boy. I've had lots of proposals. Let's count them up: Philippe, Georges, Foucarmont, Steiner, that makes four, not counting the others you don't know. . . . That's all they can think of. As soon as I'm nice to them, they all start singing, 'Will you marry me, will you marry me?'" She was becoming agitated. She burst out indignantly: "No, I won't! Do you think I was made for that? Look at me: I wouldn't be Nana any more if I saddled myself with a man! And besides, it's too dirty. . . ."

She spat and made a grimace of disgust, as though she had just seen all the filth on earth spread out before her.

One night La Faloise disappeared. A week later it was learned that he was in the country with his uncle, who had a mania for botanizing; he was mounting his specimens for him, and stood a chance of marrying a very ugly and very pious cousin. Nana shed no tears for him. She merely said to the Count, "Well, my little muff, there's one less rival for you. You can be happy today. . . . He was getting serious, too: he wanted to marry me."

Seeing him turn pale, she laughed and put her arms around his neck, sinking each one of her cruelties into him with a caress.

"That's what bothers you, isn't it? You can't marry Nana. . . . While they're all annoying me with their proposals, you fret and fume all alone in your corner. It's impossible; you'll have to wait till your wife dies. . . . Ah, if your wife died you wouldn't waste any time, would you? You'd kneel in front of me and propose to me in grand style, with sigh, tears, and vows! Wouldn't that be nice, darling?"

Her voice became soft; she was mocking him with a ferociously affectionate expression. Deeply moved, he blushed as he returned her kisses. Then she cried out:

"My God, it's really true! You've been thinking about it, you're waiting for your wife to die! . . . You're even worse than the others!"

Muffat had accepted the others. He now attached the last of his dignity to having the servants and the habitués of the house continue to refer to him as "Monsieur," the man who was the official lover because he gave the most. And his passion persisted. He maintained his position by paying, buying even smiles at exorbitant prices, constantly robbed and never getting his money's worth; but it was like a disease that was destroying him, and he could not help suffering from it. When he went into Nana's bedroom he contented himself with opening the windows for a moment to drive out the smells of the others, the exhalations of dark and blond men, the acrid cigar smoke that choked him. That bedroom was like a crossroads; boots were continually wiped on the threshold—and no one was ever stopped by the bloodstain in front of the door. In her concern for cleanliness, Zoé was still preoccupied with that stain. It annoyed her to see it there, but her eyes always turned to it anyway. She never went into Madame's bedroom without saying, "It's funny it still hasn't gone away. . . . And yet plenty of people come here."

Nana had been receiving better news about Georges, who was then convalescing at Les Fondettes with his mother. She always made the same reply: "Oh, it takes time. . . . The footsteps are wearing it away."

And indeed each one of the gentlemen—Foucarmont, Steiner, La Faloise, Fauchery—had carried away a little of the stain on the soles of his shoes. And Muffat, who was as preoccupied with it as Zoé, studied it in spite of himself, in order to determine, from the extent to which its pinkness had faded, how many more men had passed over it. He had a secret fear of it; he was always careful to step over it, seized with a sudden fear of crushing something living, a bare limb stretched out on the floor.

Then, when he was in the bedroom, he was intoxicated by a heady excitement. He forgot everything: the mob of men who were always going in and out of the room, the mark of mourning which blocked its door. When he was outside in the open air of the street, he sometimes wept with shame and revolt and swore never to go back. But as soon as he stepped across the threshold he was recaptured, he felt himself melting in the warmth of the room, his flesh penetrated by a perfume, overwhelmed by a voluptuous desire for annihilation. Devout and accustomed to the ecstasies of ornate chapels, he experienced exactly the same sensations as when he knelt beneath a stained-glass window and succumbed to the rapture of the organ and the censers. That woman possessed him with the jealous despotism of a God of wrath, terrifying him, giving him a few seconds of joys as acute as spasms in exchange for hours of horrible torments, visions of hell and of eternal suffering. It was the same stammerings, the same prayers, the same despair, the same humility of an accursed creature crushed beneath the mud of his origin. The desires of his flesh and the need of his soul were mingled and seemed to rise from the dark depths of his being in a single blossoming of the tree of life. He abandoned himself to the power of love and faith, whose double lever moves the world. And always, despite the struggles of his reason, that bedroom of Nana's filled him with madness; he sank quivering into the omnipotence of sex, just as he resigned himself before the vast unknown of heaven.

Then, when he felt so humble, Nana became tyrannical in her triumph. She had an instinctive urge to debase everything. It was not enough for her to destroy things, she also dirtied them. Her delicate hands left abominable traces, decomposing everything they had broken. And he idiotically lent himself to this game, with a vague remembrance of saints who were devoured by lice and ate their own excrement. When she had him in her bedroom with the doors closed, she treated herself to the sight of man's infamy. At first she jokingly gave him a few light taps and made him do comical things, such as lisping like a child and repeating ends of seentences.

"Say this: '. . . and anyway, Coco doesn't care.'"

He was docile to the point of reproducing her accent: ". . . and anyway, Coco doesn't care."

Or else she would get down on all fours on the fur rugs and pretend to be a bear, in her nightgown, growling as though she wanted to eat him up; she would even give him little bites on the legs, just for fun. Then, standing up: "Now it's your turn. I'll bet you can't act like a bear as well as I do."

It was still charming. She amused him as a bear, with her white skin and her mane of blond hair. He also got down on all fours, laughing and growling, biting her legs while she ran away from in mock terror.

"We're silly, aren't we?" she finally said. "You can't imagine how ugly you are, my dear! Oh, if only they could see you like that at the Tuileries!"

But these little games soon took a bad turn. It was not

out of cruelty on her part, for she was still a good-natured girl; it was something like a wave of insanity that gradually swelled in the closed room. A kind of lust threw their minds into disorder and plunged them both into delirious imaginings of the flesh. The old devout terrors of their sleepless nights now turned into a thirst for bestiality, a furious impulse to get down on all fours, to growl and bite. Then one day when he was acting like a bear she pushed him so hard that he fell against a piece of furniture; and she burst into involuntary laughter when she saw a bump on his forehead. From then on, having already acquired a taste for it by her experiment with La Faloise, she treated him like an animal, beating him and kicking him around the room.

"Giddap! You're a horse! Giddap, you dirty nag, get moving!"

At other times he was a dog. She would throw her perfumed handkerchief to the other end of the room and he had to crawl over on his hands and knees to pick it up between his teeth.

"Bring it here, César! I'll give you a good thrashing if you dawdle! . . . That's a good boy, César, you're nice and obedient. Now sit up!"

And he liked his baseness, he savored the enjoyment of being a beast. He longed to descend still lower.

"Hit harder!" he cried. "Bow-wow, I'm a mad dog, hit me!"

She had a whim: she demanded that he come one evening wearing his chamberlain's costume. She laughed and mocked him when she had him in his full regalia: sword, hat, white knee-breeches, red dress coat trimmed in gold, with the symbolic key hanging from its left tail. She was particularly amused by this key; it launched her into a wild fantasy of obscene explanations. Still laughing, carried away by disrespect for grandeur, by the joy of debasing him beneath the official pomp of that costume, shaking and pinching him with shouts of "Come on, chamberlain!" which she accompanied with kicks in the behind; and she heartily directed those kicks at the Tuileries, at the majesty of the imperial court, enthroned high above the fear and humiliation of everyone. That was what she thought of society! It was her revenge, the unconscious family rancor bequeathed to her with her blood. Then, when the chamberlain was undressed and his costume was spread out on the floor, she told him to jump, and he jumped; she told him to spit, and he spat; she told him to walk on the gold, the eagles, and the decorations, and he walked on them. Crash, bang! There was nothing left, everything was falling apart. She could break a chamberlain as easily as she broke a perfume bottle or a candy box, and she could make him into a lump of filth, a heap of mud in the street.

The goldsmiths did not keep their word: the bed was not delivered until the middle of January. Muffat was in Normandy, where he had gone to sell one of the last remnants of his property. Nana demanded four thousand francs immediately. He was not expected back until two days later, but, having settled his business, he hastened his return and went straight to Nana's house without even stopping by his own. It was ten o'clock in the morning. Since he had a key to a little door opening onto the Rue Cardinet, he went in freely. Zoé was upstairs in the drawing room, wiping off the bronzes. She was thunderstruck when she saw him. Not knowing how to stop him, she began telling him in long sentences that Monsieur Venot, looking terribly upset, had been trying to find him since the day before, and that he had already come twice to beg her to send Monsieur home in case he came to Madame's house first. Muffat listened to her without understanding what she was saying. Then he noticed her agitation. Seized with a jealous rage of which he had thought himself no longer capable, he threw himself against the door of the bedroom, from which he could hear laughter. The door flew open. Zoé withdrew, shrugging her shoulders. So much the worse for Madame! Since Madame was going mad, she could get out of the mess by herself.

And Muffat, on the threshold, cried out at what he saw. "My God! . . . My God! . . ."

The newly redecorated bedroom was resplendent in its regal luxury. Silver buttons were strewn like bright stars over the tea-rose velvet hangings, which had the pink flesh-color that the sky assumes on clear evenings when Venus begins to glow above the horizon against the light background of the dying day. The gold tassels hanging in the corners and the gold lace that framed the panels were like delicate flames, loose reddish hair, half covering the bareness of the room, whose voluptuous pallor they enhanced. And the gold and silver bed shone with the new brightness of its chasings. It was a throne broad enough to enable Nana to spread out the royalty of her naked limbs, an altar of Byzantine richness, worthy of the omnipotence of her sex, which she was now displaying in the religious immodesty of an idol held in awe by all men. And beside her, in the snowy reflection of her bosom, in the midst of her goddess-like triumph, sprawled a shameful and decrepit object, a comical and pitiful ruin: the Marquis de Chouard in his nightshirt.

The Count had clasped his hands. Trembling violently, he kept repeating, "My God! . . . My God! . . ."

It was for the Marquis de Chouard that the golden roses on the sides of the bed were flowering, those clusters of golden roses blossoming in golden foliage; it was for him that the cupids, dancing in a circle on a silver trellis, looked down with amorous, roguish smiles; and, at his feet, it was for him that the faun was uncovering the sleeping nymph wearied by sensual pleasures, that figure of Night copied from Nana's celebrated nudity, even to her overly developed thighs, which made it recognizable to everyone. Thrown there like a piece of human rubbish, decayed and disintegrated by sixty years of debauchery, the Marquis gave the impression of a corner of a charnel house appearing amid the glory of Nana's dazzling flesh. Seeing the door open, he had sat up, seized with senile terror. This last night of love had stricken him with imbecility, he had relapsed into childhood. Unable to speak, half paralyzed, stammering and quivering, he remained in an attitude of flight; his nightshirt was pulled up over his skeletal body, and one poor, livid leg, covered with gray hairs, was outside the bedclothes. Despite her annoyance, Nana could not help laughing.

"Lie down, get under the covers," she said, pushing him back and burying him beneath the sheet like a bit of dirt that ought not be seen.

She jumped up to close the door. She had no luck with her little muff! He was always coming in at the wrong time. And why had he gone off to Normandy to get money? The old man had brought her four thousand francs and she had given in to him. She shut the door in the Count's face after shouting, "It's your own fault! Is that the way to come into a room? I've had enough, good-by!"

Muffat stood in front of the closed door, still overwhelmed by what he had seen. His trembling grew still more violent, a trembling that rose from his legs to his chest and into his head. Then his whole body went limp and, like a tree shaken by a great wind, he staggered and fell to his knees. Desperately stretching forth his hands, he gasped, "It's too much, dear God, it's too much!"

He had accepted everything, but he could go on no longer. He felt himself without strength, in that darkness into which man plunges with his reason. In an extraordinary surge of emotion, holding his hands still higher, he sought heaven, he called out to God.

"Oh, no, I won't . . . Oh, come to me, dear God! Help me, or make me die! . . . Oh, no, not that man, dear God! It's finished, take me, carry me away, let me never see or feel again. . . . Oh, I belong to you, my God! . . . Our Father, who art in heaven . . ."

And he continued, burning with faith. An ardent prayer escaped from his lips. But someone touched him on the shoulder. He looked up: it was Monsieur Venot, surprised at having found him in prayer before that closed door. Then, as though God Himself had answered his call, the Count threw his arms around the little old man's neck. His tears were able to flow at last; he sobbed and said, "My brother . . . my brother . . ."

All his suffering humanity was relieved in that cry. He wet Monsieur Venot's face with his tears, kissing him and uttering words broken by sobs.

"Oh, how I'm suffering, my brother! . . . Only you are left to me, my brother. . . . Take me away forever. . . . Oh, please, take me away!"

Monsieur Venot pressed him to his chest and also called him his brother. But he had another blow to deal him: he had been seeking him since the day before in order to tell him that Countess Sabine, in a supreme burst of madness, had just run off with a shopwalker in a dry-goods store, a horrible scandal about which the whole city was already talking. Seeing him under the influence of such religious exaltation, he felt that the moment was favorable, so he immediately told him about this occurrence, this prosaically tragic ending in which his house was foundering. The Count was not even touched by it; his wife was gone, that meant nothing to him, he would see later. Then, gripped by anguish again, looking at the door, the walls, and the ceiling with an expression of terror, he could only voice this supplication: "Take me away. . . . I can't go on, take me away."

Monsieur Venot led him away like a child. From then on he belonged to him entirely. Muffat returned to the strict duties of religion. His life was shattered. In the face of the offended modesty of the Tuileries, he resigned from his position as chamberlain. His daughter Estelle was beginning a lawsuit against him for a sum of sixty thousand francs, which had been left to her by an aunt, and which she should have received at the time of her marriage. Ruined, living frugally on the remains of his great fortune, he allowed himself to be gradually finished off by the Countess, who was devouring the leavings that Nana had disdained. Sabine, corrupted by that woman's promiscuity, driven to extremes, had become the corruption and final collapse of her home. After various adventures she had returned, and he had taken her back, in the resignation of Christian forgiveness. She accompanied him like his living shame. Having grown increasingly indifferent, however, he no longer suffered from such things. Heaven had taken him from the hands of woman and placed him back in the arms of God. He experienced a religious prolongation of the voluptuous pleasures once given to him by Nana, the same stammerings, prayers, and despair, the same humility of an accursed creature crushed beneath the mud of his origin. In the depths of churches, his knees chilled by the flagstones, he recovered the enjoyments of the past, the spasms of his muscles, and the delightful perturbations of his mind, in the satisfaction of the obscure needs of his being.

One evening after Nana had broken off with the Count, Mignon came to her house. He was now becoming accustomed to Fauchery, and he found countless advantages in the presence of another husband in his home. He let him deal with all the little details of domestic life, relied on him to maintain an active surveillance, and used the money that came from his dramatic successes to pay the daily expenses of the household. And since Fauchery behaved reasonably, without ridiculous jealousy, showing himself to be as accommodating as Mignon himself whenever Rose found a good opportunity, the two men got along with each other better and better, pleased with their association, which was so fertile in all kinds of happiness. Each made his little nest beside the other, in a home where they both felt quite at ease. The whole thing was carefully regulated and it worked out very well. They vied with each other in working for the common good.

Mignon had come to Nana's house, in fact, prompted by Fauchery's advice, to see if he could take her maid away from her. The journalist had often appreciated Zoé's exceptional intelligence. Rose was in despair: for the past month she had had a series of inexperienced girls who kept putting her in embarrassing situations. When Zoé received Mignon, he immediately pushed her into the dining room. At the first few words, she smiled. Impossible, she was about to leave Madame and go into business for herself; and she added with an air of discreet vanity that she received such offers every day: the ladies all wanted her, Madame Blanche had done her best to get her back. Zoé was going to take over Tricon's business. It was a plan she had been nursing for a long time, an ambition in which she was going to invest all her savings. She was full of grandiose ideas. She was thinking of expanding the business, of renting a house and combining all sorts of amenities and pleasures in it. It was with this in mind that she had tried to recruit Satin; but the foolish girl had ruined her health to such an extent that she was now dying in a hospital.

Mignon tried to change her mind by speaking of the risks involved in business. Without specifying the nature of her establishment, Zoé smiled primly, as though she were going to take over a confectioner's shop, and said, "Oh, luxury businesses always succeed. . . . You see, I've been in other people's houses for a long time; now I want other people to be in my house."

And a ferocious feeling made her curl her lip. She would at last be "Madame"; for a few louis she would have at her feet those women whose basins she had been rinsing for fifteen years.

Mignon asked to see Nana. Zoé left him for a few moments, after telling him that Madame had had a very bad day. He had been there only once before, so he did not know the house. He was amazed by the dining room, with its Gobelin tapestries, its sideboard, and its silverware. He familiarly opened the doors, inspected the drawing room and the winter garden, then returned to the vestibule; and that overpowering luxury—that gilded furniture, those silks and velvets—gradually filled him with a feeling of awe that made his heart beat faster. When Zoé came downstairs again, she offered to show him the dressing room and the bedroom. In the bedroom, Mignon was fired with tender rapture. That Nana astounded him, despite his long experience in such matters. Amid the downfall of the house, in the waste and savage pillaging of the servants, there was still a pile of wealth that stopped up the holes and overflowed the ruins. Near Marseilles he had once been shown an aqueduct whose stone arches spanned an abyss, a gigantic work that had cost millions of francs and ten years of struggle. At Cherbourg he had seen the new harbor under construction, an immense undertaking, with hundreds of men sweating in the sun and machines filling in the sea with blocks of stone, erecting a wall in which workmen were occasionally crushed to a bloody pulp. But all that seemed small to him; Nana exalted him more. As he contemplated her work, he was seized with the same sensation of respect he had felt one night at a reception given in a château that had been built by a sugar refiner, a palace whose royal splendor had been paid for entirely by sugar. With Nana it was something else, a bit of folly that one laughed at, a little of her delicate nudity; it was with this shameful yet mighty trifle, whose power moved the world, that all alone, without workmen or machines invented by engineers, she had shaken Paris and built that fortune beneath which corpses were sleeping.

"My God, what a tool!" Mignon exclaimed ecstatically, with a return of personal gratitude.

Nana had gradually sunk into great sorrow. First the

meeting between the Marquis and the Count had thrown her into a fit of feverish nervousness that bordered on gaiety. Then the thought of that old man going off in a cab, half dead, and of her poor little muff whom she would never see again, after having driven him so wild, gave her the beginning of a sentimental melancholy. Then she had become indignant on learning that Satin was ill. Satin had disappeared two weeks earlier, and Madame Robert had reduced her to such a state that she was now dying in the Lariboisière hospital. While Nana was waiting for her carriage to be made ready so that she could go and see that little slut once again, Zoé calmly gave her a week's notice. This plunged her into despair; she felt as though she were losing a member of her family. Good God, what would become of her when she was all alone! And she begged Zoé, who, flattered by her despair, finally kissed her to show her that she was not leaving in anger. She had to go: the heart could not be allowed to interfere in business. This was a day of annoyances. Thoroughly disgusted and no longer thinking of going out, Nana was wandering aimlessly around the little drawing room when Labordette came in to tell her about some magnificent lace that could be bought at a very low price. In the course of his remarks he happened to mention that Georges was dead. She was stunned.

"Zizi's dead!" she cried. Her eyes involuntarily sought the pink spot on the carpet; but it had vanished at last, the footsteps had worn it away. Labordette gave her a few details: the cause of his death was not known for certain; some said that an old wound had opened, others that he had committed suicide by jumping into a pond at Les Fondettes. Nana kept repeating, "Dead! . . . Dead! . . ."

Her throat had been tight ever since morning; she now relieved herself by bursting into sobs. She felt infinite sadness, something deep and immense that was overwhelming her. When Labordette tried to console her about Georges, she silenced him with a gesture and said, "Oh, it's not only that, it's everything, everything. . . . I'm so miserable. . . . Oh, I understand! They're going to call me a wicked woman again. . . . That mother who's grieving for her son, that poor man who was moaning outside my door this morning, and the others who are ruined now, after spending all their money on me. . . . That's right, blame it all on Nana! Everything's always my fault! I can hear them already: Nana is a dirty whore who goes to bed with everybody, she ruins some men and kills others, she makes all kinds of people unhappy. . . ."

Her tears choked her and she had to stop. In her anguish she fell across the sofa and buried her face in a cushion. The miseries she felt around her, the misfortunes she had caused, enveloped her in a warm, continuous flow of pity for herself and others. Her muffled voice uttered a childish lament: "Oh, it hurts, it hurts! . . . I can't go on, it's choking me. . . . It's too painful not to be understood, to see people turn against you because they're stronger than you are. . . . But when there's nothing for you to feel guilty about, when your conscience is clear . . . No, by God, no!"

Her anger became mingled with revolt. She stood up, wiped her tears, and began pacing agitatedly around the room.

"No, by God, it's not my fault, no matter what they say! Am I cruel? I give away everything I've got, I wouldn't hurt a fly. . . . It's *their* fault! I never wanted to be unpleasant to them. They were all hanging onto my skirts, and now they're dying, or begging, and they all claim to be in despair. . . ."

She stopped in front of Labordette and tapped him on the shoulder. "You were here, tell the truth: did I lead them on? Weren't there always a dozen of them trying to see who could think up the dirtiest trick? They disgusted me! I refused to go along with them, I was afraid. For one thing, they all wanted to marry me. A fine idea, eh? Yes, my friend, I could have been a countess or a baroness at least twenty times if I'd wanted to. But I refused, because I was sensible. . . . I spared them all kinds of crimes and filthy actions. They would have stolen, murdered, killed their parents . . . I only had to say a word, and I didn't say it. And now you can see my reward. . . . Take Daguenet, for example. I kept him for weeks and weeks when he didn't have any money, then I arranged his marriage for him and set him up in the world. Well, I met him yesterday and he looked the other way! What a pig! I'm not as dirty as he is!"

She had begun walking again. She slammed her fist down on a table.

"It's not fair, damn it! Society's all wrong. Women get blamed when it's men who demand things. . . . Listen, I can tell you this now: when I was with them I didn't enjoy it at all, not at all. It bored me, I swear! . . . So I ask you: did I have anything to do with it? They were always annoying me! If it hadn't been for them and what they made of me, I'd be praying in a convent right now, because I've always been religious. . . . No! If they've lost their money or their lives, it's their own fault! I had nothing to do with it!"

"Of course not," Labordette said with conviction.

Zoé ushered in Mignon. Nana greeted him with a smile; she had had a good cry and now it was all over. Still warm with enthusiasm, he congratulated her on her house; but she gave him to understand that she was tired of it. She was now dreaming of something else. One of these days she was going to get rid of everything. As a pretext for his visit, Mignon told her about a benefit performance that was going to be given for old Bosc, who had been tied to his chair by an attack of paralysis. She expressed great pity and took two boxes. When Zoé told her the carriage was waiting, she asked for her hat. As she was putting it on she told them about poor Satin's mishap. "I'm going to the hospital," she said. "Nobody ever loved me the way she did. Oh, it's true that men are heartless! . . . Who knows? Maybe she's already dead. But I'll ask to see her anyway. I want to kiss her."

Labordette and Mignon smiled. She was no longer sad. She returned their smile, because those two didn't count, they could understand. And they both admired her in reflective silence while she finished buttoning her gloves. She alone remained standing amid the piled-up wealth of her house, with a host of men lying stricken at her feet. Like those ancient monsters whose dreaded domains were covered with bones, she trod on skulls. She was surrounded by catastrophes: Vandeuvres' furious conflagration; the melancholy of Foucarmont lost in the China seas; the disaster of Steiner reduced to living like an honest man; the satisfied idiocy of La Faloise; the tragic downfall of the Muffats; and Georges' white corpse watched over by

Philippe, who had been released from prison the day before. Her work of ruin and death was accomplished. The fly that had flown up from the filth of the slums, bringing with it the ferment of social decay, had poisoned men merely by alighting on them. It was right, it was just; she had avenged the paupers and outcasts from whom she had sprung. And as her sex ascended in a halo and shone on her fallen victims like a rising sun illuminating a field of carnage, she retained the insensibility of a superb animal, ignorant of her work, still good-natured. She remained big and plump, healthy and gay. All that meant nothing to her now; her house seemed idiotic, too small, full of furniture that got in her way. A mere trifle, only a beginning. She was dreaming of something better. And she went off in all her finery to give Satin one last kiss, clean, solid, looking brand-new as though she had never been used.

14

$\mathcal{N}$ana suddenly disappeared—another escapade, a spree, a flight to exotic lands. Before her departure she had treated herself to the excitement of selling everything: her house, her furniture, her jewelry, even her dresses and linen. Figures were quoted; the five-day auction had brought in more than six hundred thousand francs. Paris had seen her one last time in a spectacular play, *Mélusine*, at the Théâtre de la Gaîté, which Bordenave had boldly rented without a sou in his pocket. She again shared the stage with Prullière and Fontan. She had no lines to speak, but her part was the chief attraction of the play: three plastic poses of a powerful and silent fairy. Then, in the midst of this great success, while Bordenave, avid for publicity, was exciting Paris with colossal posters, one fine morning it was reported that she had left for Cairo the night before—an argument with her producer, a word that had displeased her, the whim of a woman too rich to let herself be annoyed. Besides, for a long time she had been taken with the idea of going to see the Turks.

Months went by. Paris began to forget her. Whenever her name was mentioned among her friends, they all told strange stories and gave prodigious and contradictory information. She had captivated the viceroy, she was living in a palace, reigning over two hundred slaves, beheading a few of them whenever she felt like having a little fun. Not at all, she had ruined herself with a big Negro, carried away by a vile passion that had left her penniless in the foul debauchery of Cairo. Two weeks later there was great astonishment when someone swore he had seen her in Russia. A legend was forming: she was the mistress of a prince, her diamonds were talked about. All the women soon knew them through the descriptions of them that were circulated: there were rings, earrings, bracelets, a necklace as wide as two fingers, and a queenly diadem surmounted by a central brilliant as big as your thumb. In the remoteness of those faraway countries, she assumed the mysterious radiance of an idol laden with precious stones. She was now mentioned seriously, with the dreamy respect aroused by that fortune acquired among the barbarians.

One July evening, toward eight o'clock, Lucy was riding along the Rue du Faubourg-Saint-Honoré in her carriage when she saw Caroline Héquet, who had gone out on foot to give an order to a tradesman of the neighborhood. She called her over and said, "Have you had dinner yet? Are you free? . . . Good, then come with me. Nana is back."

Caroline got into the carriage. Lucy went on: "And you know, my dear, she may be dead right now, while we're talking."

"Dead? What an idea!" Caroline exclaimed in amazement. "Where? Of what?"

"In the Grand-Hôtel, of smallpox. Oh, wait till you hear the story!"

Lucy told her coachman to drive fast. Then, while the horses trotted swiftly along the Rue Royale and the boulevards, she related Nana's adventures in broken sentences, without stopping to catch her breath.

"You can't imagine . . . Nana came in from Russia, I forget why, something about a quarrel with her prince. . . . She left her baggage at the station and went to her aunt's house, you remember, that old woman . . . Well, she found her baby dying of smallpox. He died the next day and she had a fight with her aunt about some money she was supposed to have sent. Her aunt said she never got any of it. It seems the child died because of that. Anyway, he wasn't taken care of. . . . Nana left her and went to a hotel, then she ran into Mignon when she was on her way to get her baggage. Suddenly she felt strange all over and started shivering and feeling as if she was going to vomit. Mignon took her back to her hotel and promised to look after her things. It's funny the way it all happened. . . . But here's the best part: when Rose found out Nana was sick she was outraged at the idea that she was all alone in a hotel room, and she went off to take care of her with tears in her eyes. You remember how they used to hate each other—they were like two wildcats! Well, my dear, Rose had Nana taken to the Grand-Hôtel, so that she could at least die in a luxurious place, and she's already spent three nights there, at the risk of losing her own life. . . . Labordette told me about it. I wanted to go and see—"

"Yes, yes," Caroline interrupted excitedly, "let's go to her room!"

They had reached the hotel. On the boulevard, the coachman had to rein in the horses amid a tangle of carriages and pedestrians. During the day the legislature had voted to declare war. A crowd was coming in from all the side streets, covering the sidewalks and overflowing onto the pavement. In the direction of the Madeleine, the sun was setting behind a blood-red cloud whose fiery glow was reflected in the high windows. Dusk was falling. It was a heavy, melancholy hour; the avenues were already dark, but not yet lined with the bright sparks of the street-lamps. And among those people on the march, distant voices were growing louder, eyes were gleaming in pale faces, while a great breath of anxiety and amazement spread over the crowd and carried away every mind.

"There's Mignon," said Lucy. "He'll give us some news."

Mignon was standing under the vast porch of the Grand-Hôtel, looking nervous and staring at the crowd. As soon as Lucy questioned him he flew into a rage and shouted, "How should I know? For two days I've been trying to get Rose out of that room! It's stupid for her to risk her life that way! She'll look nice if she catches it and has holes all over her face! That's just what we need!"

He was exasperated by the thought that Rose might lose her beauty. He had abandoned Nana to her fate, unable to understand the stupid devotions of women. Fauchery was crossing the boulevard. He, too, was worried. When he came up to Mignon and asked for news, each tried to incite the other to action. They now spoke familiarly to each other.

"Everything's still the same, my boy," said Mignon. "You ought to go up there and make her leave."

"Thanks very much!" replied the journalist. "Why don't you go up there yourself?"

Then, when Lucy asked for the number of Nana's room, they begged her to make Rose come down; otherwise they would end by getting angry. But Lucy and Caroline did not go up immediately. They had seen Fontan strolling toward them with his hands in his pockets, highly amused by the faces of the people in the crowd. When he learned that Nana was lying ill upstairs, he said with affected feeling, "Poor girl! I'll go up and shake her hand. . . . What's she got?"

"Smallpox," answered Mignon.

The actor had already taken a step toward the courtyard; he turned back and murmured simply, with a shudder, "Good God!"

Smallpox was no laughing matter. Fontan had nearly caught it when he was five years old. Mignon told about one of his nieces who had died of it. As for Fauchery, he could talk from personal experience. He still bore the marks: three spots at the base of his nose, which he showed to the others. When Mignon again urged him to go up, saying that one never caught it twice, he opposed this theory violently; he cited cases and called the doctors fools. Lucy and Caroline interrupted him, surprised by the growing mob.

"Just look at all those people!"

The darkness was deepening. Streetlamps were being lighted one by one in the darkness. Curious onlookers could be seen at the windows, while under the trees the human flood was swelling from minute to minute in an enormous stream that extended from the Madeleine to the Bastille. The carriages were moving slowly. A buzzing sound arose from the compact and as yet inarticulate mass of people who had been brought there by a need to flock together, shuffling along, excited by the same fever. Then a great commotion made them fall back. Jostling groups made way for a band of men wearing caps and white jackets, uttering this cry in the cadence of a hammer striking an anvil:

"To Berlin! To Berlin! To Berlin!"

The crowd looked on with gloomy mistrust, but they were already beginning to be attracted and stirred by thoughts of heroic deeds, as though a military band were passing.

"That's right, go get yourselves shot!" Mignon exclaimed in a burst of philosophy.

But Fontan thought it was noble. He spoke of enlisting. When the enemy was at the border, it was the duty of every citizen to rise up and defend his country; and he struck a pose that suggested Bonaparte at Austerlitz.

"Well, are you coming up with us?" Lucy asked him.

"Of course not! I don't want to catch smallpox!"

Sitting on a bench in front of the Grand-Hôtel, a man was hiding his face in a handkerchief. Fauchery, on arriving, had drawn Mignon's attention to him with a wink. He was still there; yes, he was still there. And the journalist held the two women back for a moment to point him out to them. When he raised his head, they recognized him and uttered an exclamation. It was Count Muffat. He was looking up at one of the windows.

"He's been sitting there since this morning," said Mignon. "I saw him at six o'clock, and he hasn't moved. . . . As soon as Labordette told him about Nana, he came here with his handkerchief over his face. Every half-hour he drags himself to the door and asks if the person upstairs is better, then he goes back and sits down. . . . After all, that room isn't healthy. You can love people without wanting to die for them."

The Count was sitting with his eyes raised, apparently unaware of what was taking place around him. He no doubt did not know that war had been declared; he neither heard nor felt the crowd.

"Here he comes," said Fauchery. "You'll see . . ."

The Count had left the bench and was approaching the tall doorway. But the doorkeeper, who had by now become accustomed to him, did not give him time to ask his question. He said abruptly "Monsieur, she just died."

Nana dead! It was a blow to everyone. Muffat went back to the bench without a word, his face in his handkerchief. The others cried out. But their voices were drowned by the shouting of another band of men passing by:

"To Berlin! To Berlin! To Berlin!"

Nana dead! Such a beautiful girl! Mignon sighed with relief; at last Rose was going to come down. A chill fell over everyone. Fontan, who had been dreaming of a tragic role, took on a grief-stricken expression, turning down the corners of his mouth and showing the whites of his eyes. Fauchery, deeply affected despite his journalistic cynicism, nervously chewed his cigar. The two women continued their exclamations. The last time Lucy had seen her was at the Gaîté; Caroline also, in *Mélusine*. Oh, she had been dazzling when she appeared at the back of the crystal grotto! The men also remembered her very clearly. Fontan had played the part of Prince Cocorico. And once their memories had been awakened, they launched into endless details. What an impression she had made in that crystal grotto, with her voluptuous figure! She hadn't said a word. The authors had taken out the one line she had, because it detracted from the effect she produced. No, not a word, it was better that way; she drove the audience wild just by showing herself. A body like hers would never be seen again—those shoulders, those legs, that waist! . . . How strange that she should be dead! . . . Over her tights she had worn only a band of gold cloth that scarcely concealed her in front and in back. The grotto, made entirely of glass, shone all around her. There were cascades of diamonds, and strings of white pearls streaming down among the stalactites overhead. In that transparency, in that limpid spring, illuminated by a broad ray of electric light, she had appeared like a sun, with her skin and hair of flame. Paris would never see her again like that, shining in the midst of all that crystal, poised in the air like a goddess. No, it was stupid of her to let herself die when she had reached that position! She must be pretty up there in that room now!

"And think of all that pleasure lost!" said Mignon in a melancholy tone. He did not like to see good and useful things wasted.

He sounded out Lucy and Caroline to learn whether they were going up anyway. Of course they were; their curiosity had increased. Then Blanche arrived, out of breath, exasperated by the crowd that was blocking the sidewalk. When she heard the news, the exclamations began again. The three women moved toward the staircase with a great rustling of skirts. Mignon walked after them and called out, "Tell Rose I'm waiting for her. . . . Tell her to come down right away."

"It's not known whether the danger of contagion is greater at the beginning or at the end," Fontan was explaining to Fauchery. "And a friend of mine who's an intern once told me that the hours immediately after death are the most dangerous of all. The body gives off miasmas. . . . I'm sorry she died so suddenly; I wish I could have shaken her hand one last time."

"It would be pointless now," said the journalist.

"Yes, it would be pointless," repeated the two others.

The crowd was still growing. In the light from the shop windows, beneath the flickering glare of the streetlamps, a current could be seen moving along each sidewalk, with hats drifting on its surface. The fever was spreading rapidly. People were falling in behind the groups of men in white jackets, the pavement was swept by a constant onward surge; and the same shout was bursting from every throat, rhythmically, stubbornly:

"To Berlin! To Berlin! To Berlin!"

The room on the fifth floor of the hotel cost twelve francs a day. Rose had wanted something decent though not luxurious, for luxury is useless when one is suffering. Hung in Louis XIII cretonne with big flowers, the room contained the mahogany furniture common to all hotels, and a red carpet strewn with black foliage. It was filled with heavy silence, broken only by a whisper, when voices rang out in the hall.

"I'm sure we're lost. The bellboy said to turn right. . . . What a place!"

"Just a minute, we'll see. . . . Room 401, room 401 . . ."

"It's this way. Here's 405, and 403. . . . This must be it. Yes, at last, 401. . . . Come on. Quiet!"

The voices fell silent. There was a little coughing and a short pause. Then the door slowly opened. Lucy went in, followed by Caroline and Blanche. They stopped: there were already five other women in the room. Gaga was stretched out in the only armchair, a red velvet voltaire. Simonne and Clarisse were standing in front of the fireplace, talking with Léa de Horn, who was sitting on a wooden chair. Seated on the edge of the woodbox in front of the bed, to the left of the door, Rose Mignon was staring at the body lying in the shadows of the curtains. All the others were wearing their hats and gloves, like ladies who had come to pay a social call. Only Rose's hands were bare; her hair was in disorder and her face was pale from the fatigue of three sleepless nights. She was dazed and swollen with sadness in the face of that sudden death. A shaded lamp on one corner of the dresser was casting its bright light on Gaga.

"It's a terrible thing, isn't it?" murmured Lucy, pressing Rose's hand. "We wanted to tell her good-by."

She turned her head, trying to see her, but the lamp was too far away and she did not dare to bring it over. There was a gray mass on the bed; she could distinguish only the blond chignon and a pale spot that must have been the face.

"I hadn't seen her since she was at the Gaîté, in the grotto," Lucy added.

Rose emerged from her stupor, smiled, and said, "Oh, she's changed, she's changed. . . ." Then she relapsed into her contemplation, without another word or gesture. Perhaps they could look at her a little later; and the three women joined the others in front of the fireplace. Simonne and Clarisse were discussing Nana's diamonds, in low voices. Did those diamonds really exist? No one had seen them, they were probably only a myth. But Léa de Horn said she knew someone who had seen them. They were enormous! And that wasn't all, either, she had brought back other riches from Russia: embroidered fabrics, precious knickknacks, a gold dinner service, even furniture; yes, fifty-two huge crates, enough to fill three vans. It was still in the station. What bad luck to die without even being able to unpack it! And she had money, too, something like a million francs. Lucy asked who would inherit it. Distant relatives, and her aunt, probably. What a shock it was going to be for the old woman! She did not know yet; Nana had stubbornly refused to send word to her, because she had still held her responsible for her son's death. The women all expressed pity for the little boy, remembering having seen him at the races: he had been full of disease even then, and he had looked so worn-out and sad; he was one of those poor little babies who had not asked to be born.

"He's better off in the grave," said Blanche.

"Yes, and so is she," replied Caroline. "Life isn't pleasant."

Gloomy ideas were taking possession of them in the severity of that room. They were afraid, it was silly to stay there talking so long; but a desire to see kept them rooted to the floor. It was very warm; the chimney of the lamp cast a little round moon on the ceiling, in the damp shadows that filled the room. Under the bed, a dish full of phenol gave off a stale odor. Now and then a breath of air swelled the curtains of the window, opened onto the boulevard, from which a dull murmur arose.

"Did she suffer much?" asked Lucy, who had been contemplating the picture on the clock: the three Graces, naked, smiling like dancers.

Gaga seemed to awaken.

"Yes, she did! I was here when she died, and I can tell you it wasn't a pretty sight. . . . She started shaking . . ."

Her explanation was cut short by a cry from outside:

"To Berlin! To Berlin! To Berlin!"

Lucy, who was stifling, opened the window still wider and leaned out. There it was pleasant; a coolness was descending from the starry sky. Across the street, windows were blazing and reflections of gaslights were dancing in the gold letters of signs. And below, it was amusing to see the crowd flowing like a torrent along the sidewalks and the pavement, amid the tangle of carriages, through the great moving shadows sprinkled with sparkling lanterns and gaslights. The shouting group that was approaching had torches; a red glow was coming from the Madeleine, dividing the mob with a trail of fire, spreading above the heads like a sheet of flame. Forgetting herself, Lucy called out to Blanche and Caroline: "Come here, you can see very well from this window!"

All three of them leaned out, greatly interested. The trees interfered with their view; the torches occasionally disappeared beneath the leaves. They tried to see the men they had left downstairs, but the front door was hidden beneath a balcony. They could only see Count Muffat, slumped on the bench ilke a dark bundle, his face buried in his handkerchief. A carriage stopped in front of the hotel. Lucy recognized Maria Blond, another friend of Nana's who had come to see her. She was not alone: a fat man got out of the carriage behind her.

"It's that thief Steiner!" said Caroline. "What! Hasn't he been sent back to Cologne yet? . . . I want to see his face when he comes in."

They turned around. But ten minutes later, when Maria Blond finally appeared after having taken the wrong staircase twice, she was alone. Lucy questioned her, surprised.

"Steiner?" said Maria Blond. "You didn't think *he* was going to come up, did you? It's a wonder he even went with me as far as the front door. . . . There are nearly a dozen of them down there smoking cigars."

All the gentlemen had gathered in front of the hotel. Some of them had been taking a stroll to have a look at the boulevards. They called out to one another and exclaimed over poor Nana's death. Then they talked politics and strategy. The group had been augmented by Bordenave, Daguenet, Labordette, Prullière, and still others. They listened to Fontan while he set forth his plan for capturing Berlin in five days.

Meanwhile Maria Blond, moved to pity in front of the bed, murmured as the others had done, "Poor girl . . . The last time I saw her was at the Gaîté, in the grotto. . . ."

"Ah, she's changed, she's changed," repeated Rose Mignon with a smile of dull weariness.

Two more women arrived: Tatan Néné and Louise Violaine. They had wandered around the Grand-Hôtel for twenty minutes, being sent from one bellboy to another. They had gone up and down more than thirty flights of stairs, caught up in the flood of travelers who were hastening to leave Paris, in the panic caused by the declaration of war and that commotion on the boulevards. And so when they came into the room they sank onto chairs, too tired to concern themselves with Nana. There was an uproar coming from the next room: trunks were being shoved across the floor, furniture was being knocked around, voices were making barbaric sounds. It was a young Austrian couple. Gaga said that during the death agony the neighbors had played at chasing each other, and since there was a door between the two rooms, they had been heard laughing and kissing each time one of them caught the other.

"We may as well leave," said Clarisse. "We're not going to bring her back to life. . . . Are you coming, Simonne?"

They all looked at the bed out of the corners of their eyes, without moving; then they began patting their skirts in preparation for their departure. Lucy had gone back to the window alone. Sadness was slowly gripping her throat, as though a profound melancholy had risen from that howling mob. Torches were still passing, throwing off sparks. Groups were milling around in the distance, extending into the shadows, like flocks being led to the slaughterhouse at night. And those confused, giddy masses, carried along by the stream, gave off a feeling of terror, of great pity for future massacres. They were working themselves into a frenzy, their shouts burst forth from the fever that was driving them toward the unknown, beyond the dark wall of the horizon.

"To Berlin! To Berlin! To Berlin!"

Lucy turned around and stood with her back to the window. Her face was pale.

"My God! What's going to become of us?"

The others shook their heads. They were serious, apprehensive about what was taking place.

"For my part," said Caroline Héquet with her sedate expression, "I'm leaving for London tomorrow. My mother's already there, getting a house ready for me. . . . I'm certainly not going to stay in Paris to get slaughtered."

Her mother, being a prudent woman, had invested her whole fortune abroad. One never knew how a war might end.

Maria Blond became angry; she was a patriot, she spoke of following the army.

"What a coward you are! . . . Yes, if they'd take me I'd put on a uniform and go off to shoot those Prussian pigs! We might all get killed, but what of it? Our lives aren't so valuable!"

Blanche de Sivry was exasperated. "Don't say anything bad about the Prussians! They're men the same as any others, and they're not always annoying women, the way your Frenchmen are! . . . The young Prussian I was living with just got expelled from the country. He's a very rich boy, and very gentle. He wouldn't have hurt anybody. It's an outrage! I don't have any money now. . . . If anybody gives me any trouble, I'll go to him in Germany!"

While they were quarreling, Gaga said plaintively, "It's the end for me, I never have any luck. . . . Only a week ago I finished paying for my little house in Juvisy, and God knows it wasn't easy for me! Lili had to help me. . . .

And now war's been declared! The Prussians will come and burn everything. . . . How do they expect me to begin all over again, at my age?"

"Oh, it makes no difference to me!" said Clarisse. "I'll still find what I need."

"Of course," said Simonne. "It's going to be funny. . . . Maybe things will go even better. . . ."

She completed her thought with a smile. Tatan Néné and Louise Violaine were of the same opinion. The former said that she had already had some very good times with soldiers; they were good-hearted men who would do anything in the world for women. But the ladies had raised their voices too much. Rose Mignon, still sitting on the woodbox in front of the bed, silenced them with a gentle "Sh!" They were startled, and cast a sidelong glance at the corpse, as though that call for silence had come from the shadows of the curtains. And in the heavy peace that fell over them, that peace of death in which they felt the stiffness of the body lying near them, the shouts of the crowd burst forth again:

"To Berlin! To Berlin! To Berlin!"

But soon they forgot once more. Léa de Horn, who presided over a political drawing room in which former ministers of Louis-Philippe gathered to exchange political epigrams, shrugged her shoulders and said softly, "What a mistake this war is! What bloodthirsty stupidity!"

Lucy immediately leapt to the defense of the Empire. She had once gone to bed with an imperial prince, so to her it was a family matter.

"Stop talking that way, my dear. We couldn't go on letting ourselves be insulted. This war is for the honor of France. And I'm not saying that because of the Prince, either. He was terribly stingy! He always put his money in his boots when he went to bed at night, and he used to bet beans when we played bezique, because one day I'd grabbed the stakes, just for fun. . . . But that doesn't stop me from being fair. The Emperor is right."

Léa shook her head with the superior air of a woman who repeats the opinions of important personages. "It's the end," she said, raising her voice. "They're all out of their minds in the Tuileries. . . . France should have driven them out yesterday, instead of—"

The others interrupted her violently. What was the matter with her? What did she have against the Emperor? Wasn't everybody happy? Wasn't business good? Paris would never be so lively again.

Gaga, reawakened, flew into an indignant rage: "Keep quiet! It's idiotic, you don't know what you're talking about! . . . I saw Louis-Philippe's reign, my dear: it was a time of paupers and misers. Then came '48. Oh, what a disgusting thing their republic was! After February I was starving to death! . . . If you'd been through all that, you'd fall on your knees before the Emperor, because he's been a father to us, yes, a father to us. . . ."

They had to calm her. She went on, in an outburst of religious fervor: "O God, please let the Emperor win the war. Keep the Empire for us!"

They all repeated this wish. Blanche confessed that she burned candles for the Emperor. Caroline, infatuated with him, had spent months strolling around places where he was likely to pass, without being able to attract his attention. And the others spoke out furiously against the republicans and advocated exterminating them at the border so that Napoleon III, after having beaten the enemy, could reign in peace, amid universal rejoicing.

"That dirty Bismarck—there's another pig!" Maria Blond pointed out.

"And to think I used to know him!" cried Simonne. "If I'd known what was going to happen, I'd have put poison in his glass."

But Blanche, still upset by the expulsion of her Prussian, dared to defend Bismarck. Maybe he wasn't a bad man. After all, everybody had his own job to do. "And he adores women, you know," she added.

"What do we care about that?" said Clarisse. "You don't think we want to pick him up, do you?"

"There are always too many men like that," Louise Violaine declared gravely. "It would be better to do without men than to have anything to do with such monsters."

The discussion continued. Bismarck was pulled to pieces. In their Bonapartist zeal, each of the women gave him a kick.

"Bismarck! I used to get so sick of hearing about him!"

said Tatan Néné. "I hate him! . . . I never knew that Bismarck. You can't know everybody."

"Just the same," concluded Léa de Horn, "that Bismarck is going to give us a good licking . . ."

She was unable to continue. The others attacked her heatedly. What! A licking! Bismarck was going to be booted back to his own country before he knew what was happening to him! She had better keep quiet, she wasn't worthy of calling herself a Frenchwoman!

"Sh!" hissed Rose Mignon, offended by their uproar.

They were again seized by the cold of the corpse. They all stopped at once, ill at ease, brought face to face with death again, filled with a secret dread of evil. On the boulevard the cry was passing, hoarse and frenzied:

"To Berlin! To Berlin! To Berlin!"

Then, as they were making up their minds to leave, a voice called from the hall: "Rose! Rose!"

Astonished, Gaga opened the door and disappeared for a moment. When she returned she said, "My dear, it's Fauchery out there, at the end of the hall. He won't come any closer. He's beside himself because you're staying with the body.

Mignon had finally persuaded the journalist to go upstairs. Lucy, still at the window, leaned out and saw the men on the sidewalk, looking up and making signals to her. Mignon was furiously shaking his fists. Steiner, Fontan, Bordenave, and the others spread their arms in a gesture of anxiety and reproach. Daguenet went on smoking his cigar with his hands behind his back, to avoid compromising himself.

"Yes, my dear, I'd forgotten," said Lucy, leaving the window open, "I promised to make you come down. . . . They're all down there signaling to us."

Rose laboriously got down from the woodbox. She murmured, "I'm going, I'm going. . . . She doesn't need me any more. A nun will come . . ."

And she looked around without being able to find her hat and shawl. She absent-mindedly filled a basin on the dressing table with water and began washing her hands and face. She went on: "I don't know . . . It was a terrible blow to me. We weren't very nice to each other. And yet it's knocked me flat. . . . Oh, all kinds of ideas! . . . I want to die too, I feel as if it's the end of everything. . . . Yes, I need air."

The corpse was beginning to fill the room with a stench. The women's long unconcern abruptly turned to panic.

"Let's go, girls, let's go," said Gaga. "It's not healthy in here."

They began leaving quickly, casting a parting glance at the bed. But while Lucy, Blanche, and Caroline were still there, Rose looked around to make sure the room was in order. She drew the window curtain shut. Then it occurred to her that the lamp was not proper: there ought to be a candle. She took a brass candlestick from the mantelpiece, lit the candle in it, and placed it on the night table, beside the bed. Nana's face was suddenly illuminated. The women were all stricken with horror. They shuddered and hurried out of the room.

"Ah, she's changed, she's changed," murmured Rose Mignon, who had stayed behind for a moment.

She walked out and closed the door. Nana remained alone, her face turned upward in the candlelight. She was only a piece of carrion, a mass of pus and blood, a shovelful of putrid flesh, thrown there on a cushion. The pustules had invaded her whole face, touching one another; and, faded and sunken, with the grayish hue of mud, they already seemed to be a moldering of the earth on that shapeless pulp in which her features were no longer recognizable. One eye, the left one, had been completely swallowed up by the seething purulence; the other, half open, was like a black, fetid hole. The nose was still suppurating. A reddish scab had spread from one cheek to the mouth, drawing it into a ghastly smile. And above that grotesque and horrible mask of death, the hair, the beautiful hair, still blazed like sunlight and flowed in a golden stream. Venus was decomposing. It was as though the virus she had brought from the gutter, from the decaying carcasses left in the street, that ferment with which she had poisoned a whole people, had risen to her face and rotted it.

The room was empty. A great breath of despair rose from the boulevard and swelled the curtains.

"To Berlin! To Berlin! To Berlin!"